SO BY MEREDITH TATE

Confession of Autumn Casterly

Freedom Trials

Missing Pieces

The Red Labyrinth

The Last

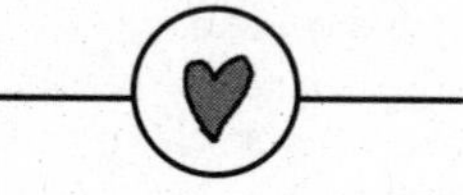

MEREDITH TATE

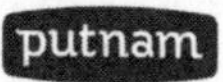

G. P. PUTNAM'S SONS

G. P. PUTNAM'S SONS
An imprint of Penguin Random House LLC, New York

Visit us online at penguinrandomhouse.com

Library of Congress Cataloging-in-Publication Data is available.

Manufactured in Canada
ISBN 9781984813527
1 3 5 7 9 10 8 6 4 2

Design by Suki Boynton
Text set in Berling LT Std

To everyone who has ever loved a fictional world
so much that it became real.

To Jamie Howard, an amazing critique partner and friend,
who has supported me from the beginning.

And to Vincent and my parents, Jessica and Paul,
because every book I write is for you.

// APRIL 24, 2017 //

✦ FOR IMMEDIATE RELEASE ✦

For the last year, SFFStream has enjoyed bringing you *Warship Seven*—a show that is often referred to as "Robin Hood in Space." In *Warship Seven*, young space rebel Captain Jill Brighton and her mismatched crew risk their lives to raid wealthy military bases tightly controlled by the tyrannical Central Elite forces and redistribute their resources to the poorer outer planets. It has reached striking popularity in its first season.

While the show has found many fans, we have made the difficult decision not to renew *Warship Seven* for a second season.

"It has been a great honor to work on this show," producer William Jackson says. "*Warship Seven* brims with heart, action, and questions of humanity and morality. We would like to take the opportunity to thank the cast, crew, and viewers for making the past year such a memorable journey."

Captain Jill Brighton, Sergeant Aaron Lewis, and their quirky crew aboard the *Revelry* have become beloved characters, and the show has been dubbed a "cult phenomenon." It will be missed. We wish the cast and crew the best in their future careers.

COMMENTS

JBStan12: you've got to be kidding me

Fleetlover9: NOOOO. WHAT?!

LewtonOTP: Honestly, I hope you rethink your decision. Ending one of the greatest shows of all time after one season is a disservice to its loyal fans. Aside from the fact that season one ended on a cliff-hanger, these characters have so much more of their journey left to complete. Canceling now proves that SFFStream cares more about revenue than viewers. Maybe I will take my subscription money to Hulu instead.

danversisendgame: oh get off your high horse it's a tv show lol I love this show but I'll get over it, we'll always have those twenty amazing episodes to fall back on

theeighthwarship: ^there are two types of fans

CoNDORsBackup: lmaoooo the show had gone downhill anyway, no surprises here

LewtonOTP: @danversisendgame I won't just "get over it," thanks though. Capt Jill and Serg Lewis were finally about to get together after TWENTY episodes of pining. You don't just end a show with the main character heartbroken after the man she loves abandons her for no reason.

danversisendgame: @lewtonOTP um, there was no love. he left her. Were we watching the same show?

LewtonOTP: @danversisendgame woooow. Clearly he was going to come back. He didn't want to leave, he was protecting her. He loves her. You're wrong.

danversisendgame: @LewtonOTP He hooked up with her and then left in the middle of the night. He's not coming back. Wham bam thank you ma'am

LewtonOTP: @danversisendgame well now we will never know because the show is canceled so stfu #Lewton is OTP

danversisendgame: @LewtonOTP there was literally no chance Jill and Aaron would end up together. They hate each other.

LewtonOTP: @danversisendgame They didn't *hate* each other. It was sexual tension.

danversisendgame: @LewtonOTP no. It wasn't. Sometimes people are just incompatible.

LewtonOTP: @danversisendgame Hate is a strong emotion. Love is a strong emotion. Are they really that different?

1 STELLA

There is an orangutan at the Cornerview Zoo that's infamous for flinging his poop. It's, like, a thing. Catch Orange the Orangutan mid-throw and post the photo on the zoo's Facebook page. Sometimes they pick an entry to win a free water bottle or something.

I'm pretty sure a speech from Orange the Orangutan would be more coherent than the crap currently being flung toward me, straight out of Wesley Clarke's mouth.

Wesley leans against the podium in front of our Public Speaking classroom, wearing a wrinkled green T-shirt. There is literally a giant Charizard on it. "And for my closing arguments, I'd like to reiterate that school uniforms stifle creativity and personal expression. How can I focus on my education when my clothing puts me in a box?" Several people clap their approval; I keep my hands firmly in my lap.

His teammates smirk at the other end of the room, because clearly everyone thinks Wesley Frickin' Clarke has the argument in the bag, just for being Wesley Frickin' Clarke. Breaking news: when you're the heir to a big local candy factory and host parties in your gigantic game room with a Ping-Pong table and old-school Pac-Man arcade machine, everyone basically thinks you're a god.

"In the same way that every student has the right to be comfortable in their learning environment, every student also has the right to wear what makes them comfortable." Even Ms. Hatley nods.

"I thought the Geneva Convention outlawed this sort of torture," I mutter under my breath.

Dahlia snickers beside me. "He's milking it, too."

I know Wesley was assigned Team No-Uniforms, but showing up to class in a ripped Pokémon T-shirt and board shorts is pushing it. I cross my arms, leaning back in my chair.

"Your initial argument decimated him," Dahlia says. "We've got this."

I wish she was right. But everyone knows Team No-Uniforms always wins at public schools. Plus, okay, here's my deep, dark secret: I suck at public speaking.

"Imagine growing up knowing you can party your way through school and still wind up rich and successful because your last name is Clarke."

"I don't know." Dahlia cocks her head, her dark curls swinging with the movement. "He's pretty smart."

"He's rich and knows how to string a few words together. That doesn't make him smart."

"He gave a pretty good presentation in AP Euro last year. He called out some obscure battle stat that Mr. Bridges didn't even know."

I pretend to gag. "Okay, he's good at history. Who cares?" It's easy to get straight As when you've got private SAT-prep classes and don't have to work at the ice cream parlor after school. "I'm just saying—"

"Girls." Ms. Hatley shoots us a warning look. She makes the opposing side sit in the front row during the other team's arguments, but I do not need such a clear view of Wesley's smug face. I hate how everyone thinks he's just *so* hot. Okay, I kind of get it—his cheekbones could basically cut diamonds—but I'd never admit that. I covertly click my phone under the desk—fifteen more minutes of class.

Captain Jill greets me on my lock screen, signature rifle slung over her shoulder. I have a pair of earrings that match the sigil on her jacket, of the *Revelry* encircled by a four-pointed gold star. I got them at last year's Sci-Con—which reminds me, I still need to find a pair of Captain Jill's boots for this year's cosplay. That Sci-Con ticket basically cost a kidney, my left arm, and the blood of my firstborn, so there's no way I'm showing up in anything less than prizewinning.

Dahlia casts a glance toward the other side of the room, and a smile twitches across her face; I follow her eyes, landing on Brandon Nguyen, Wesley's best friend, who smiles back at her. I shift in my seat.

I know it's cliché, but Dahlia's been my best friend since kindergarten, when we took gymnastics together and both sucked at it and couldn't cartwheel straight. Her first crush was on this kid Luke, who got yelled at in fourth grade for making gloves out of the class's entire stock of rubber cement. Clearly her taste in guys hasn't improved. Anyone even remotely connected to Wesley Clarke does not get my stamp of approval.

"These are meant to be the best years of our lives—not a military tour," Wesley continues. Last night, he had the audacity to post on his Instagram story that he was playing board games at Brandon's house with a bunch of track guys, drinking root-beer floats; meanwhile, I was doing actual work preparing for this debate. It's kind of insulting that he's my competition—for this, *and* for valedictorian.

"Take, for example, Stella Greene." Wesley gestures at me. I freeze. "Should school really be a place where a person looks *that* uptight and miserable?" Laughter rings around me. "No. It should not."

Heat flares through my face. I grit my teeth. *He did not.*

"All right, all right." Ms. Hatley shoots a warning glance at Wesley. "Stick to the topic, please."

"In conclusion, that is why Gene Connolly Memorial High School should *not* institute a mandatory school uniform policy." Wesley bows, to cheers and applause from the rest of the class. His eyes meet mine and he winks. I clench my hands in my lap. *The absolute nerve.*

"All right, settle down." Ms. Hatley waves her hand. "We've got five minutes left. Stella, Wesley, up at the podium for closing remarks."

I push to my feet, maintaining eye contact with Wesley as I take the front of the room, clenching my index cards so tight they're creasing. My heart pounds with every step. If I read the cards, I'll be fine. Maybe the plaid skirt and button-down were overkill, but I needed to show dedication to my assignment. Dahlia nods at me, crossing her fingers.

I shouldn't care about this project. It won't affect my GPA. But the thought of losing to Wesley Clarke makes my blood boil. I set my cards down on the opposite podium.

"As entertaining as your argument is, Wesley"—I force the fakest smile I can muster and dart my eyes to my first card—"it's not logical. Statistics prove that school uniforms foster a more positive, uh . . . learning environment, because they even the playing field. They eliminate some of the barriers created by factors like socioeconomic status."

Wesley raises an index finger. "But they *create* barriers by limiting self-expression."

"If by self-expression you mean the right to show up at school in swim trunks, then sure. Which, by the way, it's thirty degrees outside."

A few kids snicker.

"I go by the theory that we'll be dressing professionally for work for the rest of our lives," he says. "Why start now, at a time when we should be discovering our identities and expressing ourselves?" Some people nod in agreement.

"Well, *I* go by the theory that school is our current profession, um, and that you should dress for the job you want, not the job you have. So far, you're doing a great job dressing for life as a bum."

He leans closer to me. "A bum who has the same GPA as you."

"You do *not* have the same GPA as me."

Ms. Hatley stiffens. "Let's just—"

"Last time I checked, we were tied for valedictorian, Stells."

"Well, last time *I* checked, there were still four months left in the school year, *Wes*."

"Maybe you should get off your high horse and let people dress how they want."

"Maybe you should—"

The bell rings, cutting me off. Everyone rushes to gather their notebooks and jackets.

"Make sure to cast your vote for the winner before you leave," Ms. Hatley calls out. "Stella, try not to read straight off the cards next time. Great speech, Wesley."

"Thanks!" he says. "My tutor rehearsed it with me for like an hour last weekend."

He gets a private *tutor*? "Seriously?" I hiss.

"Excuse me." Wesley clears his throat, still at the front of the room, and most people stop rustling to look at him. "I'd like to thank Stella for being such admirable competition." His voice is thick with sarcasm. "When I become valedictorian and get my Porsche, I'd like to take Stella out for a celebratory hot beverage—you know, to melt off the scowl that's permanently frozen on her face."

"Mmm, tempting, but I'll be clipping my toenails that day, sorry."

"Her argument today was just . . . well, it was something. Friday night!" He raises his voice. "My place. Hot tub and Ping-Pong, who's in?" Several people rush toward him, already claiming first round with the Ping-Pong table.

"My argument was *what*?" I slam my index cards onto my desk. "Well researched? The product of actual work, rather than a few pull quotes you yanked off Wikipedia five minutes before class?" I grab my pen and make a big show of checking off *Pro-Uniform* on my ballot.

"Yes, Stella Greene, everyone." He gestures toward me, ticking off *Anti-Uniform* on his own sheet. "Always the smartest person in the room."

"When you're in the room, yes."

"Nice outfit."

I flip him off before grabbing my stuff and plowing out the door.

–♥–

"Can you believe I was alone for Valentine's Day *again*?" Dahlia asks on our way to her car. Our school runs on the "early bird gets the parking space" system, and since Dahlia is usually lucky to squeak in before the bell, that means a hike to reach her little

Honda. I would bitch about the uphill trek in the snow, but to be honest I'm grateful Dahlia drives me home, since my alternative is the bus.

"I mean, my only date this weekend was with our English essay, so"—my breath clouds in the air—"you can be my Galentine."

"Well, yeah. But that's not the point." Dahlia's puffy white Michael Kors winter coat blends into the snow piled on the side of the road. I can't help fidgeting, too aware that my pink jacket came from the clearance rack at Walmart three years ago. You know those Hallmark movies where the pretty girl has the quirky, awkward, and sarcastic best-friend-slash-sidekick? Yeah. That's me.

"I actually forgot yesterday was Valentine's Day." I did, however, remember that *today* marks an important date—it's exactly three months until this year's Sci-Con, which means I'm running out of time on my cosplay. I force my frozen fingers to pound out a reminder in my phone before burying them back in my jacket pockets. "Why, did you have something special in mind?"

Dahlia sighs. "No. Not really."

"Trust me, having a boyfriend—or girlfriend, person, whatever—for Valentine's is overrated." I hold up a finger. "First of all, the societal pressure of *needing* to have one, ick. Secondly"—I hold up another one—"it distracts from the real holiday today, which is half-off candy at CVS."

She rolls her eyes, fishing through her purse for her car keys. "Always the romantic."

"It's just not my priority right now."

There are three guys who *could* make me reconsider: (1) Sergeant Aaron Lewis, who is, unfortunately, fictional; (2) Ethan Martone, who plays Sergeant Aaron Lewis, and is, unfortunately, married; and (3) Kyle Nielsen, who, unfortunately, doesn't even know I exist, despite sitting two rows over from me in AP Bio.

But with valedictorian on the line, I can't lose focus. In a few months I'll be at MIT with a bunch of hot engineering majors, and it will all be paid for by a big fat scholarship that I earned by working my ass off for the past eternity.

Dahlia's mitten-clad fingers fumble with the unlock button, and we quickly climb in. New Hampshire's seasons are basically colors: fall is orange, summer is green, and we're currently in the middle of gray, which means we shiver in our seats while the heater decides whether to kick into gear.

"I don't really care or anything, but . . . I don't know." She flicks on the radio, keeping her eyes on the console. "I guess part of me was hoping this one guy would ask me out."

I set my backpack down at my feet. "Does his name start with *B* and rhyme with *Schmandon*?"

Dahlia looks like I just correctly guessed a number she was thinking between one and a bazillion. "How did you know?"

Because I can imagine her face becoming one of those memes—*find someone who looks at you the way Dahlia Johnston looks at Brandon Nguyen*. "Lucky guess? Why don't *you* just ask *him*?"

"I would, but—I don't know. I don't care." She shrugs it off a little too quickly. "I'd rather be single when I start college anyway."

I don't buy that for a second. But I don't argue, either. "That's the spirit."

WARSHIP SEVEN PILOT:
"The Man in the Dungeon" (2016)

SCENE CLIP: The crew has just captured a Central Elite (CE) soldier, SERGEANT AARON LEWIS, and taken him prisoner in the ship's makeshift dungeon, where he sits on a metal storage trunk. CAPTAIN JILL BRIGHTON leads an interrogation, accompanied by second-in-command MARKUS HARRIS.

JILL: He had this in his pocket. [holds out badge depicting a silver eagle with blue-tipped wings]

AARON: How do you know that's mine?

JILL: [completely ignores him] But there's never just one CE, which is what's making me nervous. They travel in pairs.

AARON: Maybe I stole that badge off the last ship I hit.

MARKUS: [completely ignores him] You think he's got a tail?

JILL: Can't be sure, but we weren't followed. Gemma checked.

AARON: [puts his booted feet up on the table] Or maybe I'm reporting your exact position to my partner right now.

JILL: [whips out a pistol and points it directly at Aaron without looking at him] Shut. Up.

MARKUS: So, what do we do with him?

AARON: Might I make the bold suggestion to let him go?

JILL: [growing increasingly irritated by Aaron's interruptions] I'm going to find out what he knows, and then we'll come up with a plan. We can't just keep a prisoner on the ship; we don't have the space or the resources. But I'm not about to send him back to the Elites to tell them everything he knows about us.

MARKUS: You can't mean you want to kill him.

JILL: I may not have a choice.

MARKUS: [clearly uncomfortable] Well, get Skulls to do it, then. He's got more than a handful of notches in his murder belt.

JILL: I won't pass a death sentence and then make someone else do my dirty work.

AARON: If I may interject—

JILL: [whirls around, knocking his feet off the table] You're on my ship. I've got no reason to keep you alive, beyond my good graces, which are wearing thin, Cescum.

AARON: Cescum? [makes a face] That's harsh, don't you think?

JILL: CE-scum. Not harsh enough for the crimes the Central Elite have committed against innocent people. And if you can't promise to keep your mouth shut, I can't promise to keep you alive.

AARON: I'm not afraid of dying.

JILL: Everyone's afraid of dying.

AARON: Not everyone, sweetheart.

JILL: I'm not your sweetheart.

AARON: You're something, though.

JILL: I don't suffer judgment from small minds. [Nods at Markus, who follows her out of the makeshift cell. They close the heavy iron door behind them.]

AARON: [Waits for the footsteps to fade. He leans back, clearly pushing his tongue around inside his mouth and engaging the tiny comm chip hidden between his back teeth.] Michele. Michele, are you there? [He mutters, barely audible.] I'm in. I'm on the *Revelry*. I'll get the info and come back to you . . . Yes . . . See you soon, baby.

[Scene cuts to MICHELE CORDOVA, her hair tied back, sitting in a cloaked two-person shuttle a short distance away, watching the *Revelry* through a pair of binoculars. She smiles.]

MICHELE: And don't forget to kill the captain.

2 WESLEY

You'd think watching fourteen pages spill from the printer would be satisfying, since I'd never have to write another sentence of this terrible essay again. But I spent the better part of the last month researching, and I'm about ready to bid farewell with my tallest finger.

My knee bounces against my hand under the desk. I force it still. So many people are already doing the whole "senioritis" thing; it must be nice to let your brain take a vacation after you get accepted into college.

My Stanford acceptance letter covers a good chunk of my bulletin board, but I can still see the corner of my Columbia acceptance letter poking out behind it. In AP Euro last year, we learned about how Mary, Queen of Scots, was once betrothed to Prince Edward of England, a guy she'd never met, in the 1500s when she was just a little kid. That's kind of what this feels like, only my parents betrothed me to Stanford University long before I even knew what college was.

Three months ago, I did something bad. Or, I guess, good. I accepted Columbia's offer and turned down Stanford. I haven't told my parents, because they'll flip.

My eyes wander to the "Natural Wonders" calendar hanging on my green wall, with May 15 circled in blue Sharpie: Sci-Con weekend. Some days I feel like it's the only thing keeping me going.

Three months to Sci-Con. Four until graduation. And then I'll be valedictorian, and I can get the hell out of here. Unless that terrible stick-in-the-mud Stella Greene manages to pull ahead of me.

Which she won't. She can't. Because I *need* that scholarship.

I scroll through Insta while waiting for the printer to finish. Brandon's parents got him a Mazda for his birthday, and he's posted so many photos of it I'm surprised the company hasn't hired him to be a spokesperson.

> If you post one more picture of that stupid car, people are going to start to think you're secretly a Transformer. Parking passes for Sci-Con just went up, I'll buy one if you drive (it's $25, don't bitch about gas).

Within seconds, he texts me back.

> You're the one getting the Porsche—that means you're driving, sorry, I don't make the rules.

Funny how he thinks my parents would give me anything without strings attached.

> I'm not getting anything unless I'm valedictorian. Won't be by May anyway. It's the Mazda or the bus. Or your mom drives.

I open Safari on my MacBook, clicking into the *Warship Seven* forum and tabbing into Fanart. Back in the day, this website was the place to be. The hard-core fans are still on it, and ideally at least a handful of them are coming to Sci-Con. It would be good to have people to hang out with, since Brandon's probably going to ditch me to see some *Star Wars* actor who's going to be there.

My phone chimes with another text from Brandon.

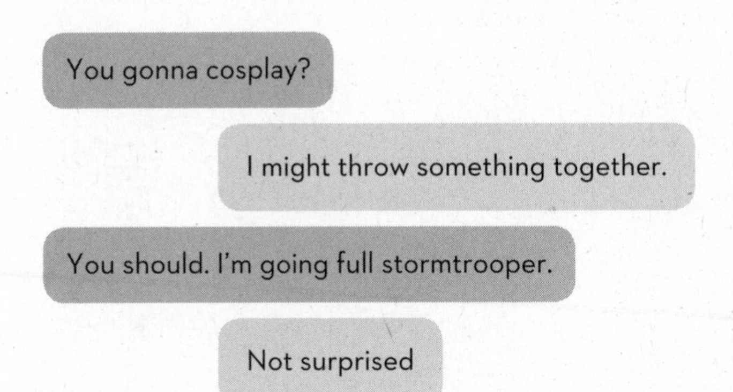

I'll be even less surprised if he shows up with not one but two lightsabers—canon be damned.

I do a double take at my notifications at the bottom of the screen. Okay, I did *not* know my random half-asleep portrait of Sergeant Aaron Lewis gripping his pistol would be the picture that got me more than a thousand likes. Seriously, I didn't even give it a decent caption. I just posted "Quick sketch of Aaron ready to kick ass," and now it's got dozens of comments. Still can't compete with the smutty fanart that people draw of Aaron and Jill, but I don't care.

Allhailtheship617: Love him—and this drawing—so much!

GemmasBodyguard11: Whoa, you did a great job capturing the expression in his eyes.

Season2orbust: Our captain probably has this drawing hanging in her bedroom

CaptainJillsBFF22: this is great!! Love Aaron. Wishing we had a few more scenes with our OTP #Lewton. Imagine them side by side fighting!?! swoons

Just once I wish I could post a drawing without an Aaron/Jill shipper turning it into a Lewton thing. Of course, CaptainJillsBFF22's thumbnail pic is a fanart of Aaron and Jill making out. That's one thing that seriously bugs me about this fandom. Aaron and Jill are the two most incompatible characters ever. Both badass and awesome, but not meant to be together. I'm sure they'll dredge it up during the *Warship* panels at Sci-Con.

As if on cue, my phone vibrates with a new text from Brandon.

> Bad news—I just found out my grandma's 80th bday party is May 15. Gonna have to bail on Sci-Con, sorry.

I stare at the text for forever. *Oh, come on.* Well, this sucks. I'm going to have to sell my ticket or something. Dad will be happy. When he saw the charge on the credit card statement, his first comment was "Isn't this science fiction stuff for children?"

Footsteps tap downstairs, and I know Mom's about to tell me to come down for dinner.

Three . . . two . . . one . . .

"Wes! Are you coming? Your father made pork chops."

"Be right there," I call back.

I snap the stapler over my freshly printed essay and slap the finished thing down on my desk. There's something almost sadistic about the fact that this paper took me two weeks to write and now lies limply on the table, ready to be read and graded by my English teacher before being tossed into the trash.

Plates clink downstairs, the only sound echoing into the hallway.

I hesitate over my open computer screen. I *really* want to go to Sci-Con. I've been dying to meet Ethan Martone for forever. I could go alone—lots of people go alone. But that could also be super weird.

I quickly shoot out a message onto the forum's home page.

Anyone going to Sci-Con in Boston this May? My first time. Looking for some fellow #Warshippers to hang with.

I shut my screen, greeted by the four stickers I added to it last year—one of the CE eagle and one of the *Warship* symbol. And then a sticker for Imagine Dragons and another for AC Milan, my favorite soccer team.

Dad's standing by the stove in slacks and a polo, typing on his phone. He puts it facedown on the countertop when I enter the kitchen. "Hey. How was school?"

Mom carries a platter of pork and a bowl of mashed potatoes to the table.

"Fine." I reach to take the plates out of her hands. "Mom, sit down, I'll get it."

"I already tried," Dad says. "She won't let anyone help. Typical."

"It's fine. Just sit." My mom's up at the crack of dawn, in the law office by 7:00 a.m., home at 6:00, and still won't take a break. "Did you have a good day, Wes?"

"Yeah. We had our debate."

"Oh? How'd it go?"

"It was okay. I think Stella Greene's team won."

"Stella Greene! Haven't heard that name in a while." Mom shuts the fridge. "What's she up to these days?"

Being an insufferable pain in the ass. "Not much."

Dad takes a seat and helps himself to some mashed potatoes. "Have you started writing your valedictorian speech yet?"

I shrug. I feel like if I start presumptuously writing the speech, the universe will conspire against me and Stella I-Know-Everything Greene will get valedictorian and mess up all my plans. "Not yet."

"Well, I'm proud of you. It's not every father who gets to say he was high school valedictorian, then had two valedictorian sons."

I sit down in my usual chair and scoop some food onto my plate. "Sure." The thing about my dad's praise is that he always says it like there's an asterisk attached, and it leads to a list of conditions longer than that godforsaken paper I just printed.

A vintage Clarke Gourmet Chocolates sign hangs by the fridge. Back in sophomore year computer class, they made us take these aptitude tests to see what our ideal career would be. It was kind of a waste of time, filling out all the answers, because it's not like I have a choice anyway. When the computer spat out "English literature professor" and "artist," I felt like it was making fun of me. *You don't need to stay in the family company, but the future's in business and engineering*—I've heard it so many times, it'll probably be the phrase they scrawl on my tombstone.

"Hon, you didn't take out the dinner rolls," Mom says to Dad as she slides a potholder over her hand. She wrestles the tray out of the oven, and a buttery scent fills the air. "They could've burned."

"You could've taken them out yourself, then."

Mom's mouth thins to a line, but she doesn't respond. Her pantsuit is still perfectly pressed, despite the long day at her law firm.

"Did you remember to take your Prozac today?" she asks me.

I roll my eyes. "Yeah. With breakfast."

"Good." Mom collapses in the seat across from me and starts serving herself. "Before I forget, I was thinking we could go back to St. Maarten this summer, before Wes heads to college."

I pick at my broccoli. Something hard settles in my chest, and it's not the food.

Dad looks at her skeptically.

"Dr. Bryce said we need to take family time," Mom says, not looking up. "You know that."

I'm not sure what marriage counselor thinks going to a happy place and pretending it's the good ol' days will make everything better.

"It's a possibility," Dad says. "Trev loves cruises—remember that Mediterranean cruise we took when you boys were kids, and we could barely pry him out of that pool?"

It's been two years since Trevor left for college, and my parents are still in denial about him not living here. The house feels emptier. Or louder, because it's always full of shouting.

"Can't see Trevor saying no to a trip," Mom says. "What about you, Wes? You up for it?"

"I guess." The thought of spending a week trapped with my

parents makes me feel seasick without ever setting foot on a ship.

"You know, I like this plan. We can take a cruise, have some fun," Dad says, checking his phone, "celebrate your being named valedictorian and heading out to Stanford."

"Or just celebrate my graduation." It comes out harsher than intended, but I don't correct it.

"Of course," Mom says gently. She shoots Dad a death glare.

"We're at dinner, babe." He slides his phone back onto the table.

We eat in silence for a moment, forks scraping against plates.

"I have a feeling we'll be making a trip to the Porsche dealership this June." Dad nods at me. "You'll need a good car for the drive out to California."

"I thought we agreed to fly," Mom says.

"With all his boxes for school? No airline would allow that."

"Why don't we just buy everything he needs once we're out there?"

I love it when they talk about me like I'm not sitting right here.

"What, you think I have unlimited time away from the office? You already want to do a vacation," Dad says. "We'll send Wesley's college stuff out on a truck ahead of time, drive him there, set him up, and fly back."

Mom shoots him a wide smile. "You've got lots of time away from the office for golf. Or is that what you mean when you say you're working?"

Dad grumbles, but doesn't respond, so Mom continues, "I mean, it's not like California is a short walk from here."

I shift in my seat. "Or, you know. New York." If I go to Columbia.

The wrinkles in Dad's forehead trench deeper. "I thought

Columbia was your fallback. Not that I thought Stanford would turn you down, when we've got a long line of Clarkes wearing Cardinals sweatshirts."

I have several safeties, and none of them are Columbia. "It's not my backup choice," I mutter.

Dad snorts. "I'm not paying for you to gallivant around New York City. Might as well not even go to college at that rate."

"You'll love Stanford," Mom says, taking a bite. "The business program is top notch. And it'll be nice for us to visit our alma mater again."

"Yeah." I drag my fork through my potatoes. "Sure."

I know why my parents want me to be valedictorian: so I won't soil the Clarke family's perfect record of being number one. But that's not why I *need* it. I *need* that valedictorian full-ride scholarship so I don't have to rely on my parents to pay for school—no pay, no say.

The pendulum on the grandfather clock swings back and forth, back and forth. Tick, tock. Tick, tock. It's hard to believe this house was once full of my dad's jokes and my mom's laughter. Seems like ancient history now.

Dad's phone vibrates, making the edge of his plate rattle. He sneaks a glance at it before placing it back on the table.

It crosses my mind that I should text my little cousin, Devin. He had a math test today.

Hey, how'd your exam go??

Dad's eyes narrow, but I've got him here—he can't yell at me for texting at the table, since his own phone has basically become a second fork in his place setting.

My phone vibrates.

Good, I think. I hate math.

Oh, sweet summer child, still doing seventh-grade math.

Wait until you have to do calc.

He responds with a vomit emoji.

My mom arches an eyebrow at my father. "The food's not going anywhere, Ted."

My dad stops shoveling food into his mouth and swallows. "You were just implying I wasn't working hard enough for this family. I'm trying to eat quickly so I can get back to work."

Mom mutters under her breath, stabbing a broccoli floret with more force than necessary.

Dad throws his fork down. "You have something to say, Bev?"

I stand up from the table so abruptly, the chair legs scrape against the tile. "I have to finish my English paper."

Mom's brow creases. "Wes—"

Dad tries to catch my eye, probably pissed I'm storming out in the middle of dinner, but I can't take this right now. I rinse my plate in the sink and slide it into the dishwasher before plowing back upstairs.

I used to sit in the living room and watch TV with my parents every night, but now they both work late and I've always got homework. I put my elbows on the desk and rest my head in my hands.

Sergeant Aaron Lewis never falters. He is fiercely loyal to those he loves.

I've got to focus on something. Anything.

I tab back into the forum. My Sci-Con post only got

three comments. The first is some dude saying he went last year but moved out of state, but still felt the need to comment. The second is someone saying they think cons are a waste of money, as if I outright asked for their opinion. Finally, there's a comment from that Lewton shipper, CaptainJillsBFF22.

I'll be there! Can't wait.

I roll my eyes. Of course that's who would be going. My knuckles tap against my desk.

I'm not sure what makes me do it, but I click the username and open a new message.

3 STELLA

I can barely keep my eyes open, glued to the AP American History textbook splayed open on my desk. I've read the same line about Teddy Roosevelt at least half a dozen times, and if I have to read it half a dozen more, I'm going to gouge my eyes out. Seriously, the name Roosevelt looks really weird if you see it too many times.

I push back, doing a quick swivel-spin in my desk chair and letting my bedroom blur around me. My walls blend together with the beige carpet. I tuck my legs into my chest until the chair stops spinning and I'm facing my bed, the purple sheets tangled in a nest at the end. I'd love nothing more than to swan-dive into it right now.

But I've still got to wash the acne cream off my face, brush my teeth, floss—and, oh yeah, finish this reading.

Pandora plays softly from my phone, streaming the Taylor Swift station. They've hit a string of acoustic songs, and I swear my eyelids grow heavier with each guitar strum.

Focus.

My phone buzzes with a text from Bridget.

> Do you know if we still have any of those peanut butter crackers?

My sister's contact picture fills my screen; she's wearing her Burger Blitz uniform, holding my niece, Gwen, up to the camera. Gwen was so small in that picture, only a couple months old. It's hard to believe she'll be two on her next birthday.

I roll my eyes and type back.

Did you really just text me from the other room? You know you could walk two feet into the kitchen and check yourself, right?

Gwen finally fell asleep and I'm soooo hungry.

More like you're soooo lazy.

I quickly add a wink face at the end, because in all honesty, Bridget is the least lazy person I know. Which makes it even worse that she screwed up her life, because I swear, she would have made an amazing doctor or lawyer or something.

Mom bought a new box on Sunday.

She responds with a smattering of kissy-face emojis. Within seconds, a door in the hall creaks open and footsteps patter in the hallway. That's a fun thing about living in a tiny subsidized apartment; anything someone does, everyone else knows about it.

I let my chair spin until that cursed book is back in view. Twenty more pages. That's it. Exhaustion drapes over me like a cloak. I should remember this book next time I can't sleep; history reading is an amazing cure for insomnia.

I have to finish it. Mr. Bailey loves giving pop quizzes to see if we've done our reading, and I've got a perfect streak I'd prefer to keep.

Valedictorian.

Scholarship.

College.

First in the family.

I repeat the words like a prayer in my head and force myself to take another crack at the book.

My first mistake was letting myself change into pajamas, and the second mistake was coming to my room to work, where my bed looks oh-so-comfy and enticing. But Dave's snoozing on the couch in the living room, and Bridget will distract me if she sees me, so this is the best place.

Theodore Roosevelt was the . . .

Theodore Roosevelt was . . .

Theodore Roosevelt . . .

Theo . . .

I slam the book shut, then rub my eyes under my glasses. This isn't working. I'll just wake up extra early tomorrow. My fingers are fighting me when I set the alarm on my phone for four forty-five, but I do it.

I will be valedictorian. I *deserve* to be valedictorian. I will show everyone that I *earned* this, and it doesn't matter where you come from—only where you go.

I'll check on my fic and go to bed.

I log in to the *Warship* forums, and sure enough, the fic I uploaded this morning has sixty-two views and twelve comments. A sleepy smile spreads across my face. This was just a quick one I wrote over the weekend, a Jill/Aaron alternate universe fic where they meet working at an ice cream shop in Seattle. I'm not even sure why I picked Seattle; I've never been there—I've never even been on a plane. But it looked nice, so why not? Jill's his boss, and they clash a ton. It ends with their wedding on a boat, strategically named—wait for it—the *Revelry*. The ending we deserved.

I keep a folder of bookmarked fluff fics for when I need an escape, and a collection of fix-it-fics for *Warship* rewatches. Twice a year, the forum hosts a livestream and everyone rewatches the episodes and posts their reactions. Last time, I wrote up episode recaps with my thoughts; pretty sure I got at least like a handful of readers. I love it, but I also always need a palate cleanser of a fluff fic after that terrible ending.

I'm about to click out of Chrome when I catch a new message notification.

CERanger11: hey. Saw your comment on my post. You're going to Sci-Con? I'm going too. First time.

Well, I definitely wasn't expecting this dude to full-on slide into my DMs. Kind of concerning. At least he didn't open with something like "hello cutie." My friend Brooke purposely keeps her username gender neutral, and her forum pic is just a stock photo of the *Revelry*. We once did an experiment where we both posted the same complaint on the forum—that despite having a woman main character, more than half the *Warship* episodes don't pass the Bechdel test. I got a personal record of mansplaining in the comments about why I was overreacting; Brooke got some "likes," but was otherwise left alone.

My fingers hesitate over the keyboard. Part of me wants to x out of the message. Cold messages from random men never lead anywhere good.

But I remember my first con; I didn't know anyone, and it

sucked. I got Leigh Stanton's autograph, though. Her picture looks back at me from across the desk, a shot of her in full *Warship* attire grasping her pistol; the actress's swirly signature scrawls across the middle. Loving an obscure thing can be very isolating; it's not like being a *Star Wars* fan or a Harry Potter fan where there are actual theme parks for the people who love them. If I tell someone I have a Captain Jill Brighton costume, they mostly gape at me. But stepping into Sci-Con and seeing so many people wearing the *Warship* sigil, or dressed as the characters, or adorned in sloganed T-shirts bearing Jill's famous quote made me feel like I belonged. All day, people complimented my costume and took photos with me, and it was great. Who am I to deny that to someone else?

CaptainJillsBFF22: Yeah it'll be my third year in a row! Sci-Con is great. Lots of Warshippers.

Within two seconds, another message pops up.

CERanger11: Nice. You cosplay?

So far, no gross comments and no mansplaining. We're on the right track.

My Jill cosplay hangs off the pink hanger poking out of my slightly ajar closet door. I sewed the *Warship* patch onto the front of the fitted gray overcoat myself, and embellished the jacket with the closest things I could find to the big brass buttons on Jill's.

CaptainJillsBFF22: I go as our dear captain every year ☺ You?

CERanger11: Thinking of putting together a Sergeant Aaron Lewis costume. Idk. I've never cosplayed before. But his uniform seems simple enough.

Okay, not going to lie, I'm (1) not surprised he's going as Aaron, because he's every dude's favorite character, but (2) also kind of wondering if he's some fortysomething sleazebag who purposely threw out Captain Jill's love interest as part of some pervy plan to get into my pants. I would not put it past some of these fanboys. But I guess I should be happy he didn't toss a dick pic into my inbox like the last random guy who messaged me on here; I responded by taking a photo of my poop in the toilet and sending it back to him, and then he blocked me, so I consider it a win.

CaptainJillsBFF22: Oh? He your favorite?
CERanger11: Yep. Since episode 1.
CaptainJillsBFF22: Cool! He's pretty great.

There's a soft knocking on my bedroom door. "Stella, honey, I just got home and saw your light on. Are you still up?" My mom's voice barely penetrates the wood. Even though she's whispering, I can hear the yawn in her voice.

"Yeah," I call back. "Sorry, finishing up some reading for AP History. I still need to brush and floss."

The door cracks open and she pokes her head in, still wearing her SpongeBob scrubs. She only got her medical assistant license a year ago but has about a bazillion different scrubs, all with various cartoon characters on them. "You have a good day?"

I shrug, rotating my chair to face her. "I guess. Almost ripped Wesley Clarke a new one in Public Speaking."

Her eyebrows shoot up. "Again?"

"Yes, must be a day that ends in *y*." I pull my knees up to my chin, stroking my soft pink pajama pants. "But it was fine. How was your day?"

A heavy sigh wracks Mom's body. "Well, the rent is due in two weeks, and the car started squeaking when I brake, so honestly not great."

"Jeez."

"Either going to have to talk to Cynthia and tell her the rent will be late or say a prayer every time I stop at a red."

"I can pick up an extra shift at The Scoopery next week and—"

"No," she cuts me off. "You need to focus on school. I can ask Bridget if I need to." Bridget, the dropout who makes minimum wage while raising a kid. I *need* to get a good job after college.

Time for a subject change. "How's the nursing home?"

"Had to clean up my body weight in puke, but otherwise not bad."

"Glamorous." I pick at my fingernails. "You know, I think the credit union is hiring. You could get a nice desk job. I guarantee your day would consist of much less urine and blood."

"Stella, you know I *love* my job. Blood and urine and all."

Someday I hope I make enough money so she won't have to do this anymore.

"Did you eat dinner?"

"No, Dave is starving us."

Mom deadpans at me, so I continue, "Yes, of course. He heated up some frozen eggplant parmesan. Gwen even tried a little. We saved some for you in the fridge."

"Good." She smiles. "Now *please* get some rest."

"Will do, if you do." She kisses the air twice, and I do it back, our little ritual.

She slips into the hall and shuts the door. I've barely turned back to the screen when an alert pops up.

CERanger11 would like to share an image with you.

Oh, here we go. I roll my eyes so hard they're practically scraping the back of my skull. Why do guys do this? Has it ever actually helped pick someone up? Like, *Yes, son, I took a picture of my junk and sent it to a woman with a hot profile picture, and surprise, that's how I met your mother.*

My finger hesitates over the button. Against my better judgment, I hit Accept—only because I still have that poop picture saved on my phone somewhere, and I'm not afraid to use it.

I'm scrolling through my phone searching for my ammunition when a black-and-white picture fills the screen. But it's actually G-rated—it's a pencil sketch of Aaron Lewis sitting in his escape pod, flying away from the *Revelry* and Jill forever. The last scene in the show.

CERanger11: Working on this one. Haven't posted it yet.

My heart sinks. Episode twenty. Oh, episode twenty. It never ceases to break my heart.

I'm not sure why it bothers me so much that he left her. I know it's just a TV show. I guess because, in the real world, romances end like it did for Bridget and Ben—Gwen's father: a giant hot mess. Jill and Aaron were supposed to be endgame. And if my OTP doesn't work out, what hope does that leave for the rest of us?

This guy caught the look in Aaron's eyes perfectly. He's glancing up to his rearview, turmoil written across his face.

I signed the viral petition for season two, even though it felt futile, because I really, really wish we could've seen them get back together. I have to believe Aaron was going to come back for her.

CaptainJillsBFF22: That's really good. Love the way you got his smirk but still show the reservation in his eyes.
CERanger11: Glad you like it. It's one of my favorite scenes.
CaptainJillsBFF22: Wait, really? That's the saddest scene in the show. He's leaving.
CERanger11: I guess it's only sad if you don't like where he's going.

Of course this dude is a Lewton anti. It honestly blows my mind that there are people who ship Aaron Lewis with Michele Cordova instead of Captain Jill. I contemplate sending him my twelve-point theory on why #Lewdova is the inferior ship, but I think better of it.

CaptainJillsBFF22: Okay, well, bedtime. Good night.

4 WESLEY

The second-to-last thing I want to be greeted with when I arrive at school is my AP Bio test lying on my desk with a giant 88% scrawled on top. I swallow hard and scan my answers. I should have studied harder. I had two calc assignments due the next day, so I kind of blew it off. One test can't mess up my GPA too much, right? My fingers drum against my leg.

I'm barely on question three—which is entirely circled in red pen—when the number-one last thing I want to be greeted with struts into the classroom.

Stella glances at the paper on my desk when she walks by. "All hail Mr. Valedictorian, king of the B-plus."

I shove the paper into a crumpled mess in my backpack. "Let me know if you need help with that salutatorian address; I know public speaking isn't your strong suit."

"Actually, I think Number Two is a more fitting title for *you*, Clarke. I think of you every time my dog takes one on the side of the road."

"Aw, you were thinking of me? That's adorable."

She flips me her middle finger before taking her seat, two rows away.

I subtly scratch my neck, trying to catch a glimpse of Stella's grade. She gives me a smug grin before holding up her paper, which has a 96% on top. My shoulders tense.

It's just one test. And this *is* her best class.

Okay, one thing about Stella Greene. If someone's going to discover the cure for cancer, it'll be her. Her brain is like a sponge for AP Bio, and last year she corrected our chem teacher on some theorem like a boss. But she absolutely sucks at English Lit and History, which is where I can make up for lost points. This isn't over.

I *need* that full-ride scholarship.

I let my face fall into my hands. I hate that my whole plan falls apart if I can't lift my AP Bio grade.

"Hey." Laura McNally drops into the seat beside me, and my pulse kicks up. "Can you believe this?" She slaps the surface of her desk. "I studied three hours for this stupid test and I got a C."

"Test kicked everyone's ass. I wouldn't worry."

"I *am* worried." She bites her lip, and my mind immediately shoots to that night we made out in the back of her dad's sedan at the mall parking lot. We got busted by a mall cop who pounded on the window with a flashlight, probably assuming we were boning. It's suddenly way too hot in this classroom. "NYU is gonna waitlist me, I just know it."

"Nah." I go to fake-punch her arm, but draw my hand back at the last second, because touching her still feels weird. "You'll get in." My heart starts racing, and I want to rip the whole thing out of my chest and throw it in the garbage.

It just stopped being awkward with Laura like a month ago, and I don't want to screw it up. She flicks a lock of long blond hair behind her back, and I shift my eyes to the front of the classroom. It's not like we dated that long. I think it was four months total. But I still get this tight feeling in my chest when she's around. Part of me is still holding out hope she'll ask me to prom. Holly D'Angeles asked me yesterday, and I said no, but now with my luck I'll probably end up going alone.

"All right, settle down." Mr. Hardwicke strolls into the classroom wearing a checkered tie and clutching a Coke Zero. "Have you all enjoyed looking over your tests?"

He must have a different definition of the word *enjoyed*.

Five hands immediately shoot up around me, including Laura's.

"Yes, yes, I thought so." He sets his Coke down on the front lab table. I guess the whole no-food-in-the-lab rule doesn't apply to him. "We'll go over it answer by answer. You'll want to keep them to help you study for the final."

The hands go down. Stella still hasn't wiped the smug look off her face, and it kind of makes me want to scream.

"But first, we have to go over spring projects—rat mazes."

Several people groan. I lean back in my seat and cross my arms. The infamous rat mazes are the sole reason half the class chooses to take AP Bio and the sole reason the other half hates this class. It is kind of a weird assignment, I guess. My parents would flip if I brought home a pet rat in any other scenario, and I'm not thrilled about it myself. Forced proximity with rats: isn't that what killed half of Europe back in the day? Cruel and unusual punishment.

"Galaxy Pets on Willow has our rat friends in stock, so make sure you take a voucher and go pick up your rat and supplies by next week."

I whip out my notebook and jot down the name of the pet store. It's really close to my house.

"You've got three months to build a maze out of cardboard"—he gestures toward the lab table at the back of the room, where a heap of broken-down boxes is draped haphazardly off the sides of the counter—"and train your rat to complete its maze."

More groans. I don't know why people are complaining. This

is an easy task: just bribe it with food. It's basically how my parents get my brother to do anything. I don't even have to touch the rodent.

"When we test them at the end of the project, your rat must be able to go from beginning to end without help, direction, or food. It's an easy A, honestly. They're very intelligent."

"What do we do with the rats after the project?" Kyle Nielsen blurts out, without raising his hand.

"That's up to you. You can keep them as pets or bring them back to the school, where we'll do a spring adoption clinic in partnership with the ASPCA."

Jen Martin's hand shoots up. "What if my parents won't let me keep a rat in the house?"

"You can leave the rats in this classroom. Just label your cage and I'll come feed them on nights and weekends. Or see if your partner can take it home instead."

"Partners?" Stella frowns. She always gets this weird little indent in her forehead when she frowns.

"Rat mazes are a group project."

More groans.

Laura gives me a quick smile.

Maybe a group project won't be so bad.

Mr. Hardwicke tugs a folded sheet of paper out of his pocket. "I'll be assigning your partners."

This time, I actually join in the groans.

"Settle down, it's a project, not marriage. When you have a job, you'll have to work with all sorts of people, so get used to it." He slides his glasses on. "First up, Laura McNally and Johanna Yolanski."

My heart sinks a little. Laura smiles at her partner across the room. I can't help wishing she would look that way at me.

"Kevin Dooley and Ally Knight. Kelly Pierce and Serena Hutchings. Wesley Clarke and Stella Greene."

Stella jumps up. "No. Wait."

I raise my hand. "Can I have a different partner?"

"Excuse me?" Mr. Hardwicke lowers his gray eyebrows. "No, you may not."

Stella glares at me. "Can I just work by myself, since I basically would be anyway?"

"No. Sit down, Ms. Greene."

Stella sinks into her seat, her cheeks bright red and a scowl stretching across her face.

"What if—"

"No." Mr. Hardwicke cuts me off.

Kyle actually raises his hand this time. "It's kind of unfair, pairing the two smartest people in class together."

I slap my hand on the desk. "Yes. That."

"He's right," Stella says. "We should be split up."

"The pairings were randomly assigned by the computer. Now, you can calm down or take a zero for the day and wait in the guidance counselor's office for the rest of the class."

I make a point to look literally anywhere but at fuming Stella.

He keeps reading names. Three months partnered with Stella Greene. Great.

—♥—

Stella's waiting for me in the hall when class ends, still wearing the scowl.

"What?" I ask her.

She releases a heavy sigh when she sees me, like it physically pains her. "I'll go to Galaxy on Saturday to get our rat."

I shift my backpack onto my shoulders. "I'll do it. It's on the way to my house."

"Um, no. I want to pick the rat."

"You don't trust me to pick a *rat*?"

She snorts. "I wouldn't trust you to flip my hamburger."

"Fine. Whatever. Are you keeping it at your house, or am I?"

"I don't think my mom will let me. Also, our dog would definitely eat it. Can I drop it at yours?"

"What? No." Stella Greene stomping around my house? "Bring it to school; Hardwicke says you can leave it in the classroom. I can bring it home Monday."

Her brown eyes go wide. "But . . . I don't want to leave the rat here all weekend. Something could happen to it."

"Seriously?"

"Seriously. I'll bring it to your house."

"So, let me get this straight." I cross my arms. "You're going to go out of your way to go to Galaxy Pets, which is closer to my house than yours, to pick the rat yourself, which you're then going to bring to my house."

"Correct."

"Suit yourself. Don't come before noon. I'm meeting with my public speaking coach, then running with the guys."

"Public speaking coach, yes, how dare I interrupt."

"And don't come after four, I'm going to Brandon's house."

"Love that you have time for that." She rolls her eyes. "I need your phone number for when we have to meet up."

"Keep it in your pants, Greene. This is a school project."

"Shut up." She yanks the phone out of my hand and enters her number, then thrusts it back at me. I quickly add her to my contacts.

"Hey!" Stella leans in. "What are you putting my name as?"

I rotate the phone toward her so she can see it.

"*Stick*? What the hell does that mean?"

"It's the giant stiff thing always up your butt." I text her. "There, now you have mine."

She enters my contact info into her phone, then tilts the screen toward me so I can see.

Salutatorian. She saved my name as Salutatorian.

Topic: ***WARSHIP SEVEN* REWATCH!!!**
Username: **CaptainJillsBFF22**

W7

Is everyone here? Did you enjoy last night's episode one rewatch as much as me?? I think I've seen that episode more than any of the others, and it never gets old.

Tonight we're watching episode two: "Two Wrongs Make a Right (Turn)." I think my favorite thing about this episode is that we really get to know the *Revelry* crew. We've got our Captain Jill, of course, but then there's pilot Gemma, mechanic Sonny, gunman Skulls, droid C0ndor, and second-in-command Markus.

In the episode, pirate cruisers box them in, and teen pilot Gemma has to pull off some serious moves to escape. I love Gemma in this episode (all the time, but especially here) because we see all the crap she deals with, but it doesn't stop her from being a badass pilot. It's also the first episode we see some hard-core battle action.

There's one scene in this episode that bugs me, though: when the crew is sitting around the dinner table. Jill and Markus ponder ways to get information out of the CE hostage, Aaron, in the dungeon, while the others weigh in. Gemma is helping C0ndor the droid, who keeps glitching, but her twin brother, Sonny, and ship-gunman Skulls keep harassing her about her upcoming date. I've always found it problematic that Sonny is kind of a man-whore who's lauded by the others, but the minute Gemma gets a boyfriend, they're all telling her that her shirt's too low cut and joking about keeping her locked on the ship? Ew. It's one of those scenes you *know* was written by a man. I swear, I love this show, but sometimes it makes me so mad.

COMMENTS

Rangerdanger69: "sometimes it makes me so mad" you know what makes me so mad? Misandrists in Warship fandom.

CaptainJillsBFF22: lmao

men: **write really misogynistic stuff**

women: **call it out**

men: **omg misandry**

aarongotrobbed99: not all men are misogynists

CaptainJillsBFF22: But "all men" apparently feel the need to be all up in my rewatch blog tonight. Go pound sand.

5 STELLA

"Will you come to Brandon's birthday party with me?" Dahlia asks as we're walking to her car. I stop dead in my tracks, right in the middle of the sidewalk.

"Ugh. Why?"

"Pleeeease?" She clasps her hands together like she's praying. "I don't want to go alone."

"Can't you go with Em?"

"She's got indoor soccer games every weekend for the next eternity."

I sigh, subconsciously tugging at my necklace that hangs just below my shirt. The three-pointed sword symbol digs into my skin. "When is it?" I don't have time to party on weekends; I'm not Wesley "Private Tutor" Clarke.

"March twentieth."

"That's like a month away."

"It's laser tag at Space Arena," she says. "C'mon, you love that place. I'll pay for unlimited air hockey."

"And Tylenol."

Her forehead crinkles. "Tylenol?"

"For the headache I'll get from hanging around Wesley all night." I keep walking.

"You know, Kyle Nielsen might be there . . ."

My heart does a weird little dive-bomb. I shift my bag strap from one shoulder to the other, trying to keep my face blank. "Really? I didn't think he was friends with Brandon."

"I think Brandon's blanket-inviting half the class."

She knows me too well. I can suffer through a few hours of Wesley if it means a few hours of Kyle. "Fine. I will make an appearance." When I pull my hand back, Captain Jill's three-speared sword is imprinted on my palm.

–♥–

Bridget is still wearing her Burger Blitz hat when I get home. The smell of grease and French fries lingers on her clothes like she was bathing with the burgers instead of flipping them. A few strands of dyed-red hair burst from underneath, framing her tired face. I hate it when people act like hard work automatically gets you out of poverty, as if the only reason we're poor is because we didn't work hard enough; Mom and Bridget work harder than anyone I know.

My sister stands at the counter, vigorously stabbing a fork into a bowl. A round pit lies on the counter beside half an avocado shell.

I kick off my shoes. "Don't worry, that avocado is already dead."

"It's all she'll eat." Bags hang under my sister's eyes. "She's been screaming for hours."

Gwen giggles on the living room carpet, no sign of a tantrum in sight. Dave sits beside her, pointing out pictures in a book with a beagle wearing a baseball cap on the cover.

"Gwennie Bear has never done a thing wrong, ever, in her entire life," I say.

Bridget rolls her eyes. "Spoken like a true aunt who doesn't have to deal with this kid at three a.m." The words *Gwendoline*

Stephens has my whole heart are scrawled across her upper arm in fancy black script, next to a heart bearing Gwen's birthday. Espeon, our Westie, sits at Bridget's feet, staring up hopefully at the counter for any raining bits of avocado. I tense, since avocado is toxic to dogs, but Bridget keeps all scraps firmly on the counter. I scratch Espeon's fluffy white ears before making my way into the living room.

"Hey, Stells," my stepdad calls, still watching the baby. If you take your eyes off Gwen for five seconds, suddenly our whole apartment is mummified in toilet paper.

"Hey." I press a quick kiss to the top of my niece's fuzzy head, then return to the kitchen, scoop up the avocado carcass, and dump it into the trash. A teetering pile of dirty dishes waits in the sink. "Do you need a break? I can take her for a walk."

"It's all right, I've got her." Dave points out something in the book, which makes Gwen smile even wider. His cane is propped against the sofa behind them.

"Dave's got her occupied, finally," Bridget mutters.

Gwen's happy squeal cuts her off. Even though she's not quite two, she's already got a full head of curly blond hair, just like her father. Her ears poke out like his, too. I wonder if it bothers Bridget that her daughter looks identical to her ex. I hope his personality isn't also hereditary.

As if reading my mind, Bridget wipes down the counter, keeping her eyes down. "I heard from Ben today."

I tense. "And you told him to pound sand, I hope?"

"Stella—"

"Or asked him where his, I don't know, last six child support payments are?"

"I'm taking Gwen to see him at the mall on Sunday; there's that kiddie play area."

I look back at my niece, who's still focused on the book. "Are you sure that's a good idea?"

"He's her father." She grinds the fork extra hard into the bowl.

"Father?" I snort. "That man is a glorified sperm donor, just like Dad."

"Stella. We aren't talking about this."

"He's not going to change."

My sister shoots me a warning look, which I should know by now to abide by, but I can't help it. My scumbag meter goes through the roof whenever Ben comes up. Seriously, who ghosts their pregnant girlfriend? It's not like Bridget impregnated herself.

"Last time you saw him, you came home crying." I slide my backpack off and put it on the kitchen chair. "Remember the first time you broke up, then got back together? And I had to go with you to Planned Parenthood for a pregnancy test? And the second time you broke up and got back together? And, like, every time since?"

"Stella."

"You'll run right back to him and he'll do it again. Can you really afford to keep wasting all your time on this douchebag? He's a loser, and he wants you to be a loser, too."

She full-on glares at me. "For fuck's sake, Stella. It's not marriage. It's just an hour so his daughter can see him."

Gwen giggles from the carpet. "Fuck sake," she repeats, looking up at her mom with a glint of mischief in her eyes.

We both blink down at her, a laugh threatening to burst out of me. Dave manages to distract her with some blocks, so I turn back to Bridget. "I just don't want you to make another mistake."

"Gwen wasn't a mistake."

I open my mouth to respond, but think better of it. "You're right," I say finally. "She wasn't."

If he screws her over again, I swear. I've got a shovel and no one would miss him.

"I have class, then closing shift at the theater tonight," she says. "I'll be home late."

"Do you need me to watch Gwen?"

"Dave said he could." She raises her brows at our stepdad. "You still okay for tonight?"

He gives her a salute. "Grandpa duty is activated."

Bridget sticks a baby spoon into the bowl of mushy avocado and sets it on the table. "C'mon, Gwen, it's time to eat." She scoops up her babbling daughter and slides her into the high chair.

I love my sister, and I hate saying this, because it sounds terrible, but Bridget is who I look at and think, *This is why I work so hard*. Because I do *not* want to end up like her—a hot mess with no future.

Maybe my sister wouldn't be in this situation if she'd spent more time reading books and less time chasing Ben. Priorities.

I clomp down the hall to my room, suddenly motivated to do my homework. Watching the way Ben acts has completely put me off the whole boyfriend thing.

It's not that I've never had a boyfriend. I've had exactly three-point-five relationships.

Victim number one: Derek Banks in the sixth grade. We held hands once, waiting for the bus. It was very chaste. I think we "dated" for a month, but I'm not sure I can call it that, since we barely spoke to each other.

Then there was Arjun Patel at the beginning of eighth grade.

We slow-danced at the winter ball, he asked me to be his girlfriend, and then his family moved to Illinois. Tragic.

Jeff Givens was the highlight of my sophomore-to-junior-year summer. We were camp counselors for the YMCA's summer program and had to lead the kids in kickball four days a week. Then school started and it just kind of died.

Last but not least, the point-five. Mark Statler, Chloe Sanderson's cousin. We made out at Chloe's New Year's party when the ball dropped, and I never saw him again. Still counting it.

The color-coded tabs poke out of my bio and history books, and I've got a fresh pile of index cards just begging to be made into flash cards. Plus I've got like eight yearbook pages to format by Monday, and I have to update the account register for NHS.

But when I get to my room, all I can focus on is staring at my to-do list as if it will magically start checking itself off. I tab into the *Warship* forum instead.

Two new fanarts are up, posted by a couple of regulars. The first one features Gemma cradling C0ndor like a baby. The other is of Jill and Aaron, bloody and beaten, sitting in adjacent cells, episode sixteen style. He's got his eyes closed, leaning his head against the glass separating them. She's glancing over at him, clearly trying not to show how concerned she is about the gashes on his face and shoulder. This is the episode where I think they truly started caring for each other—or, at least, realizing what they already felt deep down. The caption reads, ***Our captain and our soldier—I don't believe anyone who says they aren't in love!***

Ow, my heart. It's one of my favorite scenes in the show, even though my favs are in pain. Maybe it's because I'm a sucker for a good old-fashioned hurt/comfort scene. I add the drawing to my Favorites, shooting out a quick comment to the artist:

> This is beautiful. Don't listen to the antis. Didn't Leigh mention in that director's commentary that this is when Jill first caught feelings for Aaron? (I mean, if you believe they weren't #awkwardflirting the whole time, which they were.) Tim Lacey even said that, and he wrote the episode. Lewton is OTP—it is known!

I wish I could draw. I have so many ideas.

But since I have zero artistic ability whatsoever, I do the next best thing and open a clean Word doc. Last year, my fix-it-fic where I rewrote the entire ending of the show—the season two we never got—got over fifty thousand views. Sometimes, when I'm feeling down, I go back and reread it. It's pretty sad that my fanfic ending is more coherent than the BS the show-runners gave us.

Twenty minutes. I can spend twenty minutes writing.

I'm thinking this will be another fix-it-fic, right after the mess of episode twenty. Maybe Aaron flies away at the end of the episode as planned, but then he turns on Michele Cordova instead of going back to her. Then he flies back to the *Revelry* and apologizes. Yes. That's what my new fic will be—an apology. With a happy ending.

FANDOM > *WARSHIP SEVEN*

Pairing: Captain Jill Brighton / Sergeant Aaron Lewis

Tags: post episode 20, fix-it-fic, angst, #Lewton, canon compliant, episode 20 sucked let's be real

I think for a moment. Jill would be super pissed with him for leaving, and rightfully so. Maybe she'll fight with him for a bit, and then they work it out, and in the end they make out on the *Revelry*'s bridge. Then Jill and Aaron go raise their family somewhere.

I'm starting to type the first sentence when a new message notification pops up.

CERanger11: so do I really have to pay $90 for a photo with Ethan Martone?

I roll my eyes. This dude again. I love how he could easily find this information on the website, but messages me instead for some free labor. I start typing "do I look like Google?" but stop. It's his first con; maybe he honestly doesn't know where to find the info.

CaptainJillsBFF22: that's the advance pass rate, yes. If you buy at the con, it's $100 I think. Worth it though! Ethan's super fun with his fans.

CERanger11: Are you doing a pic?

CaptainJillsBFF22: I hope so! Saving up for one with Leigh (got her autograph last year but didn't get a photo) and hopefully Krista Pollack—I wore my Gemma pin last year and totally missed her.

CERanger11: Do they sell group shots? Would love to get one with the whole cast.

CaptainJillsBFF33: I think only Leigh, Ethan, and Krista are coming this year? So maybe the three of them? Idk. Probably super expensive though.

He doesn't respond, so I open my fic.

I'm thinking this one will be from Aaron's point of view.

Darkness fills the small shuttle I stole off the ship. The moment I'm out of the *Revelry*'s radar, a strange hollowness fills my chest. What am I doing? I got the information Michele needed, and now I can bring it back to her. But all I can think about is Jill. Jill and her stupid, stubborn captain resolve, and that ugly necklace dangling down her chest.

A little red *1* pops up in the corner of the screen.

CERanger11: Thanks. Sorry to keep bugging you. It's just kind of overwhelming, you know?

CaptainJillsBFF22: No worries! I totally get it. My first con I just kinda wandered around gaping at everything for hours lol

CERanger11: Already bought a parking pass, too, and now I don't even know how I'm going to get there lol no car

CaptainJillsBFF22: There's a bus that lets off right outside the arena. Depends where you're coming from, of course

CERanger11: I go into Boston via rt 3. I'll check out the bus. Otherwise I'd need to borrow my mom's car

I cock my head. Okay, that's weird. So he's coming from up north, too. I guess I shouldn't be surprised. Lots of people from New Hampshire probably go down for Sci-Con. And if he's borrowing his mom's car, maybe he's in high school too?

CERanger11: btw, Tim Lacey didn't write episode 16. Sean Heard did.

I jolt back from the screen.

CaptainJillsBFF22: wtf. Are you stalking me?

CERanger11: No! I went to comment on that new fanart and noticed you already had.

CERanger11: Sorry, didn't mean to sound like a stalker ☹

My finger hovers over the Block button.

You know what? No. I'm not kowtowing to fanboys today. So instead, I open Chrome and pull up IMDB. Episode sixteen—"Light in a Dark Place"—written by Tim Lacey. I *knew* it.

I copy and paste the link into the message.

CaptainJillsBFF22: You might find this link interesting! 😍

CaptainJillsBFF22: And PS—the next time you think about jumping into a girl's DMs trying to correct her Warship knowledge, DON'T.

Then I hit the Block button.

6 WESLEY

I blink at the screen. ***CaptainJillsBFF22 has blocked you.***

Okay, I saw that going differently in my head.

Nice one, Clarke. Now I won't have anyone to hang with at Sci-Con.

Also, did she just . . . out-*Warship* me?

I close my laptop and throw my head back. This day couldn't get any worse.

My history homework, calc homework, and English lie in a heap at the end of my desk, waiting to be done. I guess I also should go over the reading for the AP History quiz. And after that test result, I probably need to go over the AP Bio reading again. My pulse starts ticking up a few notches.

Columbia. I need to do it for Columbia.

Sometimes, when I'm feeling unmotivated, I remind myself of the big city. Being surrounded by skyscrapers and bakeries and awesome pizza places. Hanging out in coffee shops in Brooklyn. And most of all, sitting in the Columbia library with a book and feeling like it's exactly where I'm meant to be.

One summer my parents signed me up for basketball camp. I'm not sure why. I think because Trevor and I had spent all of June fighting over the Nintendo, so finally Mom and Dad got fed up and wanted us out of the house for a while. I suck at basketball and felt so awkward the entire week. I sat there pretending to care about practicing layups, but really I just wanted to go home. The next year I begged my parents to let me go to photography camp instead, and that was a week I never wanted to end.

That's kind of what it felt like visiting Stanford, and then Columbia a month later. There's a difference between forcing it and feeling like it's coming naturally. Columbia already felt like home to me before I'd even applied. It's not that there's anything wrong with Stanford, it's just that some people prefer red and others prefer blue; some people prefer California, I love New York.

It's okay. I don't need to sleep tonight. The sheet of paper about that stupid rat assignment pokes out of the pile. I forgot about that, and about Stella Greene coming over on Saturday. Mom's going to flip when she finds out I'm bringing a beady-eyed rat into our house. And a rodent, too.

I grab my sketchbook and flip to the next clean page. I know—*I know*—I don't have time for this right now. Procrastinators don't become valedictorian.

I let the charcoal dance across the paper, drawing Sonny and Skulls sparring on the bridge. The fact that they have some sort of rivalry is my favorite headcanon about them.

My phone buzzes with a new text—Laura. I sit up in my chair, grabbing the phone so fast I almost fumble and drop it on the carpet.

> Hey–did you do the AP Bio homework yet?
> I'm really nervous since I bombed that test.

I think for a second.

> Yesterday. You need help?

My heart pounds in my chest. I'm not even sure I understood the homework either, and realistically, if she needs bio help, she should probably ask someone else. But, damn.

I might. Let's see how I do.

My knee bounces against my hand. Laura was the first girl who ever asked *me* out, the first girl I ever hooked up with, and the first girl I ever seriously liked. And the first girl to dump me in the TGI Fridays parking lot last summer. I still remember exactly what she said: "I don't want a boyfriend right now," which was ironic, because not even three months later she was making out with Mitch Greenfield at a football game. I got her a necklace for Valentine's Day last year, and she wore it every day for those four months, so seeing her show up in Latin on the first day of senior year, only a little while after our breakup, her neck bare, felt like a shard of glass plunging into my chest.

Oh, also, guess what I just got in the mail??
omg. NYU?
I got in!!!
CONGRATS!

I immediately spam her with every happy GIF I can find, including that one of C0ndor doing his weird little droid dance. Laura's not a Warshipper, but everyone loves C0ndor.

Thanks 🙂 They gave me a scholarship too!! So no giant pile of loans, at least for the first year haha

That's awesome!!

I can't believe it. NYU. I've been mentally pulling for her to get in there for months now. Obviously I want her to get in because it's important to her, but I'm not going to lie, I had some ulterior motives.

You'll be close to me

The moment I hit Send, I immediately regret it. What if she doesn't want to be close to me? What if she forgot I'm hoping to go to Columbia, and now she wants to change her mind and decline their offer?

Yes! A short subway ride away!

To be honest, I'm kind of overwhelmed by the idea of NYC. It helps knowing I'll have a friend nearby. I heard you can get any type of food there at any time of the day or night!

I'm staring at the screen so hard, my bedroom door swings open and I nearly jump a foot in the air, scrambling to my feet. Mom is standing in the doorway, and here I am, clutching my phone like she just caught me with my pants down.

"Sorry, I'm sorry!" She covers her eyes and turns her back. Oh God, she legitimately thinks I was watching porn in here.

"Jeez, Mom. You scared me."

"Are you decent?"

"Yes!" This is humiliating. "Come in." I sink into the chair.

She slowly turns back around. "Okay. Phew. Hi!"

"Hi." I squint. "Why are you wearing a name tag?"

"Oh. I forgot." She peels the sticker off her sweater. "We had a luncheon at the office today, interviewing a few potential first-year associates." A thermos is clutched in her right hand, bearing the Stanford crest. Of course.

My phone vibrates, and I literally have to press it against my thigh to keep myself from checking it. I don't need Mom's third degree on the Laura situation right now. She only met Laura a couple of times, but still. "How'd it go?"

Large diamond studs sparkle in her ears, Dad's gift when she made partner. "It was great! Found three who I think will be amazing additions—one's a Stanford guy, obviously."

My chest tightens, and I can't look her in the eyes. So I stare out the window instead, down at the pool in the backyard, still covered in its winter tarp. "That's awesome."

Yesterday, I opened my online Columbia application and started browsing art courses. But then Mom shouted something from downstairs, and I x-ed out of the tab, just in case she decided to pop into my room.

The thing about my family's legacy is that we actually have one; Grandpa Clarke met my grandma at Stanford, which is also where my dad met my mom, and where my brother is currently a sophomore. The damn Stanford crest is framed in the living room. There's even a baby picture of me wearing a little Stanford jersey at one of the football games.

Mom takes a seat on the edge of my bed. "So, are you going to tell me what's been bothering you?"

"Nothing's bothering me." I keep my eyes down. I'm such an asshole. Mom will be so crushed when she finds out I went behind her back and rejected her alma mater. "Just stressed about school."

Mom stands up, resting her hand on my shoulder. She used to joke that she never has to worry about me sneaking out of the house because my eyes say exactly what I'm thinking all the time. But I don't think that's true anymore, because lately she has no idea what I'm thinking. Otherwise this exchange would be a lot different. "Try not to let it get to you. We're both very proud of you, no matter what."

I force a smile. "Thanks." I wonder if the "what" extends to breaking off a decades-long family legacy.

I sneak a glance at my phone when I think she's not looking, but it's too late; a new text lights up, and Mom's eyes are basically magnetized toward it.

"Is that Laura McNally? What's she up to these days?"

I kind of stare at her for a second. Mom is *so* nosy about this stuff. "She's good."

"Where's she going next year?"

"NYU."

Mom gives me a knowing look. "That's not far from Columbia. I hope that's not the reason you're so interested in that school."

Interested is a soft way of saying *already sent in the first payment with my savings*, but okay.

"Yeah. It's not. I like Columbia, and I like the city." I shift in my seat, eager to talk about literally anything else. "Laura just got a scholarship."

"That's great. Hey—doesn't the valedictorian get a scholarship too?"

"Yep. Full ride to the school of their choice." We've got one of those benevolent multimillionaires in town. Some guy whose grandpa started a hotel chain and now he's super rich, so they give out a scholarship every year.

"It would be great if you got that. We've got that trust fund for you, but extra cash never hurts. Stanford isn't exactly cheap. We can invest what's left."

I swallow hard. I guess Mom missed the *of their choice* part. "Sounds good."

But no pressure, right?

–♥–

I don't know what being drunk is like, but I bet I know what being hungover is like. I pounded an energy drink last night at like eleven. At cross country in the fall, we always do a "Sunrise Sprint" once a year where we jog up Mount Major in the middle of the night, reaching the top in time for sunrise. Watching that sunrise peeking over the pine trees was a lot more enjoyable than watching it this morning through my cracked-open eyelids, my AP Bio textbook still spread open in front of me. It might as well have been written in Swedish for how much I understood what I was reading.

I plow into school, my Canon hanging around my neck, the strap sweaty against my skin. I almost forgot it at home. Yearbook club is one of those simple college-app fillers that makes you look well rounded, according to my mother.

"Hey, man." Brandon catches up to me as I'm walking into school. "What's with the camera?"

"I was supposed to submit a bunch of candid pictures to the

yearbook like a week ago. And I haven't taken any of them yet."

"Nice."

"Yeah, I know." I adjust the strap around my neck, not thrilled about being GCMHS's resident paparazzo today. Especially on half an hour of sleep.

"You going to the meet Sunday?" he asks.

It takes me a second for my brain to catch up. "Uh . . . the meet?" Shit. JV indoor track made New England regionals. I totally forgot.

"Um, yeah. Brian and Aidan are making signs. Huntington Academy qualified too; they'll be there."

I do varsity track to look good on college applications and to stay in shape. Our team sucks, and to be honest, organized sports aren't really my thing. I'd much rather go running on my own. But the JV indoor team is actually pretty good this year, so I guess that's promising for the school's future or something.

"I'll try." I push open the front door. "I've got like eight papers due in the next month, so no promises."

The giant window of the main office greets us the second we walk in the door, plastered with senior portraits of everyone who's gotten into college so far—we call it The Wall. Colored labels list the college acceptances under each one. Stanford, Columbia, UPenn, Dartmouth, Syracuse, and BC are posted under my photo, with Columbia highlighted in yellow. If my parents show up at school for some reason, I'm gonna need to come up with an excuse real fast.

I really hate that picture of me. The photographer my parents hired made me look like a walking douchebag, with a stupid curl hanging down my forehead.

Brandon sighs. "You're putting everyone else to shame."

For a second I think he's talking about the picture, but then he keeps going.

"Six schools. I didn't even apply to six schools."

I shrug, turning away. I'm not sure why I feel so awkward about it. Probably because my list is at least twice as long as everyone else's. My guidance counselor and my parents had this whole elaborate application strategy, and I just kind of went with it.

"Stella Greene didn't even get into that many."

In her Wall photo, she's got her brown hair loose around her shoulders, standing with what looks like the White Park fountain behind her. Her pink glasses frame her eyes, and I can't help noticing she actually has really nice eyes. It's probably the first time I've seen her with her hair down. Under her name it just says MIT and UNH, with MIT highlighted. Okay, that's a little weird. I'd have thought Stella I'm-Better-than-Everyone Greene would have a list twice as long as mine, just to shove it in everyone's faces.

Screams rip through the hallway, jerking our attention. It takes me a few seconds to realize no one has tumbled to their death off the fifth-floor lookout or something. Several guys from the drumline march down the hall, tapping out a drumroll that echoes in the tiny square reception area by the main office. A couple of freshmen cover their ears.

Laura and a bunch of the other band kids follow behind them in a cloud of laughter.

"Oh my God, stop!" Her freckled face is beet red, but she's laughing, trying to grab the sticks away from one of the drummers, a junior who I think is named Collin. A knot tangles itself inside me.

"Attention, everyone!" Collin taps his drumsticks together,

and everyone lingering in the hall who was previously pretending to ignore them isn't anymore. "We have an announcement to make."

My jaw tenses. I hope the announcement isn't that he's going to prom with Laura or something. Not that I care.

The group of band kids crowding around Laura starts clapping, and she buries her face in her hands.

"Today, our drum major, Laura McNally, joins The Wall!" Everyone around her cheers. A couple of underclassmen in the hallway clap half-heartedly. Laura's now hanging off Collin's shoulder. Not that I'm looking.

Joining The Wall is a weird GCMHS tradition built to publicly humiliate everyone.

Collin takes his snare drum off and sets it on the ground. "NYU's getting a good one next year!" He wraps his arm around Laura's shoulder and tries to ruffle her blond hair, but she shoves his hand away, still laughing.

One of the other guys pulls out a roll of Scotch tape and tacks Laura's senior portrait to The Wall, while another scrawls out "NYU" on one of the blank labels waiting in the empty soup can hanging off the main office doorknob.

I hesitantly join the clapping, the band's cheers and drumming drowning it out.

She's not even looking over here. She's too busy looking at that Collin kid.

"This place is a cluster," Brandon says. "I'll see you later, man. I've got to get to the library before class anyway." He shoulders his way through the crowd, almost knocking over one of the band freshmen. I'm too busy watching Laura, who's drifting down the hall with Collin, still laughing. One of the guidance counselors has started trying to get them all to shut up and get ready for class.

"They're not supposed to play instruments in the hallway."

Stella stands beside me with her arms crossed, glowering at the celebrations unfolding before us.

"You the hall monitor now, Greene?"

The crowd starts to dissipate.

"Congrats on MIT." I point to her picture. "I thought for sure you'd apply to like a bazillion colleges just to say you got into more than everybody else."

She rolls her eyes. "You were supposed to have sixty candid photos submitted to the yearbook by last Thursday."

"Wow, yearbook monitor too. They give you a badge for that?"

"I really, sincerely hope that's why you brought that giant camera to school today and you're not flaking on me, right?"

"Nah, I brought this because I was hoping to take it for a swim."

She presses her lips together. "Just have the memory card ready tomorrow when I stop by your house, okay?"

"You got it." I raise my camera and snap a photo of Stella, scowling at me. "Fifty-nine to go."

7 STELLA

My left leg is falling asleep, curled under my butt on the couch. I'm still wearing my pajamas and it's almost noon, but Mom and Bridget are at work and Dave took Gwen to the park, so no one's here to annoy me about it. For the first Saturday in ages, I'm not working; I'd say I've earned a relaxing Saturday morning. Nothing like a few moments of peace and quiet before I have to deal with Wesley later.

The smell of burnt toast wafts from the kitchen. Mom always leaves pieces of bread in there and then they pop up jet black and gross. It reeks for hours. Toys and crumbs litter the floor, some partially ground into the carpet. My ancient laptop hums angrily on my lap.

FAFSA: Apply for Aid. New User? Register here.

I click the button. Man, they do not make this simple. I wish I could trade all those lessons about isosceles triangles into one how-to info session for student loan applications.

I hope I won't need them. More than anything, I hope I get that full-ride scholarship. But right now, I can't afford to risk it, with Wesley basically breathing down my neck. Mom would help if I asked, but she has enough to deal with, and she's hardly ever home anyway. Dave tried to help me with my MIT application a few months ago, but he kept asking a million questions about it, so I fired him pretty quickly. And Bridget never even finished high school.

My grandma grew up poor, my mom grew up poor, my sister's in this constant downward spiral, and now, not only am I going to a top college, but I have a shot of being number one on the way there. Of beating out all the kids with money and big houses and European vacations. I *need* to be valedictorian.

The key rattles in the front door to our apartment, and slowly, it cracks open. The front of Gwen's stroller knocks awkwardly into the door frame, followed by a muffled curse. I set my computer down and get up to help Dave bring the stroller inside.

"You should've texted that you were on your way. I would have come downstairs."

"It's no big deal." He reaches down and unbuckles Gwen, who's already squirming to get over to her heap of toys. "I got her into the elevator."

Dave's basically been my dad since I was six. My biological father—aka "the sperm donor"—vanished when I was four. Bridget remembers him more than I do. When we were kids, Bridget used to tell me Dad was coming back, like he'd gone on vacation or something. Then she told me he was dead, which I found out was a lie after I went crying to Mom about it. Then my sister just settled on calling him a jerk and saying we didn't need him anyway. I think it was Bridget's version of the five stages of grief, if the stages ended with her starting the cycle all over again by getting knocked up.

"How was your walk?"

Dave can't drive because of severe epilepsy. Sometimes he gets seizures, and a few years ago, he got one while driving and crashed his car into a tree. Now he's a full-time grandpa and gets SSDI. A few nights a week he volunteers at the veterans' food pantry with his old army buddies, but otherwise he hangs out here.

"We saw a hawk, didn't we, Gwennie?" He places her on the carpet, and she toddles toward her foam blocks. "Went on the slide—well, she did. Did some swinging."

"That sounds fun." I sink down to the carpet and start stacking blocks with my niece.

"You still doing those loan applications? Need help?"

I shrug it off, like loan apps are the easiest things in the world. "I'm all set—thanks, though."

"I'm here if you need me." With a groan he folds the stroller and heaves it into the hall closet.

My phone buzzes with a text from Bridget.

Hey–I'm coming back now. Shift went a little long. You can have the car for an hour, that enough?

Whoops. I lost track of time. I'm supposed to drop off the rat at Wesley's in two hours. The rat, which I don't have yet.

Yes! Just have to do some errands for school.

I conveniently fail to mention that the errands involve bringing a live rat into her car, but whatever. That thing is like twenty years old anyway, and Gwen's puked in the back seat at least eight times, so. A fuzzy little rat is the least of Bridget's problems.

Once Dave's settled into his usual spot on the floor with Gwen, I head into my room to get dressed, laptop under my arm, and leave it open on my desk while I shower. When I get back, I do a quick forum browse while drying my hair. There's this amazing forty-two-chapter fic I've been following for a year now, and last week's installment ended on a cliff-hanger—Jill and Skulls were abandoned on a planet infested by cannibals. Maybe she posted the next part.

People make fun of fanfic, but many famous writers have gotten their start that way. Some of these fics are legit books, basically. I'd put their quality up against anything on the shelf at Barnes and Noble. And yet, whenever I'm reading fanfic, Mom asks me why I'm not reading a "real" book. Sucks.

No luck, but the author added a note that there'll be a new chapter up tomorrow. Which reminds me, I need to finish *my* new fic. Maybe a wedding? Yes, a Lewton wedding would brighten my day.

Someone posted new fanart, though. I click the link, labeled "A Peace Offering." A hand-drawn comic appears, with a description at the top of the page.

CERanger11: Two drawings: the first is a peace offering I drew for a Warshipper friend. Hope you like it. And the second is a simple Aaron/Michele sketch.

I start reading the comic, and suck in a sharp breath. He's drawn a few panels of *His Biggest Mistake,* one of my most popular fics. Aaron sits in prison in the first panel, negotiating with Jill—just the way I wrote it. My shoulders relax. Okay, this is pretty cool. The whole scene I wrote is there, in comic form, complete with my verbatim dialogue. Oh my God. He drew fanart . . . for my fanfic. I need to save this immediately. And get it printed on a T-shirt or something.

He said it was a peace offering. Was it a peace offering to *me*?

I tab to the next page—the "simple Aaron/Michele sketch,"

which looks anything but simple to me—but the art is a photo of a drawing someone's holding up to their phone camera. Wow. He seriously took a picture of the drawing rather than doing it digitally.

> ***ARTIST CAPTION: CERanger11: Scanner crapped out half-way through uploading, so had to do it this way lol***

Sergeant Aaron Lewis sits in his cruiser with his feet up, while Michele Cordova pilots. Ugh. It's a nice-quality drawing, I suppose, and that's a huge compliment coming from me, considering that Michele is totally wrong for Aaron. She represents his past with the Central Elite, not his future as a good upstanding citizen. Of course the captain of the #Lewdova ship would draw this.

I do feel a little guilty for blocking him—if I blocked every male who mansplained, my life would be entirely full of girls. Not that I'm convinced that would be the worst thing in the world.

Nice job, I type in the comment bar. That's all he's getting from me. Sorry, I don't make the rules.

But when the photo is open, something catches my eye. In the corner, past the sheet of paper, I can see the OP's wall, painted a really abrasive shade of green. I click to zoom in, and sure enough, that's the corner of an exam schedule taped up on their wall—with the GCMHS shield right there for all to see. It's blurry, and clearly not intended to be included in the picture he posted online, but there it is.

I suck in a breath.

Does he . . . does he go to my high school? That's so weird. I guess I shouldn't be too surprised. He did mention Route 3, and it makes sense he'd be going to Sci-Con an hour away. I try to zoom in to see if there's any identifying information, but it's too fuzzy.

Against my better judgment, I unblock him.

CaptainJillsBFF22: hey—random question—do you go to GCMHS?

The second I hit Send, I'm staring at my message. Oh my God, I just sounded like the sketchiest creep to ever walk the internet. If I was him, I would re-block me forever.

CaptainJillsBFF22: I realize that sounds SUPER creepy—I saw the schedule in the background of your fanart

CERanger11: welcome back. My scanner is, I believe, a relic of the Jurassic period. Its time had come.

CaptainJillsBFF22: Scanner? Jeez, 2005 called, they want their technology back.

CERanger11: and yeah, I do go there—do you??

I blink at the screen. I *must* know this guy. And I know for a fact he's a dude, because a girl would never have told a stranger the name of her school so quickly. That's a quick recipe for ending up on *Dateline*.

But who *is* he?

I've never met a Warshipper from GCMHS before. I mean, I'm sure they exist. We're not *unicorns*.

Okay, I believe this guy. Really, I do. But it's the internet, and I've seen too many episodes of *CSI* to know I can't be too careful. I glance up at the old football calendar hanging on my bulletin board—last year's homecoming game was against our rivals, Huntington Academy.

CaptainJillsBFF22: No, I go to Huntington

CERanger11: oh, well, I guess I can't speak to you anymore. Sorry.

CERanger11: (that was a joke)

A half smile cracks across my face. What a dork.

CaptainJillsBFF22: The only joke I know about is your school's football team.

I don't even feel bad about it; the GCMHS football team sucks. Everyone goes to the games for the halftime show and the fries. Our food stand makes awesome fries, and our band is pretty good too.

CERanger11: Harsh. But I can't be mad. We do suck.

Our football players would never admit that, so I can cross out twenty possibilities.

CaptainJillsBFF22: Wow, trashing your own team! That's treason.

CERanger11: Treason of the highest order. Jill would've pelted me out of the airlock by now.

CaptainJillsBFF22: She'd give you a warning strike.

CERanger11: if she's feeling generous. So what year are you in?

CaptainJillsBFF22: I'm a senior! Graduating soon ☺

CERanger11: Nice. Me too.

My heart jumps. Okay, I definitely know him.

But who is it?

Someone raps on my door. "Yo, I'm home. You can have the car."

"Thanks," I call back to my sister.

"One hour, seriously, my boss will disembowel me if I'm late." I hear her clambering into the bathroom.

"What is this, Braveheart?"

Something pounds on the thin wall separating my bedroom from our shared bathroom, and I'm pretty sure it's Bridget's fist. "I mean it, he'll make me work late and then I'll be late for my study session."

"I know, I know. One hour. I promise."

I'm one hundred percent sure my sister would give me a kidney in an instant, but trying to borrow her car is like pulling teeth.

It hits me that I'm not dressed, so I quickly throw on some leggings and a T-shirt, my hair still half wet. Not like it matters. I'm not seeing anyone important.

–♥–

A floral air freshener pumps out lilac-scented chemicals from the half-broken AC in Bridget's car, but it doesn't help the smell. Gwen's empty car seat keeps rattling around in the back. I merge onto the highway, checking the time. Hozier booms from the radio, and it's like a heavy dose of nostalgia injected into my ears.

I didn't discover *Warship Seven* until the month after the final episode premiered. Nana and I had made plans to go to the flower show that weekend, our annual tradition, but she had died three weeks earlier when her pancreatic cancer turned out to be a late stage four rather than a stage two, like we'd thought. I was such a mess. I was searching YouTube for a Hozier song, and up popped a fan video set to "Arsonist's Lullabye," put against footage of Aaron and Jill's relationship. I didn't know anything about the show, but I got invested in the characters before even watching a single episode. I immediately binged the whole thing, two episodes a night. Every time I hit Play, I felt a little bit of relief, because I could escape, if only for a little while. When I saw episode twenty, I cried for like a week straight. All I could do was watch YouTube video edits and read fanfics.

I'm not sure why it hit me so hard. Maybe because I saw myself in Jill more than any other character. People underestimate her, and she basically comes from nothing, but she's the fiercest captain in the galaxy. I wanted to see her get a happy ending, but she closed the show heartbroken and confused. It wasn't right.

I pull into the strip mall under the red Galaxy Pets sign. For a while last year, the letters *lax* were burned out, so it read "Gay Pets," and now that's what everyone calls it. Mom buys dog food for Espeon here since it's always a couple bucks cheaper than the grocery. This is a weird part of town because the rich neighborhood where Wesley lives is like half a mile away, but *this* is the part of town where you worry about getting stabbed the moment you leave your car.

I slam the car door shut, and something inside rattles.

SATURDAY HOURS: 12–6

I click my phone; it's only 11:50. I've got ten minutes. Bridget is going to murder me if I'm late. And I've still got to drop the rat off at Wesley's house. A smattering of cars are parked near the shoe store two storefronts down.

CLEARANCE: UP TO 90% OFF FALL BOOTS.
EVERYTHING MUST GO!

Oh, wow, there's my Bat signal. If I can find some cheap Captain Jill knockoffs for my cosplay, this ridiculous errand will have been worth it.

The bell dings over my head when I push open the door. A strong burnt-rubber smell fills the air.

I make a beeline for the clearance aisle. Lo and behold, a pair of black knee-highs is waiting for me, a shiny silver buckle adorning the side. I lunge at them so hard, I knock the pair of heels in the box beside them to the ground.

Size five. Not ideal. I'd be like the stepsister in *Cinderella* trying to cram my giant foot inside.

There's this weird side effect of being poor, where you always feel guilty about spending. I should be saving for college, or food, or something else. Even with my minimum wage from the ice cream parlor, I don't have much to spare. But man, a killer pair of boots would complete my Jill look—I'm pretty sure my pink Converse were the death knell on my contest entry last year.

"Do these come in size seven?" I slap the black boots onto the counter.

The young woman puts her phone down and stares at me, and I can tell she'd rather be anywhere else today. "You can order them from our online catalog. Full price, though."

My heart sinks. "Why full price?"

"The sale's only for what's in stock. And those are scuffed."

A tiny black mark stretches across the side of the left boot. I never would have even noticed it. "Oh."

"Do you want me to go ahead and order those for you?" She types into the computer, then swivels the screen toward me. $79.99.

Yikes.

"No, it's okay. Never mind." I leave the size fives on the counter and walk back outside, into the piercing sunlight.

–♥–

You know how they say astronauts can see the Great Wall of China from space? That's kind of like Wesley Clarke's house. I have to use my phone's GPS to find it, but it's not like mansions do a good job of hiding. There is a snazzy red Porsche just chilling in the driveway.

Sometimes I wonder what would have happened if my mom had been the one creating candy back in the eighties. My life would be perfect like Wesley's. It must be nice not having to worry about stuff like rent or food or whether your mom's crappy income will be enough to pay for internet *and* heat that month. Whoever said money can't buy happiness has never been poor.

My new best friend, aka Lint the fuzzy gray rat, sniffs the air inside her cage, glaring up at me. I can't help feeling like she's castigating me for leaving her with Wesley; frankly, I'd be pissed too.

"Don't worry, Lint, I'll bring you home as soon as I persuade Mom to let you stay and find a way to keep Espeon from swallowing you whole." Or I could just keep her cage on my dresser and cover it with a blanket or something when Mom comes in? Lint's fuzzy face is so cute, I snap a photo and update my lock screen picture for the first time in like a year—sorry, Jill.

I clamber out of Bridget's car, which looks like a "one of these things is not like the others" puzzle in this driveway. I sling the shopping bag of Lint's food over my left arm and balance the cage on my right. The school only gave us a voucher for the rat, cage, water bottle, and food, but I shelled out seven dollars for an exercise wheel and some bedding. That's basically a whole hour of work at The Scoopery, gone. It's kind of weird they made us get live animals but wouldn't pay to make them comfortable.

"You okay, girl?" I reach my finger through the cage and pat her fur—soft and gray, like dryer lint. I maintain it's a very fitting name for her.

I ring the doorbell, and it echoes outside. My feet shuffle from side to side as I survey the well-manicured lawn. After an eternity, a woman with blond hair, laugh wrinkles, and a kind smile answers. Thick glasses frame her eyes. There's a hint of Wesley in her face. "Hello there." She shoots a glance at the rat, and I'm suddenly wondering if Wesley told his parents about this little project. "Can I help you?"

"I'm here to see Wesley." Oh God, those are five words I never would have expected to come out of my mouth.

"Oh." Her face softens. "For school?"

"Yep. Here to drop off some stuff for our bio project."

"Wes! You've got company." She opens the wooden door wide. "Here, why don't you come wait in the foyer."

"Thanks." I maneuver across the threshold, careful not to ding the metal cage against their white door frame.

This is exactly how I'd always imagined rich people's houses. A large staircase winds up from the center of the foyer. There's a grandfather clock standing in the corner, its massive pendulum ticking in time with my heart. Pictures of Wesley and some other kid I assume is his brother are blown up everywhere on the walls. A giant puffy white sectional sits in front of a massive flat-screen TV, and I'm suddenly paranoid I'm going to somehow spill something on it, even though I have nothing to spill.

"Wes!" Mrs. Clarke calls up the stairs, but it's like a crypt in here. "I'm sorry," she mutters at me. "He was in the shower a few minutes ago. Why don't you take a seat?" She gestures at the sofa, and I awkwardly sink onto the edge, as if I'll damage it if I lean back too far, keeping Lint's cage on my lap. My black leggings, covered in a different type of lint, stick out horribly against this pristine couch. I feel too informal to be in this room. "Do you want anything to drink or eat?"

I force a smile. "No, thanks, I can't stay. I'm just dropping this stuff off." I check the time on my phone, jittery; I've got fifteen minutes to get back home before Bridget kills me. And I'm not about to get a speeding ticket because Wesley Clarke was in the frickin' shower.

"Okay, then. I'll be in the office if you need anything."

There's this awkward part of episode twelve where Jill and Markus are trying to bargain with a bounty hunter from the CE, and they wander right onto the hunter's ship. They're in enemy territory, and even though they aren't being attacked, they're very aware of everything, flinching at every noise. That's kind of what this is like.

A poster for Clarke Candies is framed on the wall next to the portraits of Wesley and his brother. It's like the Clarkes put all their children's photos up here, and I'm hoping the fact that the chocolates come first isn't a sign of their priorities. I realize awkwardly that his mom has drifted off somewhere in the cavernous house, leaving me all alone. In Wesley Clarke's living room.

Large, colorful glass vases are positioned carefully on top of the sprawling mantel. Each one looks like it's worth more than everything in our entire apartment. He could probably pawn one and pay my whole tuition.

My feet tap against the hardwood floor.

After an eternity, footsteps thump on the stairs. "Hey, Stick. Welcome to my humble abode."

"Your living room looks like it wants to ask to speak to my manager."

"If that's your way of saying you like my home, then thank you."

Wesley collapses onto the recliner to my right. His wet hair clings to his forehead, and he's got a hoodie and jeans on. I stiffen. I sometimes forget how attractive he is. In a certain light. I suppose. "How nice of you to join me."

"I just ran six miles." He stretches his legs out in front. "Then I took a shower."

"That time of the year again?"

"Guess you'd prefer I came out here sweaty and stinking, huh?"

"Wouldn't be much different from normal."

"That the rat?" He nods at the cage on my lap. I can't help noticing that he hasn't taken his eyes off Lint since entering the room.

"No, this is a dog, actually." I have to force myself to take a breath. I will *not* lose my temper with him.

"Did you really have to get a pink cage? You know I have to carry this thing to school, right?"

"Is your masculinity really that fragile, Wesley? It's a color. Where do you want this stuff?"

"Upstairs. I made room for him on the guest room dresser."

"Her, actually. Her name is Lint."

He arches a brow at me. "Lindt? As in, the chocolate? Did you really name her after one of Clarke Candies' competitors?"

"No, Lint as in, the stuff that comes out of the dryer." I'm waiting for him to make fun of the name I picked, but he just stands up.

"Okay. Come upstairs to the spare bedroom."

"Jeez, at least buy me dinner first."

He whirls toward me. "Did you . . . did you just make a joke?"

"Keep walking, Clarke."

I follow him up the winding staircase and can't help noticing how big and open everything is. But in a weird way. Like it's never been lived in before. Goose bumps prickle up my arms, and it's not even cold in here.

"I made a feeding schedule so you don't forget." I pass him the sheet of paper I wrote out yesterday after school.

"Did you seriously color-code this?"

"Wasn't sure how strong your reading skills are."

"Oh my God. There's even a timetable." He waves the paper in my face. "How long did this take you?"

I feel the blush spreading across my face. "Well, you know I have a dog, so I . . . care about making sure Lint is happy."

"I do not believe you have a dog."

My face scrunches up. "Why not?"

"You're too much of a perfectionist neat freak."

"Excuse me? I absolutely have a dog. He's a Westie. And I'm not the one who lives in this untouched palace, so don't even start with the neat-freak BS."

"What's his name?"

I shift in place. "Espeon."

Wesley watches me a moment, then bursts out laughing. "You named your dog after a Pokémon. That is amazing."

"My sister named him." I glare at the carpet beneath his feet.

"Hey, I'm not judging. Espeon is my favorite Eevee evolution."

"More than Umbreon?" It comes out of my mouth before I can stop it.

A smirk juts across Wesley's face. "You're a Pokémon fan."

"I mean, I wouldn't say I'm a *fan*."

"You absolutely are if you know about Eevee evolutions."

I smile a little. "Okay, maybe a bit. I used to watch it when I was home sick." I unpack the rat food and accessories from the bag, then unlock the cage and gently pick Lint up to hold. Wesley takes a half step backward; it's subtle, but I notice.

Lint sniffs the air for a moment before wriggling out of my hands, climbing up my chest, and nestling against my shoulder.

Wesley raises his brows. "Are you sure you want to leave it here?"

"*Her*. Leave *her* here."

"Yes. Her."

"Here, give me your hands. I'll show you how to hold her."

He thrusts his hands behind his back. "I'm not touching that."

"Seriously? You're afraid of rats? You know we have a three-month project during which we're going to have to occasionally hold her, right?"

"Rats caused the bubonic plague."

I roll my eyes. "Yes, Wesley the history expert, I forgot."

"You can do all the rat touching. And all the plague catching."

"Thanks. You know, I better not be doing all the work for this project. Just because you're afraid of rats doesn't mean I'm doing everything."

"Noted." He gives me a sarcastic salute. "Wouldn't want the salutatorian doing all the work by herself."

"When I'm *valedictorian*," I correct, "I'll be sure to note your *many* contributions in my graduation speech."

"When I become valedictorian and get that Porsche, I'll be sure to wave at you as I drive by."

"And then you'll be distracted and crash into a tree and total it, and I promise to pretend to be concerned about it."

I gently set the rat back in her cage and close the door, making sure she has a nice nest of hay first. We wind back through the hallway and go downstairs. "Before I forget, do you have those pictures for me?"

"Oh. Yeah. Hang on." He leaves me awkwardly hovering in the foyer while he tramps back upstairs and comes running down again. "Here." He hands me a SD card.

"Sixty photos, right?"

"Um. Give or take."

"What do you mean, *give or take*?"

"I mean . . . there *might* not be sixty."

"You promised to give me the photos."

"I got the photos! There's just . . . maybe not sixty, I don't know, I wasn't counting." He shrugs.

If my eyes could shoot lasers, Wesley Clarke would be dead on his back right now. "They better be decent quality."

"Only the highest quality for you, Stick."

"Look." I anchor my hand on my hip. "I know why you signed up for yearbook, the same reason everyone signs up for yearbook. You wanted an easy college app fill-in."

"Bingo."

"But I swear to God, if there aren't at least fifty usable pictures on here, and I have to go around and retake them myself, I'm banning you forever from the yearbook club and kicking your ass."

He snorts. "You can't ban me from yearbook."

"I can too, I'm the president of the club."

"You are not president of the club. Jeremy Wheeler is."

"Jeremy Wheeler hasn't done jack shit for yearbook since sophomore year. So I appointed myself."

"So, you're more like dictator of the yearbook club."

"Yearbook is not a democracy, Wesley."

"Okay, so let me get this straight. You're class president, yearbook"—air quotes—"*president*, play something in orchestra—"

"Viola."

"National Honor Society, some role there . . ."

"Treasurer. And they *asked* me to do it. Ally Martin got sick and resigned."

"You do drama club."

"I just do the sound and microphone stuff, it's not like I'm involved with the musicals or anything."

"You are milking this college application prep so hard, Stick."

"Will you quit calling me that?"

"What, worried you won't stand out on your *academic merits*?" His voice is thick with sarcasm.

I blink. "I'm also vice president of Students Against Climate Change."

We look at each other a moment.

"Doesn't that feel like overkill?" he asks. "Like, how do you have time to breathe?"

"Not all of us automatically get into six colleges because we have private tutors and money leaking out of our assholes, Wesley."

He's still gaping at me when I charge back outside and speed home to face Bridget's wrath, because I'm officially fifteen minutes late.

When I get home, I check my phone and find a new text from Wesley.

Salutatorian: Enjoy my photos! ☺

I clench my teeth. Something tells me I am *not* going to enjoy the photos.

8 WESLEY

Okay, so I did something kind of bad. Half of the pictures on the SD card I gave Stella Stick-in-Her-Pants Greene are shots of Brandon and the cross-country guys making stupid faces. And then there are a couple of Mr. Donahue the Geography teacher picking his wedgie. And near the end of the day I had to rush and just snapped a bunch of random candid shots; I'm pretty sure half of them are either blurry or include someone photo-bombing with a middle finger in the background.

I shouldn't feel guilty about it, because Stella is a monstrous pain in the ass, but I kind of do. Because she *did* seem overwhelmed. And I don't want her to think I can't even take a stupid picture properly. I make a mental note to bring my camera to the next track meet and try to get some usable shots. I don't want to open my yearbook in forty years and be immediately reminded that in high school I was a giant jackass.

My phone vibrates, and my stomach does a somersault when I see the name.

> **Laura:** Remember last summer when my car was making that weird noise?! Mystery solved—$500 later *groans* my poor parents

That sucks. Do you need a ride?? I can come get you in like ten mins.

Wow, desperate much?

it's okay, Collin Anderson offered! Thanks though ☺

Well, that's a punch to the gut.

The next time my phone vibrates, it's like all the air came pouring from my lungs.

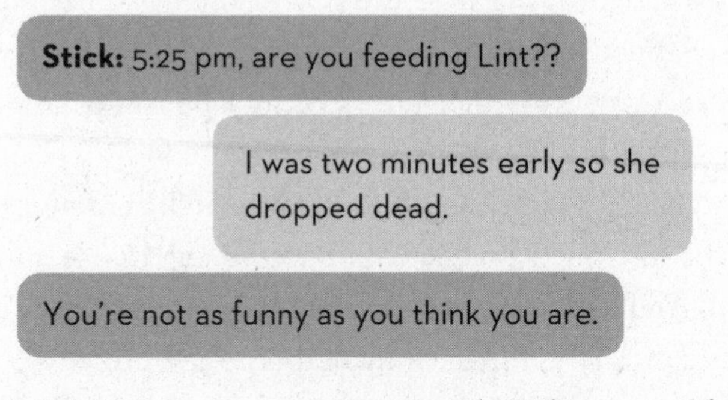

Stick: 5:25 pm, are you feeding Lint??
I was two minutes early so she dropped dead.
You're not as funny as you think you are.

Wouldn't want to upset Her Royal Highness, so I head into the guest room, where the rat is waiting.

I am every bit as funny as I think I am. PS—Lint says hi.

I take a quick picture on my phone and send it off to her.

"All right, who's hungry?" I hold my breath, slide open the cage door, and dump a few pellets and some veggies inside before quickly locking it again. The rat's beady eyes seem to follow me as I leave the guest room. I can't believe that thing is in my house.

There's a message waiting on my screen when I get back to my room.

CaptainJillsBFF22: So how did you become a Warshipper?

I sink into my desk chair and type.

CERanger11: My brother discovered it first, back when it aired. I used to watch it with him every Wednesday night. I don't think he loves it like I do, but he does have a mini Revelry on the desk in his dorm room.
CaptainJillsBFF22: Nice!
CERanger11: What about you?
CaptainJillsBFF22: I didn't find Warship until after it was already canceled, unfortunately. And actually, I got into it from watching fan videos on YouTube lol.

I'm only half paying attention to the calculus question set, lying open in the textbook on my desk.

CERanger11: So many people didn't know about Warship when it aired. I think if they had advertised it properly and it had found its fanbase at the time, maybe we would have gotten a season 2.
CaptainJillsBFF22: Right?
CERanger11: So what hooked you from the fan video?
CaptainJillsBFF22: You're gonna laugh
CERanger11: I won't!

CaptainJillsBFF22: It was this great montage of all of Aaron's scenes, paired against the song "Arsonist's Lullabye." I felt like I knew him, just from that, you know?

CERanger11: Idk that song. YouTubing it now.

CaptainJillsBFF22: OMG. No. Wait. I have a playlist. All the music!!

A link comes through, leading to a Spotify playlist titled "Warshipping." I immediately hit Play on the first song—"Poison and Wine" by the Civil Wars. Okay, this is actually really good music.

CaptainJillsBFF22: What do you think??

CERanger11: Only on the first song, but I like it so far. I've never heard this band before.

CaptainJillsBFF22: They're one of my favs!

CERanger11: I'll have to make a playlist for you now

CaptainJillsBFF22: yesssss

CERanger11: I have to ask—what's this playlist labeled Lewton?

CaptainJillsBFF22: It's the songs that remind me of Aaron/Jill!

CaptainJillsBFF22: When I'm feeling down or whatever I just listen to the Lewton playlist and it makes me think of how cute those two are together. They are the classic example of the enemies to lovers trope. The angst! The banter! The hatred! Teaming up against a common enemy! Realizing they loved each other the whole time! Proof that love still exists, you know?

It's probably the wrong time to remind her that the Lewton ship crashed and burned in episode twenty.

I guess I never really understood why people care so much about a fictional couple, but because of the dedication she put into curating this list, it almost makes sense.

CERanger11: Okay so, why do you ship #Lewton?

CaptainJillsBFF22: Are you asking so you have an excuse to make fun of me?

CERanger11: No. I honestly want to know.

CERanger11: Aaron just seems so perfect with Michele Cordova, with all their history, I never really got the Lewton thing.

CaptainJillsBFF22: Okay, so, I've thought about this A LOT.

CERanger11: I had a feeling. Lol.

CaptainJillsBFF22: Michele represents Aaron's past in the CE. Hunting people down, making them pay up, fighting for a dictatorial regime, representing a cause that is more than a little problematic.

CaptainJillsBFF22: When he meets Jill, it's his chance for a new life, even if he doesn't know it at the time.

CERanger11: But the CE is what gave him opportunity. Everything he worked for.

CaptainJillsBFF22: It gave him everything he thought he wanted (power, status, etc.). But it didn't bring him happiness.

Damn. Okay. She wasn't kidding when she said she's put thought into this.

CaptainJillsBFF22: Which I guess leads back to: Michele was everything he thought he wanted because she represents something he thought he wanted.

CaptainJillsBFF22: (but this isn't to say that I dislike Michele, because I love Michele, and I think in an alternate universe she and Jill would be best friends)

CERanger11: But Michele and Jill hate each other . . .

CaptainJillsBFF22: They hate each other because the writers are a couple of dudes.

I hadn't thought of that. Huh.

CaptainJillsBFF22: IRL, Leigh and Lisa are BFFs and Lisa always says Michele and Jill should've gotten together and left Aaron behind! Haha

CERanger11: I could see it

My phone buzzes with a new text from my brother.

hey. Coming home for spring break after all. You'll be around?

Well, that's a shock I didn't see coming. I'm pretty sure Mom had something to do with this.

I thought you were staying in LA with Mike?

Mom flipped when I mentioned it. Then I checked my email and all of a sudden there was a plane ticket for me lol

Good to see my parents are still succeeding in micromanaging our lives, even from afar.

If you google "helicopter parenting," Mom's picture comes up.

I'm not surprised. Trevor dated a few guys in high school, but Mike's his first serious relationship. He spent Thanksgiving in Indiana with Mike's family, and Mom almost blew a gasket when he told her. He came home for Christmas, but he was on the first flight out to Indiana on December 26 so he could do a second Christmas with Mike's family. I don't think my parents were too thrilled. It's not that they care that he's gay—seriously, Mom got him a rainbow-frosted ice cream cake when he came out—it's more that they'd be happy if he was gay, with a husband, in the house next door to them for the rest of his life. They want us to be ridiculously successful—just not so successful that we get jobs far from home or make our own decisions about literally anything. Which is ironic, seeing as they're currently trying to force me to live on the other side of the country for the next four years.

Could Mike come here for spring break? We could all do something?

I asked, but I guess his sister is probably getting engaged over break and wants the whole family there? Idk.

Sorry, man

He doesn't respond, so I knock off a few more calc questions, then write back to the *Warship* girl.

CERanger11: So is your Jill cosplay ready?

CaptainJillsBFF22: Just about! Still need to get the right shoes

CaptainJillsBFF22: What about you?? Still going as our sergeant??

CERanger11: the one and only. Do you think I could pass it off with brown pants, a black T-shirt, and Aaron's Central Elite flight jacket?

CERanger11: (got one off eBay already)

CaptainJillsBFF22: ooooh! Yes. Also, check this out!

She sends me another link, to Etsy. Oh my God. It's an exact replica of Aaron Lewis's silver pilot helmet. Whoever made it also hand-painted the CE logo on the side in dark purple.

DESCRIPTION: Warshippers—Look just like our favorite sergeant with this hand-painted pilot helmet! One size fits all. Made to order.

There's a tinted visor on the front, but otherwise it looks like it covers the whole head, just like Aaron's. It would match my CE jacket perfectly. I need this immediately, and it's only $70. Hope Dad doesn't mind the little charge on his credit card.

CERanger11: Ordered! Excited for Sci-Con

CaptainJillsBFF22: YAY!

CaptainJillsBFF22: I can't decide if I want to dye my hair auburn, or wear a wig, or just rough it and hope the judges don't notice.

CERanger11: Judges? It's a contest?

CaptainJillsBFF22: Yes! I always enter but never place. Basically they give you tasks to do—anyone cosplaying can enter—and you have to be fully in character while doing it. So like for example, as Jill, I try to be very stoic and controlled, like she is.

CERanger11: What kind of tasks?

CaptainJillsBFF22: Last year they had us give a monologue about ourselves onstage, then go to a "tea party" (you had to pay for the tea or pretend, lol) as your character. There's a gift card for the winner, plus a couple of vendors usually offer free art of the winner's character.

CERanger11: That is super intense. What if your character would never actually drink tea?

CaptainJillsBFF22: Oh don't worry, Aaron Lewis would drink all the tea.

CERanger11: I think he's more of a coffee guy

CaptainJillsBFF22: But the real question—are YOU more of a coffee guy? Or a tea guy?

CERanger11: Black tea, no sugar. Sometimes I'll get a latte.

CaptainJillsBFF22: You know, you can tell a lot about a person by whether they prefer coffee or tea. (I'm a coffee girl myself)

CERanger11: And what do my preferences say about me?

CaptainJillsBFF22: Hmmm . . . I think they say that

you're a straight-to-the-point kind of guy. You don't do drama, and you like when people are honest.

CERanger11: Me and Aaron have that in common.

Sometimes. Except when I lie to my parents for three months straight.

CaptainJillsBFF22: So was I spot-on??

CERanger11: Scarily so.

CaptainJillsBFF22: But Aaron absolutely loves drama, btw. My fav headcanon of him is the one where he's super sassy to Jill during their *ahem* personal time.

CERanger11: I see someone's been reading the smutty fics

CaptainJillsBFF22: I mean, it's a tough job, but someone's got to do it.

CERanger11: So who won the contest last year?

CaptainJillsBFF22: Last year the two winners were some guy dressed as Batman and this really badass older woman dressed as Peggy Carter! It was so cute. Some real-life twins came as Gemma and Sonny the year before though and came in second!! There was also this really amazing drag queen dressed as Sailor Moon.

CERanger11: Ha. I'm not sure I could do those things onstage. I'd feel stupid.

CaptainJillsBFF22: Lol that's the point! It's so much fun though, people get really into it.

I don't know why I started chatting with this random Huntington girl, but she seems nice. It's kind of weird not knowing her name.

CERanger11: Can I ask you something? I don't think you ever told me your name . . . ?

She stops typing, and I freeze. Did I overstep?

CaptainJillsBFF22: you're right, I didn't. Lol. (sorry I just think it's weird)

CERanger11: Okay. No worries. But what am I supposed to call you?

CaptainJillsBFF22: You may call me Our Dear Captain Jillian Brighton 😍

Okay, message received. No real names.

CERanger11: Only if you call me Sergeant Aaron Lewis

CaptainJillsBFF22: I salute you, Sergeant! The Central Elite thanks you for your service

CaptainJillsBFF22: How about I call you Aaron2?

CERanger11: Only if you can be Jill2

I can't help smiling, and then I realize it's the first time I've smiled all day. Only a couple months to Sci-Con. It feels like forever.

CERanger11: So tell me about this fanfic stuff. I've never written it before. What kinds of stuff do you write?

CaptainJillsBFF22: Mostly fix-it-fic, obviously, since that ending needs alllll the fixing. Here's my most popular one.

She pastes a link, and I click it.

A MISTAKE UNDONE
By: CaptainJillsBFF22
Pairing: Captain Jill Brighton / Sergeant Aaron Lewis
Words: 198,000
Tags: fix-it-fic, angst, OTP, #Lewton, so much kissing, they belong together, I want amnesia to forget the ending of episode 20, he comes back this time!, season finale was a mess, we deserved better, seriously I hate that ending

I can't get over the fact that she wrote 198,000 words of this. My last English essay was like 5,000, max, and I thought that thing was going to kill me.

CaptainJillsBFF22: (you don't have to read the whole thing, lol)

I skim the first couple of pages, taking place minutes after the end of the show. Two hundred and twenty Warshippers left comments at the end; I scroll through them, mostly fangirling over Lewton, with the occasional jerk thrown in commenting about how the fic's perfect ending is unrealistic.

CERanger11: Whoa. Okay, I'm impressed.
CaptainJillsBFF22: *bows*
CERanger11: How many of these have you written?
CaptainJillsBFF22: Ummmm . . . 17? I also have an NSFW account where I post smutty ones lol
CERanger11: . . .

CERanger11: Where's the link to that collection?

CaptainJillsBFF22: You want me to send it to you?

CERanger11: Absolutely

CaptainJillsBFF22: hahahahahahaha

CaptainJillsBFF22: No.

CERanger11: So you won't tell me your real name, you won't let me read your smut fics, how do I know you're a real person at all? 😉

I'm totally joking when I say it, but she sends me an embarrassed GIF anyway.

CaptainJillsBFF22: Okay, I'll tell you something. But you can't be mad.

I don't even know how to respond to that, but she's too fast, and before I can type anything, she's replied.

CaptainJillsBFF22: I panicked and lied.

CaptainJillsBFF22: I don't go to Huntington. I go to your school.

WARSHIP SEVEN: Episode Four

"An Illicit Trade"

SCENE CLIP: The crew, dejected, sits in the ship's dining room, trying to come up with a plan to rescue their stolen droid, after C0NDOR was kidnapped in the previous episode.

JILL: [head in her hands] Come on, we're better than this. We've raided Central Elite hospitals, strongholds, military bases. We can rescue our navigator from a black-market dealer.

GEMMA: [face blotchy, eyes wet with fresh tears] I just don't understand how this happened. He was right there with us.

SONNY: Maybe if you'd been paying attention to him instead of flirting with some guy—

GEMMA: Can you shut up? For one second?

SONNY: All I'm saying—

JILL: *Stop it.* [jumps to her feet] I don't want to hear another word out of any of your mouths that isn't productive, got it?

MARKUS: [standing stoic in the corner] She's right. This isn't helping.

SKULLS: [from out in the hallway] One wrong move, and this bullet gets lodged somewhere in your anal cavity, got it? [The door swings open and SERGEANT AARON LEWIS appears, his hands bound, SKULLS trailing behind with a gun pointed at his back.]

AARON: The amount of trouble a guy's got to go through to take a piss around here.

JILL: [visibly tensing] If you don't like it, piss your pants back in your cell, Cescum.

AARON: [walks into the small bathroom, SKULLS follows] I hardly think I need a chaperone.

SKULLS: Last time, you sawed through half your bindings with a rusty pipe.

AARON: I must say, that was some fine ingenuity on my part. Well, okay. If you insist. [He drops trou, smirking, and proceeds to pee into the metal toilet bowl, the door wide open for everyone to see.]

JILL: [keeping eye contact with him, her lips pressed together] These childish antics only make shoving you out the airlock sound more appealing to me.

AARON: Let me guess. [finishes, pulls his pants back up] Good ol' black-market shopkeep wouldn't accept your money for the stolen droid. Running a nice little illegal operation.

JILL: [with a slight look of surprise that she tries to hide] What are you talking about?

AARON: I've dealt with that guy before. Name's Marty. [washes his bound hands in the sink, then flicks off the water] He doesn't care much for money. But I know what he does care about.

GEMMA: [gasps] You know how to get C0ndor back?

AARON: [smirks, not breaking eye contact with Jill] I do.

JILL: [crosses her arms] If you're lying . . .

AARON: I'm not lying. But I'm also not giving you any information without a price.

SKULLS: Shut your trap. [slaps his hand to Aaron's shoulder, roughly leading him toward the exit] You don't get to bargain with us. You're our prisoner.

JILL: [holds up her hand] Wait.

9 STELLA

Wesley doesn't see me when I come up behind him at his locker. The second he pulls it open, I reach over his shoulder and slam it shut. The crashing metal reverberates in my ears.

"What the hell are these?" I thrust a handful of shitty photos in front of his face.

"Whoa, good morning to my favorite stick-in-the-mud." He grins, running a hand through his light brown hair. "They appear to be photographs."

"They *appear* to be trash."

He places his hand over his heart. "Are you saying you don't like my contribution to the yearbook? That hurts, Stick."

"I'm saying you probably spent the better part of five minutes taking these, and now I wasted my printer ink on pictures like this." I slap a picture of a urinal against his locker, which he wrenches back open. A sheen of sweat clings to his forehead from early morning track practice.

"You know, I bet those will be worth something someday, after I die."

"Oh, good." I smile sweetly at him. "Maybe I can arrange that day to come sooner rather than later."

"Wow, so you'd resort to murder to get valedictorian? Good to know. I'll have to keep one eye open in bed tonight."

"Like I'd get anywhere near your bed." Before he can retort, I'm storming back into the hallway and almost crash directly into Brandon Nguyen. I can't even look at him now without thinking of all those photos Wesley so kindly bestowed on me, half of which include Brandon pretending to flash the camera. I can never un-see that—and I probably can't tell Dahlia, because she would actually *love* to see that.

"Stella!" He gives me a half wave. "You coming on March twentieth?"

I have no idea what he's talking about, so I say the first thing that pops into my head. "Is Wesley going?"

"Well, yeah."

"Then no." I plow past him without another word.

It could be a free money festival where they're literally handing out fistfuls of cash, and if Wesley was going, I would still say no.

Okay, maybe for fistfuls. I do need those Jill boots.

The second he's out of view, I actually do remember what's happening that Saturday: laser tag at Space Arena. And I promised Dahlia I'd go. My brain is practically spilling out of my head today.

I can't stop thinking that maybe I shouldn't have told CERanger11 where I go to school. I still haven't totally ruled out that he's going to start stalking and murdering me like that guy on *You*.

It's okay. He doesn't know who I am. Our class has over four hundred people, which means around two hundred girls, so unless he's a master sleuth, he's not going to figure it out. I could be anyone.

He *could be anyone, too.*

What would happen if he figured it out?

I whip out my planner as I'm walking, open to the pink tab, and start scratching items off my list: I need to find sixty replacement yearbook photos (and never trust Wesley with anything ever again), finish some paperwork for the National Honor Society, finish the calc problem set, and start researching for that history paper due at the end of the semester.

Maybe it wouldn't be the worst thing in the world.

I don't know what the hell is wrong with me, but suddenly I'm picturing some weird Cinderella scenario, where my mystery man compares every girl in school with the profile he's chatted with, like it's some sort of glass slipper and he needs to find the right fit.

My feet autopilot me, slaloming around all the groups of people milling about in the hall. I half catch a few saying hi to me, but I don't have time to chitchat. I'm paging back through my planner to check the due date for that rat maze assignment when I slam directly into someone and my agenda goes flying.

"Can you watch where you're—"

Kyle Nielsen beams at me. "Oh, hey." He bends to pick up my notebook, dusts it off, and passes it back into my hand. "Sorry about that."

I'm gaping at him like a fish. "Kyle. Hi."

"I'm all over the place today." He laughs. "Up late."

"Up late . . . doing anything fun?"

"Nah. Been trying to get a group together for this convention thing in the spring, but no luck so far." He shrugs. "Well, I'll see you in AP Bio?"

He's already around the corner when I shout after him, "See you!"

Wow, could I have handled that any worse? I tip my glasses up and press the heels of my palms into my eyes; they come back stained with my purple eye shadow. Great.

This convention thing in the spring.

My jaw drops. Oh my God. It couldn't be . . . could it?

Kyle is Aaron2.

Maybe?

No. I'm getting ahead of myself. He didn't even say which convention. There could be loads.

I plow ahead and don't even realize I'm outside the main office until Ms. Rossi, the secretary, nearly decapitates me with a giant rolled poster she's got slung under her arm while she balances precariously on a stepladder.

"Well, good morning, Stella." She slowly unrolls the poster and presses it to the wall.

"Hey, Ms. Rossi." The giant *FINALS ARE COMING* poster in the *Game of Thrones* font she's trying to staple to the bulletin board hangs lopsided on the right. "Here, let me help." I pull up the leveler app on my phone and press it to the poster; the little bubble darts to the left side of the screen.

"Oh, thank you." She adjusts the side, and I hold it steady while she staples it to the board. "Will you be doing any more morning announcements this year? We miss having you down at the main office."

"Sure, if you need me to." Because I love adding more commitments to my super-open schedule.

"You did such a great job last year. And now this year, with the whole valedictorian thing, you're practically a celebrity around here."

"Oh. Thank you."

She clicks the stapler to the far corner. "You know, I've been at this school twenty-two years now, and I don't think we've ever had a couple of students as driven as you and Wesley Clarke."

I realize I'm unintentionally deadpanning at her and snap

out of it. "Oh. Yeah." But don't ever lump me into the same category as that rich douchebag.

"You guys are a lot alike!" She laughs.

Wow, I didn't ask for this personal attack. I don't even try to wipe the horrified look off my face. "No, I really don't think we are, Ms. Rossi. Sorry."

"You might be surprised. That boy's got a good head on his shoulders." *Yeah, that's what happens when your parents buy you eight thousand private tutors.* I wonder if she would still think he has such a *good head on his shoulders* if I showed her the collection of bathroom photos in my bag right now. She climbs back down the stepladder. "Thanks for helping me with this. I'll see you later, Stella."

The three meanest things she could have said to me: (1) Stella, you're not getting valedictorian. (2) Stella, you're going nowhere and bound to become just like your family. (3) Stella, you and Wesley Clarke have a lot in common. How dare she insult me like this? What did I ever do to you, Rossi?

My phone buzzes—Dahlia.

You here yet? We're at The Wall.

I barely turn the corner before all the senior photos greet me, taped up to the section of the front office reserved for college announcements. My face burns when I see mine, and the abysmally short list below it. Maybe if I'd had private tutors and public speaking coaches and money for application fees and parents who could afford to hold a Porsche over my head, I'd have a long list too.

"You look like you have smoke shooting out of your ears." Dahlia leans against the wall, covering at least five senior portraits.

Em stands beside her, fidgeting with her purse strap that looks like it's carving a crater into her shoulder; she decided back in ninth grade that she was too cool for backpacks, and now she shoves all her books into her giant Michael Kors purse instead.

"You okay?" she asks, her hand clenched around a Starbucks cup. It's weird, my two best friends think I hate coffee, but really I'm just too poor for those six-dollar-venti-whatevers they drink every day.

"Yeah, what happened?" Em's one of those soccer fanatics who plays year-round; she even found an indoor team for winter, and basically wears jerseys to school every day. The name *GONZALES* stretches across the back in red letters.

"Wesley Clarke happened." I thrust the photo stack toward them.

Em starts thumbing through it. "I don't get it. Did I miss something?"

"Wesley submitted these for yearbook club. Like, to publish inside our *senior yearbook*."

Em keeps flipping through, until both she and Dahlia recoil at once. "Is this . . . is this someone's bare ass?"

"I honestly don't want to know."

"This one belongs in the Louvre." Dahlia holds up a photo of a toilet. He actually submitted a picture of a toilet.

"No, you know where it belongs?" I find Wesley's senior photo on The Wall, right on top of that long college list, looking like he walked out of a Calvin Klein ad, and slap the toilet picture right over it. "Right here."

Em and Dahlia burst out laughing.

I peel back the tape from the original senior picture and slide the new one directly into place, so it's stuck on the wall and fully covering Wesley's face. "It's his final form."

I take a second to scan the photos. Unless I'm being catfished, one of the guys on this wall could be CERanger11. *But which one?*

I find myself staring at Kyle's picture. University of Connecticut, UMass–Amherst, and Keene State look back at me. I swallow hard, focusing on his soft brown eyes. *Are you Aaron2?*

No. I can't get ahead of myself. It could be anyone. Maybe someone who isn't even on The Wall.

"What did you guys do this weekend?" Em asks.

"I had to pick up my rat for AP Bio."

"I forgot you're in that class," Dahlia says. "I always see people walking around with rats on their shoulders this time of year."

Declan Detton beams back at me, his shaggy hair dyed blue for his senior portrait, which looks like it was taken with a selfie stick. I cringe; he seems like a possible option—he's a TV buff, so why wouldn't he love *Warship Seven*?

"I spent all weekend doing homework," Dahlia says. "Then drove down to Boston with my parents to get lunch with my sister."

Em takes a swig from her coffee. "How's she liking BC?"

Connor Jacobsen's senior photo looks like it was taken in the public library; he's gazing pensively into the distance, his chin resting on a stack of pretentious-looking library books. He's one of those guys who manages to make horn-rim glasses work. I'm pretty sure he's gay; I vaguely remember him saying something about it at Cory Ellison's birthday party last year—but then again, why am I assuming CERanger11 is straight? He's never indicated an orientation.

"She loves it." Dahlia flicks her hair over her shoulder. "She was on the dean's list last semester and probably will be again."

"I wonder if I'll run into her in Boston next year," I muse. "Maybe she knows some good coffee shops."

"I'm so jealous you'll be nearby," Em says. "I won't know anyone in Savannah."

Dahlia scoffs. "You picked a school that's so far away."

Kyle Nielsen walks by again, chunky red headphones covering his ears. Dammit, I try to think of anything else, and he has to keep popping up. Em and Dahlia keep talking about colleges or whatever, but I've spaced out.

It could be Kyle. What if it's Kyle?

My heart speeds up a little.

He gives me a shy wave. "Forgot my calc book in my locker."

I smile and nod back, heat flooding my cheeks.

"Would it be weird if I asked him to prom?" I say, low enough so only the girls can hear me.

Dahlia's forehead wrinkles. "Why would it be weird? This isn't 1952."

"I'm asking Leah to prom." Em shrugs.

"She's already your girlfriend," I say. "That doesn't count."

"I'm hoping Brandon Nguyen will ask me," Dahlia says.

"Shocker," Em says, and Dahlia gives her a friendly push.

"But if he doesn't, I'm going to suck it up and ask him myself," she continues.

"That's the spirit," I say.

"Hey, I heard Wesley Clarke doesn't have a date yet." Em ribs me in the side. "At least four different girls already asked him. Maybe he's holding out for his one true love, Stella Greene."

"Very funny. Hilarious."

"Okay, here's a question," Dahlia says. "If you had to choose between kissing Wesley Clarke or kissing Mr. Hebert the gym teacher, who would you pick?"

"Hebert. Hands down."

They both crack up.

"Okay, no, I've got one." Em's ponytail swishes as she walks. "Kiss Wesley or lose valedictorian?"

"Is death an option?"

"Nope."

"Ugh. I don't know . . ."

"Okay, okay. One more." We reach our lockers, and Dahlia spins the combination lock on hers. "Would you rather sleep with Wesley Clarke or die?"

I slide the planner into my locker, making a mental pros and cons list for the question. A photo of Dahlia, Em, and I at last year's homecoming stares back at me, tacked to the metal with a pink daisy magnet. My calendar is taped beneath it, but it looks more like one of those football charts where everything is circled and scribbled on with red pen.

I realize I'm grimacing when Em looks at me and starts laughing. "An answer?"

"I'm thinking!"

–♥–

"Can you not do that?" I snap at Wesley after his knee knocks into mine for the bazillionth time under our lab table.

"Not do what?" He's taping cardboard chunks together to form the outer edge of our maze, and it's already leaning precariously to the right. "Work on our project?"

I reach down and shove his leg away.

"Whoa." He grins. "Keep your hands to yourself, Stick. This is a classroom."

I roll my eyes. "Just hold this so I can tape it."

"I still think we should have done my idea."

"We're not constructing a maze based on a Muppet movie."

"Okay, *Labyrinth* is not a Muppet movie. It's Jim Henson. There's a difference."

"You are *such* a nerd."

"You named your dog after a Pokémon."

"How's it coming, everyone?" Mr. Hardwicke paces between lab tables, examining cardboard labyrinths.

"A-*maze*-ing," Kyle says from across the room.

When no one else laughs, I catch his eye and give him my widest grin.

Corny humor. Sergeant Aaron Lewis is the king of it.

Wesley snorts, stabilizing a cardboard corner with a giant strip of Scotch tape. "Speaking of nerds."

"What's that supposed to mean?"

"Nothing. Nothing at all."

I press my lips together but don't respond, dragging my pencil over the giant slab of cardboard to map out our maze. When the whole thing's finished, I grab my planner and open to May. Of course this stupid project is due right after Sci-Con.

"Okay, so, we've got about a month to finish building, which should give us two months to train her to go through it."

"Whoa, whoa, whoa." Wesley rips the planner out of my hands, thumbing through the pink, orange, yellow, and blue stickies poking out of it. "Are these color-coded tabs?"

I yank it back. "Some of us like to be organized."

"You could just wing it."

I can't believe he's my competition. I really, really can't.

Wesley unzips his black North Face backpack and pulls out an energy shot, then knocks it back like tequila. "Cheers."

"You know those things are terrible for you, right?"

"Some of us were up late working on our Latin translation."

"*Personae sunt molestissimi tellus*, Wesley."

He makes a face. "Person what?"

"Clearly all those long hours studying Latin didn't pay off, huh?"

"Yes, now that you're proficient in *speaking* the dead language, you can go fulfill your life dream of filing papers at the Vatican." He tosses the empty plastic container toward the recycle bin; it makes a perfect arc before sinking into the basket.

Kyle's hovering at the next lab table over, chatting with Madison Benson, his lab partner. I realize I'm staring when he looks up and his eyes lock with mine; I quickly pretend to be fiddling with a chunk of cardboard instead.

"How's Lint doing?" I ask. Our fuzzy companion watches us from her cage at the end of the table. I gently press my finger between the bars, touching her nose.

"She's fine." Wesley keeps his eyes on the cardboard strip his scissors are slowly carving through. "Eats a lot."

"You still afraid of her?"

He snorts. "I'm not afraid of her."

"I'll take that as a yes."

"It's just a rat."

"Cool." I unlatch her cage and she happily crawls onto my palm, sniffing and clawing her way up my arm. "So I assume you'd have no problem holding her, right?"

He flinches away. "You have fun keeping that plague all to yourself, Stick."

I let Lint perch on my shoulder. "This is for you, sweet thing. I hope you like mazes." I stroke her soft fur.

"She'd like it a lot better if it was based on a Jim Henson classic."

"Hey, can I borrow your Scotch tape?" Kyle stands at our lab table. "We ran out." He's wearing a vintage-print T-shirt with a sea monster on it, and it's pretty adorable.

"Oh. Yeah. Of course." I totally fumble it and it slides across the table, where Wesley stabs his finger onto it to stop it from hitting the floor. "Sorry."

"Hey, congrats on being appointed NHS treasurer," he says, and it takes me a second to realize he's talking to me. "I voted for you."

My stomach does a somersault. "Oh. Well. Thank you. It was kind of a last-minute thing." Ally Martin was treasurer for the last year and a half, but then she had to step down because of a medical condition.

"I voted for you, too," Wesley says. "I mean, you were the only name on the ballot. I did seriously contemplate writing in Oscar the Grouch instead."

"Great insult—you think that one up all by yourself?" I snap back.

"Well, thanks for the tape." Kyle looks at Wesley. "By the way, earlier she said you're the most annoying person on the planet. In Latin."

Kyle was listening to us?

Wesley presses his hand over his heart. "I'm flattered."

"Hey, cool necklace." Kyle nods at me before heading back to his table.

"Bye," I say, a little too loudly. He rejoins his own lab group.

I find myself subconsciously tugging at my three-pointed sword necklace. When he said *cool necklace,* did he mean like, a three-pointed sword is cool? Or like, *That's Captain Jill Brighton's necklace, from my favorite show?*

It could be him. It could really be him.

Wesley tapes a corner, joining two mismatched ends of cardboard. "You know, if you google the word *tool,* Kyle Nielsen's face pops up in the image search."

"You're doing it wrong." I knock his hand away. His fingers brush mine, and I pull away. "And he's *nice*. I'm sorry that *offends* you so much, up there on your giant chocolate throne."

"He doesn't seem nice to me."

"Maybe you don't know any nice people."

"Or maybe I know how to recognize a douchebag."

"Takes one to know one."

The bell rings, and it isn't soon enough. I set Lint gently back in her cage and stroll out of the room without saying goodbye to Wesley.

Topic: ***WARSHIP SEVEN* REWATCH PARTY**
Username: **CaptainJillsBFF22**

How're all my Warshippers doing? Have you checked out #RevelryRadio podcast this week? They're doing a really awesome live-watch. Jess's reactions are spot-on.

Today we're talking about episode five—"Two Hours in the Black Market." This is kind of a part two to episode four, "An Illicit Trade"—we finally get C0ndor back, and we see Aaron's master plan!

Turns out, ol' Marty doesn't care about money. His planet is slowly dying from a disease that's already been eradicated on the central planets. Our Sergeant Aaron came through—he knew all Jill had to do was offer up the medication, and boom! C0ndor's back with the crew, in all his glitching glory. If only it were that easy. Of course, Marty's not exactly the honest type. His bodyguards attempt to steal the medication without keeping up their part of the deal and returning the droid. But Aaron saw this coming and warned Jill of the dealer's dishonesty. The medicine vial was empty, and by the time they realized it, Gemma was far away with her favorite little robot son, C0ndor! A job well done for the *Revelry* crew, all thanks to their NEW ALLY, Aaron Lewis.

Well, sort of. We know they aren't exactly besties yet. But we're getting there! I bet it stung Jill deep down to have to admit Aaron was right about something. LOL she's quite proud.

Markus is there too, just as shy and awkward as always lol, although this is the ONLY episode where they show us he's gay, and it's like one line. Did SFFStream think we would all pat them on the back for having Markus imply in one offhand comment that he dated guys back on Earth? C'mon! Give Markus Harris a boyfriend, people! I'm the first to complain the final #Lewton love scene is too short, but at least they got something. Anyway. I digress.

10 WESLEY

"Dude, what happened to your Wall photo?" Derek Cooper asks as we're heading back from track practice after school. Sweat drips down his face like rain, and I make sure to stay out of splash distance.

"What do you mean?"

"Someone replaced it with a picture of a toilet."

It takes me half a second before I have to choke down a laugh. Well played, Stella. "Oh, yeah. That's my senior picture. Didn't you know?"

The group of us wind toward the locker room. I made my best time today for the mile—4:48. A dull ache spreads down my calves, but I'm feeling pretty good right now.

And unfortunately for Stella, I still have that amazing paparazzi shot of her scowling at me. "Hang on, I'll be right there." I grab my bag and make my way to the main entry, where the wall of senior portraits and college announcements stares back at me.

Stella's portrait isn't hard to find, and the moment I do, I whip out my special picture. Smiling Stella doesn't fit her personality anyway. This one is way better.

I slide the scowling picture over her senior portrait and add a few quick alterations.

I can't wait to see the expression on her face tomorrow.

–♥–

"Dad, can I take the car?" I shout up the stairs to his closed office door.

Something rustles upstairs. "How long do you need it?"

"Just wanted to take Devin out for some ice cream." When I was a kid, I used to ask my parents for a little brother; it didn't happen, but I *did* get a little cousin. "Aunt Diane's working late, and I don't want him sitting at home by himself all night." It's a total lie—not only is my aunt probably home, but I'm going to need to find a way to hide all the amazing banana bread and cookies she'll give me; it's a dead giveaway they came from her. But I just need to get out of this house.

"All right. Have it back by six. You should be doing schoolwork," he calls down without opening the door. "You don't become valedictorian by going out for ice cream."

"Fine. Whatever."

It takes a good twenty minutes to drive to Devin's condo. A couple of kids hit a Wiffle ball on the street, and the soft thump of plastic hitting plastic echoes around me when one of them finally manages to strike it with the bat. They look up when I drive by.

Devin is perched on the front steps, playing his DS. He finally wrenches his attention away from the screen when I tap the horn. My cousin is still trapped in that awkward-obnoxious preteen phase where he's a brat to everyone.

"Hey, man," I say as he opens the door and climbs into the car. "Nice haircut."

"I hate it." He slumps against the window. "My mom made me."

"Wow, what's with the mood?"

"There are too many people in my house today." Devin sighs like he just lost all his money in a gambling tournament. "It's way too crowded in there for just one bathroom."

"Oh, yeah, I forgot your grandparents are in town." On his dad's side. The dad we don't talk about, because he had a midlife crisis and walked out on Diane, never looking back. Mom won't even say his name.

"I got a B-plus on that math test, though."

Do you know why they call it a B? My dad's voice rings in my head. *Because* B *stands for "bad."*

"That's awesome!" I reach across the console to give him a high five. "You studied really hard for that."

"Yeah. I'm just glad I didn't fail."

"I knew you wouldn't."

I turn the radio on and keep flipping stations until I find a Lizzo song.

"Remember when we played HORSE at the park last summer?" Devin asks. I take a turn out of his development and onto the main road.

"I remember you annihilating me at every shot." Watching a seventh grader kick my ass at hoops was not my finest moment. He kept telling me not to let him win, and honestly I would have felt a lot better about myself if I had been.

"Do you think I should try out for the team?"

"The middle school basketball team? Absolutely. If you want to." Then he can beat people his own age.

He's quiet for a few moments, fiddling with his seat belt. "What about the musical?"

"What musical?"

"They're doing *Guys and Dolls*."

"Oh man." I cruise to a stop at a red light. "We did that

one in seventh grade, too. My friend Brandon was the lead, Sky something. Why—are you thinking of trying out?"

"I want to." He fidgets. "There's this . . . girl."

"Oh?"

"She's trying out, too." I'm suddenly praying his mom had the birds and the bees chat with him so I don't have to. But then he adds, "Have you ever had a girlfriend?"

"A few." I think for a moment. "There was this girl Olivia, and this other girl Laura." It's sad how boring my dating life is now. It's even sadder that at school, the girl I spend the most time with lately is Stella Greene. "I also went to the movies with Katie Jett in the second grade, but I don't think that counts. I did hold her hand all through *Kung Fu Panda 2*, though."

He twiddles his thumbs around the seat belt. "I think I like her."

"What's she like?"

"She's really cool." Devin absentmindedly tugs at one of the light brown curls dangling over his forehead. "She color-codes her binders with labels and highlighters." I can't help thinking about Stella and her giant planner and almost burst out laughing. Maybe Devin would get a crush on her, too.

"That's cool."

"Yeah, she's super smart."

Dad's boring candy key chains clink together. I know it sounds weird, but I already bought a key chain, even though I don't have a car yet—it's this little brass C0ndor that lights up when you press his ass. No one will get the reference, but whatever. C0ndor is the best. Besides Aaron.

We pull into The Scoopery parking lot, under the giant ice cream cone sign. This is probably the only ice cream shop in the whole state that's open year-round, but it's also the one with the most flavor choices, so I'm cool with it. I slide into a spot near the back, far away from other cars. Dad will kill me if I ding his Carrera.

"What are you getting?" I ask as we join the line at the stand.

"Mom gave me four dollars." He digs into his jeans pocket.

"Nope, put that away. I'm getting this one."

"Are you sure? Mom says I shouldn't let you pay for me all the time."

Aunt Diane works two jobs and won't let anyone help her out. This is the least I can do. "No way. Ice cream is always on me. But you should add sundae toppings, because I kind of want fudge sauce but don't want to be the only one."

Old music blares from the speakers outside. White paint chips off the walls, thick with nostalgia. This is the ice cream place every kindergarten class took field trips to and everyone got to scoop their own ice cream. Good times.

"Would it be weird if I put gummy bears on top of cookie dough?"

"Kinda. But do it anyway. I mean, I put peanut butter sauce on top of my strawberry ice cream."

Devin's face scrunches up. "That's disgusting."

"What? It's like a PB and J."

We reach the front of the line, and I'm still looking at the menu written in multicolored marker beside the window. The girl inside riffles the plastic cups under the counter. She stands up suddenly and our eyes lock. The universe is determined to mess with me.

"Are you kidding me?" Stella's eyes narrow. "What do you want?"

"We *wanted* some ice cream, with a side of grump, and it

appears we've come to the right place." I thump Devin on the back. "What are you getting?"

Stella crosses her arms, covering the pink T-shirt with *The Scoopery* twirling across the front in swirly letters. "No. Go away."

"Now, that's no way to speak to a customer." I lean against the counter. "I'm conflicted. What do you recommend?"

She scowls. "A different ice cream parlor?"

Devin's eyes dart back and forth between us. "Are we ordering, or . . . ?"

"What flavor do you think I should get?" I ask her.

"Whatever flavor gets you out of here fastest."

"I want the Stella Specialty."

"With extra spit?"

Devin clears his throat. "I'd like a one-scoop cookie dough, with gummy bears and whipped cream, in a cup, please. No spit."

She quickly scoops Devin's ice cream into a dish and carefully hands it to him.

I glance back at the menu. "I'll have—"

"I thought you wanted the Stella Specialty." She smiles sweetly at me. "One Stella Specialty, coming right up." She immediately turns her back and starts scooping. I lean in, but can't see which flavors she's getting.

"Okay, on a scale of one to ten, how likely is it that she poisons me?" I mutter under my breath. It's a Sergeant Aaron Lewis quote.

"Like, an eleven," Devin says, taking a giant spoonful.

"Here." Stella slides a bowl across the counter to me. Looks innocuous. I'd probably guess coffee ice cream with hot fudge—no visible spit that I can see. I cautiously pick it up like it's ready to detonate.

"What is it?"

"A surprise."

"That's promising." I dig out my wallet. "How much?"

She pounds some numbers into the register. "That'll be two fifty for the one-scoop, and ten dollars for yours."

I nearly choke on the spoonful. "For one bowl?"

"It's the Stella Specialty."

I force a smile and thrust fifteen bucks over the counter. "Keep the change."

"Thank you for the generous tip." She takes the ten-dollar bill and slides it directly into the tip jar. The receipt prints out, reading two $2.50 ice cream charges.

"Well played." I take a big bite, half expecting my mouth to catch on fire. Weirdly, it's actually pretty good? "What is this?"

Stella shrugs. "Caramel toffee with caramel drizzle. You asked for the Stella Specialty, and it's my favorite."

Okay, so Stella Greene didn't try to poison me. Consider me shocked. "It's good. See you tomorrow."

When Devin and I are back in the car, he lets out the biggest snort.

"Whew. Could you flirt any harder with that girl? Jeez."

Um. What? "Okay, I was not flirting with Stella Greene." I laugh, but it turns really awkward really fast. *Was* I flirting with Stella Greene?

–♥–

"Okay, foul beast, enjoy your supper." I fling a few pellets into Lint's cage. I'm about an hour late—nobody tell Stella, she'll have a conniption. Wouldn't want to upset the color-coded schedule. A yawn rips through me. Sometimes I wish I could punch Yesterday Me in the face for assuming I could handle pulling three hours of sleep to finish that English paper.

Lint cocks her head, then starts munching on one of the pellets. I stand several feet away, watching. "You're a hungry little thing, aren't you?"

She ignores me, nibbling. Her wormlike tail is curled behind her.

Okay, she's kind of cute. Which is a word I never thought I would use to describe a rat. I take a hesitant step toward her cage and press my finger to the cold metal bar. Lint extends her head and sniffs at it, and I quickly pull away. My heart pounds.

"Well, goodbye." I race out of the guest room and shut the door behind me, almost plowing right into Dad. He's still in his work clothes, his eyes fixed on his phone, which he immediately stows in his back pocket.

"Wes, why is there a rat in my spare bedroom?"

I blink at him. There's been a rat in his spare bedroom for a while now. "It's for school."

"They make you get pet rats now? What, do you dissect them?"

I picture Lint's fuzzy little face, and the thought makes me cringe. "No. We train them to go through a maze."

"Waste of time." He claps a hand on my shoulder, and I tense. "But I'm proud of you for the dedication you put into your school projects. You deserve that valedictorian spot."

"Oh. Thanks."

"And that new car." He winks at me. "Mom thinks you should get the white, but I'd recommend silver. Gotta make their heads turn when we cruise out to Cali this summer."

"Oh. Sure."

"Have they mailed your course catalog yet? Or is it online now?"

"Um." That would have required looking on the student portal, which I haven't. Because I don't have a log-in. Because I turned them down. "Not yet."

"I want to go over them all before you choose. We need to make sure your schedule has at least two business courses in your first semester."

I already know the answer, but I blurt it out anyway. "What if I don't want to major in business?"

"Then we'll make it engineering classes instead. Chemical, electrical, so many options—I'm sure you'll find the right one." He gives my shoulder a squeeze before heading back down the hall into his office. The door closes with a soft thud.

Sometimes I feel like I had two dads growing up. There was the guy who put up a tent in the backyard and told us spooky stories by the firepit, who kissed the top of Mom's head and danced with her in the kitchen. And then there was the guy who threw away my colored pencils when I was drawing instead of doing math homework and who screamed at the referee for yellow-carding me in soccer games. Still, even when he's that jerky second guy, I don't want to lose him. And I can't fight the feeling that when he finds out about Columbia, I will.

I head back into my room and collapse into my rolling desk chair. Suddenly I feel like a weight is pressing on my chest. I spin, watching the carpet blur beneath my feet. My laptop dings.

CaptainJillsBFF22: how's your cosplay coming?

I jolt the chair still. It's been a few weeks, and I'm no closer to knowing who this girl is.

CERanger11: helmet should be here soon, gonna look badass
CERanger11: What about yours??

CaptainJillsBFF22: I'm still saving up for the boots, but otherwise I'm good to go!

A heavy silence fills my room. Even from upstairs, I hear that damn grandfather clock. Tick, tock. Tick, tock.

I'm not sure what makes me type it, but I do.

CERanger11: Do you ever feel trapped?

CERanger11: Like, in your situation. The hand life dealt you, so to speak. Like everyone expects you to be something you're not.

CERanger11: Sometimes I feel like I'm a different person on the outside than I am on the inside. Like, I smile a lot, when I don't mean it.

CERanger11: I feel like I'm supposed to be happy, but I just feel . . . empty.

I'm kind of surprised I said that. Nice one, Wesley. Way to get all philosophical on a stranger. She starts typing, then the little dots disappear. Why do I always manage to make things awkward?

CERanger11: Sorry, is that a weird question to dump on you?

Aaron Lewis always had an answer for everything, always had a retort. And then there's me, barely finding the right words. I pull out my sketchpad and start to draw, not really thinking about it.

CaptainJillsBFF22: All the time.

WARSHIP SEVEN: Episode Six
"The Cost of Winning"

SCENE CLIP: AARON sits pensively in his makeshift cell, still chained up. Footsteps pound on the stairs, and JILL enters the room.

AARON: So I take it my black-market-Marty idea worked, then?

JILL: You got lucky. [She slaps a hastily made sandwich onto the crate.] Eat.

AARON: [smirking] Oh, you're making me sandwiches now?

JILL: Skulls made it.

AARON: [His grin melts into a frown.] On a scale of one to ten, how likely is this to contain poison?

JILL: [sits on the opposite crate] Two. He's happy C0ndor is back and he doesn't have to navigate for us.

AARON: [takes a bite] Your gunman isn't winning any culinary awards anytime soon.

JILL: That's why he's our gunman and not our chef.

AARON: You're being awfully nice to me.

JILL: Yeah, well, you promised to get our navigation droid back, and you did. I promised to take the chains off your legs so you can stretch them out, so. [She unveils a key from her pocket.] You kick me and I'll kill you.

AARON: [grins] I wouldn't dream of it.

[JILL kneels down and removes his ankle chains.]

AARON: [stretches out his legs with a hearty, appreciative groan] Now, how about these chains binding my hands…

JILL: Don't push it.

AARON: Is it just me, or is our ship slowing down?

JILL: Gemma's entering a contest planetside, so we're docking for a couple hours.

AARON: May I ask, how did someone as young as you become a captain?

JILL: The same way someone as young as you became a CE sergeant. Lots of work, and a bit of luck.

AARON: You seem like you don't take any crap.

JILL: A woman in my position can't afford to. You mess up once, they hold it against you forever.

AARON: Well, that's admirable. You've kept your whole crew safe for all this time. Even when you've probably got the whole CE after you.

JILL: Of course. [stands to leave] Enjoy your lunch.

AARON: [calls after her] Are you ever going to tell me what that sword necklace means?

JILL: As soon as you tell me the name and location of your partner.

AARON: So, never, then.

JILL: So you admit you have a partner? Interesting. I'll keep that in mind.

AARON: [realizing his error, tries to hide the brief veil of panic crossing his face]

JILL: That's what I thought. [The door locks behind her, leaving the CE alone in his cell.]

AARON: [activates the comm chip in his mouth] Michele... are you there? Yes... good. I've made some progress. I think the captain is beginning to trust me. All I have to do to come home to you is retrieve their stolen medication... and kill Captain Jill Brighton.

11 STELLA

Bridget is already wearing her Burger Blitz uniform when I get into the kitchen in the morning. A thick black streak of mascara is smudged under her left eye. She sandwiches her phone between her ear and her shoulder while sliding a K-cup into the ancient Keurig. The machine whirs to life. Mom dodges around her, throwing together her lunch for work. Gwen squirms in her high chair, letting out a small whine.

"I don't give a . . . No, you don't get to decide." Bridget's voice gets louder. "Her father? Ha! You've done nothing, you don't even know your own daughter's birthday . . . Because you weren't there, that's why . . . What? Bullshit!"

"Don't swear in front of your daughter," Mom hisses at Bridget.

Bridget covers the phone receiver and hisses back at her, "Where do you think I learned these words, Mom?"

"Good morning." I kiss the top of Gwen's fuzzy head. "Not even seven a.m., it's way too early for Ben drama."

Dave sits across the table, reading the paper. I always find it kind of endearing that I have a stepdad who still reads the actual newspaper every morning, even if it's because he is too technologically challenged to know how to use the CNN app. "That boy's called her eight times this morning," he mutters under his breath. "Trying to get her to drop Gwen with him next weekend."

"What?" I slap my hand protectively on Gwen's high chair. "No. No way."

Mom shakes her head, whipping open the fridge. "I told you not to talk to him again."

"Mom, I'm on the phone! . . . No, you listen," Bridget thunders into her phone. "I'm late for work, I don't have time for this." She hangs up, then releases a loud groan before muttering to herself. On the morality scale, my sister ranks chaotic good about ninety percent of the time. Emphasis on the chaotic. The moment she sets the phone down on the kitchen table, it immediately starts vibrating again. Fire rages in her eyes, and before she can take it out on the phone, I quickly slam my finger down on Ignore, taking great pleasure in seeing Ben's name disappear.

I grab a granola bar and a banana, and slide into my backpack straps. "All right, ready to go?"

Bridget jerks her attention toward me. "Yeah. Hang on."

"This is why you shouldn't have gone to see him," Mom chides, throwing her hair into a messy ponytail while her breakfast rotates in the microwave. "He's a mess."

"I said the same thing," I mumble.

"Mom, stop," Bridget snaps. She wipes Gwen's mouth with a towel. "None of you think I'm capable of making my own decisions."

Dave raises his hands. "Hey, leave me out of this, I didn't say anything."

"Well, if you'd make one good decision every now and then . . ."

My sister levels a finger at me. "Okay, can you not?"

"Stella, be nice to your sister."

"I'm just saying," I mutter. "This family could use some good decisions once in a while."

Mom huffs. "Seriously, Stella? We're doing our best around here. You could try to be a little kinder."

"Fat chance." Bridget throws her towel on the ground. "You can walk to school."

I open my mouth, then close it. She doesn't mean it. But I probably should shut up for a little while.

"Are you working today?" Mom asks me. "I finish at eight, I can pick you up after."

"No, they just cut all our shifts. I'm not working again until next week." Of course, right when I need those boots, The Scoopery screws me over. "Whatever, it's not like I want to work there forever. It's just a stupid high school job."

Bridget tenses, lifting Gwen out of her high chair. Without a word, she sweeps from the room.

"Are you . . . still driving me to school?" I call to her.

After an eternity, she calls back, "Ten minutes, then we leave." There's no spark of affection in her voice.

A twinge of guilt prickles to life inside me, but I swallow it down. I can't end up like my sister. I won't.

–♥–

"Wow, that's *attractive*," Greg Carlson says as I walk into school. A group of guys is clustered around The Wall, laughing.

I squint to see what's so funny, and that's when I notice it—it's my own face, scowling back from The Wall, looking like I'm ready to punch someone. I shove past the gawking crowd and take a closer look.

Yep. It's the picture Wesley took of me last week, in this very hallway. Devil horns crown my head in black Sharpie, and there's a curly mustache stretched across my face.

With one swift swoop, I tear it off The Wall, revealing my real senior portrait behind it. The guys whoop and holler behind me.

I will annihilate him.

"That Public Speaking project is due today," some guy mumbles behind me. "I totally forgot."

"You didn't write your speech yet?" his friend replies.

"No, which means I gotta do it in two hours."

I roll my eyes. I've had that speech drafted, proofread, and practiced for a week now.

When Ms. Hatley handed back our school uniform debate cards—Wesley's team won, shocker—she had written in big, bold letters, *Don't read straight off your notecards next time, Stella* followed by the most passive-aggressive red smiley face I'd ever seen and a giant *-5 points*.

I touch the three-pointed sword necklace dangling under my sweater and think of Jill. She wouldn't take this lying down. She'd do something about it.

An idea hits me.

Hope you're ready for your speech today, Wesley.

Because I'm going to be ready for you.

–♥–

Ms. Hatley sits in the front row of the auditorium, thick red glasses perched on her nose and a clipboard clamped in her hand. "Okay, we have time for about half the speeches today. We'll finish up on Friday."

Everyone settles into seats, scattered between the first, second, and third rows of the auditorium. Our classroom always seems overpacked with the thirty of us crammed into desks, but the huge auditorium looks next to deserted. Hatley says it's to practice our voice projection or something, but what she doesn't realize is that everyone is going to use this as an excuse to nap or text or work on stuff for other classes.

I catch sight of the back of Wesley's head in the second row, his stupid perfect hair, and of course, he's sitting next to Brandon. Lord help me if he and Dahlia ever actually start dating.

I pull out my stack of green, pink, and yellow index cards, each numbered in the corner in case I drop them.

Card #1 *Short welcome, address the crowd*
Card #2 *Opening argument: climate statistics, natural disasters, etc.*
Card #3 *Explain how temperature has shifted over the last hundred years*

I read through all twenty-eight cards for the eight thousandth time. No verbatim notes today. I'm going to do the whole thing from memory. My heart rate spikes just thinking about it.

"Why did I have to get a cold right before this stupid test?" Dahlia plops down next to me, holding a crumpled tissue.

"Want a cough drop?" I unzip my bag, revealing my neatly organized collection of necessities.

Dahlia starts pawing through it. "Jeez, look at all this stuff. Tampons. Pads. Tylenol. Cough drops. Tissue packs." She grabs a honey-herb cough drop, unwraps it, and pops it into her mouth. The smell of thyme and lemon fills the air. "You're a walking pharmacy."

"You never know when you'll need something."

"What do you think Brandon's presentation is going to be?" She sits up super straight, surveying the rows in front of us until she sees where he's sitting.

"A point-by-point argument about why you should be his girlfriend?" I mean, technically Ms. Hatley let us choose our own persuasive essay topics, so it wouldn't be *too* outlandish. "What did you decide to do for yours?"

She pulls out a few sheets of computer paper stapled together. "Sexism in the school dress code policy. Why do guys get to walk around with their boxers showing but I get written up if my bra strap pokes out? Or yanked out of class for being a *distraction* to boys, like that's my problem? And also, they don't even *make* girls' shorts fingertip-length, so if the school has an issue with that, they can install air-conditioning that actually works, or take it up with clothing manufacturers."

"Yes! This! I can't wait to hear it."

"Thanks. You doing the carbon footprint presentation?"

"Yep." I tap my stack of cards. "Twenty-eight notecards."

A look of horror crosses her face. "You're not using the projector?"

I shrug. "I mean, maybe? Hatley made a comment about how I read off notes too much." Although now that Dahlia said it, my pulse ticks up another notch and I'm starting to regret not emailing Ms. Hatley my bullet points so she could project them on the giant screen in the back like everyone else did.

"We have a few freshman English classes joining us," Ms. Hatley says, waving her hand over her head to quiet everyone down. "They'll be observing you as part of their persuasive essay unit. It'll also be good practice, putting the *public* in *public speaking*, if you will."

A brick forms in my stomach. This was not part of the deal. What if I vomit right on the stage?

She's barely finished speaking when the back door swings open and dozens of freshmen filter in, laughing and talking amongst themselves. They climb into seats.

I raise my hand. "Ms. Hatley, do you need someone to run

the sound system and microphones? I do it for the musical every year."

"Thank you, that would be very helpful, Stella."

"Since when do you volunteer to run sound?" Dahlia whispers. "You hate doing it."

"No reason. Just wanted to add some . . . spice . . . to Wesley's presentation."

"Oh no."

Before she can talk me out of it, I get to my feet and make my way to the back of the auditorium.

"Yes, yes, settle down," Ms. Hatley says to the ever-growing crowd.

I flip some switches and adjust the sound balance before shooting my teacher a thumbs-up.

"Who wants to go first?" she asks, addressing the crowd.

"I'll go." Katie Pelham stands. I adjust the sounds to amplify her voice; she's a few inches short for the microphone, so I make it louder. Every few seconds, my eyes flick up to the projection screen hanging over my head, which broadcasts Katie's notes across the room to her. After a spirited three-minute presentation about why the school board should fund the lacrosse team's trip to Florida, she takes a bow and heads back to her seat.

Jordan Fisher goes next, with a pretty lackluster argument for why downtown should have free parking after two. I lower the volume near the end when he picks up steam and starts shouting. Parking meters really get some people going, apparently. You can learn a lot about someone by the topics that are important to them.

Wesley Clarke raises his hand. "I'll go." I jolt to attention. He looks like he hasn't slept in days. He's wearing a green long-sleeved polo and jeans, which is at least an improvement from our last Public Speaking test.

"Wesley, thank you." Ms. Hatley scrolls down her iPad. "Let me get your notes keyed up on the projector."

He takes his sweet time slogging up those stairs to the stage. This is going to be so good.

The screen over my head displays a long list of Hatley's emails. It scrolls down until Wesley's name is in view, and a document opens on the screen, revealing a page of detailed bullet points.

"Imagine this." He stands in the center of the stage, his projection perfect. I don't even have to tamper with the sound system. Yet. "You get home from school, it was a long day, and all you want to do is sit down and catch the next episode of your favorite TV show." He's so comfortable doing this, I hate it. "You know the one. Maybe the main character embodies all that you wish you could be. Maybe it's an escape, a way to leave all your problems behind for forty-five minutes. Maybe you've grown so attached to the characters, they feel like your friends. It's become your home. Or maybe it's just a good story, and you're dying to see how it ends."

I think of Aaron Lewis, flying away from the *Revelry*, leaving Jill behind. The familiar knot twists in my chest.

"But then, everything changes!" He flares his hands out dramatically. "You stick with a show for two seasons, or five, or eight, only for the ending to tank. Or maybe your favorite actor leaves the show, and its whole tone changes. Or worst of all, you see an article on *Deadline Hollywood* that says your favorite show's been canceled."

My hands are frozen over the buttons on the table.

"And suddenly, that thing that brought you so much happiness—that gave you an escape, a place to connect, and a place you felt seen—is gone." He shifts in place. "Maybe you mourn a little. It's only natural, right? You've lost something important to you."

He looks up, and I feel his eyes searing into mine; but no, he's just looking at his notes on the screen. It only lasts half a second before he's scanning the crowd again, making eye contact with everyone in the audience like Ms. Hatley taught us.

I text Dahlia. A few rows down, I catch her subtly checking her phone.

What show is he talking about?

"They tell you to get over it, it's just a show, there are other shows out there, stay in the real world. But that show was never just a show to you. It was a place you belonged." I hate how much sense this makes. I *hate* how good he is at this. "So you search, and you find out you're not alone. Because other people are mourning, too. And they understand."

I think about my fanfic, and the *Warship* community, and how I log in whenever I'm feeling stressed or sad or alone. Wesley's right. *He's right.*

Wow, that is painful to admit.

My phone vibrates from Dahlia.

Doesn't he always quote reruns of The Office? Or maybe Game of Thrones? The 100? Pitch? Sense8? Dexter? I don't know. It's probably just generic, you know?

I relax. That's true. *Warship* wasn't the only show that had a crash landing or a premature cancellation.

"And maybe you write fanfiction. Or draw fanart. Or make video edits. Or maybe you just lurk, absorbing it all and, for a minute, feeling connected to someone else. Someone who understands." He pauses. "But then someone sees you writing your fic, or drawing your fanart, or being involved, and they tell you to stop. They don't understand, they think it's silly or childish, or immature. They tell you to move on and focus on something *important*. Read a real book, they say. Work on something meaningful, they say. Focus on real world issues. Well, what do I say? Screw them." The audience cheers. I let my hands clap quietly under the sound table.

Wesley tells a story about a woman on the news who met her best friend—the maid of honor at her wedding—through a fandom website. And finally, he talks about how skills made from fandom—whether it's designing a cosplay, or writing a fic, or editing a video—can help with skills needed later in life.

For the first time ever, I feel like I'm seeing a different side of Wesley. A side I maybe, sort of understand. Part of me doesn't want to do it. Maybe I should take the high road, be the bigger person, stop this ridiculous war between us.

"So that is why I, Wesley Clarke, believe that fandom is valid and that you—*generic you*—shouldn't belittle it." He scans the audience, looking directly at me. "And, Stella, I loved the new addition to your senior portrait, by the way—it's a big improvement."

Laughter echoes around the room as necks crane to look at me. I clench my jaw so tight, my teeth might fall out. *He. Did. Not.*

"Thank you." Wesley lowers into a bow.

Seething, I ram my fingers across the soundboard and crank the volume all the way to the top. And right as Wesley straightens back up, a loud fart sound rips through the entire auditorium.

12 WESLEY

I have to admit, that was well played. And maybe I kind of deserved it, but to be fair, Stella violated *my* senior picture first. But I still killed that persuasive speech, and Hatley won't dock points for farting, so whatever.

"Nice one, Wes." Dylan Smith from the cross-country team thumps me on the back as we wind out of the auditorium after class, shouldering through the crowd. "Way to end the speech with a flourish."

"Thank you."

"You practice that bit at the end, Clarke?" Matt Hopkins asks as he passes by. A bunch of guys laugh as they pass, and I laugh too.

Some freshmen girls snicker, still loitering in the aisle, and I give an exaggerated bow as we pass.

"There you are." Brandon slams his arm down on my backpack so hard, I almost fall over. "Been looking for you."

"What'd you think of my speech?"

He shrugs. "I agree, man. You know I've got like three stormtrooper costumes in my closet."

"Yes, sadly, I do know this."

"You're still coming to laser tag, right?"

Brandon reminds me so often, I won't even be able to pretend I forgot. "Yeah, I guess."

"Well, good, because we're in luck." He pulls out his iPhone and opens up a Groupon page. "Half off if we can persuade thirty people to come."

"Dude, do you even talk to thirty people?"

"Won't be an issue. Watch—hey! Courtney and Jackie! You ladies want to play laser tag with a bunch of us on Saturday, March twentieth, at Space Arena? Eight p.m.?" The junior girls look at each other before shrugging and nodding. "See? Everyone loves laser tag."

—♥—

I find Stella at a table in the library after lunch, sitting way too close to the computer screen. Why is she *always* working?

"Yo, Greene." I pull up a seat beside her. "You keep staring at the screen so close, you're going to ruin your eyes."

She leans back in her seat and crosses her arms. "Entertaining speech today. Better cut down on the baked beans next time."

"I was looking forward to hearing yours," I say. "Too bad we ran out of time. But I'll be on the edge of my seat for Friday."

"I'm sure you will. It'll be good practice for my valedictorian speech."

"All that practice for nothing." I shake my head. "It's a shame, Stick."

She smiles sweetly, turning her attention back to the computer screen. "Keep telling yourself that."

"You know this means war, right?"

"I thought war was already declared. You should probably surrender, because you will never outsmart me, Clarke."

"We'll see."

A girl I don't recognize—probably a freshman or something—sits across the table from us.

"So, what show was your speech about?" Stella asks, shifting in her seat.

I guess I could tell her about *Warship*. But what if word gets around that I love the show and it gets back to Jill2? I'm not sure I'm ready to broadcast who I am yet. I want to get to know her better first. If my online friendship crashes and burns, I don't want awkwardness at school. "Nothing specific. Could apply to lots of shows. My brother and I were pissed when they ended *Schitt's Creek*. And *The OA* deserved another season."

Stella deflates a tad. "Oh, okay. Worthy choices."

"Why, were you expecting something different?"

"My sister, Bridget, was really upset about *Game of Thrones* a few years back. I thought maybe you were talking about that." She goes back to typing. "Bridget also loved some space show called *Warship Seven*." Her eyes flit up to mine.

Well, Stella's sister has good taste. Not that I'd ever open that can of worms. "Never heard of it."

She shrugs and looks back at her screen.

It takes me a few seconds to realize Stella's typing up a bullet point list in Word. I bark out a laugh. "Oh my God. Did *the* Stella Greene seriously not have her persuasive essay notes prepared for class today?" I slap my hand over my heart. "You're going to give me a heart attack."

She ignores me and keeps typing.

"What would you have done if Hatley had made you do yours today?"

"I would have done it from memory, like I'd planned. This is a precaution."

"Did Hatley give you crap for reading too closely off your cards last time?"

Her face flushes. "No."

"Always the overachiever." I reach out to pretend to press some buttons on her keyboard, and she slaps my hand away.

"Can you not?"

"Hey." The freshman looks up at us. "Do you know where the reference section is? I'm supposed to find three sources."

"Here." Stella stands up. "I'll show you." She leads the freshman back to the reference desk at the other end of the library.

I'm about to leave when I notice Stella's document, lying wide open on the computer. Well, this is just begging for it. My eyes dart to the other end of the room and back.

This is too perfect. I quickly tab into Find and Replace, make some alterations, and get the hell out of there.

Your move, Greene.

—♥—

CERanger11: Okay, what's your favorite episode?

CaptainJillsBFF22: OMG. How can you ask me that???

My MacBook sits open on my desk, with a bunch of tabs open. Exhaustion is draped over me like a shroud. I need to do homework. But I can barely keep my eyes open.

CaptainJillsBFF22: I know everyone says episode 16, but I actually kind of like the duel episode? TO. THE. DEATH.

CaptainJillsBFF22: I also love the finale . . . well, aside from the last ten minutes, which I'm pretending NEVER HAPPENED!!! What's your favorite?

CERanger11: Ah, the duel. Poor Aaron getting his ass kicked

CERanger11: (I like the duel episode too lol)

CaptainJillsBFF22: I mean, he should have known better than to try to pull one over on Our Captain!

I want to know who she is. My mind flits through all sorts of possibilities. Kara Gordon. Preeti Agarwal. McKayla Grant. Who in our grade would be a secret Warshipper?

CERanger11: Speaking of the duel, here's one for you . . . it's not quite done yet, but:

I attach a picture I sketched in the middle of the night of Aaron and Jill dueling. She's got her pistol pointed at Aaron in one hand, and a knife clenched in the other. Aaron's wielding his own stolen pistol, desperate to escape out the back door and onto the shuttle. I'm not going to lie, I'm pretty proud of this one.

CaptainJillsBFF22: OMG. I love this so much.
CERanger11: Thanks!
CaptainJillsBFF22: Did I tell you I have an alternate-reality fic about this scene??
CaptainJillsBFF22: It's basically the same scene, but they don't get captured by the pirates at the end. They end up in the infirmary instead lol had to make it a hurt/comfort
CERanger11: And let me guess, Jill and Aaron end up making out in the infirmary?
CaptainJillsBFF22: Spoiler? 😉

She pastes a link into the chat, which I click.

CERanger11: This thing is practically a novel!

CaptainJillsBFF22: haha yeah it's long. Not as long as that other giant fix-it-fic I sent you before.

CERanger11: I don't think there are encyclopedias as long as that fic.

CaptainJillsBFF22: I know lol. Took me forever, but I put everything into it, you know? You don't have to read it!!

CERanger11: I'll save this one for later.

I still have her last fic bookmarked, the super-popular one. Reading a novel of Lewton boning doesn't really appeal, to be honest. And I still haven't wrapped my brain around the fact that she wrote 198,000 words of it.

My attention drifts to the stack of books on the side table. I have so much to do. I can't slack, not now. I let my forehead fall into my hands. Only a few more months. Then I'll be valedictorian, and none of this will matter. I'm not sure why, but I let my fingers say what my mind is thinking.

CERanger11: Currently swamped with homework. I have no motivation left. Is it June yet?

CaptainJillsBFF22: I take it you're a chaotic good.

CERanger11: . . .

CERanger11: Was that an insult? Lol

CaptainJillsBFF22: No! It's the morality scale! Look!

She sends a photo someone obviously Photoshopped, with all the *Warship* characters categorized by their personalities. Apparently Aaron is also chaotic good, so I take that as a compliment.

CaptainJillsBFF22: I'm lawful good.

CERanger11: Like Jill!

CaptainJillsBFF22: Exactly! 😍

CERanger11: I feel like my head isn't screwed on right half the time, so it's fitting.

CaptainJillsBFF22: Ugh, I feel that so hard. I feel like I've been working for years and then it'll suddenly be . . . over? Well, until college.

CaptainJillsBFF22: I have to do well, though. No one in my family has a college degree. I'll be the first one.

CaptainJillsBFF22: I've worked SO hard, and I got into my dream school and . . . idk. If I fail, I'll feel like I've failed my whole family.

I know how that feels.

CaptainJillsBFF22: Sorry for dumping all that on you, lol

CERanger11: No, I get it! Families can be . . . complicated

CERanger11: That must be so much pressure.

CaptainJillsBFF22: I need to get like a zillion scholarships. Being poor sucks, you know?

I hesitate. Honestly, I *don't* know. And I feel kind of weird admitting that. I drag the charcoal pencil across my sketchbook, shading in Aaron's face. By this point in the episode he'd been a prisoner for a while, and had more than a little scruff.

CERanger11: you'll do awesome, I believe in you!

CaptainJillsBFF22: haha thanks

CaptainJillsBFF22: What about you? You planning

to hibernate for a month after graduation like me? Zzzzzzz

The thing is, I can see my graduation going one of two ways. Either I'm valedictorian and my parents are happy and buy me a Porsche, or Stella gets it and Dad acts like he just saw my mug shot on the front page of the paper. And that's not even the part where they learn about my college decision and disown me.

I press the charcoal into the paper a bit harder than necessary, and the tip chips off.

CERanger11: I hope so.

CERanger11: if my parents don't kick me out lol

CaptainJillsBFF22: . . . wait, seriously? Why would they do that????

CERanger11: I was jk

CERanger11: (sorta)

CERanger11: My dad just has these really unrealistic expectations. I get it. He wants me to do well. But I feel like a massive disappointment to him most of the time because I didn't turn out like a mini version of him, the way my brother did.

CERanger11: And sometimes it's like I don't even recognize my dad anymore.

I swallow hard, remembering how excited I was at the soccer tournament when I was six. Our team had come in second out of the whole state. I had even scored a goal. I ran off the field clutching my little plastic trophy, and shoved it in my dad's face.

"Look!" I beamed at him, holding up the trophy.

"That's not a real trophy, Wesley," Dad said. "That's what they give the losing teams. They give everyone something for participating. Keep working at it, and maybe next year you'll place first."

The trophy ended up in my sock drawer. I threw it out eventually.

CaptainJillsBFF22: If it helps, I'm proud of you! 😍

CaptainJillsBFF22: and Aaron would be, too!

For some reason, it does help.

CERanger11: who are you? I start to type. My fingers hesitate, and finally, I delete it unsent.

A soft knocking sounds on my door, and I tense. Dad creaks open the door before I can reply.

"Hey, do you have a minute?"

My mind shouts *No!* but my head nods, and he comes in.

"I wanted to give you this." He sets a small package on my bed, wrapped in a grocery bag. "From your mom and me."

I push off in my chair and roll over to the bed. "What is it?"

"Don't worry, it's not your graduation gift. Just something small." He keeps his eyes glued to the ground. "For college."

I peel open the bag and find a small rectangular box. When I slide the box open, a shiny silvery pen greets me. *Wesley Daniel Clarke, GCMHS senior class* is inscribed in the side. My stomach clenches a little. "Thanks." I pick it up. "That's really nice."

"For your college classes and future internships. Everyone respects you more when you sign your name with a really good pen."

I appreciate that he didn't say, *For your Stanford classes*. The cold silver is heavy in my hand. "That's really cool."

My phone vibrates in my lap.

> **Laura:** hey so omg I totally forgot to tell you remember how you always kept trying to get me to watch Warship Seven? WELL...

"Ending high school can be a rough transition, and I want you to know we're always here for you," Dad adds. He scratches the back of his neck. "I realize we put a lot of pressure on you, but it's paying off. You're going to be very successful, just like your mother and me."

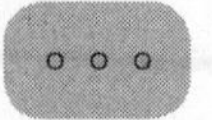

"Thanks." I'm only half paying attention to him. *Type faster*.

Dad glances at my desk, where my portrait of Aaron and Jill dueling is lying out, a piece of broken charcoal covering half of Aaron's face. "But you're not going to get anywhere if you keep wasting your time with these spaceship doodles."

There he is again—Dr. Jekyll and Mr. Dad. After he leaves, I'm still glowering out my open bedroom door when my phone vibrates again.

> I actually got really into it last fall!! That Aaron Lewis, 😍

What? Why didn't she tell me sooner? I answer my own question: because we barely talked last fall.

I quickly type back.

What made you start watching? Because I wouldn't stop talking about it ever?

LOL no. You're going to laugh.

I actually got into it because I found this fan video online. On YouTube.

No. It can't be.

It's her. It's Jill2.

The whole room basically collapses around me.

13 STELLA

It's after eleven by the time I finish my homework. I open my agenda and check off every assignment I finished (orange), and mark progress on the papers I worked on, too (pink).

Something clatters in the hallway, and the sound of crying Gwen permeates the apartment, followed by Bridget's soft voice.

I tiptoe out of my room into the darkened hallway. A single light shines in the kitchen, illuminating the otherwise dark apartment. Papers, a calculator, and a mug of something that looks like it used to be hot litter the kitchen table. My sister gently rocks Gwen, hushing her softly.

"What happened?" I whisper. "I heard a noise."

"Nothing." Bridget's voice is hoarse. "I dropped a spoon and the sound woke Gwen up." Her eyes burn red.

I put my hand on her arm. "What's going on? Were you crying?"

"It's nothing . . . Shh, go back to sleep, *please*. You're going to wake up the whole building."

Another wail rips from Gwen's tiny mouth.

"Do you want me to take her?" I hold out my arms.

Bridget shakes her head. "No, it's okay." She's still wearing her Burger Blitz T-shirt, plus her black pants from the movie theater, which are covered in popcorn grease.

I wash the notorious spoon in the sink, then leave it in the dish rack and take a seat at the table. What looks like Bridget's GED study guide is spread across the entire surface, a few brown droplets of coffee splattered on one of them. I compulsively tuck the pages together until they're in three neat stacks, organized by assignment.

"Seriously?" Bridget mutters at me.

I jerk my hand back to my lap. "Sorry, habit."

She sets Gwen into her bouncy chair by the table. "Look at this." She holds her phone screen out to me, showing a slew of texts from Ben.

I'm really sorry

Can I see u guys this weekend?

I messed up

are u seriously ignoring me right now

wow bitch really? I just want to see my daughter

I'll get a lawyer and take everything from you. You'll never see Gwen again.

"I told you not to—"

"If you're going to lecture me, go back to bed."

My mouth snaps shut. "Okay. No lecture."

"I already have one of my coworkers looking into it, she knows a lawyer."

"That's good."

"I just don't know what to do anymore." She sits opposite

me, her head in her hands. "I don't want to keep him away from her, but he makes it so hard."

"You didn't do anything wrong." I rub her arm. "You're doing great—working two jobs, taking classes, *and* raising a badass girl?"

"I don't feel like I'm doing great. I feel like I'm barely hanging on."

"I know it's not the life you wanted, but you're killing it either way."

She straightens up for a moment and gives me a weird look. "I've got to finish this."

"You know where I am if you need anything."

She drags her highlighter across the textbook and doesn't give me another glance.

—♥—

"Okay, settle down." Ms. Hatley takes her seat in the front row of the auditorium, ready for day two of our persuasive essays. I filter inside with the rest of our class and the freshman observers, who seem to be taking it like a free period.

"I'm not sure I can sit through another hour of this," Dahlia says, plopping down in the seat beside me.

"I think there are just five left, including mine."

"Thank God."

"Stella, would you like to run the sound system again?" Hatley lowers her glasses, scanning the auditorium. "Stella?"

"I'm here." I stand. "Sure." I wasn't expecting to get sound again after last class's misdeed, but okay. I start walking up the stairs to the back of the room, but Hatley interrupts me.

"Actually, you know what? We're going to have to do without. I completely forgot you're on today's list," she says. "Do you want to go first?"

I pivot midstep, almost face-planting on the stairs. "Okay." I work my way down to the front of the room, feeling everyone's eyes on me, cold as ice. All I can hear is my heart, slamming in my ears.

I woke up at five o'clock this morning to press my skirt and button-down especially for this presentation.

My stomach plummets when I catch Wesley's eyes in the front row.

He's smirking. Why is he smirking?

I glance up at the sound system in the back of the room, my pulse pounding. No. Don't panic. There's no one working the sound system, and there's nothing he can do to me from down there.

That's right, Wesley. There's absolutely *nothing you can do*.

"When you're ready," Ms. Hatley says from the side of the room.

Rustling fills the room, but darkness obscures the faces in the crowd. Hot spotlights from above burn into my skin. High over everyone's heads, the projector beams, my carefully curated bullet list waiting for me.

I don't want to use the slides. I want to show Hatley I can do it on my own.

But the second I open my mouth, it just hangs open. Someone coughs in the audience.

"I . . . I'm . . ." I swallow hard. My eyelids fall shut, and I force myself to take a deep breath. Relief cascades over me, and suddenly, I'm grateful I decided to send it in after all. I can do this with the slides. Hatley can deal with it.

> ***INTRODUCTION****—Hello! My name is Stella Greene, and I'm a senior. Today I want to talk to you about things you can do to reduce your carbon footprint.*

I'm kind of judging myself for typing this verbatim, but I'm so grateful it's there, I don't even care. I let myself read it aloud.

"Hello, I'm Stella Greene, I'm a senior, and today I want to talk to you about things you can do to cut"—my voice cracks—"to reduce your carbon footprint."

I feel like I can hear the crickets chirping and any minute now a hooked cane is going to swing out and pull me offstage, like in old cartoons.

Climate change is real. You can see it in the increasing numbers of natural disasters that have been sweeping through our country for the past few years.

"Climate change is absolutely real, and you can see it in the increasing number of natural disasters that have been sweeping through our country for the past few years." I realize I'm holding the microphone way close to my mouth, and pull it back. "Hurricanes can be devastating. In 2018 alone, they destroyed . . ." I keep going, following my bullet points word for word.

It's just reading. Reading aloud. That's all this is.

I hate how easily this came to Wesley. Why am I so tense?

But the more I talk, the more I relax, and the easier the words come. All I have to do is read it and not look like I'm too high-strung, and boom, A+.

Remember that viral photo of the starving polar bear that went around a few years ago? Glaciers have already begun melting, stranding animals like polar bears and leaving them without food.

"Remember that viral photo of the starving polar bear that

went around a few years ago? Well, glaciers have already begun melting, stranding animals like polar bears and leaving them without food."

I keep going, rattling off my carefully researched facts and talking about the thin bears.

Closing arguments

A knot inside me slowly unwinds when I see those two sweet words. "That is why you should be concerned about the imprint you're leaving on the world, and why you should practice those few basic changes in your everyday life to help make a difference." I pick up steam, charging into those final arguments on the slides. "Remember, we only get one planet, and we can't afford for it to become uninhabitable. So many animals, plants, and future generations of humanity depend on it. So go out there, and make a fucking difference!"

The second I say it, I gasp into the microphone so loudly, it makes a high-pitched shriek. I slap my hand over my mouth. Cheers erupt, along with whoops and hollers in the crowd.

How? It's not possible.

There it is. The F-bomb, right there on the screen as if I wrote it myself.

Wesley cheers in the front row. The library. He messed with my paper.

I am going to kill him. I am going to murder him. No one will ever find his body.

Ms. Hatley's voice cuts in. "Ms. Greene, may I see you after class?"

WARSHIP SEVEN: Episode Nine

"Too Many Tales"

SCENE CLIP: AARON is lying on his back in his makeshift cell, staring at the ceiling. Camera cuts to MICHELE, parked in her shuttle.

MICHELE: Aaron . . . Aaron, can you hear me?

AARON: [sits up quickly, muttering into his comm chip] I'm here. Any news?

MICHELE: Nothing. How're you doing on the mission?

AARON: I'm close. I just need them to drop their guard so I can get the upper hand. I'll take out the captain first, then whoever else I can hit on my way out, grab the stolen medicine, and be on the shuttle back to you.

MICHELE: Good.

AARON: And then we can be together. [Something rattles in the background, and Aaron jolts to attention.] Someone's coming. Got to go. [He hangs up.]

[SONNY unlocks the door and strides into the cell.]

SONNY: Cozy down here?

AARON: Oh, you know. Can't complain.

SONNY: The captain's invited you to join us for dinner.

AARON: [raises his eyebrows] Really? I didn't think our dear captain was overly fond of me.

SONNY: She isn't. She feels bad you're stuck eating Skulls' stale sandwiches for every meal.

AARON: I suppose pity is better than hatred, so I'll accept.

[He follows SONNY upstairs and into the main area, where GEMMA, JILL, SKULLS, and MARKUS are already at the dining table. C0NDOR wheels in the background, rummaging through kitchen drawers.]

SONNY: Here he is, our guest of honor.

MARKUS: [nods curtly]

JILL: [rolls her eyes, seated at the head of the table] This is a one-time thing. You helped us get our droid back, and you deserve our thanks. But you're still Cescum and an enemy of this ship.

AARON: Yes, yes. Big enemy of the ship. [sits at the empty seat across from JILL] What are we having?

GEMMA: [places plates in front of everyone] Hydrogenated beef and broccoli. I made it myself.

SONNY: Take cover, it has a fifty-fifty shot of killing you.

AARON: [takes a bite, considers it a moment] Definitely better than Skulls' sandwiches.

JILL: That's a low bar.

SONNY: Pretty sure your cooking is the reason I got food poisoning on Hutton-2 last month.

SKULLS: [polishing his pistol] Those are some mighty big words from an unarmed man.

SONNY: I'm never unarmed as long as I've got these guns. [flexes his biceps]

GEMMA: [rolls her eyes] Please, our grandma has bigger muscles.

JILL: [starts eating absentmindedly] C0ndor, get out of the trash.

C0NDOR: [His bottom half is visible, poking out of the trash can.] I will not.

AARON: I've been on this ship several weeks. I've never seen you all together before.

[SONNY and GEMMA have begun flicking food at each other, bickering.]

MARKUS: Guys, come on. Seriously?

JILL: Yes, Cescum, welcome to our circus.

AARON: It's kind of nice, to be honest.

GEMMA: Why?

AARON: [shrugs] You all just seem really cool together.

JILL: [rubbing her forehead] They're a bunch of monsters insistent on driving their captain mad. Hey! C0ndor, what did I just say?

AARON: It's nothing compared with the CE training barracks, I'll tell you that.

SONNY: So, you want to tell us how you came to be involved in the Central Elite?

AARON: [takes a swig] It's a long story, and not a very good one.

MARKUS: We've got a four-day flight to Penzon, so we have time.

JILL: You've got twenty minutes before you're back in that cell, so better tell it quickly.

AARON: [thinks for a moment] Have you heard of the explosion on the Polygon satellite?

MARKUS: Bunch of pirates blew up a space station a few years ago? That one?

AARON: Yes. That one.

JILL: We heard about it.

GEMMA: [softly] I think the whole galaxy heard about it.

AARON: My... my family was on it, when it exploded. [The whole table is watching him.] And when you're a kid with no family, what choice do you have? [laughs awkwardly] Join the CE, or . . . join a pirate ship. Like this one. Like the one that killed everyone in my family.

JILL: [staring at her plate] I'm sorry.

AARON: You didn't do anything.

[The table is silently eating. When AARON finishes his food, JILL stands.]

JILL: I'll take you back to your cell.

14 WESLEY

"Did you hear? Stella Greene dropped an F-bomb onstage during Hatley's Public Speaking assignment." At least five different people say the same exact thing as I wind my way to the cafeteria. That worked out way better than I had planned. Honestly, I thought she'd see it, stumble a little, finish the argument, then come freak out at me after class.

"Here comes R-rated Stella!"

"No, you're allowed a PG-13 rating with only one."

"I agree with her, climate change is a big effing problem."

Everyone's talking about it, and okay, I feel a little proud of myself.

"You."

Stella plows through the crowd, and they part like the Red Sea to let her pass. I don't bother to wipe the smirk off my face. "Nice speech. You really persuaded me to unplug my electronics when I'm not home."

"Shut up." She jabs me in the chest. "You did this." Dahlia Johnston and Emma Gonzales flank her like a couple of bodyguards.

"Did what?"

"You know what."

"Put a gun to your head and forced you to drop obscenities in front of two hundred people?"

Brandon comes up behind me. "Stella! Did Hatley give you detention?" He sees Dahlia, and his expression softens. "Hey, Dahlia."

"Hey."

"No." Stella scowls at him. "I told her it was a mistake, and she praised me for my passion and dedication to the topic."

His eyebrows shoot up. "Whoa. That's awesome."

She smiles back at him. "Please tell your friend that his days are numbered. He's not going to see it coming, and then I'm going to flatten him."

"Can't wait," I answer, only to be met by her middle finger as she shoves past me to get into the cafeteria.

Brandon laughs. "What did she mean by that?"

"Let's just say, Stella should really learn not to read out every word she sees on her script."

We traipse into the cafeteria. Laura sits alone at a table, reading a book. *Jill2*. "Hey! There's Laura."

Before Brandon can respond, I'm already making my way over to the table. I wonder if I can get her to slip up and admit she's my mystery girl. I know there are a million reasons why I shouldn't suspect her—Laura said she got into the fandom last fall, but Jill2 cosplayed as Captain Jill in the spring. Still, it's possible. Jill2 already lied once about her school; who's to say she didn't lie about Sci-Con too?

Laura smiles up at us. "Hey, guys. You want to join us?" She moves her backpack off the seat. "Right now it's just me, Julia, Tim, and Collin."

Collin. Of course. My shoulders tense, but I force a smile. "Sure. Thanks." Brandon and I take seats beside her. Tim comes over, too, and sinks into a seat across the round table.

"So, you're a *Warship* fan now?" I try to keep the enthusiasm out of my voice, focusing instead on squirting a packet of Italian dressing onto my salad.

"Fairly recently, but oh my God, I'm already writing Lewton fics." She laughs.

I realize I'm staring at her and quickly look the other way. It's her.

"Wait, *Warship Seven*?" Tim arches his brows. "That show is the best. What's your favorite episode?"

" 'To the Death,' " I say without hesitating.

Laura taps her lips, and it kind of makes me want to kiss her. "I love the one where they rescue C0ndor from that black-market dealer."

" 'The Worst Laid Plans'?" I grin. "Great choice."

Tim rolls his eyes. "You can't call yourself a *Warship* fan if you don't know the episode titles from memory."

I don't think I've ever been asked once to prove my fandom status. So why does he care about Laura's? My forehead creases. "Hey, man—"

Laura bursts out laughing. "Oh my God, do *not* give me that *not a real fan* BS. I watch the show, I enjoy the show, I'm a fan. Go crawl back under your rock, Tim."

Brandon shakes his head, fighting back a laugh. He's not the biggest fan of Tim.

"Did you hear what happened with Stella Greene in the Public Speaking class?" Laura's eyes grow wide. "I couldn't believe it."

"Yeah." Brandon snorts, ribbing me in the side. "We heard."

Laura takes a bite of her Caesar wrap. "I feel kind of bad for her," she says, mid-chew. "She shouldn't get in trouble for that, everyone gets nervous onstage. She probably just slipped."

"Yeah," Brandon says. "*Slipped.*"

"I don't think she got in trouble," I say, watching Stella across the cafeteria. Weirdly, I can't help noticing her hair is wavy today. It looks nice wavy.

"Or sabotage," Brandon says, wiggling his eyebrows. "Dun dun dun."

Laura laughs. "I don't know who would sabotage her."

Brandon starts to open his mouth, but I shoot him a death glare and he doesn't say it.

"She's staring at you," he whispers in my ear.

"Who?"

I follow Brandon's eyes across the cafeteria to where Stella sits with her friends, glaring daggers at me. I give her a friendly wave, at which she takes the plastic knife she'd been using to smear cream cheese on her bagel and stabs it directly through the hole in the center.

"I wouldn't want Stella Greene on my bad side, dude," Brandon says.

I wave him off. "It's fine. What's the worst she could do?"

–♥–

Over two weeks have passed, and so far, Stella hasn't retaliated. In fact, she's barely spoken to me at all, outside of our bio project. *Checkmate, Stick.*

AP History smells like oranges in the mornings, because Mr. Bailey is always peeling and eating one at his desk. This is my favorite class, because it's like stories about the past. Mr. Bailey has all these quotes on the walls by famous people in history, presidents, and world leaders, and I read through them every day, even though I've already read them a million times.

"Wesley, good morning," Mr. Bailey greets me between slices

of orange. "You ready to dissect World War I?"

"Of course."

I take my assigned seat in the corner and pull the textbook from my backpack. I forgot about the reading until last night at like midnight, so I was up until after two doing it.

I open my agenda book and flip through all the blank lined pages in the back, but end up counting down the days until Sci-Con instead.

One by one, people filter into the room and take their seats. The first thing I notice is that Stella's seat is empty. That's weird. Stella is late, well, never.

Mr. Bailey finishes his orange, slides the pile of peels into the trash, and starts writing on the board.

"Where's Stella Greene?" The words burst out of my mouth before I can stop them.

"She's helping with the morning announcements in the main office." He keeps his back to us, still writing historical dates on the board. "You know Stella, always volunteering to help."

A sinking feeling balls up inside me. Stella hasn't done morning announcements since last year. I don't know why she would randomly—

The speaker at the front of the classroom crackles, and a long beep rings out. "Good morning, students and teachers of GCMHS!" Stella's overly cheery voice greets us, and everyone's whispers fade to silence. "I'm senior Stella Greene, here with your morning announcements. The day is Wednesday, March seventeenth—happy St. Patrick's Day to all who celebrate." Several whoops ring out from students wearing green. My family is super Irish and I always wear green, but I totally forgot today.

"First, our wonderful custodial services team wanted to remind you that they're trying to grow grass on the front lawn, so please stick to the picnic tables if you want to eat your lunch outside for the duration of the school year. Seniors intending to graduate, please make sure you file an intent to graduate form by next Thursday."

I quickly scrawl out a note to myself to remember to do that. Would be pretty ridiculous if the valedictorian didn't graduate because he didn't turn in a stupid form.

"And, *prom*! We're just a few months away from the big night, and your prom committee wants to inform all juniors and seniors that we've tallied your votes, and the theme this year is officially . . . drumroll . . . Under the Sea!" Several people groan. One girl smugly announces that she voted for that one, while someone else mutters about the votes being rigged. "In fact, we've got the big open room in the aquarium all booked and ready. We'll be dancing with the fish, everyone. So dress in your best seaworthy attire, and come ready to party."

I roll my eyes. Prom. Great.

"The senior class is looking for volunteers who would be willing to help clean up after prom. If you're willing to donate about an hour of your time, please contact Jen Meyer, head of the prom committee. All volunteers will attend prom free of charge. French Club, there is no meeting today. And anyone planning to go to Greece with the Latin Club this summer, please come to an information session in the cafeteria next Wednesday at seven p.m."

I went to Greece with my family once. Back before my parents started spending every waking minute fighting and trying to dictate my future. The memory leaves a bittersweet tinge behind.

"And finally, to Wesley Clarke, in Mr. Bailey's AP History"—everyone's eyes dart to me—"please come to the main office after class. Your mother dropped off your anti-diarrhea pills and a clean pair of pants—she knew it was urgent. Thank you."

15 STELLA

Not my most mature moment, I'll admit. But imagining the look on Wesley's face was totally worth it. If only Dahlia had been in that class to film it.

"What was that about?" Ms. Rossi confronts me, eyes wide. "We don't generally publicize messages to individual students."

I grab my bag. "Sorry. I didn't know."

Before she can protest, I'm out of the main office and headed to History. The bad thing about doing morning announcements is that I miss a few minutes of class. AP History is my weakest subject, too, so I need all the minutes I can get.

Brian Coombs walks toward me in the hall, drumming in the air with invisible drumsticks. AirPods protrude out of his ears, and whatever he's listening to gets louder with each step, the bass practically reverberating from his head. I have no idea where he's supposed to be right now, but I'm guessing the answer isn't dancing in the hallway.

"Sup, Greene." He walks straight past me.

"Hey, Brian." I open my mouth to tell him he should really lower that music to protect his ears, when the beat catches my attention.

My heart jumps. The *Warship Seven* theme song blares from his headphones. At least, it sounds like it. Was it? I turn to call out to him, but Brian's already turned the corner and disappeared.

Okay, I need to mark this down. CERanger11, I have a new suspect, and his name is Brian Coombs.

Maybe I'm getting ahead of myself, but how else am I supposed to find Aaron2 if I don't take every clue I can get? I know, in the grand scheme of things, I don't really know Aaron2 that well—I mean, I'm still not entirely convinced I'm not being catfished. But Aaron2 doesn't see me as uptight stick-up-her-ass Stella Greene—he sees *me*. Just me. I get this little flutter in my chest whenever his screen name pops up.

It could still be Kyle. There is always that chance.

I picture us at prom together, dancing to the *Warship* theme song. The rest of the class would part in a circle, leaving space for just the two of us. *I always knew it was you*, I'd say; *I hoped it would be you*, he'd respond.

I hum the theme song as I make my way to class, not bothering to wipe the smile off my face. It's dangerously catchy, and now it's going to be in my head all day. The smell of fresh oranges greets me the second I get to the room.

"Ah, Stella, welcome." Mr. Bailey slouches against the table at the front of the room, a bunch of random dates scribbled on the whiteboard behind him in red and blue marker. I'm yawning already. "You were about to miss a riveting journey through history."

"I'm sure." I hand him my tardy slip and head to my seat. My eyes immediately dart to Wesley.

His expression is indifferent when I sit down two rows away from him. Every few seconds, his pencil scratches across his paper, taking diligent notes like a good salutatorian. Finally, he meets my gaze, and the edge of his mouth curls into a grin.

I roll my eyes and face front.

Mr. Bailey's voice sounds like static, droning on about dates and names and places, and I just can't make myself pay attention.

Less than two months until Sci-Con.

I click open my Notes app under my desk, where I have an important running document.

NATE BUCKLEY—made a comment in Latin about how all the good space shows get canceled

MARK SANDERS—said Leigh Stanton was hot. Could've been referring to Warship7 OR her new movie, unsure? She's not THAT famous?

KYLE NIELSEN—proud nerd, mentioned going to a convention in the spring (!!!)

I type quickly under my desk.

BRIAN COOMBS—suspected of listening to Warship theme song in hallway

"Anyone know what year the treaty was signed?" Bailey scans the room. "Anyone?" No one responds. "Bueller? Are you too young for that reference? C'mon, I know someone did last night's reading."

I jolt. I did, actually, do the reading. I did it last week, when it was assigned, and the information leaked out as quickly as it got absorbed. I need to bump up my participation score in this class, but I can never remember anything. Finally, it hits me—*1919*—and I shoot my hand up.

"It was 1919," Wesley says. He says it to the teacher, but his eyes are trained on me. "Five years after Franz Ferdinand's assassination arguably started the war in the first place."

"Excellent, Wesley." Bailey turns and scribbles that on the board. His handwriting rivals the quality of Gwen's. "See? I knew *someone* had done the reading."

My face gets hot. I did the reading. I *did* the reading. When Mr. Bailey's back is turned, Wesley shoots me a smug look.

I hate history.

And I *hate* Wesley.

—♥—

A huge bruise stretches across my knee, thanks to an hour of hell, aka gym class flag football. Dahlia's lover Brandon tried to grab my flag, so I quickly spun around and tripped over a rock, landing knee-first on a hard patch of still-frozen ground. Now I cringe every time my left foot hits the floor. After spending half of fifth-period Latin in the nurse's office with an icepack pressed against my knee, I now have a ton of makeup work to do, which means no lunch for me. My mood has taken a spectacular turn to the negative, and I'm about ready to murder someone.

I force myself not to limp as I shove open the door to the library. Of course, every table is full; groups of freshmen and sophomores huddle closely around them, some giggling and some doing actual work, but hogging every spot.

Except at the two-person table in the corner, where I can only see the back of one person's head.

Wesley is hunched over our bio textbook, his stuff spread out over the entire tabletop, his backpack taking up residence on the other available chair. I hobble over and, with a huff, shove his backpack onto the floor.

"My bag was there."

"Tough shit." I grimace as I sit down, trying not to let the pain show on my face.

"How was gym?"

"Terrible. Not that you would know—did you seriously cut today? You know they count that against your GPA, right?"

"Nope. In case you missed this morning's riveting announcements, I was instructed to head down to the main office after History." He grips his stomach. "Bad indigestion, you see. I got a late pass for it."

"It took you ninety minutes to go down to the main office for a fake announcement?"

"Well, I got to chatting with those sweet ladies in the office. You know how they are." He winks at me. "Hope you enjoyed flag football, though. I bet it was a *blast*."

I force a smile. "Yep. It's my favorite."

Wesley gets up to grab some books while I put my headphones on and spread out my Latin work on the table. When he sits back down, I slide his messy stack of papers over to his half of the table. "Stay on your side, Clarke."

"Hey." He puts his finger in the center of the table and pushes my textbook back toward me. "That was in the neutral zone. You know, the place where all territories can—"

"I know what a neutral zone is," I snap.

"Oh, sorry." He grins. "Didn't know if you'd been paying attention in History. You usually look bored."

"You can make fun of me when you get that AP Bio grade back up."

Wesley laughs. "Oh man, you *hate* this."

"Hate what?"

"That we're evenly matched."

"In your dreams. You're evenly matched with a potato, maybe."

"It bothers you *so* much." He sets his pencil on the table. "You just can't take knowing that I might beat you to this valedictorian thing."

"*This valedictorian thing,*" I repeat, mocking him. "Or maybe you're going to lose. And it'll be the first time you didn't have everything handed to you, and you're going to *cry*."

"Why do you assume things are handed to me?" The humor leaves his voice. "Seriously, why do you think that?"

"Um, let's see." I hold up one finger. "Because you've got private tutors and SAT prep." I hold up another. "Because your family is rich." I hold up a third. "And because you get all of that, automatically, without having to work for any of it."

"You know what happens when you assume things about people, Stick?" He leans back in his seat. "You make an *ass* out of *u* and *me*."

"Yes, great joke." I scoff. "You don't know anything about my life."

"I know you're a giant snob who judges everyone and has no life because you spend each waking minute buried in homework even when we don't have any."

"I don't need this." I stuff my Latin notes back into my bag and stand.

"Finally," he mutters.

"God, will you two get a room?" Some sophomore at the next table rips his earbuds out. "I'm trying to write an essay over here."

Wesley laughs.

"I don't suffer judgment from small minds," I mumble under my breath as I walk away.

"What did you just say?" Wesley calls back to me, a hint of amusement in his voice.

"Nothing you would understand." I storm toward the exit, walking right through the security stand. An alarm pierces the air, and I freeze. All eyes in the library drift toward me, and a blush flares across my face. Did I forget to put something back on the shelf? No, I didn't take any books out. I sling the backpack off my shoulder, right as I catch Wesley grinning and watching from across the room—along with everyone else.

Oh no.

Oh no.

"You want to open your bag for me, Stella?" Mrs. Kendall, the librarian, slides on her thick blue glasses and reaches out a wrinkled hand for my bag.

With horror, I hand it over, and she pulls out three books I've never seen before.

A Teen's Guide to Safe Sex

Puberty: A Time for Change

Condom Diaries: What to Expect During Your First Time

A few snickers ring out behind me.

"I . . . don't know how those got in there." It's a lie; I know exactly how they got in there. And he's going to pay for this.

"Hey, Stick," Wesley calls. "You can't just walk out with those! But good for you for wanting to be informed."

I whirl around. "Are you fucking kidding me, Wesley?"

Whispered *ooooh*s float around me.

"What?" He places his hand over his heart. "I didn't have anything to do with this."

"You had everything to do with this." I plow across the library toward him.

"That's quite an accusation."

"I swear to God, I'm going to wipe that smug look right off your—"

"Ms. Greene." I'm two steps away from him when a low booming voice echoes behind me. I pivot to see Principal Woods with his hands on his hips. "And Mr. Clarke. My office. Now."

16 WESLEY

You know those movies where delinquents get called to the principal's office for doing stupid shit? Yeah, I never expected that to be me. And yet here I am, sitting in this uncomfortable wooden chair, my hands in my lap and my knee bouncing up and down, like I'm a little kid who just punched someone on the playground.

Stella sits beside me, fuming.

"Now, would either of you like to explain what's going on?" Principal Woods glowers at us from behind the desk. Of course, he's got one of those comfy rolling chairs for himself. When Stella doesn't answer, I don't, either.

"I've been getting comments from teachers all week." He slaps two pieces of paper onto the desk. I lean forward in my seat, and there's the toilet picture, right next to the defaced photo of Stella scowling. "Neither of you have anything to say? That wasn't the case fifteen minutes ago, in the library—a place intended for quiet learning, not for feuds and pranks."

Stella inhales deeply, and for a second, I think she might finally say something, but with a sigh, she lets it all back out again.

"This is not a lecture I thought I'd be giving my two top students. You're both better than this. I mean, fart jokes? Tricking each other into saying curse words? Sex-ed books? Are you in twelfth grade or third?"

I fix my eyes on a piece of dust settling on the dirty linoleum floor. My face is on fire. What if he calls my parents? They already think I'm a disappointment.

"You're at the top of your class, and that means you should be setting an example for the lowerclassmen, *and* your peers, too. If you can't stop being disruptive, I'm going to have to issue you both in-school suspensions, and do you know what that means?"

I clench my jaw. Stella sucks in a sharp breath.

"You can't be named valedictorian with disciplinary marks on your record. Do you understand?"

"Yes," Stella says, right as I say, "Of course."

"If you can't behave, the title and the valedictorian scholarship will go to the number three in your class, Marisa Cooke-Allen."

If I lost out to number three, my parents would probably keel over.

Stella closes her eyes for a moment, and part of me wonders if she's about to cry, but she straightens back up. "I'm sorry. I'll be better."

"I'm sorry, too," I mutter. My stomach churns.

"Good." He stands. "I think you've both got AP Biology now, correct?"

"Yes," Stella says, and I nod.

"Okay. Go to class. Let's hope the next time I talk to you both, it's to congratulate you on valedictorian and salutatorian."

I keep my head down as I exit the room. Stella stays behind an extra moment before joining me in the hallway, cringing every time her left foot hits the ground.

"So, that was fun," I say.

She sniffs. "Yep. Highlight of my day, for sure."

"You hurt your leg?"

"No. I'm fine." She stares straight ahead, her eyes glassy. "I don't want any more. No more pranks, no more jokes. I've got too much at stake."

"Agreed." I hold out my hand to her. "Truce?"

Stella watches my hand, her face blank. "I don't trust you enough for a truce." She pushes past me toward the staircase, leaving me standing alone in the hallway with my hand out.

–♥–

I've typed like twelve different things to Jill2, and deleted them all. If this is Laura, I need to choose my words carefully.

If she likes Aaron2—*really* likes Aaron2—then maybe she'll like me again, too.

I'm trying to think of a witty way to propose meeting up at Sci-Con, when Jill2 beats me to the message.

CaptainJillsBFF22: You have a better day than mine, I hope?

My English paper sits open, untouched on my computer screen. A sketch of Aaron Lewis, slumped in a cell, lies on my sketchbook in my lap. Scars and blood dapple his face. His hair is a stringy mess, and he's got his head in his hands. I shade in the shadows stretching beneath his body. I've always thought long, dark shadows can make anything seem lonelier, and in this horrible episode sixteen scene, it applies. For some reason, I relate extra hard to this tonight.

CERanger11: No. I had a bad day too. What happened in yours?

CaptainJillsBFF22: Stupid stuff at school ☹ You got any new art to cheer me up?

It's kind of cool to think my sketches could cheer someone up. And thinking of that actually manages to cheer *me* up.

CERanger11: Just this one. Episode 16

I send along the drawing, holding my breath. I've been posting art on here for a couple years now, and most people just gush about anything you post, and that's part of the reason I love this fandom so much. But for some reason, I really want *this* girl to like my drawings.

I never showed them to Laura when we dated. It feels weirdly exposing to send them now.

CaptainJillsBFF22: WTF???

My stomach drops. Wait, what did I do? For half a second, I worry I sent the wrong thing, like that time I drew that NSFW sketch of Aaron and Michele making out and couldn't bring myself to post it. But when I check the file, it's just Aaron, disheveled and broken.

I start typing out an apology, but she gets there first.

CaptainJillsBFF22: How could seeing my baby in pain cheer me up??? Sobs

She follows it with a GIF of someone crying into a pillow.

CaptainJillsBFF22: (it's really good, but seriously how dare you break my heart like this???)

CERanger11: hahaha sorry!

CaptainJillsBFF22: I think as payback, I'm sentencing

you to read an ENTIRE fluff fic that's all #Lewton being adorable and soft.

CERanger11: I accept my punishment. I shall endure it bravely. Which fic?

CaptainJillsBFF22: Stand by. I'm digging through my bookmarked fics.

For some reason, I kind of love that she has a bunch of bookmarked fluff fics. Sometimes I try to picture what Jill2 really looks like; I can't stop seeing a slightly younger version of Leigh Stanton, and man, I'm one hundred percent okay with this.

My mind immediately jumps to Laura, and seeing her in a Jill cosplay at Sci-Con. I blink at the screen for a moment and shake out of it.

What if she sees it's me and gets super pissed? Or disappointed?

I need to figure out a plan of action. While Jill2 is looking for fics, I head downstairs for a snack. It's only seven, but it feels like midnight around here. My house is big, and it feels hollow. Even the pool looks lonely, covered with its winter tarp.

I open the fridge, and someone slaps a hand over my mouth. My heart jumps into my throat. I whirl backward with my fists raised, and Trevor grins at me.

"Surprised you?"

I knock his hand away. "I almost punched you in the face."

"Like you could take me." Trevor wraps his arm around my shoulders, and I shove him away.

"What are you doing here?"

"Spring break. I told you I'd be home."

"I thought that was next week."

"Technically, but I finished midterms and decided to move

my flight up a few days." He digs around in the fridge and pulls out a string cheese. "Think I'll go surprise Mom next. Never told her I was coming."

"Mom," I shout up the stairs. "Your second-favorite son is home."

"What?" Mom shouts back from upstairs.

Trevor scoffs. "Way to ruin my surprise."

"You would've given her a heart attack."

Soft footsteps patter and Mom appears, draped in a pink bathrobe, her wet blond hair knotted on her head. She screams and throws herself at Trevor, who wraps her in a hug.

"Oh my God, why are you early?"

"Spring break." Trevor pulls back, holding Mom at arm's length. "Missed you, so I switched my reservation."

"I thought you were going to Mike's for the first half of break." Mom's still holding him, as if terrified he's going to vanish out to California again. Which is ironic, seeing as she's basically already planned a way to shove me into a car and get me out to the West Coast too.

He shrugs. "I'll stay with him this summer."

"Why doesn't he stay with us this summer?" Mom says. "Your father's been wanting to take us all on a cruise again."

Trevor makes a weird face. "You want Mike on our family vacation? After making such a huge deal about Thanksgiving?"

"Why not? He's family, too."

Trevor groans. "You guys are going to scare him away. Remember that Royal Caribbean cruise where Dad spilled an entire tray of piña coladas in the pool while trying to limbo? Yeah, I do."

Mom laughs. "I remember them having to evacuate the entire pool because of broken glass."

In the movie *Inside Out*, happy memories are yellow and sad memories are blue, but some memories are tinged with both. That's kind of how I feel when I remember that cruise. It was a week where we were all together, and no one was working, and no one was fighting.

"Anyway." She straightens his collar. Because only my brother would still be looking sharp, in a crisply pressed button-down, after a six-hour flight. He hasn't even graduated and he looks like a Wall Street douche. Or a Clarke Candies douche, I suppose, since he's already announced plans to take over the family business, which is perfectly fine by me. Living the dream. "I missed you so much."

Trevor goes in to hug her again. "Missed you too." He pulls back. "Where's Dad? Am I allowed to surprise him, or is that against the rules too?"

"You're going to put our poor old parents in the hospital."

"We're not *that* old." Mom swats my arm. "He's on a golf retreat with Al for the next three days." Her voice sours.

Trev and I exchange glances.

"Golf is more important than seeing your own family, I suppose," she adds stiffly. "Glad you're home."

WARSHIP SEVEN: Episode Eleven
"More Alike than Different"

Description: "Captain Jill Brighton and the Revelry crew plan a raid of a Central Elite transport ship, but it goes awry."

SCENE CLIP: JILL and crew prepare to leave the ship on a heist mission. She visits AARON in his cell.

JILL: We're going planetside for a bit. [She cocks her pistol before sliding it into her holster.] Sonny's staying on board, so don't try anything.

AARON: Shooting puppies today, are we?

JILL: [raises her brows] What in the hells is it you think we do when we're planetside?

AARON: [shrugs] Stab small children? Kidnap innocent people? Blow up space stations?

JILL: No.

AARON: If you don't tell me what you're doing, I'm going to draw my own conclusions based on the bundle of weapons you've got strapped to your belt.

JILL: Not that it's any of your business, Cescum, but this is a humanitarian mission.

AARON: Is that what they call it these days?

JILL: You heard of the green pox?

AARON: [shudders] Nope. I remember the first epidemic, though. Felt like everyone had the nasty thing.

JILL: And why are you still alive?

AARON: Parents got me vaccinated. Why?

JILL: There are hundreds of children on the outer planets who don't have your vaccinations. They die every day.

AARON: [horrified] I didn't know that.

JILL: Those on the central planets rarely know, or care.

AARON: I didn't say I don't care.

JILL: We're hitting a pharmaceutical storage unit and pillaging their doses. We'll sell it to the outer planets at a fair price. It's a win-win.

AARON: That's . . . honorable.

JILL: Don't sound so surprised, Cescum. [She turns to go.]

AARON: Would it be out of line to wish you good luck?

JILL: I don't need your luck.

[She slams the door on her way out, leaving the prisoner alone.]

17 STELLA

Okay, this is the perfect fic to send him. It has three of my most beloved tags: **hurt/comfort**, **fluff**, and this special one that's a personal favorite, **just-kiss-already**.

I paste it into the message box and hit Send. This fic makes me giddy. Although it's weird to think I'm sending it to someone from school. Someone whose identity I'm still no closer to learning.

Kyle. It could be Kyle Nielsen.

I could have just sent a semi-NSFW piece of literature to Kyle Frickin' Nielsen. What if he's totally weirded out?

No. There's no way it's actually him. I'm not that lucky.

But maybe it's not so far-fetched. I mean, he's (1) cute, like I imagine CERanger11 to be, and (2) geeky—I mean, he dressed full-on Gandalf for lit day last year—and (3) he's a total sweetheart. Maybe if I put the thoughts into the universe, it'll somehow be him.

My face melts into my hand, propped up on the desk by my elbow. I imagine Kyle, looking dapper in the full Sergeant Aaron Lewis Central Elite Squadron uniform. I'd be at Sci-Con, drifting between vendor tables, looking for another *Revelry* patch to add to my shoulder bag. Then I'd see him from across the room: he'd be browsing, maybe looking for a decal for his pilot helmet, and our eyes would lock. I'd shoulder through people to get to him, and he'd make a beeline for me, too. It would be fate. Me and Kyle. Jill2 and Aaron2, happy together, like they should be.

You know how with some things, you can't pinpoint exactly when it first started? Like dreams or career aspirations or whatever. Someone could ask, "So, Irene, when did you decide you wanted to be a chef?" and she'd reply, "I don't know, I guess I've always loved cooking since I was a little kid." But my crush on Kyle Nielsen has a defined starting point: October 16th, junior year. He had just transferred from a charter school in Massachusetts. I stood in front of him in the cafeteria coffee line and asked him to pass me the almond milk. He said, "This is going to sound really random, but weren't you the one who made that comment about Hitchcock in sixth-period Modern Media? Spot-on." His brown eyes met mine, and that was it. I was dead.

My computer makes a door-slam sound.

CERanger11 has gone offline. I deflate a little.

Or not.

Voices drift in the hallway. I poke my head outside to see what's going on.

"And I told her no, I've closed every night this week, if she's unhappy with how I leave the snack counter, she can do it herself."

"Good, I'm glad you stood up for yourself. She always does this."

I follow the voices into the kitchen, where Bridget sits at the table with a girl I've never seen before. A tattoo curls around her arm like a spiky vine, and she's got several piercings in her eyebrows, nose, and ears. Cartons of half-eaten Chinese food lie open on the table in front of them. The smell wafts toward me, making my stomach rumble. There's my sister, no money, a kid, and blowing her cash on takeout. Typical.

"Hey."

Both girls look at me.

"Oh, Stella, this is Amber, she works at the theater with me. We're doing GED prep together."

Amber shoots me a lazy wave. "Living the dream, every Thursday."

"Oh, that's exciting." I take a seat. "You taking the test with Bridget?"

"Hope to. I want to start cosmetology school by summer."

"Get this." Bridget nudges me. "We want to open a hair salon together."

Not going to lie, I'm pretty shocked to hear my sister making actual, solid life plans. "That's awesome! So you'll do cosmetology school too?"

"Going to do it the smart way like Amber, though," Bridget says, her mouth full of General Gao. "Online courses half the time." She holds the carton up to me, cheeks bulging with food. "You want some? It's still kind of warm. We already ate the dumplings, sorry."

I grab a cup out of the cupboard and turn on the faucet. "I just brushed my teeth. Thanks, though."

"Seriously, it's so much better doing it online. Cheaper, too." Amber skewers a piece of chicken with a chopstick, and I'm cringing. "Half the debt. I keep telling Bridge to take some time off after the GED. Take a break once in a while. Spend a few months with the kiddo before diving back into school."

What?

"Us Greenes don't know how to do that." Bridget ruffles my hair, and I shove her hand away. "Yeah, I definitely need a break. This studying is just such a time suck."

Oh great, another chance for my sister to mess up her life. I already don't like this Amber person—what a terrible influence.

"You're doing so great with the GED prep classes, though," I say. "Shouldn't you just go right into cosmetology school? I mean, if you're not going to do a four-year, isn't it the next best thing?"

"Why does it matter whether it's a four-year?" Bridget snaps.

I put my hands up, because I'm not getting into this with her right now.

She sighs. "It's hard enough working at the theater and Blitz, but then doing all this schoolwork is just wrecking my energy."

"I get it," Amber says. "Seriously, just take a few months off. Focus on Gwen and your burger job."

"That's a terrible idea," I say.

Bridget glares at me, but Amber keeps talking. The key clicks in the front door, and Mom bustles in wearing *Tangled* scrubs, carting an armload of groceries. Mom is the only person I know who would finish a late-night shift and brave the grocery store right after. I rush over to help.

Amber and Bridget start unloading groceries onto the counter while I stack cans in the pantry.

"Here." Mom hands Bridget a few jars of baby food and my sister's WIC card.

"Thanks." Bridget pockets the card and sets the food on the counter. "She goes through food like we're in the apocalypse or something."

"Kind of like my rat," I add.

Bridget's nose crinkles. "What rat?"

"Car's making that noise again." Mom shoves a can of green beans into the pantry a bit harder than necessary. "I'm gonna need to bring it in next week. Don't know what I'm going to tell Cynthia about the rent this month."

Bridget looks conflicted for a moment. "You could bring it to Ben's shop. Maybe he'll give us a discount."

I nearly drop the boxed mac and cheese on the floor. "No. Don't you dare."

"I'm trying to help!"

"Hey." Mom steps between Bridget and me. I open my mouth to chastise Bridget, but Mom's death glare cuts me off and I know the conversation is over. "Where's Dave and Gwen?"

"Gwen's sleeping." Bridget loads a box of off-brand Lucky Charms into the cabinet over the stove. "And Dave's at the vets' pantry with Jerome."

"Good." Mom collapses into a kitchen chair. "How was school, Stella?"

I shrug. "Fine."

"I just saw Jeff Porter's son, Ian, working at Market Basket. I wonder if he has a prom date."

"Mom, I promise, I don't need your help finding a prom date."

"I was just mentioning it." She puts her hands up. "He seems nice."

"Well, I'm going to prom with Dahlia and Em, okay?"

"It's such a big occasion, though, it might be nice to have a young man . . ."

"I don't *need* a date, Mom."

"You need to do *something* social once in a while. You're like a hermit."

"I do social things!" I retort.

She shakes her head. "Most kids your age date, Stella, it's not rocket science."

"Okay, first of all, that's not even remotely true, and even if it was, why would it matter?"

"You want some Chinese food?" Amber holds out the carton

to her—with the chopstick she'd already put in her mouth wedged into the food—but Mom shakes her head.

The hard linoleum floor burns my injured knee as I stock the bottom shelf. "Anyway." I get to my feet, rubbing my knee. I feel old. "I'm gonna go back to my room." Quickly, before my mom lobs another low blow at my dating life, or lack thereof.

She raises her brows. "Everything okay?"

I can't possibly tell her I got yelled at by the principal for my prank war with Wesley Clarke. It sounds ridiculous, even in my head. "Yeah. Just tired. Traded shifts with Becca at The Scoopery this Sunday so she could go out with her boyfriend, but I'm kind of bummed I don't get the whole weekend off anymore."

"See, Becca is dating." Mom pounces, like she was just waiting for the second I mentioned someone else's love life. "Are there any nice guys at The Scoopery you could ask to prom?"

"Mom."

Mom kicks her shoes off under the table. "Maybe you should quit. There's only three more months to graduation, and it wouldn't be terrible for you to focus on school right now. Would you mind making me a cup of tea? I'm exhausted."

"I need to work." I dig out a mug from the cabinet and fill it with water from the tap. "I'm saving up for a pair of boots from that discount shoe emporium over by Galaxy Pets."

"In all your eighteen years, I have never known you to care about shoes," Bridget says. "Usually I have to drag you shopping with me." Shopping isn't exactly fun when you've got twelve cents to your name. Bridget should know this.

"They're for my Captain Jill cosplay for Sci-Con. But they're like eighty bucks." I slide the mug into the microwave and hit the button. "Just need to pull a few more shifts."

Mom sighs. "So much time and energy you waste on that TV show."

I hate the tone in her voice when she says "TV show." Like it's some petty fixation, the way Gwen gets hung up on dandelions when we go to the park. "I like it. Let people enjoy things."

"Your costume last year was badass," Bridget says, and I'm relieved she's backing me up here, even though she always declines my invitations to the *Warship* rewatch livestream. "You doing the same thing, but with boots?"

"That's my goal! I got a new pin this year, too." The microwave dings.

"Eighty dollars is a lot of money to spend on dressing up," Mom says.

I pull out the scalding mug, steam curling from the surface. "But if I earned it, why does it matter?" It's not like those eighty dollars would be the difference between me affording college or not.

"Just make sure you remember that there are other things in the world, too," Mom says when I hand her the tea. "*Real* issues you should be caring about."

I press my lips together. As if I'm not capable of caring about more than one thing at a time. Like the fact that I'm involved in a fandom means I don't also work hard, and care about school, and hang out with my friends, and go to climate change protests, and make presentations about skinny polar bears that Wesley Clarke ruins. "Sure, Mom."

Amber leans back in her chair. "I don't know. No one ever asks a sports fanatic who spends hundreds of dollars on season tickets and paints their face for every game why they don't care about real issues."

Mom's mouth opens, then closes.

Suddenly, this Amber girl doesn't seem so bad.

—♥—

Aaron2 is online when I get back to my room, and there's a slew of messages on the screen. My heart beats a little faster.

CERanger11: Okay, this fic is pretty cute

CERanger11: don't tell anyone I said that, ever

I wonder what he looks like. If he's tall and dashing, with a killer smirk, like Aaron. Suddenly I'm picturing a young Aaron Lewis meeting me at Sci-Con. My mouth runs dry.

CERanger11: ahhhhh the bridge scene. Perfection

CERanger11: enjoying sassy Gemma in this one

CaptainJillsBFF22: it's one of my favs!! That writer has a bunch of fics, they're all great.

CERanger11: you're trying to distract me from my homework, aren't you?

CaptainJillsBFF22: #Lewton is a worthy distraction 😍

Laughter echoes in the hallway; Bridget's always going to be stuck in one place, never going anywhere. That familiar unease spreads through me. There are a lot of "what-ifs" that come with being poor: what if you can't pay the electricity this month, what if they shut off your water, what if the ancient car dies, et cetera. But lately, I've been circling another question, over and over.

What if I never escape and spend the rest of my life living paycheck to paycheck like my mom and sister?

CaptainJillsBFF22: Do you believe in fate?

CaptainJillsBFF22: Sorry, that's a weird question.

CERanger11: Sometimes.

CERanger11: Why? What's going on?

CaptainJillsBFF22: I feel like I'm doomed to end up just like my family.

CERanger11: I worry about that too.

CERanger11: Like, my parents want this one specific path for me. I'm not really interested in that life AT ALL. But what if I somehow get stuck in it anyway? Because that's what everyone in my family does?

CERanger11: But remember, things happen that you can't control. You can only control your own choices and where you go from there.

CaptainJillsBFF22: That's totally a Jill quote.

CERanger11: You caught me.

CaptainJillsBFF22: I barely know you, but I really like talking to you. Is that weird?

CERanger11: Not weird.

CERanger11: I like talking to you too.

My heart is racing like a frickin' freight train, but I type it anyway.

CaptainJillsBFF22: Maybe we could meet IRL someday?

CaptainJillsBFF22: Like, at Sci-Con.

I stare at the screen like it's going to burst into flames. I do. I want to meet Aaron2. But what if he's not into me? What if he's totally freaked I even brought it up?

CERanger11: I'd like that.

18 WESLEY

Space Arena smells like burnt pizza and looks like it was scooped right out of the seventies. Red and yellow polka dots swirl in patterns on the matted gray carpet, which is also decorated with decades-old soda stains. Top Forty hits blast from somewhere in the high drop ceiling. Little kids run between arcade games, sliding tokens into Skee-Ball and basketball-hoop machines.

And here I am, the skeevy eighteen-year-old, standing in the doorway by himself. I check the time on my phone. Either I'm way early, everyone else is late, or this is an elaborate prank and I'm about to get stood up by half my class.

Sometimes on Fridays when Trevor and I were kids, Dad would pick us up from school and bring us here. Dad used to win a ton of tickets on the bowling game and let us split them; we'd always buy a bunch of toy cars with our winnings, then line them up on the windowsill at home. I get a weird pit in my stomach thinking about it. I'm not that kid anymore. And my dad hasn't been that guy in years.

A mother shoots death glares at me, standing at the prize counter with a couple of four-year-olds who have managed to spend their four-hundred-ticket haul on thirty pieces of penny candy.

Okay, if Brandon and the others aren't here in five minutes,

I'm leaving. As if on cue, the door swings open behind me. Dahlia Johnston and Stella Greene amble in, laughing about something. The laughter melts off Stella's face when she sees me.

"Ladies. Hello."

"Hey." Dahlia waves. Stella rolls her eyes and looks pointedly at the prize counter.

I casually lean into her line of sight. "You up for a game of air hockey later? You know, after I decimate your team in laser tag."

"I think those games are more your speed." She points at the *Dora the Explorer* game over in the kiddie section.

"It's okay to be afraid of losing."

"At least I'm not afraid of rats."

Voices outside get louder until a cloud of people appear, bursting into the arcade. The sound decibel goes up by like a thousand. I relax a little.

"Laser tag!" Brandon comes up to the front and jostles my shoulders.

"You are way too excited right now."

"Did you see Dahlia Johnston is here?" he mutters under his breath.

Dahlia stands with Stella by the prize counter, eyeing the row of toys. Stella's got her hair knotted up in some elaborate braid thing. It's nice.

"Teams!" Adam Yang cups his hand around his mouth. "We need teams."

A good chunk of our graduating class as well as a handful of juniors mill about, laughing and chatting and buying game tokens.

"Everybody get your laser tag passes and meet in front of the room," Brandon shouts over the noise of the crowd.

It takes about fifteen minutes to get everyone to buy their tickets, as a couple of strays have found their way to the pizza counter instead of the laser tag booth.

"What'd you put as your code name?" Brandon asks, shoving a fistful of change into his back pocket.

"Ranger-A. What about you?"

His face scrunches. "Is that a spaceship seventeen reference or whatever?"

"*Warship Seven*. Yes."

"I should have known. I did CaptPhasma."

"Isn't that a girl stormtrooper?"

He shrugs. "She's badass, and so am I."

"That's true."

The door swings open, and Laura McNally saunters into the arcade. My stomach plunges. Did not know she was coming. I'm about to suck it up and go over there when Collin comes in after her and puts his arm around her waist. The feeling goes away.

Brandon practically has to herd everyone like sheep into the briefing area, where a couple of employees slightly older than us stand waiting.

"Okay, rules," a woman in a Space Arena T-shirt talks into her headset, amplifying her voice, but she still can't make everyone shut the hell up. "Hey! Hey, everyone!"

I put my thumb and forefinger into my mouth and blow out the loudest, sharpest whistle I can muster. The noise dulls to a handful of whispers floating around us.

"Okay, hi, everyone. Welcome to Space Arena laser tag."

Brandon cheers from somewhere behind me. He's so into this.

"Basic rules: no running, no swearing—"

"Yeah, Stella, no swearing," someone shouts from somewhere,

met with laughter. I smirk, craning my neck to catch her giving him the middle finger.

"And no physical contact—the goal is to hit your opponent with the laser *only*." She says the last part directly to the group of football guys snickering in the back.

"There are two levels in the laser arena, so you can go up and down, just please be careful on the stairs. You've got three ten-minute tag periods, during which your goal is to hit members of the other team. If you're hit, you have to go back to your team's base and tag it to get recharged. There's a three-minute break between each period, when you'll go back to your team's base and power up by scanning your laser gun on the red box. Got it?"

"Got it!" Brandon shouts, a little too enthusiastically.

"Okay! Come inside and get your gear on."

Commotion ensues as forty people elbow each other to grab their vest, helmet, and laser gun. When I slide the bulky black helmet over my head, a long, low beep sounds in my ears. Not going to lie, I feel kind of like Aaron in his CE uniform. I practice holding up my laser pointer, firing a shot at Brandon's chest. He holds his hands to his fake wound and cries out dramatically.

"Okay, everybody hear the beep? All your helmets and lasers working?"

A chorus of excited agreement rings among us.

"Excellent. How are you doing teams?"

"Seniors versus juniors," Olivia Stanstead offers.

"That's not fair," Alicia Monroe counters. "There's only a few juniors here."

"Guys versus girls!" someone shouts from the back.

Alex Hoffman scoffs. "What about me?" They point to the yellow, black, white, and purple striped button on their purse. "I don't play for either of those teams."

"Make Stella and Wesley captains," someone shouts from the back.

"Yes! Battle of the valedictorians." Before I can protest, Brandon grabs my arm and drags me to the front. "Stella? Where's Stella?"

Stella ambles to the front with her arms crossed, a scowl stretching across her face. "I pick Dahlia."

Dahlia crosses to the front to stand beside Stella, sneaking a grin at Brandon on her way past.

"I choose Brandon."

My friend comes up and stands behind me. "Ooh, ooh, Ryan and Josh," he hisses in my ear.

I wave him off. "Who's the captain here?"

"I didn't vote for you."

"Kelly Rothenburg," Stella says.

"Sanjay Laghari."

"Kyle Nielsen."

"Jake Cooper."

"Alex Hoffman."

"Rachel Ross-Bezelman."

"Laura McNally."

My heart sinks as Laura goes off to join Stella's team. Okay, I could have picked her first, but that would've been too obvious. She came here with Collin. The thought digs into my chest.

We go back and forth until everyone is lined up behind us.

"You ready to lose, Stick?"

She smiles at me. "Why don't we make this interesting?"

"Oh? A wager?"

"Loser uses their tickets to buy that tiara." She points to the prize case, where a bright pink plastic crown stares back at me. "And wears it the rest of the night."

"I'll do one better. Loser wears the crown the rest of the night and serenades the class with a rendition of our school song while standing on that table." I point at the pizza party table in the center of the arcade.

"Stands on the table singing until Space Arena kicks you out or yells at you." She holds out her hand.

"Deal."

"You hear that, everyone?" Brandon cups his hand around his mouth. "We get a free show later."

"Hope you've got your singing voice ready," I say.

"Yes, so I can announce your performance to the whole arcade. Because I will in fact be alerting everyone here."

"If you say so, Stick."

—♥—

Pink, yellow, and green glowing shapes illuminate the otherwise dark laser arena. My team huddles at our home base, a black post at one end of the room on the first floor. I squint, but can't make out Stella's team in the opposite corner. Pillars and walls painted to look like jagged space rocks jut out all over the place like we're on the moon, and behind us, a ramp leads to the second level of the arena.

"Okay, we need to talk strategy," Brandon says.

I click my laser pistol to the charging station. "Dude, this is laser tag, not the Hunger Games."

"Doesn't mean we just rush in there waving our guns around."

"My strategy is to hide behind the pillar and snipe everyone."

"You ready?" the Space Arena woman shouts from somewhere. "Three, two, one, go!"

We take off in all directions, strategy be damned. I slip behind the nearest pillar, peering out onto the main floor.

A soft *pew!* sound goes off in my ear.

"Got you!" Stella zips out from behind me and darts away. How the hell did she get over here that quickly?

"Oh, it's on now."

I run back to base and charge up, then head back onto the field. I'm stealthily weaving between pillars when I look up; the second floor is separated only by a grate, full of holes—and from here, I have the perfect shot of Stella's back, up on the second floor. I aim and fire.

She startles at the hit, whirling around. "Down here." I wave at her.

Stella grits her teeth and runs back to her base.

I dart up the ramp to the second floor. It's pure chaos up here, everyone running around laughing, laser beams flying every which way. Brandon and Dahlia stand on opposite sides of a wall, peeking around it at each other every few seconds and giggling. Finally, she fires at him, but it misses, and he laughs.

"Bam!" The *pew* sound goes off in my ear, and Stella high-fives Laura. Which one of them got me?

We dash around the room, hitting each other from near and far. Sweat breaks out across my forehead. I think a few guys turned on each other, because there's a loud accusation of friendly fire. At one point, I manage to ambush Stella by hiding behind the ramp, and the next, she snipes me from my own home base.

"Not even safe in my own house," I muse.

Stella pretends to blow on the end of her laser gun. "Not while I'm around."

"Quit fraternizing with the enemy!" Dahlia calls, and Stella skips back across the arena floor.

After an eternity, I'm bent over, catching my breath, when Stella comes running toward me. I whip out my laser and aim for her, but she dodges, launching herself over the side of the ramp.

I jump over to fire at her, but her loud groan catches my ear first.

Stella lies in a heap on the floor, clutching her knee.

"Stupid gym class," she mutters.

19 STELLA

My leg feels like I dropped a bowling ball on it and then an iron, and then laid it across some train tracks and let Amtrak come squish it. Okay, that's an exaggeration. But when I try to stand, a sharp pain sears through my knee.

"Whoa, Stick. You okay?" Wesley thumps down beside me.

"Go away." I hold my laser pistol up to zap him, but a jolt of pain slices through my leg when I move.

"All right, can you get up, or do you need help?"

"I'm fine. I don't need your help." I maneuver to my feet, trying to hide the pain crossing my face.

Our classmates run around us, firing lasers at each other. This is humiliating. It's not even like I broke it or sprained it, just beat the crap out of it playing flag football. You'd think I was rolling around on the ground, dive-tackling people.

Wesley's eyebrows shoot up. "Okay, well, if you're sure. Then I won't feel bad about doing this." He holds the laser gun out to blast me, but I raise mine quickly and shoot him in the chest. Wesley looks down at his vest in disbelief as the light flashes red.

I'm expecting him to swear at me, but he laughs instead. "I think I just got hustled."

"Sounds like someone's making excuses for being the inferior laser tag player."

"Those are some big words from someone who's going to be doing a lovely rendition of our school song on the nine-year-olds' birthday table in a few minutes."

The little chime goes off in my headphones, signaling the end of the round. I start limping toward my home base, but change my mind halfway there.

"Tell them I'll be back in a few, I have to go sit for a minute." I wade past my team, flocking toward the back of the room.

I've barely exited the laser arena when the door opens again behind me.

"You *sure* you're okay?" Wesley asks.

"Ugh, yes. I hurt it in gym earlier, okay?"

I sink into one of the red plastic kiddie chairs, and the edges dig into my butt. Wesley drifts off to the snack counter at the other end of the arcade. I manage to roll up the leg of my jeans enough to see the giant purple bruise stretched across my knee. Beautiful. I roll my pant leg back down.

"Here." I startle as Wesley sits down beside me, clutching a bag. "I got you some ice from the pizza stand."

I kind of stare at him for a moment. "What's the trick?"

"No trick. Ice." He opens the bag to show me.

"Oh. Um. Thank you." I take the bag and press it to my knee.

"You messed that up pretty good, huh? What'd you do, tackle someone for the ball?"

I blink. "Yep. That's exactly what happened."

"You know the point of flag football is to, you know"—he grins—"*not* do that."

"I didn't know, thank you for the bulletin."

"So, who'd you tackle? Kyle Nielsen?"

"You would know if you had come to gym."

"I would have come to gym if I hadn't been summoned to the office." He starts walking back to the laser tag arena, but stops. "What's your code name?"

"My what?"

"Your code name. For laser tag."

It's not that I'm embarrassed I named myself RevelryCap, because honestly, it's the most fitting code name for me. But I'm not ready for the jokes that would come pouring out of Wesley's mouth. "It's a secret, and I will never tell."

Before he can ask me more, the door opens and the rest of our class comes spilling out of the arena.

"Dude, where did you go?" Dahlia asks.

"It's a mass conspiracy!" Brandon presses his hand over his heart. "Stella and Wesley, conspiring team captains."

"Sorry, I took a tumble." I point to the bag of ice on my knee.

"She tried to do this duck-and-dive move to avoid my shot," Wesley adds. "It was badass."

Heat flares across my face. I can't tell if there's sarcasm in his tone or not.

"So who won?" I ask.

Wesley leans in. "More important question, who's going to film your rendition of our school anthem so I can upload it to Instagram later?"

"You're going to look so good in that pink tiara," I say. "I can't wait to take a million pictures and then my hand will slip and they'll end up plastered all over the yearbook."

"It was a tie." Dahlia shrugs.

My mouth snaps shut. "Well then," Wesley says.

"Here you go, Stella. Wes." Brandon passes us each a shiny pink tiara. "Let's hear some school pride!"

"Plot twist," I mutter under my breath, setting the pointy crown on my head. Queen of Fools.

When Wesley just holds his own crown, laughing, I yank it from his hands and set it right on his head. "If I'm doing this, so are you."

"Thank you for coronating me, Stick."

Cheers fill the arcade as everyone gathers around our table, their cell phones raised, ready to capture every moment.

"A bet's a bet, I suppose," I mumble.

Wesley offers me his hand. "You ready, Stick?"

Begrudgingly, I let him help me onto the table. "I was born ready." Because I'm not about to let Wesley Clarke upstage me. Someone in the crowd starts playing the instrumental version of the school anthem on their iPhone, courtesy of the marching band.

We simultaneously take a deep breath, ready to belt it out, but an employee with a gold manager badge rushes over.

"Get off of there right now!" He waves his arms like a human windmill. "Off the tables, come on!"

Our class groans and lowers their phones as Wesley and I climb back down. Well, that was anticlimactic.

"You got lucky, because I would have kicked your ass at this performance, Clarke."

Wesley grins. "Those are some mighty claims, Stick."

"Well, I'll tell you—"

"Do they have to compete over everything?" someone mutters, shutting us both up.

But the rest of the class has already spread out in the arcade, sliding tokens into air hockey tables and slamming plastic alligators with mallets.

–♥–

Do they have to compete over everything?

The words replay themselves in my head for the next hour as I follow Dahlia around the arcade, the tiara shoved in my purse. I'm not *that* competitive. Wesley just brings that out of me.

"You want some magic potion?" Dahlia holds out a paper cup from the pizza stand, a red straw poking out of it.

"What is it?"

"No idea. Their specialty drink—don't worry, there's no alcohol or anything, they sell these to little kids." She takes a heavy suck through the straw, her nose wrinkling. "Bit too sweet."

Wesley stands in a group by the basketball games, still wearing the pink tiara, subtly checking out Laura McNally, who's wrapped in that Collin kid's arms. Way to be obvious, Clarke. The way he's looking at her makes a weird flame burn inside me, and I look the other way.

"Should we do the game with the spinning lights next?" Dahlia asks, her arm laced with mine. "We can rack up the tickets that way."

"What are you using your tickets for?" I hadn't really looked at the prizes yet. The ice bag has become a sack of room-temperature water, so I dump it in the trash. I hate admitting it, but it helped.

"The little purple alarm clock is pretty cute, but it's four hundred and twenty tickets."

"How many do you have?"

She scrunches her mouth to the side and starts counting them. "At least a hundred."

"You can have mine." I pull out my pitiful ticket thread from Skee-Ball.

"Okay, so we're, like, almost a third of the way there?"

We head over to the light game, and Dahlia slips her token in. "Come on," she mumbles, waiting for the light to circle back to the jackpot space. "Stupid light."

Kyle slips his sweatshirt off a few feet away, starting a game of air hockey against Jake. He looks up, and I quickly pretend to be staring at the floor instead.

"Go challenge him to a game," Dahlia whispers.

"Yeah, like that wouldn't be super obvious."

"Why would it be obvious? Everyone's playing something."

"Hey, Stella!" Kyle's waving to me from the air hockey table. "You want to play winner?"

"Dahlia Johnston, what the hell kind of potion did you buy?" I murmur, only to get a wink in response.

"Yes, absolutely!" I quickly collect myself. "I mean, sure."

A smirk stretches across Dahlia's face, but she keeps her attention on the light game. "Told you."

"Who's winning now?" I ask the guys, making my way over.

Jake slams the puck, and it ricochets off the side. "Tied, two-two."

From the other end of the arcade, a jackpot alarm goes off, followed by Dahlia's distinct "Hell yeah!" I shoot her a thumbs-up as she rushes to collect her ticket haul from the machine.

I try to lean casually into the air hockey table, but of course, Jake makes the winning shot and the board goes still. I deflate a little.

"Boom!" he shouts. "Roasted."

"Good game, man." Kyle smiles.

I'm about to boldly suggest I play loser instead, but an announcement cuts through the room.

"Attention, guests. Space Arena will be closing in ten minutes.

Please make your way to the prize counter to redeem your tickets, and have a nice night."

"You still have those tickets for me?" Dahlia's clutching several new strings of tickets that drag on the floor. "I can get the clock!"

"Yeah, here." I fork them over, watching Kyle and Jake make their way toward the door, our game forgotten.

Brandon waves at us from across the arcade, sliding into his jacket. "Hey, Dahlia! Stella! We're all going back to my house for some gaming, you in?"

Dahlia's grip on my arm tightens. "I can come. My curfew's not until eleven." She looks at me. "You want to go?"

"I don't know, I'm pretty tired." I rub my upper arm. "But I can call my mom or something to come get me."

Her smile sinks. "No, it's totally cool. I drove you, I'll take you home."

"Nah, don't worry about it." I force a smile, not about to be the person who cock-blocks my best friend. "My mom can get me."

"You sure?"

"Yes. Have fun." I nudge her toward the door.

Of course—*of course*—Wesley's at the door, fiddling with his car keys. I roll my eyes and walk straight past him into the parking lot, watching as everyone loads into cars and pulls away.

"You need a ride?" he asks me, unlocking the doors to a red Porsche. Of course.

"No, I'm not going to Brandon's." A spring chill rips through the air, and I huddle into myself.

"Me neither." He opens his driver's-side door. "You sure you don't want a ride?"

I glance down at the text I sent my mom, but she still hasn't even seen the message. It's cold out here. "Okay. If you don't mind."

Wesley Clarke's car does not actually smell like candy bars, but it does smell like a new car. "This is a nice car," I say awkwardly.

"Thanks. I guess. It's my dad's."

"Oh." Weird that he doesn't have his own car. I mean, I don't have my own car, but it's Wesley Clarke. They have a frickin' pool with a waterfall outside their mansion.

We sit in silence for a moment.

"Where do you live?" he asks.

I buckle my seat belt. "Crestview Heights."

"Oh, really?" Wesley pulls out of the parking lot. I'm waiting for him to make a snide comment about the fact that I live in the poor neighborhood, as if it's something to be ashamed of, and I'm ready to fire back about how poverty isn't some moral failure and he should keep his mouth shut. But instead he says, "My little cousin lives near there."

I'm taken aback. "Oh. Yeah. He seemed like a cool kid."

"He is."

It's kind of weird to think of Wesley hanging out with some little kid after school. "You must be pretty close."

"Yeah. I try to make it to his school orchestra concerts and stuff since his mom works late."

Wesley's fingers drum against the steering wheel. He cruises to a stop at a light and flicks on the radio, connecting the audio to his phone. Music fills the car.

"I love this song." I start swaying in my seat. "The Civil Wars are the best."

"Yeah? I only just got into them a few weeks ago."

"Yeah. They're one of my favorites."

"Cool."

We sit in silence for several minutes.

"So, you have anything fun planned tomorrow?" he asks.

"I mean, if you count doing all the homework I should've been doing tonight *fun*, then sure? I guess?"

"You don't do *anything* fun on weekends? Unless someone drags you to Brandon Nguyen's laser tag parties?" He shakes his head. "For shame."

I laugh. "What should I be doing?"

"I don't know. Going out, seeing people. Taking a drive. Going to the beach."

"It's March."

"You know what I mean. Doing something other than homework."

Spending money I don't have? "Are you telling me to get a life?"

He grins. "I guess."

"Man, I haven't been to the beach since I was like eight."

"How is that possible? We're only an hour away."

I tug at my purse straps in my lap. "My sister is the one with the car, and she guards that crotchety old thing with her life."

"Well, how about this. When I get my car, I'll drive you to the beach."

I don't know what surprises me more—that Wesley just volunteered to spend at least two hours with me, or that I'm not completely repulsed by the idea. "I'd like that."

He shoots me an awkward smile that I return, but his eyes quickly dart back to the road. We're silent until Wesley pulls into my neighborhood and I direct him to my building.

"Thanks for driving me." I unbuckle, not sure where to look.

"No problem."

"Do you want to work on the maze tomorrow before I have to work at four?"

"Oh. Sure. My place at one?"

"Sounds good."

I'm halfway out of the car, but pause. I give a heavy, over-exaggerated sigh and hold out my hand to him.

He gives me an amused look. "What's this?"

"I'll accept your truce, Wesley Clarke."

"I thought you didn't trust me enough for a truce."

"I'm reconsidering."

"Is this a trap?" He hesitantly holds out his hand. "Because this feels like a trap."

"Just shake my hand, Clarke." So he does. Our eyes lock, and I get this weird hollow feeling in the pit of my stomach. I quickly look away.

What just happened?

The moment he's gone and I'm standing alone in the entryway to my building, it hits me. Did I just become sort-of-not-quite friends with Wesley Clarke?

W7

Topic: ***WARSHIP SEVEN* REWATCH**
Username: **CaptainJillsBFF22**

Hi again! I can't believe we're two weeks deep into our rewatch.

Episode fourteen, "A Tenuous Alliance," brings forward the old adage: the enemy of my enemy is my friend. The *Revelry* is stuck on the planet, held down by a strange programming code. We find the answer to the "who's been tracking us / who disabled our ship's jump capacity" of the last few episodes, and the answer is that a CE signal is pinning our ship planetside—and there's a missile headed right toward it. If they aren't able to re-code the signal, they'll all get blown to bits.

That's where Aaron comes in. Sergeant Aaron Lewis, our poor CE prisoner and the only person on board who can translate a CE code. Jill and Aaron shake hands, it's monumental, and he agrees to help free the ship to save all their lives. After all, if they don't stop the missile or unstick the *Revelry*, he'll be dead, too.

Aaron inputs the code, saving the crew. It's the first sign that he might be on our side. After all, he's choosing the *Revelry* crew over the CE (even though we learn later it wasn't actually the CE, but awful space pirates pinning them down!). Jill tells him he's earned his place among the *Revelry* crew and proven his alliance with them. I think Aaron is thrilled here, because it's what his heart secretly wants! She releases him from the brig and gives him his own quarters on board the ship.

I remember feeling so much hope after this episode, that maybe he'd become the next member of the *Revelry* crew. Maybe he realized the CE was wrong. But alas, episode twenty. I really hate how this show ends.

20 WESLEY

Trevor and I sit at the kitchen island, eating fistfuls of dry Honey Nut Cheerios out of the box. "Wanna join my fantasy baseball league?" he asks.

"You know I don't know anything about baseball."

"We need like two more people." He arranges a circle of Cheerios on the countertop and plunks them one by one into his mouth. "There's a hundred-dollar prize for the winner."

"I wouldn't even know who to put on my team."

"I could advise you. C'mon, you know you want to."

"I really, really don't."

Mom saunters into the kitchen. "I almost forgot. A package came for you," she says, thumbing through yesterday's mail.

"Which one?" Trev and I say at the same time.

"Wesley." She drops a square box on the floor by my feet.

I start tearing into the box with my bare hands before Mom sighs and hands me scissors. "It's my battle helmet!"

Her eyebrows shoot up. "Your what?"

"For my Sergeant Aaron Lewis cosplay." I hold it up, then slide it over my head. The smell of plastic smothers me, but I've got a clear view through the dark visor, and it's pretty badass. I pull out my phone camera and set it so I can see myself in the screen. My back immediately straightens. If I didn't know it was me, I could never tell; I basically *am* Aaron Lewis in this thing.

Trevor laughs. "You still doing that stuff, man? You know the show isn't real, right?"

"You literally play *fantasy* baseball, and you're making fun of *me* for liking something that isn't real?"

Mom takes a seat at the table with a mug of coffee. "Let your brother enjoy things."

I'm not sure why, but the first thing that crosses my mind is that I should tell Jill2 about this. I jump off the stool and plow upstairs, still wearing my helmet.

She's online. I jut my chin out and snap a selfie, and then I quickly go in and Photoshop out my room, replacing it with the background of the *Revelry*'s makeshift dungeon.

There are always at least six or seven Aaron Lewises at these cons, judging by the pictures that crop up online afterward, but I'm fine being one of them. That would actually be a pretty cool photo op—all the Aaron cosplayers, posing with Ethan Martone himself.

I pause a moment. Laura.

What would I even say to her? What if she finds out it's me and deletes her account or something? Before I can stop myself, I'm copy-pasting right into the message window.

CERanger11: Check it out.
CaptainJillsBFF22: OMG! I love it!!

When we were dating, I always made fun of Laura for using way too many exclamation points in her texts. When we broke up, she started putting periods at the end instead, and man, that sucked. I never knew how much I'd miss that stupid line with a dot at the bottom. Like all her enthusiasm for talking to me was gone.

And now, here's Jill2, peppering them across my screen.

CERanger11: Thanks for finding it for me!
CaptainJillsBFF22: No problem, it looks amazing!! Like you just stepped off your shuttle and reentered the Revelry to reunite with your one true love
CERanger11: I'm going to let that one slide, just this once
CaptainJillsBFF22: haha thank you

I think carefully. How can I make Laura reveal herself?

CERanger11: Reminds me of the pilot episode when he shows up on the Revelry for the very first time.
CaptainJillsBFF22: The Warship Wednesday theme this week is Cosplay—you should post your helmet!
CERanger11: Okay 😍 Maybe I'll even post it today! Warship Sunday??
CaptainJillsBFF22: Never a wrong day!

I'm procrastinating doing my homework right now, but this is too important. I can stay up tonight if need be.

Laura's in my AP Bio class, and I know she volunteered to keep her team's rat. Also they have a black Lab.

CERanger11: Do you have any pets?
CaptainJillsBFF22: One (1) doggo!!

Okay, it's possible.

CaptainJillsBFF22: but technically I also kind of have this pet rat lol. (I take it you're not in AP Bio with me?)

I can't get ahead of myself. There are four AP Bio classrooms, and probably lots of people have dogs. It's not like she has something exotic like a python that would single her out immediately.

I can narrow it down to anyone taking AP Bio this year. That much is fact.

CERanger11: I, too, am in AP Bio, with a rat.

CaptainJillsBFF22: Ooohhhh??

She follows this with a slew of eye emojis.

Part of me feels silly for this whole thing. Like, why can't we just suck it up and use our real names?

Because if Laura knows, she'll just reject me again.

I tab into the forum itself to post a photo. Little do I know I'm stepping into a war zone.

Revelry5122: Did you see they're talking about a Warship spinoff show??

DroidBystander09: I heard it was a full-on remake.

Revelry5122: Producer slipped out a comment at that German con last night.

I jerk back from the screen. Okay, it's not a big deal. Lots of rumors have been flying for years about this. Leigh and Ethan even did an April Fools' prank a few years ago, fake-announcing on Twitter that they'd signed on to do a *Warship* spinoff series together called *Sweet Home Lewton*.

Ellenj15: NO. omg. No. This is unacceptable.

Hustler717: is the original cast signed on??

DroidBystander09: Technically it's all rumors. Nothing's official.

Revelry5122: Why do they have to remake it?? Why can't they just make original material? Or GIVE US A MF SEASON 2??

Hustler717: they can't even give us a second season and they're talking about remakes? Total cash grab.

Revelry5122: There's no need for a remake. The original was perfection!!

CaptainJillsBFF22: I mean, it had its issues for sure, but the original is the classic. They shouldn't just remake it for money. Ridiculous.

Jill2 of course has an opinion on this, and that's part of the reason I like her so much. I picture Laura sitting at her computer, typing into the forum.

Hustler717: @CaptainJillsBFF22 . . . wait, what do you mean "issues"?

CaptainJillsBFF22: @Hustler717 Lol. I didn't mean anything by it. It's my favorite show.

Hustler717: @CaptainJillsBFF22 Then why did you mention issues . . .

CaptainJillsBFF22: @Hustler717 Just saying it's not above criticism, you know? Like, for example, it has issues with sexism. This is nothing new. Doesn't mean we can't enjoy it.

Revelry5122: Oh ffs. Take this somewhere else.

CaptainJillsBFF22: Examples: Sonny CLEARLY sleeps around a ton, which is cheered by the crew and used as comic relief, while Gemma is slut shamed and overprotected by the male crew because of her relationship. Then there's the issue that it's HEAVILY implied that Nat in the CE tried to sexually assault Michele (randomly, for no reason? Gotta love when male writers just shove in assault scenes to kill time), yet this is used to develop a male character (Aaron) and show how heroic Aaron is for beating him up, and Michele's feelings on this aren't explored. I mean, there's the whole portrayal of Michele's character in general, I could spend hours talking about that.

Hustler717: No hating on Lisa Rodriguez in this chat.

CaptainJillsBFF22: I'm not hating on her! I love Lisa! I'm just saying there are flaws in the way her character was written (she's depicted as a villain for being ambitious and sexy and dating Aaron etc.)

DroidBystander09: some people are just always looking for things to complain about

Revelry5122: @CaptainJillsBFF22 wow if you hate the show so much, just don't watch it

CaptainJillsBFF22: I didn't say I hated it. I can love something and still recognize that it has issues. I loved Game of Thrones, but that doesn't mean I can't say season 8 sucked . . .

Hustler717: We're here to have fun and chat about our fav show. If you want to drag Warship, do it somewhere else.

Revelry5122: ^What he said. This isn't the group for someone whose fragile ego is going to be offended that easily. It's a show. If you want to trash it, go over to Reddit.

Before I can overthink it, I'm jumping in.

CERanger11: Wow, lots of guys in here who have never had a legitimate complaint about anything in their lives *sarcasm*

Weirdly, none of them come after me.

My hands hesitate over the keyboard. I don't want to pretend I'm swooping in to save Jill2 when she's perfectly capable of handling herself, but I also feel like a douche just watching this happen. I'm about to add more to the thread, when Jill2 gets there first.

CaptainJillsBFF22: you're all saying I'm fragile but, like, you're the ones all offended because I have an opinion? Lol cheers!

CaptainJillsBFF22 has left the chat.

CERanger11: you guys are driving people out of this fandom by being asshats, fyi

I open our private chat.

CERanger11: there are a lot of butthurt fanboys in this group right now. I'm sorry.

CaptainJillsBFF22: Lol no worries, I'm used to it. My friend Brooke started using a gender-neutral name on here just so guys won't be jerks to her.

CERanger11: wow that's awful.

CaptainJillsBFF22: Yep -_- But you know. I love the show, and I call out problematic stuff because I love the show.

CERanger11: I get that.

CaptainJillsBFF22: But anyway, want to see something fun??

She follows with a shoulders-down photo of her Jill cosplay, taken in a floor-length mirror.

CaptainJillsBFF22: What do you think??
CERanger11: The purple spotted socks are my favorite, I didn't know Jill wore those
CaptainJillsBFF22: well the captain has good style (and I haven't gotten my boots yet)

I have to admit, she has a nice body, but it's impossible to tell who she is. The uniform is just baggy enough to hide any identifying features, except maybe the fact that she's short. *Laura's short.*

I wish I could see her face. But I guess with all the jerks roaming around the *Warship* forums, I'm not surprised she wants to stay anonymous.

CERanger11: But really though, it looks good! Very Jill-like
CaptainJillsBFF22: Thanks!
CERanger11: I'm looking forward to seeing the full look at Sci-Con.
CaptainJillsBFF22: Can't wait!

Me neither.

–♥–

Stella rings my doorbell at exactly 1:00 p.m. on the dot.

"You're twelve seconds late," I say when I open the door, holding up my phone to show her the clock.

"You have a long driveway." She comes inside, the cardboard maze wedged under her left arm, a pink thermos clenched in her right hand. "This thing is digging into my skin." She drops the mass of cardboard onto the kitchen table, crushing the stack of mail Mom was browsing earlier. "I think I just crushed something. What was that?" She frantically lifts the maze back up.

"My childhood photos. You destroyed them."

She gasps. "Wait, really?"

"No."

Stella rolls her eyes. "Where's our friend?"

"Who?"

"Lint."

"Here." I point to the cage on the kitchen counter. Thankfully Mom is at work now or she would kick my ass for that. Dad might care, but he's holed up in his office.

"How'd you get Mom and Dad to agree to that?" Trevor asks, conveniently sliding into the kitchen for snacks. "I'm Trevor, by the way."

"Stella. Stella Greene." She barely looks up, examining Lint through the metal bars.

Trevor laughs. "Oh, *you're* Stella Greene? That's amazing. Wesley won't shut up about you."

I smack him in the side.

Stella grins. "What does he say?"

"That you're his favorite person in the world."

"Yep," I say. "That's exactly it."

Trevor's phone rings, and his eyes light up. "It's Mike on FaceTime." He answers the phone, and Mike's face fills the screen. "Hey." I love how his tone suddenly shifts from asshole brother to smooth and collected.

"Hi, Mike," I shout.

"Who's that?" Stella whispers.

"His boyfriend."

"Hi, Mike!" It's Stella who shouts this time. Trevor quickly runs out of the room, and I hear his footsteps thudding up the stairs.

The second he's gone, I go to high-five Stella.

"What's that for?" She smacks my hand.

"Getting my brother to go away."

"He seems nice. Giving out false information, though."

"False information? Never. The slander."

She unlocks the cage and gently pries Lint out. "I can't be your favorite person in the world. That's Laura McNally's job."

I can feel my face blanch. "What do you mean?"

"I mean you were super obvious last night." She shrugs. "It's okay. Your secret's safe with me."

"I don't have feelings for Laura."

"You're a terrible liar, Clarke."

"Not sure what you saw, Greene, but maybe you should get your eyes checked. Laura's with Collin." The words physically pain me when they leave my mouth.

"I saw. But don't worry. Girls can't resist the incomparable Wesley Clarke for very long."

"Very funny." I set to work reinforcing the cardboard that's already starting to lean. "Hilarious, in fact. And Laura and I actually dated, for a few months last year."

A knowing smile creeps across Stella's face. "I thought so."

"What? No snide comment?"

"Why would I make a snide comment? I like Laura. She's got amazing taste in music. Not so much in guys, though."

"Ah, there's the Stick I know and love."

"If you call me Stick one more time, I'm going to find one outside and throw it at you."

"You want snacks?" I pull a bag of Chex Mix out of the cabinet.

"I never say no to snacks. So why'd you guys break up?"

Ah, there it is—the last possible topic I want to discuss with anyone, let alone Stella Greene. "Seriously?"

"Yes, seriously."

"Why do you care?"

"I'm curious."

Stella lets Lint crawl up her arm and perch on her shoulder. Lint sniffs the air. I can't help noticing how Stella's smile brightens when she's holding her.

"Here." I open the fridge and pull out a Tupperware container full of orange chunks. "Give her this."

"What is it?"

"Sweet potato. She likes it."

Stella jerks back. "Is that safe for rats?"

"Yes, I googled it." Every night, I boil a sweet potato, let it cool, then throw the chunks into the cage with her dinner.

"Wow, look at you. It's almost like you care about Lint."

"I don't." I scratch the back of my neck. "I just want a good grade."

I love the way she munches the sweet potato, though. Her little whiskers twitch. It's pretty cute.

"Here, do you want to pet her?" Stella puts Lint flat in her palm. "She loves attention."

I stiffen. "I don't know."

"You don't have to. Just thought I'd ask, while I'm here."

"Will she bite me?"

"No!"

Hesitantly, I reach out a finger and stroke her gray fur. It's softer than I was expecting. I quickly draw my hand back.

"She's soft."

"The softest. Like dryer lint." Stella pets Lint. "And she's going to dominate this maze, too."

"Maybe we can lure her through with the sweet potato."

"She did gobble that right up, didn't she?"

We get to work stabilizing the maze walls, and let Lint get in the maze and start sniffing around and exploring. She manages to make it around the first corner before getting distracted in the dead end. After several failed runs, Lint finally makes it past, learning not to get stuck.

"Look," Stella whispers, grabbing my arm. "She's doing it."

"So close," I say. "C'mon, girl, you can do it."

"Go, go, go!"

Lint looks up at us, sniffs the air, and heads back toward the first dead end.

I deflate a bit. "Well then."

"This is going to take some work," Stella says. "But she'll get there."

Footsteps clomp somewhere in the hallway, a little too heavy to be Trevor's.

"So this is that biology project you told me about?" Dad's brow creases when he appears in the doorway, his phone sandwiched between his ear and his shoulder.

"Rat mazes." Stella holds up Lint for Dad to see.

Dad snorts, covering the phone with his hand. "Cardboard and rats. I told your mother we should have sent you to private school. You better believe they'll have you doing *real* science projects at Stanford."

Stella shoots me a look, and I'm silently praying she doesn't drop the bomb that my picture on The Wall says I'm going to

Columbia. I give her a slight shake of my head, and she seems to get the message, because she doesn't say anything.

I force a smile. "It's a fun project. We're trying to—"

"Keep it off the counter, okay?" Dad points to the phone glued to his ear, grabs a banana, and sweeps out of the kitchen. The second he's gone, his booming laughter echoes back, enthralled with whatever the person on the other line is saying.

Stella's eyebrows shoot up and she looks straight at the countertop, like she's got eight thousand things to say but is laboring to hold them back, which I appreciate, because I already know what they probably are.

"Yeah, he can be a jerk," I say, before she can.

Stella opens her mouth, then shuts it. "Hey, I'm not here to judge. My family's got weird stuff going on." She lowers her voice to a whisper. "I would have picked Columbia too."

We sit in silence for a moment.

"She said she didn't like me anymore."

Stella looks bemused. "Lint?"

"Laura." I twiddle my fingers. "She said she liked me as a friend but there was no . . . spark."

"Ah." She sets Lint back in her cage. "Well, you have your answer, then."

"What do you mean?"

"I mean, *no spark* is a good reason to end things. It shows she doesn't want to waste your time with something that isn't going anywhere."

I shrug, plucking pretzels out of the Chex Mix. "I guess. Still sucks, though."

"I mean, it's not like she told you she's ending things because you're boring, or you smell, or because she's about to be sent to prison for manslaughter and didn't want you to be stuck waiting around for twenty years until she makes parole." She takes a Chex from the bag. "Anything like that."

"Does that happen to you often, Stick? Guys you like out murdering people and leaving you hanging?"

"All the time," Stella says. "But really, why would you want to be with someone who's lukewarm about your relationship? Everyone deserves someone who's *really* going to like them. Even you."

Stella's eyes meet mine, and she quickly looks away.

Her phone dings, and she nearly falls off her stool. A nervous smile juts across her face as she frantically types back.

"Whoa, chill out, Stick. You texting Chris Evans or something?"

"If you *must* know, Kyle Nielsen asked me a question on the calc homework. That's all."

"I can't believe you're hung up on that guy and you're being judgey about *my* relationships." I take a few pieces of Chex from the bag.

Stella makes a face. "I was *not* being judgey and I am not *hung up* on him. We're talking about homework."

"I don't make that face when I'm talking about calc homework. Just saying."

She sets Lint gently back into her cage. The rat slinks around before settling in the giant hollow plastic strawberry I picked up last week and filled with shredded paper for her to use as a bed. "You don't know what you're talking about, Clarke."

"I'm just saying Kyle Nielsen is a know-it-all. I mean, be friends with who you want. I just think he's slimy."

"Wow." She smiles smugly. "If I didn't know any better, I'd say you *care* about me."

I laugh, but it melts away the second she looks back toward the rat.

Shit. I don't know when it happened, but it's true. I do care about Stella Greene.

WARSHIP SEVEN: Episode Fifteen
"To the Death"

Description: "After his heroics earned him a spot on the Revelry crew, Aaron betrays Jill, leading them to find themselves in a life-changing predicament."

SCENE CLIP: AARON lies in bed in his new quarters after midnight, unchained, after saving the *Revelry* in the previous episode. His help allowed the crew to escape right before the explosive hit. CAPTAIN JILL had given him only one rule about his newfound freedom: do not leave your quarters at night.

AARON: [sits up in bed, pensive] Michele? Do you hear me?
MICHELE: I hear you. Are you all right?
AARON: It happened. The captain granted me limited freedom to roam the ship. I can get the goods and return to you tonight.
MICHELE: And kill the captain.
AARON: Yes. Of course.
MICHELE: I'll see you soon, Rookie.

[AARON creeps out of his quarters, glancing side to side in the darkened *Revelry* corridor. He sneaks down the bridge and toward the armory, where he disarms the security system and enters the room, quietly grabbing various weapons off the wall.]

JILL: [pointing a pistol at his back] Stop.
AARON: [freezes, slowly turns toward her, grinning] Hello, Captain. Fancy seeing you here. [Before JILL can react, he fires a pistol at her; she ducks out of the way and fires back.]

JILL: You filthy Cescum. I trusted you. [fires at AARON, who ducks behind a crate]

AARON: Ah, a poor idea. [fires back at her, misses]

[JILL and AARON duel, shooting at each other.]

AARON: Should've killed me when you had the chance, Captain.

JILL: Not a mistake I'll make again. [fires at him]

[The two hurtle over crates, racing around the ship and firing at each other. AARON manages to knock JILL's pistol from her hands; she launches herself at him, tackling him to the ground. They wrestle; AARON manages to roll away, and JILL regains her weapon. An alarm sounds, but the two are too distracted to notice. The fight continues, and eventually AARON is knocked to the ground, JILL standing behind him with her pistol.]

JILL: [seething] Get up, Cescum.

AARON: [slowly stands, hands up, turning to face her in disbelief] You had the shot. Why didn't you kill me?

JILL: [spits at his feet] I'm not going to shoot you in the back. If I want to shoot you, I'll do it in the face. [They both raise their pistols trained on each other's heads at the same time, but freeze when they see a group of pirates standing on the bridge, holding the pajama-clad *Revelry* crew at gunpoint.]

21 STELLA

"Did you get your prom dress yet?" Dahlia's bag scares the shit out of me when it thuds on the empty chair beside mine. Our English classroom always reverberates.

I shut my planner. "It's April. We've got like two months."

"You better hurry. I went to that bridal shop on Main to look for one, and they were already picked clean."

"I know, I got your snap." I'll probably wait until the mall puts some formal dresses on clearance anyway. "Honestly, I've barely thought about prom." I've been way more focused on getting my outfit ready for Sci-Con, which is only a few weeks away now.

Three weeks until I learn Aaron2's real identity. Three weeks until we finally meet face-to-face, even though we already know each other.

What if he's disappointed when he realizes it's me?

"Any news about valedictorian? You crushing Clarke yet?" She sinks into the seat.

My heart always seems to jump a little when I think about it. I'd planned to pull ahead of him by now, but he's hanging in there. "Not yet. Honestly, it's probably going to come down to finals, and that's just, ugh." I rest my head in my hands, elbows on my cold desk. "I just . . . I don't know. I want to show my family I can do it."

"I hear you." She takes a swig from her Starbucks cup. "All

my siblings graduated college summa cum laude, so my parents will freak if I don't. First Johnston Failure is not a title I want."

"At least your siblings went to college." I roll my eyes.

"Hey, Stella. Dahlia." Kyle strolls into the room, a wide smile on his face.

"Hey!"

He takes a seat at the other end of the room and tugs off his yellow jacket. My heart stops when I see what he's wearing underneath.

It's a black T-shirt, emblazoned with a giant space cruiser. Yellow letters stretch across the top of the shirt, spelling out *Warship Seven*.

My breath catches in my throat.

Oh my God.

It's him.

I was right.

It's fate. We were meant to be together. Jill2 and Aaron2.

Dahlia starts talking to Jamie Henderson, and I tune it out. All I can think about is Sci-Con, and me in my Jill costume running right into Kyle's arms.

"Hey, Stick." Wesley collapses into the seat on my other side, blocking Kyle from view. "Lint keeps staring at me when I'm at my desk at night; it's super weird."

I try to peek around him, staring at Kyle's shirt as though I could've imagined it. "She sleeps in your room now?"

"She's growing on me." He gives an exaggerated sigh. "Hate when things do that."

I don't have time for this. "Hang on." I get to my feet and take a deep breath, patting my hair. I step around the other people filing into the classroom, making a beeline for Kyle's desk.

Maybe he borrowed the shirt.

Or maybe he likes the show, but isn't Aaron2.

I realize I'm standing right in front of him, gaping, when he puts down his phone and smiles up at me. "Hi, Stella. How's it going?"

"I didn't know you were a *Warship* fan." The words fly out of my mouth before I can stop them. Across the room, Wesley arches a brow. I'm glad he can't hear what we're saying from that far away, or this would be humiliating.

Kyle grins. "Only the greatest show of all time. You watch?"

I can't form coherent words—*good job, Greene*—so I just nod and point to my three-pointed-sword necklace.

"Nice! I didn't think there were any other Warshippers at this school. That's awesome."

Ask if he's CERanger11. Just ask him.

But I blurt out something else instead. "You want to hang out after school today?"

–♥–

All day long, I'm watching the clock, barely able to focus. I'm hanging out with Kyle Nielsen after school.

I managed to accomplish three firsts today.

1. I asked a guy out. Extra points because he said yes.
2. I blanked out during fifth-period Latin and had to borrow Dahlia's notes.
3. Mr. Bailey caught me texting Em and Dahlia in the group chat and took my phone away, to which everyone *ooh*ed and Wesley full-on applauded because he's an asshole.

But none of that matters. Because after school, I get to hang out with Kyle Nielsen. When I finally get my phone back after AP History, two texts are waiting on my screen.

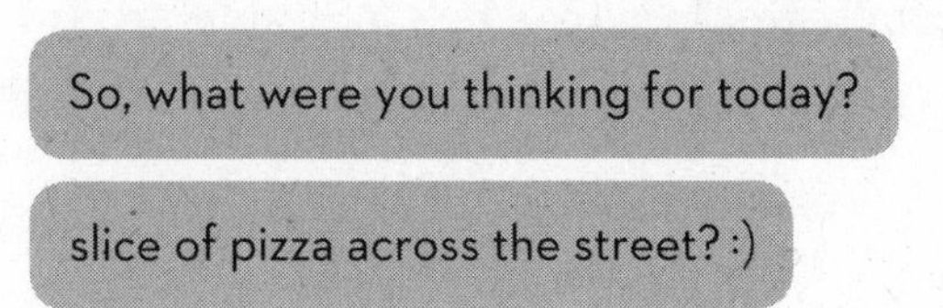

So, what were you thinking for today?
slice of pizza across the street? :)

Oh my God, he's so charming. Who else that isn't my mom's age actually types out their emojis? He *is* Aaron Lewis. So dorky and awkward and perfect.

The thing about being poor and car-less is that there are limited options for "hanging out after school." But dollar slices are a good plan.

Yes! Meet you there at 3?

sounds great! We can go down to Memorial Field if you want, walk around. It's such a nice day! :)

I'd never thought of the pizza place as romantic, except for the fact that Em and her girlfriend got busted for making out behind it last year. But now I can't think of a better date.

I have found my Sergeant Aaron Lewis.

–♥–

Kyle is leaning against the side of the building after school, texting. He's got a jacket over his T-shirt, but it's zipped a few inches down so I can still make out the *Warship* logo. I take a moment before he sees me to catch my breath.

I've already planned a whole speech in my head, sans

notecards. First I'll clear the air with some small talk, ask about school, maybe bring up the weather. Then, I'll broach the elephant in the room: the fact that he's Aaron2 and I'm Jill2. Finally, I'll bring up Sci-Con and maybe get the guts to ask him to be my date.

Okay, Stella, focus.

Mist hangs in the air, left over from this afternoon's April showers. The spongy ground squishes beneath my feet.

"Sorry I'm late." I tuck my backpack over my shoulder. "Had to talk to Mr. Bailey." Okay, it's a half lie. I stayed late so I could brush my hair and redo my mascara. But it's me, so I know he'll buy the excuse.

"No worries." He flashes me a shy smile. "I'm just glad to see you. We've never hung out before, I mean, outside of English and Bio."

"I'm glad to see you too!" It comes out more enthusiastic than I was planning. Why am I like this?

"Shall we get a slice across the street?" He raises one eyebrow at me. I always kind of adored that he has this ability to sound like a gentleman from the 1920s. Or like Aaron Lewis, stepping right off his space cruiser. I mean, without the whole jumping onto my ship to steal stuff and arrest me thing. My heart races.

"Sure. I'd love that." He holds out his arm to me—literally holds out his arm, like we're in an old movie—and I thread my arm through his. Kyle smells like those cherry cough drops, the ones that you can still smell hours after they dissolve.

I picture us walking into prom this way, arm in arm. Maybe I'd wear Jill's three-bladed-sword necklace, and he'd somehow include a CE patch on his tux, and it would be just like the show should have ended: the two of us, together.

"How . . . was your day?" I ask, trying to stop myself from grinning.

"Oh, you know. The usual. We had a gym sub, and he made us play dodgeball."

"The absolute worst." Or maybe second worst, to flag football.

"Yeah, he had to call a time-out when Liz pelted Jeremy in the nuts, though. Jeremy fell and was clutching himself for like five minutes before the coach realized he'd really been hit in the leg and was just wasting time."

I snort. "Oh my God."

"Pretty ridiculous, right?"

We walk across the quad in silence. Kyle waves to a couple of underclassmen, telling me they're in his D&D group, but otherwise, our footsteps are the only sound breaking the silence. I wish I had something interesting to say. I try to form the words, to tell him about the forum, but they all turn to incoherent garble in my mouth.

"Did you—"

"I was—"

We both stop short with an awkward laugh.

"You first," he says.

"No, you." I was going to ask him if he'd done the history homework yet, and when you're at the point in small talk when you're talking about homework, you know it's a dud. "Really, go ahead."

We stop at the crosswalk and wait for the signal, then start walking toward the pizza place.

"I was just saying, I was really happy when you asked me out today," he says.

"Well, I'm really happy you said yes."

"I mean, most girls don't notice nice guys, you know? They like jerks and jocks and stuff."

I laugh. "I'm pretty sure most girls don't like jerks."

"They all like rich asshats like Wesley Clarke."

"Okay, Wesley Clarke isn't a *total* asshat—" A fact that pains me to admit. "Just like ninety-nine percent. Ish."

He takes my hand in his. "But you're not like other girls, Stella."

I stop dead. Hold up. What does *that* mean? "What's wrong with other girls?"

"It's a compliment. I didn't mean anything bad by it."

"Oh." It didn't feel like a compliment. At least, not a compliment I want. "Okay." He didn't mean anything by it. Poor adorable, awkward Kyle.

He holds the door open for me. The smell of melted cheese, oregano, and warm crust fills the small pizza shop. "What do you usually get here? I love their mushroom slices."

He beams, showing off a row of perfect white teeth. "Me too. I'm starving. Split a whole pie?"

That's a good several dollars more than I was planning to spend today. I bite my lip, but nod.

Kyle orders two waters and a medium mushroom pizza with extra cheese. I find us a table near the back of the room by the old jukebox. I picture him plunking a few coins into the slot and pulling up the *Warship* theme song, and then we'd dance around the pizza parlor and it would be romantic and geeky all at once.

It doesn't happen. And I'm pretty sure they wouldn't even have the theme song.

A few strings of mozzarella stretch from the plate when I

grab a slice off the pie. "So, who's your favorite *Warship* character?"

He holds up his finger to indicate he's still chewing, then takes a big swallow. "Easy one. Aaron Lewis."

"Pretty sure I've only heard that from every single male *Warship* fan ever."

"Well, he's pretty cool." Kyle unzips his jacket, pointing to his T-shirt. "I keep hoping to meet Ethan Martone and get him to sign this."

Mention Sci-Con. Prove it's you.

"I met Leigh Stanton last year at Sci-Con. She was great."

"Oh, yeah? She seems awesome." He takes a sip of water. "I really wanted to hit Sci-Con last year, but I got the flu. Sucked."

"They're coming back this year. Leigh and Ethan."

"I know! I want to go."

I fidget in my chair. So far, this has been inconclusive.

"Okay, tell me." Kyle wipes his mouth on his napkin and leans back in his chair. "Are you, like, a *real Warship* fan?"

"As opposed to an imaginary one?"

"I just mean, there are a lot of people who didn't even watch the show when it first aired, you know? Or they've only seen it once and haven't even read the novelizations or anything." He rolls his eyes.

"I didn't watch the show when it aired. And I'm absolutely a real fan."

"Okay, if you're really a real fan, then who cowrote the 2018 novelization based on episode twelve?"

I blink. "You're not serious, right?"

"That's what I thought." He sighs. "Not a real fan."

My hands clench around the table's edge so tightly my

knuckles turn white. "Okay, do you ever ask male fans that? Make them prove their fandom status? Nerd cred?"

Kyle stares at me for a moment, and for the first time, he looks more dorky than cute when he does it. "Look, it's not a big deal, okay? I just don't like it when casual fans are out here talking about *Warship Seven* like they're part of it."

You know those eye tests where the screen is blurry, and then they put the glass over your eyes and suddenly the letters are clear? And maybe if your eyes suck like mine, you think you were seeing a *K* when it's really an *E*? And you're shocked to discover you were wrong? This is like that, only I thought I was looking at a guy I could conceivably date, and it turns out I'm actually looking at a piece of asparagus. And I *hate* asparagus.

I force my voice to remain light. "If I want to call myself a fan because I watch the show, then I'm still just as much of a fan as you are, you know?" I take a sip from my water, and it's way too cold going down my throat. "I mean, even if someone just discovered the show last night and they love it, they're still a valid fan. *Warship* fans are the best, and we don't need to police each other."

"As long as you're not one of those awful shippers who make everything about romance."

"What do you mean?"

"Sometimes girls watch *Warship Seven* just because they think Ethan Martone is hot or they ship Aaron and Jill or something. It's kind of pathetic."

"Ex*cuse* me?"

The bell over the door dings, and voices fill the small pizza shop, drawing our attention. The entire male track team pours inside, dripping with sweat, still in their workout clothes.

"Yo, it's the Stick!" Wesley waves at me over the crowd. I relax a little.

When did it become a *relief* to see Wesley Clarke? I can't help noticing he's kind of hot when he's been working out. And I hate myself for noticing. Ew, what is wrong with me? I give a half-hearted wave.

Wesley pulls up a chair at our table and straddles it, stealing a stray mushroom off the edge of our pizza; I smack his hand away. "You guys on a date or something?"

"Yeah—"

"Absolutely not," I correct. Not anymore, at least. I get to my feet and put my jacket on. "I was just leaving."

I start to walk away, when Kyle continues, "You owe me seven bucks for your half of the pizza."

I turn around and flip him both middle fingers. "Keep the change." I storm toward the exit, to cheers from the track team.

Kyle pushes his chair back from the table, and it screeches against the tile. I'm already dreading having to face him again outside. He starts to stand, but Wesley immediately stands too, blocking his path. "C'mon, don't follow her. That's weird."

Out of the corner of my eye, I catch Kyle glaring at me while Wesley takes another bite of my pizza.

22 WESLEY

I stare at the unsent text to Laura on my phone screen.

> hey, do you have any plans next weekend?

My intention is innocuous enough: get her to mention Sci-Con, and work that into asking if she's Jill2. But it looks like I'm hitting on her or something.

"Wes, did you take out the trash?" Mom calls from the hallway.

"Yeah, why?"

"It still smells in here," she replies. "Was something rotting in it?"

I mean, I took it out about five hours later than I should have, knowing there were leftover shrimp shells in there. "No idea. Sorry." The house has felt so much lonelier since Trevor went back to Stanford.

"Wesley Daniel Clarke."

Mom stands in my doorway, still in her work clothes, her arms crossed. "Are you really on Instagram right now? Don't you have homework?"

I quickly minimize the window, where I was definitely not creeping on Laura's pictures from when she and Collin went bowling last weekend. "I wasn't on Instagram."

"You know I can see the tab, right?"

I shut my laptop and give her a sheepish grin. "Not anymore."

She sighs, coming in to hug me. "Oh, Wesley. What am I going to do with you?"

I inhale deeply into her hair. My mom always has this weirdly comforting smell.

"Trev called, he's booking a flight home for your graduation—or rather, I'm booking it for him."

"Oh. Cool."

"I'm thinking of reserving Portman's Steakhouse for your graduation dinner, is that okay?" She pulls back, holding me at arm's length.

"That's fine." I look away. *If my parents still want to celebrate when they learn where I'm going next year. If they don't disown me first if Stella gets valedictorian.* "How was your meeting?"

"Oh, you know. The usual. Lots of associates mansplaining, think they know the law better than me."

Not so different from the *Warship* forum, I guess. "That sucks. Can you fire them?"

Mom laughs. "If I fired every man who behaved like that, I'd have no lawyers left at the firm." She changes the subject. "I see the rat project has made its way to your room." She walks over to my bureau, where Lint's cage now sits. Lint is curled up in a ball in the corner, ignoring her much comfier strawberry bed.

"Yeah, I thought I'd keep her in here. You know. So I can keep an eye on her. For school."

Mom bends, hands on her knees, so she has a clear view into Lint's cage. "Has she finished the maze yet?"

"She keeps getting tripped up near the end." Stella keeps the maze at her place, so it's not like I can have Lint practice at night. I think she keeps it so I don't feel like I have to pick Lint up to train her. Not gonna lie, I appreciate it. "The project is over in a couple weeks. I hope she figures it out soon."

Mom presses her finger between the bars; Lint sniffs at it. "Yes, hello, sweetie."

"Yeah. She is sweet."

My phone vibrates on my desk.

Brandon: Hey, what source did you cite for the English paper?

I blink at the text. Paper?

Oh no.

"Well, I'll let you get back to work." Mom kisses the top of my head before making her way into the hallway.

This six-page English paper I've been putting off for a month? Yeah, it's due tomorrow.

None yet. I'll report back. I totally forgot.

Remind me again who you paid to make you a valedictorian contender?

I send him a middle finger emoji, then get to work writing this thing as fast as humanly possible. My laptop dings.

CaptainJillsBFF22: omg. I just had the WORST day.

I type **can't chat, super busy, forgot about this massive paper**

due tomorrow, but I can't make myself press Send. The truth is, I want to talk to her. And I don't want her to have bad days. So I delete it and type something else instead.

CERanger11: what happened?
CaptainJillsBFF22: I had a crush on this guy who turned out to be a total douche.
CERanger11: Well you probably dodged a bullet.
CaptainJillsBFF22: Honestly, and don't judge me—I thought he was YOU lol.
CERanger11: glad to know total douches remind you of me lol
CaptainJillsBFF22: lmao no! I found out this guy was into W7 so I assumed. Oh well.

Not going to lie, I'm pretty flattered she was looking for me.

CERanger11: Who is it? I probably know the guy, I mean our school isn't THAT big . . .
CaptainJillsBFF22: It doesn't matter. I was just disappointed.
CERanger11: Well then I'm glad it wasn't me. I don't want to disappoint you
CaptainJillsBFF22: You don't!! ☺

For some reason, her message makes my palms sweaty. I manage to bang out a few English paragraphs that, let's be honest, are a garbage fire.

CaptainJillsBFF22: I'm also kind of bummed.

CaptainJillsBFF22: /annoyed

CaptainJillsBFF22: My mom keeps making passive aggressive comments about how I don't have a prom date and UGH. Idk.

CaptainJillsBFF22: I was thinking of asking that guy, but not anymore!

I start to type **I'd love to go to prom with you** but stop. What the hell is wrong with me? I barely know this girl. She could be some weirdo at school I wouldn't want to be caught dead with.

CERanger11: I'm sorry. If it helps, I don't have a date for prom either.

CaptainJillsBFF22: at least I won't be the only one there without a date lol

CERanger11: You excited for Sci-Con?

CaptainJillsBFF22: YES! I can't wait. Even though I never got my boots ☹

CERanger11: You going barefoot?

CaptainJillsBFF22: haha no, that floor is disgusting. I'm probably just going to wear sandals or something and hope the judges don't notice

CERanger11: I bet Jill has some kickass sandals

CaptainJillsBFF22: So, I was thinking. Since we're officially meeting IRL at Sci-Con in TWO WEEKS(!!!), maybe we should get to know each other a little better first?

CERanger11: Sure. What do you want to know?

CaptainJillsBFF22: Two truths and a lie? GO.

I think for a moment.

CERanger11: 1. My favorite foods are all cheese related: cheesecake (no strawberries or weird stuff on top), brie (best barbecued with garlic), and grilled cheese (classic: white bread, butter, American cheese). 2. I played the violin in elementary school. 3. I hiked Mount Washington last summer.

CaptainJillsBFF22: Hmmm . . . violin??

CERanger11: Yep! I did play the bass, though. It was taller than I was. Your turn!

CaptainJillsBFF22: Aaron would 100% approve of your food list, btw.

CaptainJillsBFF22: 1. My favorite movie is Coco (the Disney movie). 2. My favorite food is salmon. 3. I worked as a lifeguard for two summers.

CERanger11: I'm going to say . . . salmon?

CaptainJillsBFF22: Ding ding ding! I hate salmon

CERanger11: So, Coco?

CaptainJillsBFF22: IT'S A BRILLIANT FILM DON'T JUDGE ME

CERanger11: I'm judging you.

CERanger11: (kidding)

CaptainJillsBFF22: Okay new game. Top three things you want to accomplish in your life. And go.

The first thing that pops into my mind is become valedictorian, but for some reason, I can't make myself type it. It feels wrong.

CERanger11: I want to travel to every continent. Spend a summer backpacking in Ireland. And publish a graphic novel.

CaptainJillsBFF22: Omg. I love that. I would totally read one of your graphic novels.

CERanger11: Haha thanks. So I'll at least sell one copy. Maybe two, if my mom buys one.

CaptainJillsBFF22: Speaking of traveling to every continent: top three places you'd want to visit!

CERanger11: that's impossible, I want to see everywhere

CERanger11: Also, you cheated and asked two questions in a row.

A photo in a tarnished frame on my dresser shows my parents, Trevor, and me in front of the Colosseum ten years ago. My dad freaked out at the hotel front desk because there was a mosquito in our room. I remember, even as a little kid, looking out the window and pretending I had nothing to do with that jerk shouting at everyone in English.

CaptainJillsBFF22: WAITING . . .

CERanger11: Tokyo, for sure. Alaska. And I'd love to go back to Rome—I haven't been since I was a little kid.

CaptainJillsBFF22: I'd love to go to Rome. Or anywhere, really.

CERanger11: What's your favorite vacation place??

CaptainJillsBFF22: uhhhhh . . . Idk? I've never been on one.

We always took family vacations, often once in the summer

and again over February break. It's been a few years, though. Our last trip was back to Disney World right before Trevor went to college. My mom spent the whole trip taking work calls and arguing with my dad. We haven't gone away together since.

CERanger11: Really?
CaptainJillsBFF22: Once when I was a kid, we stayed at a Motel 6 out by the coast for a night, that was cool.
CaptainJillsBFF22: I'm gonna tell you a secret, okay?
CERanger11: . . . should I be afraid?
CaptainJillsBFF22: lol . . . MAYBE.
CaptainJillsBFF22: Okay this is awkward. But here's my dirty little secret: my family is poor. Like, food stamp poor. We slept on my aunt's floor for a month when I was five.

I shift in my chair. That's not what I was expecting her to say.

CERanger11: Why is that a "dirty" secret?
CaptainJillsBFF22: Oh, you know. Poverty is weird. It's this thing that affects so many people but no one wants to talk about it because money is such an awkward topic to bring up. But then they treat you differently for it anyway. Or try to pretend class differences don't even exist, like that making us pay $50 for a yearbook affects everyone equally.
CaptainJillsBFF22: I'm not ashamed of it or anything, I just . . . I don't know.
CaptainJillsBFF22: I'm going to break out of it, though. I want to be the first person in my family to go to

college. To prove I can. And that it doesn't matter where I came from—I deserve this.

CERanger11: Money can't buy happiness.

At least, it didn't for my family. All the trips in the world didn't make my parents love each other.

CaptainJillsBFF22: And that's how I know you've never been poor. 😉

I put my hands on the keys to type, but nothing comes out. She's right, of course, but it's weird to admit.

CaptainJillsBFF22: Money would solve a LOT of my problems. Having to choose between gas and groceries really sucks. The fact that my mom skips doctors' appointments because she doesn't have good insurance gives me anxiety all the time.

CERanger11: I'm sorry. I didn't mean anything by it.

CaptainJillsBFF22: I know.

–♥–

At midnight, I'm two pages deep, and yawns keep ripping through me. Yep, this one's going to end in an all-nighter. Nice job, Clarke.

I rub my eyes and tiptoe downstairs for some coffee. A dark living room greets me, the ticking pendulum of the grandfather clock the only noise breaking through the silence.

I'm starting up the Keurig in the kitchen when the back door creaks open. I whirl around to find my dad, still in his work suit, coming in from the garage. He was clearly not expecting to see me here.

"Oh. Wesley. What are you doing up?" There's a weird slur in his words.

I kind of stare at him a moment. "Just getting some coffee."

"Up late studying?"

Mom saunters into the kitchen. Her eyes turn to ice. "It's after midnight."

"Oh." Dad snorts. "I didn't realize I needed to ask your permission to get a drink with the guys."

"Sounds like more than one," she counters. "You do realize you have a family here, right? Your oldest son was home for a week last month and you couldn't even stick around for one meal with him."

"I'm sorry I work hard for our family and provide all these nice things you're so ungrateful for."

She throws her hands up. "Yes, you're clearly the only successful person in this house. Not like I made partner in the largest law firm in New England before I was thirty, whatever."

Their voices get louder when I round the corner, slipping unnoticed back toward my room.

I take a swig of my coffee, barely tasting the heat as it scorches my tongue.

When *Warship Seven* ended, I was signature 22,816 on the petition for a second season. I hit Refresh on that thing about that many times per day, watching the number tick higher and higher. When it hit half a million, they sent it to the execs at SFFStream and never heard back. Like, we weren't even acknowledged. They just moved right on to their next show on a different streaming service—a giant deal with Disney+. Sometimes I feel like that's the only reason they let *Warship* drop.

I felt invisible. Like my name on the list was meaningless, and this show that had been my home meant nothing but money to its creators.

That's kind of how I feel now. I live in a house glued together by my parents' futile wish for successful children. But I'm invisible. And my home is just a hollow building shined and polished and molded into the perfect façade of a happy family.

For some reason, I'm struck with a memory of sitting in my room last summer, the show streaming on repeat from my laptop, my eyes bleary. When the voices downstairs got too loud, I made the volume louder, until all that was left was the *Revelry* crew and me.

My body feels numb. Like a rock could come flying through the window and smash me in the skull and I wouldn't even feel it.

My legs propel my body upstairs and down the dark hallway like a puppet on strings. I collapse back into my desk chair.

CaptainJillsBFF22: okay, so f/m/k, Revelry crew—go.

I stare at the screen. I don't know what makes me type it, but I do.

CERanger11: sometimes I think I'm the only reason my parents don't get divorced. And I hate it.

The moment I hit Send, I realize it's the first time I've ever said it to anyone. I squeeze my eyes shut.

CaptainJillsBFF22: OMG what?

CaptainJillsBFF22: what makes you think that??
CaptainJillsBFF22: I'm sorry, Aaron2

My name's Wesley, I want to type. But I can't make my fingers hit the keys. So I type something else instead.

CERanger11: They've always kind of bickered. But now they have full-on fights. The only time they agree on anything is when they're dictating how I'm supposed to spend my life.
CaptainJillsBFF22: Oh no . . .

My knee bounces against the leg of the desk. I can't believe I'm saying all this. But once I start, I can't stop. It just keeps pouring out.

CERanger11: It's like I'm caught in a hurricane all the time.
CaptainJillsBFF22: I'm so, so sorry.
CERanger11: I think the moment I leave for college, and they'll be alone in the house, it'll be over.

I blink hard, and realize for the first time how wet my eyes are.

CERanger11: I don't know what to do.
CERanger11: Everything is going to change and I feel like shit. Like maybe I could have stopped it or something idk.

Maybe it's why I haven't told them about Columbia yet. I don't want to be the domino that pushes over all the others, toppling the whole thing.

CaptainJillsBFF22: It sucks. I'm so sorry.

CaptainJillsBFF22: But if anything happens, it wasn't your fault.

CaptainJillsBFF22: People grow apart, and change, and realize they aren't right together. That's on them. Not you.

She's right. I know she's right. But it doesn't make the hollow pit in my stomach feel any better.

CERanger11: Thanks.

I write the rest of my paper, and get it done an hour before sunrise, but I don't comprehend a single word of it.

23 STELLA

LINT THE RAT AND HER MAZE ADVENTURES

> ***Trial 1: March 21.*** *Got stuck in first corner.*
> ***Trial 11: March 31.*** *Made it halfway through and seemed to give up?* NO QUITTERS ON THIS TEAM, LINT.
> ***Trial 16: April 1.*** *Lint ate the sweet potato at the beginning of the maze and wouldn't budge until we gave her more. Not my favorite April Fools' prank.*
> ***Trial 27: April 20.*** *Lint got to the very last turn and then turned around and went back to the beginning.* ***Facepalm***
> ***Trial 36: May 1.*** *If this rat hangs out in the middle corridor for another ten minutes today, I'm going to scream.*
> ***Trial 38: May 7.*** *Okay, they can't fail* ***us*** *if she doesn't do it, right?* C'MON, LINT, DON'T LET US DOWN!!

"I think she's messing with us." Wesley's face melts into his hand.

My butt is growing numb against this bio lab stool. "Come on, girl. You can do it." I pluck her out of the middle of the maze and stick her plump, fuzzy body back at the beginning, taking a moment to stroke her soft fur.

At least three other teams finished the project weeks ago and are now hanging out around one of the lab tables, watching a video on someone's phone; every few minutes, they simultaneously burst out laughing.

"This is trial forty-two, Friday, May fourteenth," I say with exasperation into my phone camera, then point it toward the maze.

Lint looks up at me, as if to say, "You've got to be kidding, I'm not doing it again."

Wesley pops open a bag of chips under the lab table, being as conspicuous as humanly possible. He holds out the bag to me, but I shake my head. "You're not fooling anyone, Clarke."

"So, Devin. My little cousin." He takes a mouthful of chips.

"Cookie dough with gummy bears and the cool haircut." I keep the phone trained on Lint. Watch—with my luck, the one time she completes it will be the time my camera is off and we fail anyway.

"Yes. Him. He has a date to his middle school spring dance, and I don't have a date for prom. Tell me, Stick, how is that fair?"

"A date?" My nose wrinkles. "Isn't he like ten?"

"Thirteen. But that's not the point."

"Why don't you ask someone, then? Like Laura." The words taste sour in my mouth, and I don't know why. "Unless she's already going with Collin."

"She is." He gives an exaggerated shrug that's trying a little too hard to be indifferent.

"Who cares? I'm going alone, too. Well, I guess I'm not really going alone—I'm going with Dahlia, but I'll probably be tricycle-wheeling it because I'm assuming Brandon's going to ask her."

"He will. Soon. He's got some big promposal or something planned—I don't know, I think it's tacky."

"Seriously?" I throw my pencil down, furiously tapping Wesley's arm. "Oh my God, she'll be so excited. I need details."

"Yeah, you're not allowed to tell her, though." He mimics zipping his mouth shut. "Because I wasn't supposed to tell you."

"Oh, I'm absolutely telling her." I wave my phone at him. "The second we're done recording, I am texting her immediately."

"You wouldn't dare."

"Oh, I would."

"Can't text without a phone." Before I can process, he grabs my phone straight out of my hands.

I reach back for it, but he holds it over his head. "Seriously? You know we're filming, right?"

"If you want it back, you have to agree not to spill Brandon's big plan. And you have to admit that I am the rightful valedictorian."

"My mother taught me not to tell lies." I'm climbing over him, practically in his lap, and still can't reach it. Dammit, I hate being short. "You're such an ass."

"It's really only one simple sentence, and you get your phone back." He hasn't stopped smirking, which is awkward because I'm standing between his legs right now.

I lunge, reaching as high as I can, and my cheek brushes against his. Our faces are less than an inch apart. I pull back, and for half a second, his brown eyes lock with mine. My heart thuds. I quickly jerk away, and so does he.

The corner of his iPhone pokes out of his pocket. "How about this?" In one swipe, I grab his phone and hold it an arm's length away. "Hand over the phone and no one gets hurt." I wave his phone like a flag.

He grins. "Or what?"

"Or—" My eyes dart to the maze exit, where Lint sits, innocently watching us. "Oh my God. No way."

Wesley catches on. "No way," he bellows, and the whole classroom looks at us. "Lint finished the maze."

"She did it!" I'm bouncing up and down on the balls of my feet. Without thinking, I throw my arms around Wesley.

He wraps me in a hug, and in half a second, we both realize, and our arms slink back to our sides.

"Stella! Wesley!" Mr. Hardwicke's stern voice breaks the silence. "Have we forgotten that this is a classroom? Not some sort of revelry."

I wish it was the Revelry.

"I wish it was the *Revelry*," Wesley mutters.

I toss a glance at him, but he's looking at Mr. Hardwicke. "Sorry. Our rat finished the maze."

"Yes, come see!" I pick up Lint and place her back at the beginning of the maze. "C'mon, sweetheart, do it again."

Mr. Hardwicke strolls over with his hands behind his back, watching as Lint slithers through the maze, properly this time. "Well done. Excellent work. Make sure you have a video to turn in, and that you've both submitted evidence of your trials."

"You got it," Wesley replies.

I nod, scooping up Lint and placing her on my shoulder. "That video is a hot mess," I whisper.

Wesley laughs. "We can take another one."

"Speaking of your hard work, I spoke to the principal yesterday afternoon." Mr. Hardwicke gives Lint a pat. "For the first time ever, our valedictorian will come down to your final exam scores."

Well, I was afraid of that.

"Usually valedictorian is a clear shot, but in this case, you're so evenly matched that it would be a tie without finals. So study hard."

He turns to walk away.

"Wait," Wesley blurts out. "Why couldn't it be a tie? If we both earned it, why couldn't we both be valedictorian?"

The whole class is casually pretending not to eavesdrop at this point.

"Ah, in the words of the Highlander"—Hardwicke sticks up his pointer finger—"there can be only one." He walks away.

I busy myself with Lint, not looking at Wesley, who suddenly seems very interested in repairing the maze walls.

It's all coming down to our exams. Everything is on the line. Sci-Con is this weekend, and after that, I have to throw everything into studying.

From somewhere, Kyle Nielsen groans, still trying to persuade his rat to make it through. "I told you not to pair the two smartest kids in class together."

"Kyle, my dear, dear friend." Wesley presses his hand over his heart. "Shut up."

–♥–

Someone uploaded the best new video edit to YouTube. It's the Lewton love scene, on repeat, for fifteen straight minutes. And honestly, the original scene was way too short, clocking in at like ten seconds, so this loop is amazing. I'm laughing at the fact that someone had this much free time, but also grateful that this fandom cares about injustices like this and worked to lengthen it. I wonder what Leigh would think if she found this clip. Just kidding, she's said herself she's found dirty fanfics on here and texted them to Ethan. They are friendship goals.

My mind jumps to Wesley, and practically climbing on top

of him today. I quickly shake it off. Ew. No. The Lewton scene did *not* make my mind go there. So wrong.

AP Bio rat maze paper and smutty YouTube videos: Friday night of champions. I mean, I have to wake up early tomorrow to catch the bus for Sci-Con, so it's not like I can be out late anyway. I paid a lot for this ticket; I'm going to be waiting at the door the second the arena opens.

Tomorrow I meet Aaron2. The thought makes my pulse race. What if he's someone I don't like? Or someone who thinks I'm a total loser and wants nothing to do with me? What if he blows me off? What if it's super awkward?

I scroll to the video's comments and add my own.

CaptainJillsBFF22: Dear OP: thank you for your service

My bedroom door swings open. "Hey." Bridget stops dead. "Are you watching porn in here?"

I glance at the computer screen, where Aaron and Jill are hard-core making out, sans shirts. "Shit." I minimize the window, and Bridget snickers.

"Please, I don't care." She saunters into my room wearing her movie theater uniform and carrying a large box wrapped in *So fun, you're one!* balloon-printed wrapping paper. "Got you a present."

I look from the package to my sister. "That's very nice, but you're like seventeen years late to my first birthday party."

"Yeah, sorry about the paper. I had this lying around from Gwen's party. I promise it's not *The Very Hungry Caterpillar* like I bought for her."

"I love that book, though." Even after reading it to Gwen

about a zillion times last summer, to the point where I have all the words memorized—that caterpillar is *insatiable*. I slide off my desk chair. "What is it?" When we were kids, Bridget and I used to give each other "gifts" all the time—usually finger paintings and other works of fine art. Hers were always better than mine. "Giant bag of day-old popcorn?" Having an older sister who works at the theater is pretty awesome because she brings home cases of that stuff.

"You have to open it and find out." She thrusts the box into my hands, a gleam in her eyes. "Open it. Open it."

I slide the wrapping paper off the box and peel open the lid. My heart jumps. Brand-new black Captain Jill Brighton boots lie in a nest of tissue paper. They're the shiny new versions of the pair I saw in the store—the ones that were too expensive to order. "My boots!"

"These are the right ones?"

"Yes!" I rip them out of the box and slide them over my green polka-dot socks. "Oh my God, look at them!"

Bridget squeals. "I love it. They'll be amazing with your cosplay."

My enthusiasm drops a notch. "Wait, these were like eighty bucks."

"You're worth it." She shrugs. "I had some extra cash."

"But you need this money." I start to take the boots off. "I can't accept these."

"Too late! No give-backs." She throws her hands up. "I got them for you, and I better see a ton of pictures of you wearing them at Sci-Con or I'm going to riot."

"But . . . you can't afford this."

"Stella Catherine Greene." She holds my upper arms, and

our height difference is apparent. "It's fine. I wanted to get them for you. I'm an adult, and I can handle my own money."

No you can't. You've got a kid. And you're already working two jobs and still living with Mom.

I open my mouth to protest, but Bridget's mastered the mom stare, and I slink back into my desk chair. "That's what I thought," she says. "Enjoy them. Have fun at the con."

"Okay." I force a smile. They're really amazing boots. And they look just like Jill's. But I can't help feeling guilty.

"Are you going by yourself?" She takes a seat on the edge of my bed, chewing at her purple-painted fingernails.

"Well . . ." I rub my upper arm, still examining my awesome boots in the mirror. "Kind of?"

Her brows shoot up. "Kind of? I can try and get a few hours off to come with you, if you don't want to go alone. I definitely have to leave by five, though."

"There's this guy." I spin around in my desk chair, watching everything blur around me. "I met him on the *Warship* forum."

"Whoa, wait, back up." Bridget slices her hand through the air and stops my chair mid-spin. "Excuse me? Who?"

"This is why I didn't want to tell you."

"I hope you're not doing this to get Mom off your back about not having a prom date."

"I swear I'm not."

"You realize it's probably some forty-year-old pervert, right?"

"I don't think so."

"What if he tries to lure you into his basement?"

"I think that would be hard to do in the middle of the Wells Arena."

Bridget gives me a look. "You know what I mean."

"We've been chatting a ton, and just . . . I don't know. He

seems really cool." Would it be weird to say I have a crush on a stranger? But I guess he's not a stranger—at least he won't be, when I figure out which GCMHS senior I've been chatting with. "And, um. I think he goes to my high school?"

"You're meeting in a public place, I hope?"

"Yes, Mother." I roll my eyes. "We're meeting in front of the big clock at twelve forty-five, right before the cosplay contest at one." My heart flutters just thinking about it. "We think we have a better shot of winning if we enter together, since our characters are a super-popular ship in the show."

"Well, just be careful, okay?" She stands to leave. "Text me if he catfished you, and I'll come down there and kick his ass."

"Oh, don't worry." I whip out my replica Captain Jill pistol. "I'll be armed the whole time."

Tomorrow. Tomorrow I meet my Sergeant Aaron Lewis.

WARSHIP SEVEN: Episode Sixteen
"Light in a Dark Place"

Description: "Jill and Aaron are taken as hostages on the pirate ship, and must fight to survive another day."

SCENE CLIP: Prisoners of the pirate crew, CAPTAIN JILL BRIGHTON and SERGEANT AARON LEWIS are led onto the pirate ship, blindfolded, their hands chained together. At least twenty dirty members of the pirate crew line the hallway, jeering at the prisoners.

PIRATE1: Big bounty today, boys. [rubs his hands together] A CE ranger and a fugitive ship's captain in one haul? Payday.

[AARON tries to take out the nearest pirate with a headbutt, but it's sloppy, and he misses.]

PIRATE2: He's a lively one. [laughs, jolting AARON in the back with a cattle prod; he jerks forward with a grunt] The lady's not much of a threat.

JILL: [muttering] I'll show them a threat.

AARON: [also keeping his voice low] You know they outnumber us ten to one, right?

JILL: I've taken on bigger threats. Better-looking ones, too.

AARON: They're going to kill you.

JILL: They're welcome to try.

[The pirates roughly shove AARON and JILL forward, where they stumble down a short spiral staircase before finding themselves in the moldy basement of the ship. A bulletproof glass wall forms two tiny individual cells coated in grime and mold. Bits of trash coat the filthy floor.]

PIRATE1: Welcome to your new mansion, Cescum. Captain. [He rips their blindfolds off.]

AARON: [wrinkling his nose] You know, it's smellier than my usual mansions.

PIRATE2: Sorry we forgot to clean it after our last guests. They didn't last long, though. [Laughter roars throughout the pirates as JILL and AARON are unchained and shoved into individual cells. One of the pirates slams the heavy door on JILL's cell, locking her inside.]

AARON: One more thing. [He swings his fist at one of the pirates, but is easily overpowered. The pirates throw punches at him, shoving the CE ranger to the floor and raining punches and kicks on him. JILL looks on in horror from her own cell.]

PIRATE1: [spits on AARON, curled on the dirty floor] That'll teach you, Cescum. [He slams the cell door, and the pirates filter out of the basement, their cheers and laughter growing quieter until they're all back in the main part of the ship.]

JILL: [sinks to the floor in her cell, slamming the back of her head against the glass]

AARON: [Bloody and bruised, he forces himself to a sitting position and reaches around in his mouth, pulling out the destroyed comm chip. He frowns, slouching against the opposite wall.] So, Captain. What do we do now?

24 WESLEY

I can tell it's Sci-Con weekend, because I'm wearing a full battle suit and space helmet, and I was not the strangest-dressed person on the bus. I slept in a bit and decided to arrive at noon, and I'm right on the dot.

Jill2 is here, somewhere. I get to meet her. Finally.

My pulse is ticking out of my skin. I'm glancing in every direction, searching for her.

If it's Laura, what do I even say?

I need to get myself together. It's probably not her. She probably *does* go to Huntington. Maybe she lied about her school twice.

"Hey, it's Sergeant Aaron Lewis," some guy in an Aragorn costume shouts as I step off the bus in front of the Wells Arena. "Keeping the galaxy safe."

I tap my three fingers to both shoulders, the Central Elite salute, and he repeats it to me. Nerds are awesome.

The plastic helmet covering my head seals in all the heat, and I'm pretty sure my hair is practically bathing in sweat right now. Warmth from so many bodies smothers me the second I step into the large covered stadium. Vendor stands line the room in several long rows, and the buzz of chatter from a thousand people is amplified in the open space. A stage sits at the front, over which a large red-and-white banner proclaims, *Welcome to Sci-Con: Celebrating Sixteen Years*.

The second I'm through the door, I whip my helmet off.

"Aaron! My love!" A thirtysomething woman wearing a Michele Cordova costume runs over to me. "Take a photo with me?"

I grin. "Anything for you, Michele."

Not going to lie, it's pretty awesome that everyone here recognizes my costume. Some old guy at the Nashua bus station where I connected this morning shouted, "Who are you supposed to be? Neil Armstrong?" at me, so this is a refreshing change.

I shoulder through a crowd containing a Daenerys Targaryen, a Bucky Barnes, and a kid carrying at least five different lightsabers, until the giant clock comes into view at the front of the room, near the stage.

I don't know why I'm so nervous. We're just going to hang out, and then have some awkward encounters at school until graduation, and then I'll never see her again—unless it really is Laura. But it's weird. I've started looking forward to our chats. And this? This makes it real.

I walk down the row of vendors, passing a middle-aged man selling his fantasy book series and a woman with a collection of handmade necklaces, each one boasting a different slogan from a different fandom. I take a second to peruse.

Winter is coming.

Always.

One ring to rule them all.

May the force be with you.

You can't take the sky from me.

I stop at the gold circle with a CE logo engraved into the top. *I don't suffer judgment from small minds.* Is it weird to buy a gift for a stranger? I don't know if she likes necklaces, or if she's allergic to whatever metal this is, or if she would think that's way too weird of a gesture after just meeting someone.

The metal is cold against my skin when I pick it up.

"How much is this?" I ask, holding it out.

"Ten dollars," the woman replies.

I give her the money and pocket the necklace. If I like the girl and she's not totally weirded out by me, I'll give it to her.

Noise buzzes around me as I make my way to the big clock, but all I can hear is my pulse thudding in my ears.

Stop being so anxious! It's literally just some random Warshipper from the forum. It's fine.

The crowd thins the closer I get to the stage, ironically. Everyone is either browsing vendors or finishing up their noon panels. I check the schedule on the Sci-Con app, where I starred the two panels I want to attend, at three and four. Ethan Martone is on the *Warship* one; then I'm planning on grabbing his autograph at five.

A single tone rings out, signaling 12:45 on the dot. I slide my helmet back on. Hopefully the plastic will hide how awkward and sweaty I am.

I cautiously step behind the clock to get a good view, watching.

A girl stands alone with her back to me, and I know immediately it's my Jill2. Brown hair twists into a knot on her head.

My heart sinks a little. She's too short to be Laura.

The *Revelry* crest is displayed proudly on the back of her jacket, and she's got some really awesome black boots. She leans to the side, one hand on her hip, and there's something familiar about her.

I take a deep breath and adjust my helmet before stepping in front of the clock.

My stomach plunges.

No.

Oh God.

Is this some kind of sick prank?

Stella Greene is staring back at me.

"Hey." She smiles sweetly. "Are you Aaron2?"

My voice catches in my throat. I can't be here. "Yeah. Hey." I force the words out in a voice that isn't my own, already muffled by my helmet. No. It's not possible. "Sti—Jill2?"

It's like the entire universe just came crashing down around me. It can't be Stella. The charming, fun, *Warship*-loving girl on the forum is *not* the stuffy, uptight perfectionist Stella Greene.

"Yeah." She gives me a weird look. "Don't you . . . recognize me? I feel kind of awkward now."

Too much. I wish I didn't recognize you.

I kind of gape at her, which she can't see, because my whole face is hidden behind my helmet.

She gives me a sheepish look. "Are . . . you going to take the helmet off?"

"I . . . I lied about my school," I say quickly, because there's no way I'm about to tell her who I really am. "My brother went to GCMHS. I go to St. Luke's."

The smile melts off her face. "The fancy private school?"

"Yep. But everything else was the truth, I swear. I'm a senior, I'm graduating next month, I'm probably going to be valedictorian."

"I'm going to be valedictorian too."

Okay, that one stings.

"Oh. That's cool."

We stand awkwardly for a moment. Now the necklace Stella wears every day makes sense—I had thought it was a cross, some religious thing or something. Never in a million years did I think she was a Warshipper. "I love your cosplay," I say suddenly.

"I love yours too!" She reaches out and touches the sigil on my chest. "This is awesome."

"Thanks. I sewed it on myself."

"And the helmet looks awesome."

"You found it for me."

"I have good taste." She winks. "By the way, I guess I can tell you now, my name is Stella."

"I'm . . ." A guy in a Captain America costume drifts past us. "Steve." I don't know why I've never noticed how pretty she is. Is it weird that I find her super attractive when she's dressed as a fictional space captain? What does that say about me?

"You're . . . different from how I imagined," I say truthfully. Because I imagined she wouldn't look like my archnemesis.

"In a good way, or . . ."

"A good way."

"Well, you're different from how I imagined, too. Mostly because I imagined I'd see your face at some point."

"Aaron Lewis always keeps his helmet on. When he's not a prisoner on your ship."

"I—"

"Good afternoon, fans and friends!" A man's booming voice echoes from the stage directly behind us, and we whirl around. He's wearing a top hat, like he jumped out of a 1930s magic show, and a *Millennium Falcon* necktie; it's a pretty bizarre combination. "I hope you're all having a great time. At this point, I'd like to ask anyone entering our cosplay contest to make their way down to the stage."

I release a heavy breath. This guy just became my new hero.

"Never mind, you can tell me all that later." Stella grabs my arm. "Should we get into the contest?"

"Lead the way."

We weave through the crowds pouring into the stage area, passing people in all sorts of costumes and cosplays. I recognize some of them. There's a pink-haired girl I think is from some anime, and about a bazillion Jon Snows and Reys, that singing guy from *The Witcher*, Sailor Moon, Doctor Who, Harley Quinn, Captain Marvel, four women dressed as the team from *Ghostbusters*, plus a Malcolm Reynolds and some guy in a Cylon suit. One dude made a pretty convincing Iron Man outfit out of cardboard boxes. Some guy in a Deadpool costume is giving a spirited stand-up routine to anyone who will listen. A little girl in a Gemma costume flexes her muscles in the center of a circle of adults, who cheer for her. Several people have already broken out in duels using their respective swords, pistols, or whatever else their character wields. One guy is doing all sorts of spin moves with his plastic lightsaber, and I'm worried no one told him this isn't a real duel. There's even a Jack Sparrow, randomly throwing his arms around people and offering them swigs of whatever's in the giant jug he's carting around. Several other characters from fandoms I don't know also walk through the contest area, all wearing intriguing homemade cosplay.

"We've got some great costumes here," the broad-shouldered announcer says, surveying the dance floor. "It's going to be a fun afternoon. Hey—I see you over there, with the lightsaber. You could put an eye out with that thing." The crowd laughs, and the lightsaber dude bows.

Spectators from the con who aren't entering the contest—some in regular clothes, and others in fandom T-shirts and cosplay—slowly trickle toward the stage and dance floor to watch. One guy in a Chewbacca costume makes a loud Wookiee growl, quieting everyone down.

"Okay, here are the rules." The man holds up a finger. "First,

I'll tell you this year's theme—are you ready?" Half-hearted applause ripples through the crowd. "This year's theme is . . . masquerade! That's right, friends, it's a grand old cosplay masquerade."

Simultaneous groans and cheers sound around us. Stella clasps her hands together, a wide grin spreading across her face. Seeing her smile makes a hint of one twitch across my own face.

"That sounds super fun," she whispers at me. "I can whip out my Captain Jill dance moves."

"Does Captain Jill *have* dance moves?"

"Oh absolutely." She gently elbows me in the side. "Didn't you read my fic?"

That long novel of a fanfic? I skimmed the first page. "Oh yeah, of course."

Now that I know Stella wrote it, I'm kind of impressed, but then I'm also not surprised. She probably color-coded it with a million different tabs before writing it down.

I can't imagine Aaron Lewis attending a masquerade. With anyone, but least of all Captain Jill. Screw that—I can't imagine *me*, Wesley Clarke, attending a masquerade with Stella Greene.

I glance at the exit, across the room, on the other side of hundreds of people. How awful would it be if I peaced out right about now? My hands twitch at my sides.

"First things first, we're going to have a masquerade dance—but remember, you must stay in character the entire time." The announcer sticks up his finger. "Our anonymous judges will be walking among you, tracking your characters. And for the winner, we've got an amazing prize package from our sponsors, at a value of approximately two hundred dollars."

"What do you think is in the prize box?" Stella whispers.

"A lifetime supply of doughnuts."

She bursts out a laugh. "That is worth way more than two hundred dollars."

"Depends how many you eat per day."

"Oh, with a free lifetime supply? I could eat a disgusting number of doughnuts."

"Ready?" The man nods to the deejay on the side of the stage, who cranks up some hip-hop song I've never heard before. "Remember—stay in character."

"Can you imagine a real masquerade with all the characters who are here today?" she asks.

"I'd love to see Aaron Lewis go up against Han Solo," I whisper back.

"Who do you think would win?"

"Aaron. Definitely."

A guy in an R2D2 costume rolls back and forth to the beat. One woman dressed as a cantina performer from *Star Wars* just stands still, playing her plastic instrument. A woman in a Princess Tiana costume spins around the dance floor in a glamorous green ballgown. A Batman and a Daenerys Targaryen have found each other and started grinding on the dance floor, apparently making their own crossover fic right before our eyes.

"How would Aaron dance to this?" I mutter under my breath.

"Awkwardly." Stella crosses her arms and sways to the music, keeping her face expressionless. "Jill would be like this, I think."

"She would not be that stiff."

"She would when you're around."

I start moving to the music, the way I picture the sergeant dancing.

Stella bursts out laughing. "Oh my God, Aaron would not sway awkwardly like that. He'd be ripping up the dance floor."

"I'm pretty sure he'd be the world's worst dancer."

"Let's switch it up a bit," the man says into the microphone, and the music changes to something classical—like a traditional ball.

Stella grins. "I don't think they have this kind of music on the *Revelry*."

"I bet they have it in CE training, though."

"Yes, all you prim and proper Central Elite rangers"—she does a quick spin on the dance floor—"would absolutely dance to this."

The music changes, and this time, it's a remix of a Taylor Swift song.

Stella claps her hands. "Okay, I love this song."

I grin at her, even though she can't see it. "Yes, but would Jill?"

"Jill absolutely would love Taylor Swift. No doubts here." She starts jamming out to the song, waving her arms around and twisting side to side.

It's kind of ridiculous.

It's kind of adorable.

"Jill is quite the dancer."

"Quite the awesome dancer," she says, pulling an invisible rope like a fishing line to reel me in. I've never seen her like this before. It's almost like I'm meeting a whole new version of Stella—forget Jill2, this is Stella2.

Or maybe she's always been like this. Maybe I've just never noticed.

I move my shoulders in time with the beat, keeping it contained like Aaron would.

"Aaron is *not* that uptight." Stella grabs my hands. "Come on." She tugs me toward the center of the dance floor, and we start spinning around the room. A few people part to give us space, forming a sloppy circle around us.

"I don't know how to dance to this," I call over the music.

"Just go with it."

She twirls under my arm, and I do a really bad attempt at dipping her that results in both of us bursting into laughter.

"Spin move!" I tuck her into my chest suddenly and then spin her out, and she does this silly move to get back over to me.

"Okay, so they said we have to stay in character—what about episode-fifteen Jill and Aaron?" she asks.

I immediately reach for my plastic pistol, but she's too quick, already pointing hers at my head. We dodge and shoot, our fake pistols making high-pitched *pew!* noises. We somehow manage to do this all while still dancing to the music.

"Episode sixteen!" I retort.

Stella puts on a sad face and collapses to the ground; I sit beside her, our shoulders pressed together, our arms still dancing weakly.

My pulse kicks up a notch when I wonder what I'm supposed to do if Stella asks us to reenact episode twenty—the sex scene—when thankfully, she suggests something else.

"Episode nineteen?" Stella asks.

"You got it."

Simultaneously, we get up and sneak through the other dancers, pistols raised, dodging everyone else like they're the pirates who've captured us.

Stella spins and crouches in time with the music. I follow closely behind. Several other dancers have stopped to watch us, weaving around and being total pains in the ass to everyone else.

A dancer dressed like Harley Quinn steps back and accidentally rams her foot onto Stella's.

"I've been hit!" Stella grabs at her chest instead, just like where Jill got shot in the show, and falls to the floor.

"I'll save you!" I lower my voice to a whisper. "May I?" Stella nods. With one swift lift, I scoop her up and swing her over my shoulder, just like Aaron did to Jill, then dance back toward our original spot, Stella laughing the whole time. She's warm against me.

I set her down on the edge of the dance floor. Wavy brown hair has sprung free from her bun and now hangs loosely around her face, which is flushed pink.

"That was *epic,*" Stella says, through a laugh.

She's beautiful.

I'm horrified by my own thought.

"All right, we've got one last song for our masquerade," the deep voice booms over the microphone. "Are you ready for the last challenge?"

The music slows to a soft ballad.

Cosplayers rush around the dance floor to partner up. A Steve Rogers links his arms around the waist of a Bucky Barnes; a Jaime Lannister with a gold-painted glove pairs up with a Brienne of Tarth cosplayer who towers over him, and the Malcolm Reynolds makes a big deal of asking an Inara cosplayer to take his arm (she stays in character, asking if he washed it first). A couple of stormtroopers ignore the dancing and start prowling the parameters with their guns. There's the Jack Sparrow, wobbling around, cradling his jug of rum. The little girl dressed as Gemma hugs a plastic C0ndor to her chest, swaying around with him.

I swallow hard. Stella grinds her boot into the linoleum floor.

Before I can stop myself, I'm holding out my hand to her. "Would you like to dance?"

A nervous smile stretches across her face. "How could an illegal transport ship captain lower herself enough to dance with a member of the Central Elite?"

"What if I ask nicely?"

"Well, in that case, I don't think Jill, or I, could refuse." She slips her hand into mine, threading our fingers together. I lead her back into the center of the dance floor and wrap my right hand around her waist. Stella places hers behind my neck.

"I . . . would have worn my nicer CE uniform if I had known we'd be dancing."

Stella gasps in mock offense. "You Cescum are so unclassy." She lowers her voice to a whisper. "I do love the flight suit, though. I'd love it more if you took off the helmet . . ."

"The helmet you found online for me? Never."

I wonder if she can feel how hard my heart is pounding right now. Only a few inches and this damn helmet separate our faces. Stella's eyes lock onto mine, even though she can't tell. My plastic helmet suddenly feels so suffocating, and for some reason, I want more than anything to take it off.

We glide across the room, and weirdly, it's not awkward at all. Our steps just kind of fall together. Which is good, because I don't know the first thing about dancing.

I don't take my eyes off of hers.

This is wrong.

This is weird.

This is *right*.

My hands grow slick with sweat, but I don't untwine my fingers from hers.

After an eternity, the music slows, the room fading to silence. All I hear are my breaths, echoing against the plastic helmet.

Cheers and applause fill the room, indicating the end of the competition.

"All right, everyone, our judges have chosen a winner." Someone hands the announcer a folded piece of paper, like we're at the Oscars or something, and he unfolds it dramatically. "Cosplayer number thirty-one!"

The Jack Sparrow jumps into the air, then fist-pumps and starts staggering toward the stage to accept his winnings. Stella and I half-heartedly join the rest of the room in clapping for him. I'm kind of wondering if he's amazing at what he does or he actually *is* drunk.

"Oh well." Stella shrugs. "Maybe next year."

I jab my thumb over my shoulder. "I didn't think we could compete with that guy anyway. I mean, he's been carting that giant jug around all afternoon."

"How much do you bet it's actually rum?"

"Quite a lot, actually."

Stella grins at me. Her smile is so contagious. "Want to get some food?" She points to the snack bar.

"Yeah, definitely." My mind races. Food. That would mean eating, which means taking my helmet off. "Sure."

I need a plan. Stella can't know this is me. This isn't going anywhere, and she would be all weird about it at school on Monday. I stand in silence for a second as she starts walking toward the red-and-white-striped stand at the corner of the room. This really sucks.

"Hey, wait a second."

Stella pivots back toward me. "Yeah?"

"I got you this." I reach into my pocket and pull out the Jill necklace.

"Oh my God, I love it. I have this quote in a bumper sticker on the back of my laptop." She unclasps it. "Will you put it on me?"

Stella turns around, and I slide it around her neck, clasping it shut. My fingers brush her skin.

"How does it look?" she asks, turning toward me, rubbing the bronze pendant.

"Stunning," I say, and realize after I say it how corny that is. "Hey, I have to use the bathroom. Want to meet over at the stand after?" The words gum up in my throat. I hate this. I *hate* it.

"Sure!"

I watch her disappear into the crowd, making her way toward the food stand. Back in class, when Stella caught me staring at Laura, she said I was a terrible liar. But she was wrong; I've lied to my parents for months now. I'm a great liar. And sometimes I hate that about myself.

I turn around and walk straight out of the building, never looking back.

WARSHIP SEVEN: Episode Seventeen
"Captive Audience"

Description: "While the Revelry crew plot a rescue mission, Jill and Aaron find themselves at the mercy of their captors."

SCENE CLIP: JILL and AARON sit in their adjacent cells, stewing and angry.

JILL: This is your fault.

AARON: [laughs] My fault? You gave yourself up.

JILL: To save my crew. Which, by the way, wouldn't have been necessary if you'd stayed in your room in the first place.

AARON: You could have just let me leave.

JILL: I should have known better than to trust a CE. You Cescum are all the same.

AARON: I believe the correct term is Central Elite soldier.

JILL: Yes, very elite. Raiding poor planets for their water taxes is so honorable.

AARON: [sarcastically] You'd know a thing or two about honor. You could have killed me, one fewer CE in the world, but alas, the infamous Captain Jill Brighton is too honorable to shoot a man in the back.

JILL: [snorts] Yeah, well, at least one of us is.

[Footsteps pound, and three inebriated pirates stumble into the basement. JILL stands and watches them through the glass.]

PIRATE1: Look at 'em. Not so tough, are you, Lady Captain? [spits at the glass separating him from JILL's face]

JILL: I'm not Lady Captain. I'm just Captain.

PIRATE2: Ooooh, she's got a mouth on her.

PIRATE3: Big talker for someone behind glass.

JILL: You put me in here. [shrugs] Seems you're the one who's afraid of me.

PIRATE1: What do you say we teach her a lesson, eh, boys?

[The pirates grin as the leader fumbles with his keys, but AARON jumps to his feet.]

AARON: You know, they always told us at the CE academy that you pirates were ugly, but I thought it was a myth. I stand corrected.

PIRATE1: What did you say to me, boy?

AARON: Nothing. Nothing at all. You know, our general—you'd like him, big intimidating fellow—always warned us we'd be dealing with tricky pirates, but I think he was overreacting. See, you've got to have brains to be tricky.

PIRATE1: Think this boy needs a lesson of his own about respecting his superiors.

AARON: [laughs] Superiors?

PIRATE1: [whips out a different key and opens AARON'S cell] I'll teach you to disrespect me, boy. [The pirates gang up on AARON, punching and kicking him until he lies in a heap on the floor. They laugh and make their way back upstairs.]

JILL: [pressing her hands to the glass separating them] Are you all right?

AARON: [spits a wad of blood and saliva on the cell floor] Had worse.

25 STELLA

I swirl a spoon through my soggy cereal. A heavy sigh rips out of me from somewhere deep inside.

"Do you want to talk about it?" Dave asks from across the table. He bounces Gwen on his knee.

"Not really." How do I explain this, anyway? Some guy I met online ghosted me? "Just something stupid that happened at Sci-Con."

Dave's salt-and-pepper eyebrows shoot up. "Your internet boy?"

"Oh God, did Bridget tell you?"

"She was just worried."

"I'll give her something to worry about when she gets home."

I waited for him for thirty minutes. The first ten minutes, I thought maybe he got lost on the way to the bathroom—it *is* at the other end of the arena, and there was probably a line. Then I started to worry something didn't agree with him and he was blowing up the Sci-Con toilet, and maybe I should buy him some Pepto or something. Then I went to text him, *did you fall in?* and realized I never got his cell number. Or literally any info whatsoever.

Hell, he lied about his school. Why should I believe anything he told me was real? It's like I'm starring in some messed-up Cinderella reality show. I'm half waiting for someone to jump out with a camera crew and tell me I've been pranked.

No. Not a prank. He blew me off.

"Well, I wouldn't worry too much." Dave hoists himself up, gently setting Gwen into her bouncy chair beside the table. "All guys are fools at that age."

"At every age," I mutter.

He laughs, pressing a kiss to the top of my head. "There's my Stella."

The same message I sent last night is sitting on my computer when I get into my room.

CaptainJillsBFF22: hey, what happened today?

No response.

Whatever. He was just some random guy, and I'll never see him again.

What would Captain Jill do? I picture her, at the end of episode twenty, waking up alone, the bed cold, discovering that Sergeant Aaron Lewis had left in the night. I imagine her discovering the *Revelry*'s escape pod, gone—right where the show ended. And then I do what I've never done before.

I picture a world where they don't end up together. No fix-it-fic, just real life. Jill would move on. She would continue working, captaining the *Revelry*, and forget about the snarky sergeant who was once a prisoner on her ship. That's what she would do.

I push Aaron2 out of my mind and whip out my assignment book. This history chapter is not going to read itself.

–♥–

Over a week has passed since Sci-Con, and my unreplied-to message still sits in the forum. I check my phone quickly before

AP Bio, but it's still stewing there. I don't even know if he read it. Hell, part of me wonders if he even existed.

A new text pops up, and my heart nearly jumps out of my chest.

Dahlia: OMG! Brandon asked me to prom. *happy dance*
I deflate a little.
about time.
right? he was super nervous lol it was cute
I was getting worried I'd have to either ask him (lol, no) or go alone *shudders*
. . .
(yikes, that came out wrong—sorry)
Yeah, it would be a shame if you had to go to prom with *gasp* ME
we'll all go together!
I'll be the tricycle wheel, can't wait

Really, if prom wasn't some major rite of passage everyone says I'll regret skipping in like ten years or whatever, I probably wouldn't go. It's not that I don't love dressing up, it's just that I don't see the point.

I touch the necklace Aaron2 gave me, and it's cold against my skin. I should've thrown it away. I don't know why I still wear it.

I tuck it back under my shirt.

Strangely, there is someone having a worse day than me.

Wesley Clarke seems to have decided that he no longer wants to ogle Laura McNally in AP Bio; instead, he's fixated on the periodic table poster hanging on the wall. He's been so mopey lately.

"Wanna hear an element joke?" I take Lint out of her cage and set her on the lab table, letting her sniff around and explore. "What's the funniest element? Helium, helium, helium. Get it? He He He."

Wesley doesn't look up. It's like he didn't even hear me.

"Hey!" I prod him in the arm. "Earth to Wesley. You still with us?"

He snaps out of it. "Sorry."

"You missed my brilliant joke."

"Why would the helium be laughing?"

"Because its elemental abbreviation is—never mind, it's not funny if I have to explain it."

"Stella, Wesley." Mr. Hardwicke sets a stapled set of pages onto the table. "Great work." He moves onto the next lab table, and Wesley and I pounce on our grades.

Holding my breath, I rapidly flip through the sheets of our rat analysis and description of the maze trials until I reach the grading rubric in the back. Wesley hovers behind me, peering over my shoulder.

I release a heavy breath. "A-plus."

Wesley throws his head back, running his hands through his messy hair. "Oh, thank God. I hate bio."

"Good thing I was here to drag your freeloading ass."

"Yes, what would I have done without you?" He holds up his hand. "We did it, Stick."

"We did it." I high-five him.

My eyes catch his for a moment, and something passes between us. I clear my throat, drawing my hand back to my side.

"So, are you ready for your new home?" Wesley asks Lint, scooping her up and setting her on his shoulder. "I never thought the day would come when I'd miss having a rat in my house." He pets her soft fur, and she sniffs his stubbly cheek.

"You love her."

"Don't say it too loud, Stick. Wouldn't want anyone here thinking I'm soft."

"I still can't believe my mom and stepdad agreed to take care of her while I'm in college, and our landlord was cool about it," I say, scratching *rat maze grade day* off my agenda book in dark purple pen. "I'm going to need to keep Espeon out of my room for the foreseeable future."

"I . . . might have let it slip to Devin. He's pretty psyched about having a neighbor with a cool pet."

"I guess I could let him visit Lint. If he wanted to." I twiddle my fingers, keeping my eyes down. "With his older cousin."

Wesley's lip twitches into the slightest hint of a smile, and then his gaze falls to my open agenda book, which has a rainbow-colored list of final assignments and exam schedules.

AP History*—flash cards, chapters 1–16 (exam 6/2)*
(first priority)

***AP Bio**—rat maze paper, cram for final exam on 5/31 (chapters 4–20) (second priority)*
***Public Speaking**—final exam 6/1 (sixth priority)*
***Calculus**—practice problem set on pages 316–318 (exam 5/31) (third priority)*
***English**—final paper, notecards (essay exam 6/3) (fifth priority)*
***Latin**—study vocab list from chapters 6–30 (exam 6/1) (fourth priority)*

"Now you can study in all the colors of the rainbow." He follows my list with his fingertip. "Seriously, though, what do the colors mean?"

I slam my agenda book shut. "None of your business."

"They've got to mean something."

I pull out my collection of multicolored pens from my backpack, to which Wesley roars with laughter. "I just like the way they look, okay? I'm a nerd."

"I knew that already."

"And yet, you still chose to work with me."

"I mean, I wasn't given much of a *choice*." He digs around in his backpack. "I have a present for you."

"Oh God." I pretend to cringe. "Is it ticking?"

He hands me a flash drive.

I cock my head. "What's this?"

"Sixty good yearbook photos."

"Only about three months late, but just in time for the yearbook submission deadline tomorrow. I suppose I could take a peek." I slide it into my butt pocket. "You know I already got the photos from other people, right? Am I supposed to thank you?"

"I guess not, seeing as they *were* three months late."

"You should actually be groveling at my feet," I say, "because I almost submitted that toilet photo as your official senior photo for the yearbook. Something for you to look back on twenty years from now and think, Hey, maybe I should have been nicer to that Stella girl."

"I maintain that's a museum-worthy photograph."

"What museums are you going to, Wesley?"

Wesley picks up Lint and sets her gently back in her cage before locking it shut. "Finals start next week, I guess." He doesn't meet my eyes.

I catch the hidden meaning in his words; finals will determine who is the valedictorian and who isn't. After all this time, we'll have an answer.

I'm not sure why, but I feel weird about it.

"Yep. Should be a fun time."

"May the best valedictorian win?" He holds out his hand.

"Why, Wesley Clarke. How noble of you." I shake his hand. "Don't worry. She will."

26 WESLEY

My knee bounces against my hand under the lunch table. I keep darting glances at Stella, who's across the cafeteria, sitting with Dahlia Johnston, who keeps darting glances over here, at Brandon, who hasn't been able to wipe the smile off his face all day.

"Can you just go sit with her or something? You've been staring at each other across the cafeteria for the past twenty minutes."

Brandon makes a face. "I have to get a flower thingy for her."

"You mean a corsage?"

"Yeah. Do you know what color her dress is?"

I take a bite out of my bagel. "Why would *I* know what color Dahlia Johnston's dress is? You're the one going to prom with her."

He shrugs. "Aren't you friends with Stella Greene now? And they're best friends, so."

"Okay, first of all, I am not friends with Stella Greene." Am I? "And second of all, she's my bio partner. We aren't in the corner gossiping about dress colors." Over at that table, Stella is laughing with Dahlia and Emma Gonzales. It makes me think of how her eyes lit up when she laughed, twirling across the Sci-Con dance floor. That was probably the most fun I'd had in a while.

"All I know is you're accusing me of staring at Dahlia, but you're practically salivating over that table too." Brandon gathers his trash and stands. "And unless you've also got a thing for Dahlia—in which case, dude, we gotta chat—or you don't realize Em Gonzales likes girls, then you're looking right at Stella. Just saying."

He walks away, leaving me gaping at his retreating back.

It's like I got hit by a truck.

I can't even believe my own thoughts right now.

I have a thing for Stella Greene.

–♥–

I find Laura in the band wing, sitting in a practice room, her fingers gracefully tracing scales up and down the piano keys. I watch her through the glass for a moment and realize, weirdly, that I don't feel anything. She stumbles over one of the notes and swears, probably a lot louder than she realizes.

My fist hesitates because I don't want to interrupt her, but finally I make myself knock on the door.

Laura startles, but smiles when she sees me. She opens the door. "Hey, Wes! What's up?"

"I didn't know you played."

"Oh, I don't." She laughs. "I'm practicing for my music final. We have to memorize like eight different scales."

I scratch the back of my neck. "Can I talk to you for a second? I swear it'll be fast."

"Only if you play with me." Laura sits back at the piano bench and taps the seat next to her. My mind races to a million different ways I could interpret that statement, when she breaks out into the bass clef part of "Heart and Soul." I sit next to her on the bench and start playing the top part. "Are you okay? You look terrible."

"Thanks," I say. "I haven't been sleeping. Studying and all." I mean, I guess that's one way to phrase *I've probably gotten eight hours sleep total in the last five days, I'm three cups of coffee deep right now, and I still don't understand biology no matter how many times I read the textbook, and I shouldn't have procrastinated all this studying but I'm terrible with time management, and somehow the mystery girl I've been chatting with for the past three months turned out to be the rival I thought I hated but apparently actually have feelings for, and, well, here we are.*

"I found this top ten list of best cafes in NYC," she says. "I think we need to try them all. It can be part of our New York college bucket list."

And then the tiny little detail that my parents still don't know I turned down Stanford and will be attending Columbia in the fall.

"My brother told me about some pizza place we have to try, too," I say. "So maybe we should just make it a general food bucket list."

"Works for me." We keep playing, until she's interrupted by a big sneeze she manages to aim into her elbow. "Ugh, sorry. I think I'm getting that gross cold that's going around."

"Right before finals? Man, that sucks."

"You're telling me," she says with a sniffle, her nose tinged pink. "So, what's up? I'm assuming you didn't come down to the music wing to help me with my scales."

I take a deep breath. "You remember when we dated?"

Laura's hands go still over the keys for a moment. Then she keeps playing. "Of course I do. Why?"

"Why did you break up with me?"

"Wesley—"

"Please don't say the spark thing. You can be honest. I won't be upset."

"Wesley." She stops playing. "You know I really value our friendship, right? And I'm going to prom with Collin."

"No, wait." I shake my head. "I'm not trying to get back together or anything."

She visibly relaxes. "Okay, good."

"I think . . . I think I have feelings for someone else."

Laura elbows me really hard in the side. "Oh my God, who?" She grabs my arm. "Who? Who? Who? This is so exciting."

"You're going to laugh so hard."

"I swear I won't."

"Stella Greene."

Laura blinks at me. "*Stella Greene*? Really?"

"Yes? Is that weird?"

"No! She's such a sweetheart. I just always thought she hated you."

"I'm not convinced she doesn't."

"I mean, I should have known from the way you guys looked at each other all semester during those rat mazes."

Why does everyone seem to notice this but me? "Yeah, I know. It's weird."

"It's not weird! Are you going to ask her to prom?"

Stella would probably laugh in my face if I asked her to prom. "No way."

"Why not?"

"Because she'll reject me."

"Wesley Daniel Clarke. If you're so afraid of rejection that you won't take risks, you'll miss out on a lot in life." We sit in silence for a few moments before she breaks out giggling. "Wow, that was deep."

"You really think I should tell her?"

"Yep. I absolutely do."

I stand up. "Thanks, Laura. I really appreciate it."

Laura takes a deep breath. "And to answer your question, I didn't give you any other reasoning because there wasn't any. We broke up because I realized I didn't have *those* feelings for you. It wasn't personal. I just wanted something more than what we had." She rests her hand on my arm. "And you deserve something more, too."

Something more. I think of Stella, and Sci-Con, and how she threw her arms around me in bio. And how, in that moment, it felt right. "I think . . . I think I finally understand."

"Good. And I really, *really* like you as a friend. I'm glad we're going to be in New York together."

I smile at her. "Me too. And I can't wait to try all the cafes."

She wraps her arms around me in a hug, and I hug her back.

That's what I'm going to do. I'm going to tell Stella how I feel. At prom.

I won't even wear my battle helmet this time.

–♥–

The second hand on the clock ticks in time with my heart. My foot taps the linoleum. Across the room, Stella's face is practically pressed to her paper as her pencil scrawls across the page at lightning speed. She's so good at this science stuff.

Forget Stella-level sabotage, the universe is apparently determined to mess with me for final exam week. A pounding headache throbs behind my forehead. I shoot my arm up just in time to catch the cough rocketing out of my mouth with the crook of my elbow; the girl sitting to my right shoots me a dirty look. My body picked the absolute wrong week to get sick. I'm starting to regret sitting so close to Laura on that piano bench.

One by one, my classmates turn in their tests to the box on Mr. Hardwicke's desk and leave the room. I sniffle, for the eightieth time.

I'm still staring at the fourth question. Why can't I remember this equation?

Focus.

I chew the end of my pencil. It's a number two pencil.

My stomach is churning like mad. I should have eaten breakfast. Or not stayed up until four reading the same three bio pages over and over. Or taken DayQuil or something.

I cough into my elbow again.

Stella rises from her seat with a nervous smile and drops her exam into the pile. She subtly drops a couple of cough drops and a tissue pack onto my desk before walking out the door.

"Ten minutes remaining," Mr. Hardwicke says to the three of us still in class.

Kyle Nielsen huffs as he practically slams his test into the box and storms out. Okay, at least I can't do worse than him.

Mr. Hardwicke heads over to his desk and starts rummaging through the drawers. The sound is extremely distracting. One of the remaining students shoots him a death glare when a bunch of his pens hit the floor.

I wish I could remember this damn formula.

My pencil taps furiously against the desktop.

I studied. I should *know* this.

I wish I was home, in bed, gulping back chicken noodle soup.

One by one, I fill in the answers on my Scantron.

I either bomb spectacularly or pull off something in the B range, but I get it done.

The moment I'm finished, I set my test down in the pile. Mr. Hardwicke stands up, his tie slightly wrinkled, his shirt pocket stuffed with pens. "Well done, thank you, Wesley."

I nod at him, not meeting his eyes. If I say anything, I'll start hacking up a lung again. AP Bio will be the death of my GPA. Columbia's going to rescind my acceptance, and then I'll have to run back to Stanford, and they'll say no, and then I'll be stuck living with my parents forever, if they don't kick me to the curb first.

–♥–

On the second morning of exams, I gulp down some DayQuil and make my way downstairs. No fever, but I still feel like crap. I have no clue what Hatley's planning for our Public Speaking final, but I'm grateful she said it won't involve any actual public speaking, since my voice is all throaty right now.

Mom's laptop is open on the kitchen table, and a mug of coffee sits at her left.

"Where's Dad?" I ask, quickly slugging back my Prozac with a cup of water.

"Went in early."

Of course he did. "Oh." I grab a banana off the counter.

"You all ready for your exams today?" She doesn't look up from her screen, and part of me wonders if she's even listening.

"Yeah." I blow my nose and toss the tissue into the trash. "I think so."

"Whoa there." She rockets up from the chair, her brow creased. "Are you sick?"

I sniffle. "Just a cold. Took some meds, don't worry."

Panic flits across her face. "You can't take exams when you're sick." She presses the back of her hand to my forehead. "You feel cool, no fever."

"I'm fine."

"No, you're not." She takes the banana from my hand and directs me to the couch in the living room. "You should stay home. Take the tests when you're healthy."

I give her a skeptical look. One time in the sixth grade, I had the flu and a temperature of 101. My parents freaked out about me missing school and made me go anyway. The social studies teacher ended up pulling me out of class and sending me to the nurse's office because I looked like death, and they sent me home. Mom spent the whole day worrying about how the missed classes would affect my grades, while Dad called the school and argued with the principal.

Brandon used to fake being sick all the time to get out of going to school, and his parents usually fell for it; that never worked for me, because even when I was legitimately ill, my parents wouldn't let me stay home. So basically, I'm just super confused right now.

"It's just a cold, I'm really fine." I start to get back up, but Mom gently rests her hand on my shoulder.

"Wes. You need to rest. This is too important. If you can't focus on your exams, you won't do well, and you've worked too hard for that." She drapes a blanket over me. "I'll make you some tea."

"Okay, who are you, and what have you done with my mother?"

"Get some rest." She kisses my forehead and flicks on the TV. "Find something fun to watch. I'll go call the school and let them know you won't be in today."

I'm still gaping at her when another cough tickles in my throat. Maybe she's right. A bit of rest wouldn't hurt. I grab my phone and text Brandon.

Hey, I'm not coming to school today, feel like crap. Good luck on finals, hope they don't suck.

Latin and Public Speaking will have to wait.

A news reporter starts chatting about some parade on TV, but my eyelids get heavier, and I drift off to sleep. For some reason, I dream about Stella.

My phone buzzes, jerking me awake. I check the time on my phone—it's after 11:00 a.m. A now-cool mug of tea rests on a coaster on the coffee table, the string hanging over the side. The medicine must have kicked in, because I feel a lot better.

I rub my eyes and check my texts.

OMG. That public speaking final murdered me.

That is not promising for a class intended to be an easy A.

That bad?! Wtf did Hatley do?

You know those famous speeches we went over in, like, January?

. . .

no?

Wait, kind of? I think I blacked it out

Yeah, you and everyone else. That's what the WHOLE exam was on. Little tiny details about those speeches. No one even thought to study them.

Okay. Rest time is over. I need to review my super-old material, apparently. I'm not even sure I took notes on those January speeches.

I whip out my phone and text my Public Speaking coach.

hey Rob. Sorry to bother you. Can you possibly drop by later? Actually, I'm kinda sick and probably contagious, so we could chat via phone or something

My parents pay him by the hour, so I'm guessing he'll be thrilled I'm so incompetent.

Might need some help on this public speaking final, it's apparently on a bunch of stuff from January I don't remember . . .

Within a few moments, he writes back.

Absolutely! I've got the curriculum notes. I'll bring them over and leave in your mailbox, then we can FaceTime and discuss.

—♥—

Plot twist. Brandon wasn't the only one screwed by Hatley's Public Speaking final.

I sit awkwardly in the classroom, fidgeting, watching Hatley pass back finals while I wait for my makeup test. Last night, I pored over those old speeches, and judging by the groans and whispered swears around the room, I'm glad I did.

"Scores were lower than I expected," Ms. Hatley says loudly.

Stella's hand shoots up. She doesn't even wait for Hatley to call on her. "A *sixty-two*?" Her voice squeaks out. "Seriously?"

Jeez, even Stella.

Everyone in class gapes at our teacher, wide-eyed, like a bunch of frogs.

"Ms. Greene, the highest score in the class was a sixty-two." Hatley sighs. "None of you reviewed your old work."

More hands shoot up.

"Wesley, come with me." Hatley beckons me toward the door. "You can take your exam in the empty reading lab down the hall, but you can't be in here while we go over the tests."

I nod, not meeting anyone's eyes as I follow her toward the door.

"You said it would be about a speech." Stella's voice cracks. "One of our speeches from class."

"I said it would be about *a* speech, not necessarily one of yours."

"Can we make it up?" Stella asks.

"No. There's not enough time in the semester."

I scrub my hand down my face, second-guessing my studying.

"But it didn't even test our ability to publicly speak," Dahlia

Johnston whispers from somewhere behind me. "In *Public Speaking* class."

Hatley ushers me into the hall, and whatever other complaints everyone has about the test, I don't hear them.

–♥–

"There's my future Stanford grad," Dad says when I enter the house. "Don't forget to show me that course catalog."

"My first priority," I mumble, too low for him to hear.

Dad grabs the lever and straightens the recliner he'd been lying on. Sweatpants and a hoodie replace his usual business casual. "You feel better today?"

I shrug. "Yeah. Still got a bit of a stuffy nose, but my cold is basically gone."

"Good. And your exams?"

"Fine." Super thankful to Brandon for the heads-up about Public Speaking, but he wasn't exaggerating; the test sucked. At least I knew some of the stuff on there. "Public Speaking kind of screwed everyone over."

"That's a fake class anyway. Don't worry."

"Doesn't matter. It's done." I shake my head, one foot on the stair. "Why are you both home?"

"We took the afternoon off," Dad continues. "Your mother and I went down to the pond for a walk. We needed to chat about . . . a lot of things."

Mom bustles into the living room, holding a plate of chocolate chip cookies. The smell wafts over to me, and my stomach grumbles. "Wesley! Want one?" She's still in a pantsuit, day off be damned.

For some reason, it feels like bribery. I'm always suspicious if my parents are getting along. "Sure."

"You going running with Brandon and the guys today?" Mom asks. "You can always bring them over after, give them some cookies. We've got another batch in the oven."

"Yeah. Maybe. I gotta pick up my tux for prom."

A smile splits my mom's face. "You're going to look so dashing, I'm sure all the girls will ask for a dance."

Hopefully the one who matters. I swallow hard, imagining dancing with Stella at prom. I need to tell her how I feel. Prom night. If I wait until the next day, they'll announce valedictorian, and things will just be too weird. If Stella gets it, it'll be awkward. If I get it, it'll be awkward. Either way, if I don't say it, I'll regret it later.

"Yeah. I gotta go. History exam to study for." Not that it matters. Public Speaking and Bio are going to tank my whole grade.

"You'll do great," Dad says, grabbing a cookie for himself. "And you'll do great at Stanford next year."

My anxiety kicks up. I should've told them months ago, and now I don't know how to. They'll find out when they show up in California and my name's not on the list.

A pit forms in my stomach, and suddenly I can't taste the cookie at all.

Topic: **SECOND. TO. LAST. *WARSHIP*. *SEVEN*. RECAP!**
Username: **CaptainJillsBFF22**

W7

heavy breathing Here we are, folks. The penultimate *Warship* episode we've all been waiting for: Jill and Aaron's Grand Escape, aka episode nineteen, "The Pirate Guard."

Jill and Aaron are still captive in the pirate cells. I LOVE how badass Jill is in this episode, and Aaron isn't so bad himself. When the pirates come to deliver meager meals to their prisoners, Aaron distracts them with his usual sass long enough for Jill to get the upper hand and kick some pirate ass. They're no match for her, and it's wonderful. Jill engages in a fight, taking out four pirates before realizing there's a camera in the corner of the room. She shoots out the camera, preparing to flee, when she notices Aaron, still locked in his cell. (Sorry, am I rambling? I feel like I'm rambling. That was like one long sentence but OMG THIS EPISODE.)

She looks at Aaron and YOU CAN SEE HER DECISION MAKING!!! In a split second, Jill runs back to Aaron and frees him, much to his SHOCK. They start to escape, defending each other, fighting back to back like the OTP they are, when Jill gets shot in the stomach and collapses.

Now it's Aaron's turn to decide. He sees his potential exit, a chance at freedom, but he slings an injured Jill over his shoulder and runs to the shuttle with her. They chose each other. There is always a choice, folks, and this is why I know #Lewton is OTP: when their lives were on the line, when everything was coming crashing down, they chose each other.

27 STELLA

Dahlia's sisters crowd into her bedroom, helping us get ready for prom. The whole room smells like vanilla and coconut and whatever perfume Em is spritzing on herself.

I glance at the tiny clock on Dahlia's dresser. If Public Speaking turns out to be the reason I miss out on valedictorian, I'm going to scream.

Em sniffs her pits, then adds another spray. "I'm telling you guys, I bombed that AP Stats exam."

"I guarantee you couldn't have done worse than Bobby Miller, who was hard-core sweating during the whole thing," Dahlia says, wincing as her sister Bethany yanks her hair into an elaborate updo she found on Pinterest. "Are you almost done?"

Bethany scowls. "Do you want this hairstyle or not?"

"It looks really good." I nod at Dahlia. "Guys, can I pull this off without a strapless bra?" I hoist my dress up, examining the pink, slinky gown in the mirror. Looking back, I'm not sure why Past Stella wanted to go for strapless when I've got a solid A-cup.

"Here." Em waddles over, struggling to walk in her tight yellow gown. "Turn around, I'll pin that sucker so tight the girls will never escape."

I press my hands over my poor boobs. "Yes, but will they be able to breathe?"

"Dammit, hold still." Bethany slides more bobby pins into Dahlia's hair. "I swear it'll be worth it."

"It better be," Dahlia grumbles, massaging her temples.

Bridget and Amber tag-teamed my hair before I left, then took a picture of it for their future salon's website. My wavy brown hair now hangs in thick curls around my face, with a bump pushed back at the top.

"Ooh, I love your eye shadow, Em. I wish I could pull off the gold like that."

"Hey." She points at me. "You winged your eyeliner like a boss tonight."

She's right; I did, and it looks badass with my glasses. For the first time in history, I managed to make a flawless wing without having to redo it eight thousand times.

We bustle around the room, fixing our makeup and pinning hair. Bethany finally releases Dahlia, who beams when she looks at her hair in the mirror. "Okay, fine. I love it."

Bethany snorts. "Told you. Complainer."

"Here, let's take a selfie." I hold up my phone, and Em and Dahlia lean in.

I can't help but feel a pit of sadness inside me. This could be one of our last days together, all three of us.

"Cute!" Em croons. "We'll need another one once Leah and the guys get here."

"Why didn't Leah get ready with us?" Dahlia asks.

"Because we need a reveal!" Em rolls her eyes. "Also, she's going super fancy and getting her hair done at an actual salon and everything."

"It's five o'clock!" Dahlia grabs the phone off her dresser. "Final grades are up."

My heart slams into my ribs. I grab my phone and log in to

the school website; my fingers are overeager, and I punch in the wrong password at least three times.

Stella Catherine Greene
English: *94%*
AP Bio: *96%*
Public Speaking: *90%*
Calculus: *95%*
AP History: *94%*
Latin: *97%*
Gym: *95%*

A smile bursts across my face. The D on the exam didn't kill me; A-minus in Public Speaking. I quickly text the results to my mom, who immediately responds with a GIF of someone jumping up and down. My mom thinks she's really cool for knowing how to use GIFs, so she spams me with them whenever possible. Even when they're not entirely appropriate for the occasion.

Dahlia does a little dance. "I got a B-plus in AP Stats. Thank God."

"I got four As, a B, and a C-plus," Em says. "Pretty good, considering I stopped caring right before the chem final."

"What about you, Stella?" Dahlia asks.

I try to hide my grin, because I don't want to be a jackass. "I'm happy with my scores."

"Straight As?" she asks again.

"Straight As, and an A-minus in Public Speaking, because Hatley's final screwed everyone."

Dahlia and Em simultaneously squeal, and I love that I have friends who will be genuinely happy for me about this.

"So did you get valedictorian?" Em asks. "After all this?"

I swallow hard, stowing my phone back in my purse. "I don't know."

I'm proud of my scores. But I don't know if it'll be enough.

–♥–

Leah arrives at exactly six, and she and Em proceed to take the cutest possible photos together, posing on Dahlia's grand staircase. Em's mom cries, which makes Em cry, which makes Bethany usher her back into Dahlia's bedroom to redo her mascara. Eight other girls from school come by for photos, and we take pictures in a million different positions on the staircase and the lawn. Mom and Dave arrive, Mom still in her scrubs, and Bridget texts me from work, begging for photos and also to say she hopes I have an "amazing time, but remember, no glove no love." My cheeks hurt from smiling by the end. But inside, I can't help wondering how this is going to play out. My fingers drum against the silky fabric covering my thigh.

How will I know? When Wesley arrives, can I ask him what his grades were? Would that be weird?

The limo full of guys arrives fifteen minutes late, as expected. Brandon, Dylan, and a bunch of others pour out of the shiny black car, laughing about something I probably don't want to know about. I never thought I'd go to prom in a limo, but a bunch of the guys sprang for it, and since I'm the tagalong with Dahlia and Brandon, there was a spot for me. It's only a ten-minute drive from the Johnstons' house to the aquarium, but still. It's pretty cool.

Wesley steps out last, wearing a classic black-and-white tux. His floppy hair is combed, and I am ashamed to admit that he looks good. Really good. I swallow hard. For half a moment,

I don't even want to know his grades. I just want to run my fingers through his hair.

Dahlia elbows me roughly in the side and I snap out of it.

Ask him.

He joins the group of track guys making a beeline for the spread of appetizers lying out on the Johnston family's back patio. Dylan is apparently trying to break his own record for the number of mozzarella sticks he can fit in his mouth at once.

I'm getting up the courage to inquire about Wesley's grades when Dahlia's mom gets in front. "Everyone, on the lawn for a group photo, please!"

"How do we do this?" Em asks.

"How about everyone stands behind their dates?" Brandon suggests, offering his hand to Dahlia, whose cheeks flush red.

Well, this is embarrassing. I watch as everyone couples up, Em behind Leah, Brandon behind Dahlia, Dylan behind Charlotte, Collin behind Laura, and so on. I carefully maneuver to the back of the group. Maybe if I'm inconspicuous enough, it won't be super obvious I don't have a date. My silver heels sink into the damp ground.

"Stella, we can't see you," my mom says, and I kind of hate her right now. "You're too short to be in the back."

"Here, stand with Wesley," Laura says. "He's going stag too. I love your dress, by the way."

"Thank you—yours is stunning." I run my fingers down the blue sequins on Laura's back. She even used this funky, sparkly blue eyeliner that makes her eyes pop. "You look like a glamorous mermaid."

"Thanks!" She beams, flashing me her perfect white teeth. "It is under-the-sea themed, after all."

Dylan groans as loudly as possible. "All right, come on." I start to flip him off, then remember my mom is there.

"Get in front of Wes so we can get pictures and go," Brandon says.

Wesley shuffles his feet, standing at the edge of the group. I make my way over to him.

"Hey," I whisper, positioning myself slightly in front of him like the others.

"Hey."

"Can you guys get a little closer so I can fit you in the frame?" one of the dads asks from the crowd of paparazzi pointing phones at us and snapping photos.

I feel Wesley take half a step closer to me, so my back is pressed into his chest. He smells like some kind of piney cologne, and I inhale a little deeper.

"You look . . . nice," Wesley whispers.

"You too," I whisper back.

For the first time tonight, I let myself relax. I'm not sure when I started feeling comfortable around Wesley Clarke, but his presence is weirdly calming.

"Okay, we've got like five minutes before we have to get in the limo," Brandon calls. I love how he's always the ringmaster of these sorts of things.

The rest of the group breaks off to get some last-minute snacks.

I rub my upper arm and turn to Wesley. "Hey, can I talk to you for a minute?"

"Oh, yeah. I wanted to . . . talk to you too."

"Stella, you didn't tell me you were going to prom with this dashing young man." A wide grin splits Mom's face. "Can I get a photo of you with your date?"

"He's not my—"

"Of course." Wesley wraps his arm around my waist, and without thinking, I put my hand over his and lean into him. My heart thuds so loud, I'm surprised no one else can hear it. Mom snaps some pictures, and when she's finally satisfied, she pulls back to check them on her phone, as if not believing it actually happened. She's heard me bitch about Wesley Clarke so much, she'd probably faint if she made the connection that he's the guy standing beside me.

"Well, you made my mom's night," I say.

"I do what I can."

My hand subconsciously reaches out for him, but I draw it back to my side. The words all get caught in my throat.

"Hey—I do *not* want to be stuck in the middle." Laura laughs, practically wrestling with Collin as they climb into the limo. "I'll kick your ass."

Dahlia and Brandon follow, and it's a bottleneck trying to get inside. I bite my lip; I'll have to ask him later.

We join the mess of people, and before I know it, we're crammed in the limo, waving goodbye to our parents, winding toward the aquarium.

–♥–

A wall of music slams into me the second the limo pulls up in front of the aquarium, lining up behind the other cars dropping people off. Everyone is dripping in elegance. Some people wear classic white-and-black dresses with pearl necklaces, while others went for more dramatic sequined gold, silver, purple, and blue gowns resembling fish scales.

"Some people took the theme very seriously," Em observes. She tugs at her dress. "Maybe I should have gone with purple."

"Shut up, you look great. You ready for this?" Dahlia threads an arm through mine while the other latches onto Brandon. I'm grateful she didn't ditch me when she got her date.

We make our way toward the building in a giant mass of people, where Ms. Hatley stands, stamping tickets. I roll my eyes. Great: the last person I want to see tonight. Thanks for ruining everything, Hatley.

Wesley, Dylan, and Brandon stop to chat with a group of guys from the track team.

"Seriously?" Em scoffs, shoving right through them. "Blocking the whole entryway."

Last in our group, I hand my ticket to Ms. Hatley, who's wearing a gray pantsuit, indifferent to the undersea theme. "Oh, Stella, you look lovely." She punches a fish-shaped hole in my ticket and hands it back to me. *Sure, compliment me now—I haven't forgiven you for that giant sixty-two.* "Congratulations, by the way."

My heart jumps. "Thank you—for what?"

"Making salutatorian."

I feel like she slapped me. "Wait, what?"

"Yes, I know the official announcement isn't until tomorrow, but it was just too big an honor not to tell you tonight. You worked so hard for this."

No. What? How?

"I thought . . . I thought . . . Did Wesley make valedictorian?"

"I think so, yes. You'll get to introduce him at graduation."

"But . . . how?" I realize it's a childish question, but it's all I can get out.

"I heard it was very, very close." She rests a comforting hand on my arm. "He had straight As on his exams."

"Even . . . even bio?" My voice squeaks.

"I believe so."

"But I thought . . . I thought the highest grade on your final was my sixty-two."

Another limo pulls up behind me. The car doors slam, and footsteps and voices get louder.

Hatley starts talking to another teacher, ignoring me.

I blink back the tears threatening to fall from my eyes. "Well. Thanks for telling me."

"Have a great time tonight, Stella." She smiles, and I can tell she's sincerely happy for me, even though the world just crumbled before my eyes. "You deserve it."

I want to turn around and run back home and never come out of my room. But my feet move before I can process, and I'm heading into the aquarium, following the dresses and tuxes and lights and pretty things I barely register.

"Stella!" Em and Dahlia shout at me from the punch table, already dancing with Styrofoam cups clenched in their hands.

Maybe I didn't work hard enough.

Or maybe everything just comes easy for Wesley Frickin' Clarke.

I force a smile. Because acting happy is easier than the real thing.

I worked night and day, for years, sacrificed sleep and parties and fun stuff, and it still wasn't enough. No matter what I do, I will never be enough.

WARSHIP SEVEN: Episode Twenty
"A Heavy Decision"

Description: "In the highly controversial cliff-hanger ending to Warship Seven, *Aaron makes a devastating decision."*

SCENE CLIP: Upon rejoining the *Revelry*, AARON paces outside the infirmary, where unconscious JILL is being treated by MARKUS and SONNY. GEMMA comes up behind him, also watching through the infirmary window.

GEMMA: She's going to live, you know.

AARON: [startles] What? Oh. Great. That's great news.

GEMMA: We had a whole rescue plan ready, too. If you'd given us one more day, we were going to burst in there and save her. [She flushes.] And you. We'd have saved you too.

AARON: Jill's lucky to have such a dedicated crew.

GEMMA: She's an amazing captain.

AARON: She is.

[They stand in silence for a moment.]

GEMMA: So, why'd you come back?

AARON: What do you mean?

GEMMA: You had your escape shuttle. You could have taken Jill back to the CE, turned her in, gotten away from the *Revelry* forever.

AARON: [stands stoically beside her, not having an answer to give]

28 WESLEY

I'm gripping this can of Sprite so tightly, there are finger-sized dents in the aluminum. I can't stop scanning the room, looking for her. I need to tell her how I feel, and own up about being Aaron2. *We need to talk. We need to talk. We need to talk.* I've run the words in my head so many times, they've all started blurring together.

Music pounds through the floor, up my legs. The giant floor-to-ceiling fish tanks bathe everyone in a bluish glow. Colorful tropical fish flutter past, nonplussed by the dancing and music reverberating around the room.

"Wesley!" A girl I recognize from English Lit rushes over and grabs my hand. She looks nice, wearing a slinky silver dress and matching silver feathers in her hair. "Want to dance?"

I force a smile. "Maybe later?"

Dylan comes running up, already buzzed from the vodka in the flask he'd strapped to his leg that he whipped out and showed us in the limo. "May I?"

He takes her hand and escorts her onto the dance floor, shooting me a wink over his shoulder.

I can't focus on anything. I just need to find Stella.

"Hey, stop moping over there," Brandon calls from the dance floor, his arms wrapped around Dahlia. "Come dance with us."

Dahlia laughs, pulling him closer.

I wave him off. "Maybe later, man."

I shoulder through the crowd, heading to the snack table, where tiny finger sandwiches, veggies, and cheese and crackers wait. I'm not sure whose bright idea it was to put the snack table by the bathroom hall, but here we are.

A long line already snakes out from the ladies' room. Tabitha Edwards and Mitch Michaels seem to be embroiled in an argument to the side. A couple of guys take turns stealing sneaky sips from a flask before shoving it into one of their coat pockets and heading back to the dance floor. I shove a cheddar cheese cube into my mouth.

Over my head, a giant yellow fish watches me, its tail fluttering in the water.

"Having fun?"

I whirl around. Stella walks out of the bathroom, her eyes red.

"Sure." I nod at her. "You okay?"

She sniffles, but smiles up at me. "Yeah. Allergies."

"It's pretty hot in here, huh?"

"Yeah." She stands back and gazes up at the massive tank. "I haven't been here in years."

I watch as a school of small black fish sweep past.

Tell her. Just tell her how you feel.

I try to say it, but instead it comes out, "What's your favorite fish?"

"Puffer," she says without hesitation. "Like the one in *The Little Mermaid*."

"You mean Flounder?"

"No, Flounder is a *flounder*. I mean the one who plays the saxophone in 'Under the Sea.' You know." She does a little shimmy. "'An' oh, that blowfish blows.'"

"You might need to sing the whole song to jog my memory."

She gives my arm a light shove. "What's your favorite?"

"Um. Octopus?"

"That does not count as a fish."

We stand in silence for a moment, a foot apart, surveying the tank. A massive shark floats by, his beady eyes trained on me.

"I hear congratulations are in order," Stella says, keeping her eyes on the tank. "For valedictorian."

I freeze. "What?"

"I guess Hatley didn't tell you?"

Shit. Really? "I . . . what? Are you sure? Oh my God." I step back and close my eyes. No.

"Yep. It's you." She gives me a smile that doesn't reach her eyes. "Congrats."

"You're not messing with me?"

"I honestly thought Hatley would've already told you. She told me when I walked in."

A grin bursts across my face, and I throw my head back. It's real? It's over. It's me. I really got it.

I'm going to college in New York, and there's nothing my parents can say about it, because of the scholarship. I squeeze my eyes shut because tears prickle behind them and crying at prom would be super embarrassing.

I did it. I really did it. "I can't believe it."

Stella stares at her feet. "I can."

I try to say "thank you," but my voice breaks. I burst out laughing, and have to stop myself from shouting. It hits me how crappy this must be for Stella, and I force my mouth shut. *Stella.*

"Oh, um. Thank you. For telling me." I shift in place. "Congrats on, you know. Salutatorian."

Stella nods, but doesn't reply.

My smile sinks.

I'm valedictorian. I got everything I wanted, everything I

worked so damn hard for—so why do I suddenly feel so weird about it?

The loud music fades, and a slow song croons from the speakers instead. Most people rush to couple up, and I'm blasted with Sci-Con déjà vu. Stella's friend Em Gonzales wraps her arms around Leah Baker, and Dahlia rests her head on Brandon's shoulder. A bunch of guys rush off the dance floor and head toward the food table and bathrooms.

Stella watches the dance floor with her arms crossed. Her eyes flit to me, and she gives me a half smile.

"Do you—"

"Would it—"

We both stop short. "You first," I say.

"No, you."

"Okay." I lean my head back, focusing on the fish instead of her. "Would it be weird if . . . if I asked you to dance?" I hold out my hand for what feels like an eternity.

She eyes me skeptically. "Is this the part where you pretend to dance with me but it ends up being a prank and you trip me or something?"

"I mean, you don't have to." I whip my hand back. "I just thought, you know. As AP Bio partners. Who share custody of a rat."

Stella blinks. "Okay."

She takes my hand and leads me onto the dance floor. Several people crane their necks and double-take when they see us together. It's probably because of the library book thing. And the Public Speaking thing. And, well, everything.

She wraps her hands around my neck, and they're surprisingly warm. I put my hands at her waist, kind of overwhelmed by the urge to pull her closer.

Stella Greene. My worst enemy. What the hell is wrong with me?

She locks her brown eyes with mine, and we move around the dance floor. Her eyes are so pretty. Somehow, despite all the crowded bodies bumping into us, it's like we're the only ones here. It crosses my mind that the last time I danced with Stella Greene, she was Captain Jill, and I was Sergeant Aaron, and then it all blew up in my face. It feels like ages ago even though it's only been a few weeks.

"So I have to ask," she says. "How'd you get your AP Bio grade up?"

I fidget. "Studied forever for the exam."

"That's cool. Congratulations."

"Thanks. Heard you crushed that History exam, too."

She smiles. "Yeah. I used flash cards. Memorizing dates isn't so hard after all, I guess."

"Maybe someday you'll enjoy history."

"Don't push your luck, Clarke."

Just tell her how you feel.

"I have to admit, I didn't vote for Under the Sea," she says, looking around. "But this is pretty cool."

"I voted for it. I like fish."

"You would." She keeps dancing with me, the water of the fish tank reflecting in her eyes. "So, how much do you bet it takes Mr. Hardwicke less than an hour to flip all the lights on and come prowling around with his tape measure to enforce that school-sanctioned six-inches-apart rule?"

"A lifetime supply of doughnuts."

She freezes. "What did you just say?"

"A lifetime—" Oh. Oh shit. I have no poker face and it must show, because her eyes grow wide.

"Oh my God." She untwines her hands from my neck. "No." A look of sheer horror crosses her face. "It's *you*?" With a flit of panic, she runs off the dance floor.

I follow her, back to the now-empty corridor with the bathrooms.

"You're Aaron2."

"I can explain."

"You lied to me."

"Wait." I shake my head. "Stick, I can explain."

"It's been you this whole time." She slaps her hand over her mouth. "Oh my God. *How*? How did I not see it?"

"Let me explain—"

"At Sci-Con. You danced with me and then . . . you . . . you . . . *ran out*?"

"I know." I fist my hands in my hair. "I'm sorry, okay? I'm so sorry. I regretted it the moment I left. But I just . . . I couldn't tell you."

She raises her voice. "Why the hell not, Wesley?"

"I was going to tell you tonight."

"When?" Anger flares in her eyes. "After I'd babbled about pufferfish all night?"

"I don't know, okay? I wanted to tell you. I was waiting for the right moment."

"All this time, I thought I was talking to a nice guy who actually gave a shit about me."

"I *do* give a shit about you. Ten shits. A hundred."

"No." She jabs me in the chest with her index finger. "If you cared about me, you would have told me the truth."

We bathe in the silence. I wish I had something—anything—to say right now. But all I can do is stand and watch her.

"You've been messing with me this whole time. I feel like an idiot," she whispers, her eyes locked on mine. A sharp, humorless laugh escapes her mouth. "But we already knew you were so much *smarter* than me, right, *valedictorian*?"

"Okay, that's a low blow."

"I just don't get it." There's venom in her voice. "We were evenly matched in everything."

I jerk back. "What are you implying?"

"Maybe if I had all your tutors and private lessons and advantages and a mansion and a cushy life, you wouldn't have beaten me."

"Advantages?" Anger boils inside me. "Or maybe I got the spot because I worked for it and earned it."

"Yes, because there are no other factors but how hard you work." She throws her hands up. "You assume everyone has what you have, because you can't even look past your own bubble."

"And you assume your life is terrible, and can't even recognize all the good things you have."

"I was right about you from day one. You get everything handed to you because you're a rich white guy born with the right last name."

"You don't know anything about me." I raise my voice. "I work my ass off."

A group of people has stopped subtly eavesdropping and now stands around us, watching.

"I know everything there is to know about you," she shouts. "The second we graduate, I never want to see you again."

"Good. Have fun in Boston."

"Have fun being Daddy's Little Stanford Boy."

"Stick . . ."

"Stay away from me." She turns and runs toward the door.

"Stick! Wait!" I chase after her, but she bursts outside into the warm June air. "Stick!" I swallow down the lump in my throat, shouting into the empty night as I watch her disappear. "Stella!"

She doesn't look back.

WARSHIP SEVEN: Episode Twenty
"A Heavy Decision"

SCENE CLIP: Several days have passed since AARON and JILL returned. JILL, in recovery, sits on her bed, back in her own room, pensive. There's a knock at the door.

JILL: [props herself up using a metal cane and opens her bedroom door, where she is surprised to see AARON] Oh. Hi.

AARON: Hey. [He stands awkwardly in her doorway for a moment before JILL stands back, motioning for him to come in.] How are . . . you feeling?

JILL: As good as one can feel. Given the circumstances. [She settles back on the edge of her bed, rubbing her bandaged midsection.] Markus mentioned you'd like to join our crew.

AARON: Yes, I did say that. [pauses] If you'll have me.

JILL: I suppose I can find a place for you. Here, on the *Revelry*. With us.

AARON: [silent for a moment, staring at the floor] Why did you come back for me?

JILL: Because I never leave a man behind.

AARON: You are more honorable than you know. [He looks back down.] And more honorable than I deserve.

JILL: [softly] You have more honor than you think, CE.

[They watch each other for a moment, before JILL steps closer to him.]

AARON: I have to admit, you're not the person I thought you were.

JILL: And who did you think I was? [steps closer to him, so they're only inches apart]

AARON: [reaches out a tentative hand to brush a lock of auburn hair behind JILL's ear] A pirate.

JILL: [scoffs] I hope you realize now that there is a huge difference—

[She is cut off by AARON kissing her. JILL presses her hands to his face and pulls him closer. They kiss softly at first, until finally, JILL pulls back. AARON takes a breath, cautiously, worried he overstepped. They watch each other for a moment, then JILL slides her shirt off. AARON removes his own shirt. They stare at each other in silence before JILL closes the gap and kisses him deeply, maneuvering backward until they end up on her bed, and the camera fades to black.]

[FOUR HOURS LATER text shows on screen]

[AARON awakens in the darkness, JILL asleep in the bed beside him. He watches her, smiles sadly. Then he reaches out a hand to touch her, but pulls it back at the last second when a short beep pierces the air. AARON rushes to pull his clothes back on, fumbling with the comm device he'd managed to fix during the past week on the *Revelry*.]

MICHELE: Aaron? Are you there?

AARON: [hesitates] Yes, I'm here.

MICHELE: I'm outside the *Revelry* ship. Can you come?

AARON: [swallows down a lump, still watching JILL sleeping peacefully, her bare shoulder visible over the sheets] Yes. I'll be right there.

[The next morning, JILL awakens. She looks around the empty room, not sure what happened to AARON. The screen fades to black. End of season one.]

29 STELLA

The *Warship Seven* score plays in my ears, drowning out the world around me.

I am not here. I am somewhere else, far away, on the *Revelry*. Jill is my captain, and we are roaming the galaxy together, with no men in sight.

Someone rips the earbud out of my ear, and my eyes wrench open.

Bridget hovers over me. "Do you want to talk about it?"

Talk about what? How some jerk I thought cared about me actually lied to me this whole time and then took away the one thing I ever wanted?

"No." I flip over so my face is pressed into my pillow and slide the earbud back into my ear. "Go away."

My mattress sinks down, and I can tell she sat on the foot of my bed anyway. She rests her hand on my back and tugs my headphones out of my ears. "Can I help you, Bridget?"

"I'm worried about you."

"Well, don't be. You have other things to worry about." I sit up, and a burst of light sears my retinas. "Did you have to turn that on? I was perfectly fine in the dark."

"You've been moping in the dark all week. Dave almost came in with some dinner for you last night so you'd stop eating Froot Loops for every meal, but I told him to let you rest. Next time, I'm letting him plow right in here with a giant plate of salmon, extra olives on the side."

I wrinkle my nose. "I hate salmon and olives."

"That's what you get if you lie in bed for five days and don't talk to anyone. You know, I work with Cassie Palmer at the theater. She told me about . . . valedictorian."

"Remind me to get a lock on my door." I curl back up, facing away from her. "You can go now."

"I'll go if you tell me what happened at prom."

I let out the king of all sighs and hoist myself into a sitting position. My hair is matted all over my head.

"How about a hairbrush?" Bridget sniffs the air. "Or a shower?"

"Doesn't matter anymore. I'm going nowhere. I'll be a giant loser the rest of my life. Probably live at home forever and get a shitty minimum-wage job. Honoring the family tradition and all."

The moment I say it, I regret it. I snap my mouth shut, but a veil of silence has already descended over the room.

"Like me," Bridget says after an eternity.

"No," I add quickly, "Bridget, I didn't mean it like that."

"Yes you did."

"I swear, I didn't." I grab her arm. "Bridget."

"You know what, Stella, you're my sister and I love you to death. But you're a monumental snob."

Her words smash into me. I did not ask to be attacked like this. "What the hell? I'm not a *snob*!"

"Yes, you are. You think I'm some sob story because I'm a twenty-year-old single mom high school dropout who works two minimum-wage jobs and lives at home. You think I'm a failure and it's your job to save me." She laughs. "You probably get nightmares about ending up—gasp—like me."

I open my mouth, then close it again.

"Well, I love my life." She shrugs. "I wouldn't change a damn thing. And I don't care if that bothers you."

"But—"

"You're always the first one to yell about how your circumstance doesn't define you, but then you run around judging everyone else for theirs. It's fine to want to change your situation, but dammit, Stella, stop shitting on mine."

It's silent for a moment. I take a deep breath. "Bridget."

"No one put my picture on some wall at school for this—and by the way, The Wall tradition reeks of classist BS. Why don't they put up photos of all the students going to trade school? Or going right to work? That's also something to be proud of. Going to college isn't synonymous with intelligence, Stella. A person's worth isn't determined by their job or education or how much money they have. Being rich doesn't mean you're a better person. Success isn't one size fits all. Maybe a GED isn't the path I originally expected, but it doesn't change the fact that it's *my* path—and my path is just as valid as yours."

I'm still staring at her.

"So you're not valedictorian, because some stupid rich boy got it instead. Who cares?"

"Hey!"

"No. Seriously. You act like if you're not the perfect valedictorian, you're a failure. You're not. You can still go to MIT if that's what you want, become a physicist if that's what you want, be successful in the future *if that's what you want*. You think you're the first poor kid who wasn't a valedictorian to go to college?"

"It doesn't matter, okay? I wanted to *earn* it." My voice cracks. "I worked *so* hard."

"Oh please, no one cares about who was valedictorian after high school. The valedictorian of my class is backpacking in Thailand or something, don't think he even went to college. Meanwhile, this girl Vicky who went to trade school is making *bank* as a plumber right now. Amber and I? Already have plans for our salon. Because, and I'll say it louder for the people in the back"—she leans closer to me—"there is no single path to success. Stop judging people whose success looks different than yours."

"I don't care if it won't matter to anyone else. It mattered to *me*." A traitorous tear leaks from my eye, and I roughly swat it away. "I wanted it *so badly*. I wanted to earn it."

Bridget cups my cheek. "Hey. You *did* earn it. You worked so hard. *We* know you earned it, and that's all that matters. Your life is only beginning. You can still get everything you dreamed of." She stands. "And salutatorian is *really* good."

Maybe she's right. I worked my ass off to get this far, and dammit, I didn't work this hard to stop here. I *will* be successful. I've earned it.

"Bridget—wait!"

My sister stops, one foot out the door. "What's up?"

"I'm sorry. You're right."

She flips her hair. "I know."

"No, really. I look up to you a lot. And you better give me a discount at your hair salon."

"Thank you." Bridget takes a bow. "But I only give discounts for customers whose hair doesn't resemble the fryer at Burger Blitz. Take a shower." She points her finger at me like a threat. "And your family loves you, dammit. Be proud of where you came from."

I smile at her, even though she's already out of the room. "I am."

—♥—

Begrudgingly, I join humanity again for dinner. And by humanity, I mean Dave and Gwen, while Bridget and Mom are working. I even manage to brush my hair first, and accidentally yank a giant nest of it out of my scalp in the process.

The smell of Stouffer's lasagna fills the tiny kitchen. Red sauce coats Gwen's face within half a second of Dave putting the plastic bowl in front of her. Several red splatters dapple the floor under her high chair, and Espeon is already hard at work cleaning them up.

"Glad to see you back, Stells." Dave smiles at me, setting a plate of lasagna on my plastic place mat. "We're all very proud of you. I hope you know that."

"Thanks."

A loud knock pounds on the door, making me almost fall off my chair. Espeon leaps up and starts yipping. Gwen's face scrunches, and her howl joins the ruckus.

I jump up, ready to give whoever it is a piece of my mind, and yank the door open.

"Hey. Ice cream girl." Devin shuffles his feet in the doorway.

The anger floods out of me. "Oh. Um. Hi, Devin." For half a second I panic that Wesley is with him, but the hallway is empty. Gwen's cries mingled with Dave's failed attempts to get her to calm down drown out everything else, so I step into the hallway and close the door behind me. "What's up?"

"I'm supposed to give you this." Devin holds up a big plastic Tupperware container filled with orange chunks. "Wesley says it's freshly cooked sweet potato. For Lint."

"Oh. Cool." I realize my voice doesn't sound anything but cool, and quickly add, "Thanks for dropping by."

"I'm two streets away." He points to the wall. "My mom says you can come visit and bring the rat, if you want."

I'm ninety-nine percent sure he just wants to hang out with Lint but would tolerate my presence if it meant rat cuddles. "Yeah. Sure."

"Okay, well. Bye." He turns to go.

I don't know what gets into me, but I blurt it out before I can think. "What's Wesley up to lately?"

Devin stops and releases one of those heavy sighs that can only come from a thirteen-year-old. "He's been moping around all week."

I roll my eyes, the familiar anger flaring to life inside me. Of course he has. "What's he upset about? Can't decide on a color for his Porsche?"

"I don't know." Devin shrugs. "I think he was more upset about some girl who broke his heart."

W7

Topic: **DEVASTATION.**

Username: **CaptainJillsBFF22**

Yeah, I'm still pissed.

He wouldn't have left her.

I'm sorry, he just wouldn't. It's like the showrunners don't know Aaron AT ALL.

I don't even have a proper recap for episode twenty.

Warship Seven wasn't supposed to be REAL. It was supposed to be FANTASY. Because you know what? The real world sucks. I wanted Aaron and Jill to be happy, because *Warship* isn't the real world.

They deserved an HEA, and we deserved better.

30 WESLEY

My face droops against my hand. It's been five days, and I feel awful. For some reason, I can't get Stella's words out of my head. I log in to the forum, holding my breath, and click on Stella's screen name.

This user has deactivated their account.

I want to throw my computer out the window. Or punch a pillow. Or something.

Maybe if I had your advantages, you wouldn't have beaten me.

My knee bounces under the desk. The day after prom, Principal Woods called me on my cell and congratulated me for being named valedictorian. I pretended to be shocked at the news. My parents hugged each other for the first time in like a year. But I could barely even muster up fake enthusiasm.

Maybe if I had your advantages . . .

I take out my phone, the principal's number still in my call log. I'm not sure what finally makes me do it, but I hit the button and press the phone to my ear.

"Hello?"

"Hey, Principal Woods. It's Wesley Clarke."

There's a pause. "Wesley? Why . . . hello. Hi. Can I help you? You know school's out, right?" He chuckles. "You got your speech ready for Saturday yet?"

"What made me valedictorian?"

"What do you mean? Years and years of hard—"

"No, I mean, what specifically? Exams? How did I get it over Stella?"

He sighs heavily, sending a wave of static over the phone. "Hang on. Let me open my computer and look."

"Yeah. Thanks."

"You know I can't tell you specifics about other students' grades, right?"

"Yep. Not asking for that."

"Never had two students as driven as the two of you." I can hear keyboard keys clicking in the background. "Okay, here we go," he says. "Clarke. Clarke. Yes. It looks like you outscored the rest of your peers on Regina Hatley's Public Speaking exam."

My blood turns to ice. The Public Speaking exam that everyone else bombed. I would've bombed it, too, without Brandon and my tutor.

I squeeze my eyes shut. "Okay. Cool. Thanks for telling me."

"You know you're—"

I press End. Hanging up on the principal is probably frowned upon, but I don't care.

I let my head fall into my hands.

What have I done? Was Stella right? Did I earn this?

I open my desk drawer and pull out my sketchbook, but something catches my eye below it. The familiar photo of Stella scowling glares back at me from inside the drawer.

She looks fierce and smart. Like a captain.

The charcoal drags across the page, and suddenly, I'm lost in a drawing.

I tab open Stella's 198,000-word beast of a fanfic. And then I start to read it.

–♥–

Under the kitchen table, my knees won't stop fidgeting.

"Congratulations, Wesley." Dad thumps me on the back, settling into his seat at the table.

I don't respond. I just don't have the energy.

I should've failed that exam. My grade was higher because I had an advantage that no one else got.

I don't deserve it.

Stella does.

Dad looks expectantly toward the kitchen, and I follow his eyes to where Mom stands, holding a celebratory cheesecake that I don't deserve. "We're so proud of you, Wesley!"

I wish I could make it all stop.

I force myself to shovel cheesecake into my mouth until my piece is gone, even though I don't taste any it. I need to give it up. I'll call Principal Woods. Or something.

"Did you write your speech yet?" Mom asks, taking her time with her own slice of cheesecake.

I can't even look at her. "No."

Dad laughs. "I've been asking him that, but you know our Wes, always the procrastinator."

It's weird that my parents are getting along. I guess it's true. Maybe I'm the only thing they have in common anymore.

"You better hurry up," Mom says. "Graduation is in two days."

Dad gives Mom a nervous grin. "I'm sure he'll blow that speech out of the water. Then, on Sunday, we can take a father-son trip to the Porsche dealer."

"I don't deserve the spot." I force the words out from gritted teeth. "Brandon told me what was on the Public Speaking test, and then Rob helped me study for it."

Mom looks taken aback, but doesn't reply.

Dad stares at me for a moment. "It's not a big deal. You were *sick*." He thumps me on the shoulder. "We pay Rob to help you study, and that Brandon's never been able to keep his mouth shut. Hell—if that's really what happened, you should be grateful they helped you."

I know what I have to do. Doesn't make it hurt any less.

My parents have some sort of conversation with their eyes, and I can practically cut the tension.

Mom glances at Dad, then back at me. "Wes, we need to talk to you about something." She wrings her hands. "We wanted to wait until after your graduation. I know this isn't a great time, but we're all here together, and there's never going to be a perfect time for this."

I already know what it is. But it doesn't sting any less when Dad says, "Your mother and I . . . we're getting a divorce."

Silence hangs over the table. I blink. I don't know what to say. Maybe I'm relieved.

"Sometimes people grow apart," Mom adds quickly, taking my hand, "and I promise we both just want what's best for you."

I swallow hard. "You mean that?"

"Of course, honey." Mom's eyes crinkle at the side. Dad nods, not looking at either of us.

"Good." I stand and take a deep breath. "I'm going to Columbia."

"You're *what*?" Dad snaps.

"I already accepted and paid the deposit."

Mom just kind of stares. "Wesley. What? Why?"

"It's nothing personal. I just don't want to live in California.

I like New York. And the Columbia campus. And they have a great art program—and sciences, too," I add quickly. "If you don't want to help me anymore, that's fine, I can get loans, but I . . . I have to do this. I have to go my own way."

"Is that really what you want?" Mom asks softly.

"Yes, a hundred percent."

She closes her eyes, and sends me a smile that's obviously forced. "I'm sorry you felt you couldn't tell us sooner. You know we'll always support you, right?" When Dad doesn't reply, she elbows him sharply. Dad nods tersely, then stands and leaves the room.

For some reason, it's like a huge weight's been lifted off me. "I have something to take care of. I can Uber if you don't want me to take the car."

"Keys are on the counter," Mom says.

I grab the keys and rush out of the house before anyone can say another word.

WARSHIP SEVEN FORUM

W7

Topic: **THAT ENDING THOUGH**

MOD NOTE:

*This is a thread to discuss / vent about the season one cliff-hanger and subsequent cancellation news. Any posts about the cancellation outside of this thread will be deleted. **Sorry, but the sheer number of posts all complaining about the same thing just got to be too much to handle.*

WarShipper12: I'm sorry, but the writers owe us an apology. That ending ******* sucked.

WarShipper12: Wow, @mod, censoring our posts now? What happened to freedom of speech? **** you.

MOD NOTE: ***@WarShipper12, first warning. We do not tolerate aggressive speech here.***

PrincessLea19: Yeah, that ending was no good, but thank God for fanfic! Maybe someday the cast will come back and do a movie or something like they did with *Firefly* . . . In the meantime, ***reads all the #Lewton fics in one sitting***

SonnyDeservedBetter3: I actually liked the ending? Is that weird? I mean, people are angry because they didn't get the ending they wanted. But we liked the show because of how real and flawed and human the characters are, and now people want to criticize the showrunners for keeping it real by having Aaron leave? Grow up. Perfect endings don't happen in real life, they shouldn't happen here either.

JustHere4theComments: okay, I watch the show to escape. My own relationships suck IRL, I watch TV to get some happy endings for once.

Lewton4Eva: Um, no, @SonnyDeservedBetter3, actually we don't like the ending because it MADE NO SENSE. Aaron's character development was about learning to see past the propaganda they taught him in CE school. He wouldn't have gone back to Michele after all that.

WarshipofDreams: lol now your just mad your ship didn't end up together

Lewton4Eva: *you're

31 STELLA

"I really don't think we can afford this." I slide into the Applebee's booth next to Dave.

"Oh, shush." Mom sits across the table while Bridget helps Gwen into the high chair the waiter brought over. "We're celebrating."

"There's nothing to celebrate."

"You're graduating tomorrow," Dave says. "Salutatorian, that's huge. And Bridget passed her GED."

Bridget rolls her eyes, but smiles. "Only took me two years. Next stop, cosmetology school."

"The point is that you did it," Mom says. "Both of you. And that deserves a celebration."

She's right. I earned this.

"Split mozzarella sticks?" Bridget asks me.

"Like you have to ask." I page through the menu. "Ooooh, chicken tenders."

"That's what I'm getting." Bridget sets the menu down. "Don't even have to look too carefully."

"You girls have been getting the same thing here since you were Gwen's age." Mom shakes her head.

"We have good taste," I add.

"I hope you weren't feeding us mozzarella sticks at Gwen's age, jeez," Bridget says.

"Yeah, Mom." I laugh. "What were you thinking?"

My phone vibrates in my pocket, jolting me.

"No phones at the table." Mom gives me a death glare. "Seriously, how many times do I need to say it?"

"Oh, let her check," Bridget says. "It's her special day."

I don't recognize the number on the screen. I plug my left ear, drowning out the noisy restaurant, and press the phone to my right. "Hello?"

"Hello—Stella?"

My brows furrow. "Principal Woods?"

"Yes. Sorry to bother you, I know it's, what, five p.m.?"

"Yeah." I slide out of the seat, pointing at my phone, then the door. Mom nods, and I rush outside into the warm June air. "It's fine. Is everything okay?"

"Well, I know it's short notice, but you've been named valedictorian."

What? The phone tumbles out of my fingers, and I fumble to catch it before it crashes onto the pavement. "Sorry—what? How? Is this a joke?"

"No joke. You were number one in the class, and that makes you the recipient of our valedictorian scholarship."

I put my fist in front of my mouth, trying to stop the grin from bursting across my face. "But . . ."

"I know it's short notice, but if you can have a short speech prepared by tomorrow, that would be excellent. We had a last-minute change of plans."

"What about Wesley Clarke?"

"He'll be our salutatorian. Mr. Clarke asked not to have his Public Speaking exam counted toward his final grade."

"What?" My face scrunches up. "Why?"

"Now, I can't tell you specifics about students' grades, Ms. Greene."

Frustration wells inside me. What the hell? "I don't want to be handed valedictorian just because Wesley Clarke thinks I'm some charity case." I don't want handouts. Am I supposed to be gracious about Wesley trying to be a hero and coming to save me like I'm a distressed damsel? BS. If this is Wesley's way of trying to make amends for lying, he can shove it up his sorry—

"I'm not sure I'm supposed to tell you this, but he called this morning very curious about his grades. It was his Public Speaking exam that pushed him ahead of you in the first place."

I snort. "He wasn't even there for that exam."

"Well, he showed up at my office an hour ago and said another student gave him information about the test while he was home sick, which gave him an advantage when he retook it, and he didn't feel right about it. Said he worked hard for this and wanted to earn whatever position he landed in."

I blink. "Really?"

"Yep. He was practically in tears, poor kid. He'll be introducing you tomorrow onstage."

I touch my neck, grazing the Captain Jill necklace I never could bring myself to take off. "I don't believe this."

"You worked hard, Stella. Sometimes, hard work pays off."

I've barely hung up before the tears pour from my eyes.

The second I'm back in the restaurant, I wrap my arms around everyone in my family in turn.

"Is everything all right?" Mom asks, patting me on the shoulder. "Who was that?"

"Mom. Dave. Bridget. Gwen." I take a deep breath, standing at the head of the table. "You're looking at the valedictorian."

I catch the shock passing across their faces before the deafening cheers erupt so loudly, the whole restaurant looks at us.

A MISTAKE UNDONE

By: CaptainJillsBFF22

Pairing: Captain Jill Brighton / Sergeant Aaron Lewis

Words: 198,000

Chapters: 121/121

Tags: fix-it-fic, angst, OTP, #Lewton, so much kissing, they belong together, I want amnesia to forget the ending of episode 20, he comes back this time!, season finale was a mess, we deserved better, seriously I hate that ending

Chapter One

Sergeant Aaron Lewis scans the empty star-scape surrounding his shuttle, and that familiar sense of sadness overwhelms him. Aaron used to enjoy looking up at the stars, but these days, all they do is remind him of what he's lost. He can hardly believe it's been a month since he made the biggest mistake of his life.

Aaron scrubs a hand down the helmet obscuring his face. It's been no use. Since leaving the CE and going rogue, he's tried to track down his favorite stubborn, beautiful captain and her ragtag crew on that beat-up old ship—and yet, it's almost as if they don't want to be found.

A sharp beep pierces the air, echoing in the tiny shuttle. Aaron startles, examining the radar. The signal is weak, but it's there—the *Revelry*, within range. After all this time, the love of his life is just a short distance away.

She's going to kill me if I go back, he thinks. But it doesn't stop him from entering the coordinates and heading toward the warship anyway.

By the time the shuttle thuds against the side of the *Revelry*, dozens of mechanical connections sliding into place, Aaron's heart is in his throat. With a deep breath, he exits the shuttle, finding himself on the bridge of the ship he once called a prison—and then called home.

"Look who's back." Sonny stands at the other end of the bridge, pointing his pistol directly at the former CE ranger. "You've got a lot of nerve coming back here." Skulls joins him, aiming a rifle at Aaron's head.

Aaron puts his hands up. "I know. I just want to see her."

Skulls sneers. "What makes you think you deserve to see her?"

"I don't deserve to. But I'd like to."

"Well, if you think we're going to allow you to set one foot—"

"Leave him."

All three men dart their eyes to the upper level of the bridge, where Captain Jill Brighton waits, her eyes radiant in the low light of the ship's docking station. She steps toward the bridge slowly, deliberately, until she's only ten feet away from the ranger. Skulls and Sonny keep their weapons trained on him, unsure where to go from here.

Jill nods at them. "Leave."

Her loyal comrades look at each other quickly, then disappear into the belly of the ship.

"What do you want?" she snaps, keeping her pistol raised, like he's the same CE ranger he was on the day they met.

Aaron gapes at her for a moment. And in that moment, she's everything: everything he wants, everything he wants to be.

He takes a step toward her. "I shouldn't have left."

Jill freezes, not daring to lower her weapon.

"In all my years at the CE academy, I made a lot of mistakes."

Aaron takes another step toward her. "But leaving you behind was the worst one I ever made."

Jill closes her eyes. "What am I supposed to do with that? You left me. You left us. And took my shuttle."

"You are the most stubborn, annoying, beautiful captain I have ever met." Aaron takes another step toward her, until she's close enough to touch. "And I've never been able to stop thinking of you."

A rush of emotion overtakes Jill, but she forces herself to remain composed. She can't let herself fall for this man again. "If you couldn't stop thinking about me, why did you leave?"

"I shouldn't have." He brushes a strand of long auburn hair out of her face. "I will always come back for you."

"Aaron Lewis, you are the most stubborn, arrogant Cescum I have ever—"

He cuts her off with a kiss. Jill freezes for a moment, contemplating pushing him away like she should have done that night in her bedroom, so long ago. But instead, she takes a risk and falls into his kiss, wrapping her arms around him, right there on the bridge, not caring who sees.

COMMENTS:

JBStan21: BEAUTIFUL! Thank you for this wonderful story!

Revelryyyy44: loved every word. Thank you.

SonnysGF999: How it should have ended, tbh

HavingaRevelry: LMAO THIS IS SO PATHETIC AND CORNY. Won't you #Lewton stans get a life already and move on? Ffs

KillerPlanet52: This is so unrealistic lol I mean, come on, this would never actually happen! MOVE ON.

JBStan21: Wow, @KillerPlanet52 @HavingaRevelry, who hurt you??

CaptainJillsBFF22: Lol I don't care what any of you jerks say. I believe in this love story, and if you don't like it, fuck off.

32 WESLEY

A deep blue sky covers the entire football field in a cheeriness that doesn't match my mood. The navy-blue tassel hangs off the side of my mortarboard, swishing in time with my footsteps.

"We did it, man." Brandon slugs me on the back a little harder than usual. "You coming to my grad party afterward?"

"I hope so, yeah." I mean, I'm definitely not going right home. Mom and Dad had a "long discussion" last night, which included a lot of shouting and ended with Dad going to stay in a hotel. Mom said she was proud of me no matter what, then spent the rest of the night in her room with the door closed. This morning she said she'll visit me in New York and that she'll help with tuition. Dad texted me *congratulations* this morning, so at least I'm not completely chopped off the family tree, although I'm not sure if he's here right now. Maybe the issue was never about me and my college choice. Maybe it was always about them.

"Good. If you'll excuse me." Brandon wiggles his eyebrows, then goes to stand next to Dahlia, who's talking to Stella. There are a million things I wish I could say to her, but they all gum up in my throat.

I rub my forehead, then turn to face the wooden bleachers. I still can't bring myself to look at her.

"Line up!" Ms. Rossi from the main office ushers us into two lines, and it's like herding cats. I take my place beside Amanda Carter near the front of the line.

A few stray drumbeats echo in the air, and then the band cues up "Pomp and Circumstance," and we haphazardly march to our seats, to applause in the bleachers.

Principal Woods takes the microphone and starts talking about hard work and integrity, and I can't help feeling like he's talking to me. I slink down in my seat.

"And now, without further ado, to introduce our valedictorian speaker, I'd like to present our salutatorian of this year's class—Wesley Clarke."

Applause erupts from my classmates and I force myself to my feet, not daring to look at Stella sitting in the row behind me with the Gs. The podium feels about ten degrees hotter than the field, and I'm suddenly very aware of the hundreds of eyes settling on me.

I want to tell her I'm sorry. That I'm going to carve my own path, and I'm not going to turn out like my dad. I want to tell her that I've been thinking of nothing but Sci-Con. But I can't even bring myself to look at her.

"Good morning, everyone." My heart thuds against my ribs, but I force it to calm down. "My name is Wesley Clarke, and I'm honored to be number two in this year's class." My eyes catch my mom, sitting in the front row between my grandparents, with her phone camera recording me. I don't see my dad.

I take a deep breath. "When I think of the word *valedictorian*, I think of being number one. But there is a lot more to the title than that. Being valedictorian comes from years of hard work, and effort, and studying, and perseverance. There is no one in my class who better exemplifies those traits than Stella Greene." I pause, reaching into the pocket of my graduation robes where

I find a folded sheet of paper. "But Stella is so much more than that. She's kind. She's passionate about everything she loves. And she's the very best, most fun person to be around. So, without further ado, our valedictorian, Stella Greene." I look into the crowd and find her brown eyes looking back at me. "Stella . . . no one deserves this more than you." I leave the paper on the stand and take my chair, letting the applause drown out all the words I didn't get to say.

33 STELLA

I hold my head high as I make my way up to the podium. My hands grow sweaty, clenching the four sheets of stapled paper containing the speech I wrote last night. I stayed up until one in the morning, and edited it again when I woke up today.

Roaring applause follows me onto the stage.

The microphone is still pointed over my head when I reach the podium. Thanks, Wesley. I adjust it, and a god-awful screech rips through the field, making everyone simultaneously cringe.

"Whoa, sorry about that. Good morning to my classmates, family, and friends." I *have* worked so hard; I can't believe this moment is actually here. "My name is Stella Greene, and I am honored to be your valedictorian this year." I go to set my speech on the podium, but stop. A photo-quality picture is already sitting there, drawn in charcoal. I recognize the person in the drawing immediately.

It's me.

It's a drawing of that awful scowling photo Wesley took of me a few months ago.

I swallow hard.

Captain Jill's *Revelry* jacket covers my torso, and my hands are propped on my hips like I'm ready to take on an entire battalion of CE rangers. Jill's pistol is wedged in my holster, and I'm glaring at whoever dares come my way.

But for the first time, I see the look on my face differently. I don't look angry and scowling—I look *fierce*. A note is scrawled at the bottom.

Congratulations, Captain. —W

Something inside me softens. I don't know what compels me to do it, but I fold up my well-edited, well-researched, well-practiced speech. And I tuck it into my pocket.

"I hope this isn't too weird, but I'm going to wing it, okay?"

A few scattered snickers sound in the crowd.

"Don't drop any F-bombs, Stella," Kyle shouts from the middle of the pack of chairs, to laughter.

I give him a wide smile while flipping him off under the podium. "I'll try not to, Kyle, thank you."

Hundreds of eyes settle on me, watching. Waiting. In the crowd, my eyes find Wesley's; he shoots me a quick thumbs-up. I take a deep breath and pull the microphone toward my mouth.

"Who here has seen the show *Warship Seven*?"

People toss glances at each other. A few hesitant hands go up. Even Kyle, rolling his eyes, raises his hand.

"Well, it's my favorite show," I say. "For years now, I've been obsessed. It's got the best one-liners, and the romance is amazing, even though they ended it on a cliff-hanger because the stupid network didn't renew it and—okay, I'm rambling." *Slow down, jeez!* I take a deep breath. "But my favorite character in the show is the brave Captain Jill Brighton. She's the captain of the warship, the *Revelry*, and she doesn't take any crap—even from the people who belittle her and don't believe she deserves to be captain. She doesn't fight them; she just proves them wrong.

"Throughout the show, we see Captain Jill fight pirates and Central Elite rangers and, most of all, her own internalized prejudices when she finds herself with a CE prisoner on her own ship.

"For years, I have looked up to her. I have this epic cosplay I put together, and if I do say so myself, I did a great job—I even have these amazing Captain Jill boots, thanks to my sister. But . . . for someone who strives to be like Captain Jill, I was doing a piss-poor job. Am I allowed to say *piss* up here? Anyway." I clear my throat. "We can all learn a lot from *Warship Seven*. I, for one, am guilty of making preconceived judgments about people. I don't like admitting when I'm wrong." I take a deep breath. "But I was wrong.

"Today, I promise that I'm going to be better at that, and I hope you'll try, too. Maybe there's someone you don't like—you think they're arrogant, or stubborn, or a jerk, or whatever else, because you don't know them. I say, give them a chance. I think there's a lot more that brings us together than that separates us. So go out there and be like my favorite captain: fight for what you believe in, live those big dreams, and do all the wonderful things you're capable of." I scan the audience, and my eyes lock with Wesley's in the third row. "But never forget that sometimes, the ones you judge the most harshly are the ones who will surprise you the most. Thank you."

I traipse back to my seat to scattered applause.

The rest of the ceremony passes way too fast, and before I know it, we're throwing our caps in the air, I'm holding a diploma, and Dahlia is practically tackling me in the field for a hug.

I wrap my arms around my friends and we take so many photos, in so many different poses. Then my family comes over, and we take even more pictures. I put my graduation cap on Gwen's head, even though it's way too big for her, and we take some more. My cheeks hurt from grinning.

When most people have started breaking off to their respective graduation parties, Dahlia comes running up to me. "Are you coming to Brandon's house?"

"Maybe. I'm kind of tired." I'm not sure I can handle seeing Wesley right now, no matter how badly part of me wants to.

"Meet up later, then? Em's up for ice cream at The Scoopery."

"As long as I don't have to do the scooping."

We hug, and she leaves with her family.

Mom and Dave go over to the picnic bench by the parking lot, where Bridget is letting Gwen toddle around in the grass. My niece is way overdue for a nap, which means she's probably cranky, which means Bridget will be cranky too. Time to go. My feet squish in the spongy grass as I make my way over to them; but then I see Wesley, sitting by himself on a bench.

I'm not sure what makes me do it, but with a swift pivot, I walk toward him instead.

Wesley gets to his feet. "Hey."

I look at the ground. "Hey."

"I, uh, I loved your speech."

"Thanks. I'm pretty sure you're the only person who got the *Warship* references, so."

"I think Kyle Nielsen did."

"Oh, well, I meant the only person whose face doesn't look like a shovel."

Wesley snorts. "That's a new one."

"Yeah."

"Look. Stella." He digs his sneaker into the muddy grass beneath us. "I'm really sorry. For everything."

I reach out to touch him, but withdraw my hand. "Thanks for . . . you know."

"You earned the spot, Stick."

We stand in silence for a moment.

"Friends?" I hold out my hand. Wesley shakes it, his eyes locked on mine. For a moment, I don't want him to let go, but he does. "Are you going to Brandon's party?"

He shrugs. "Maybe. Are you?"

"I don't know."

"Well. Maybe I'll see you there?"

"Maybe." I turn to walk away, but stop and turn back toward him. "Thank you for the drawing."

"Oh, it's no problem." He swings his arms at his side, decidedly not meeting my eyes.

"I always loved your fanart. No one captures Aaron quite like you do, Aaron2."

"Well, I love your fics."

I laugh. "Please, you did not read those dictionary-length fics I sent you." With a wave back toward Wesley, I head toward my family in the parking lot.

"Wait. Stella," Wesley calls behind me.

I stop walking, peeking back at him over my shoulder.

"I . . . I shouldn't have left. At Sci-Con."

I swallow hard, not sure how to respond.

Wesley takes a step toward me. "In all my years at the CE academy, I made a lot of mistakes. But leaving you behind was the worst one I ever made."

Those words. I recognize those words.

I wrote them.

"You read my fic?" Wesley Clarke read my 198,000-word fix-it-fic?

Wesley watches me, his fingers twitching at his sides. It's almost like he's . . . nervous? Wesley Frickin' Clarke. Nervous. Because of me?

"Well, what am I supposed to do with that?" I step closer to him. "You left me. You left *us*. And you took my shuttle."

"You are the most stubborn, annoying captain—and valedictorian—I have ever met." He takes another step toward me. "And yet, for the past few weeks"—Wesley's Adam's apple bobs up and down—"I haven't been able to stop thinking of you."

I blink hard. Wesley Clarke couldn't stop thinking about me. "But . . . why?"

"Because I like you. I really like you. I don't know where it came from, but there it is, okay?" He throws his hands up and lets them slap back down against his sides. "I like you, Stick. I like all your funky hairstyles and the way you make everything into a bad joke, and the way you keep your agenda book rainbow-color organized, and the way you put Lint on your shoulder, and the way you were so nice to me online even when I didn't deserve it. I like you, okay?"

My heart slams against my ribs. "Well . . . if you couldn't stop thinking of me, why did you leave?"

"I shouldn't have left." He brushes a strand of long brown hair out of my face. "I will always come back for you. Like I should have done the first time."

"Wesley Clarke, you are the most stubborn, arrogant Cescum I have ever—"

I know what comes next. The confusion and weirdness and all the scary things that come from admitting I like Wesley Clarke.

But you know what?

I really don't care.

I get up to my tippy toes, and then, just like that, I'm kissing Wesley Clarke, and he is kissing me back, right there in our graduation gowns. I wrap my arms around his neck and pull him closer. Everything inside me feels so fluttery and *right*.

I can't help it—I'm smiling into his kiss. He pulls back, grinning. "What?"

"I just realized what this means." I run my hand through his hair.

"What does it mean?"

"You're officially a Lewton shipper."

He gives an exaggerated sigh. "Maybe your ship has some merit. Or maybe I'm just an *us* shipper."

"Just shut up and kiss me, Clarke."

He grabs me around the waist and picks me up, and we're twirling around the field, my lips pressed to his.

Maybe this time, the love story gets an ending. Or maybe, just maybe, it's the beginning of a new one.

SAN DIEGO COMIC-CON 2018

— PANEL TRANSCRIPT —

Fan Questions with Leigh Stanton and Ethan Martone

Moderated by Halley Stewart

Halley: Okay, we only have time for a few more! [reading submissions on her phone screen] This question comes from Lisa S. in Montana. Lisa asks, "When you filmed the twentieth episode, did you realize it would be the last one?"

Leigh: Definitely not.

Ethan: None of us did. I mean, we all wanted the show to go on forever, but, you know, it doesn't always go that way.

Leigh: We've stayed in touch, though, and we all became really good friends through this whole experience. We still have a group chat going on WhatsApp.

Ethan: [snorts] Leigh's the sentimental one.

Leigh: Shut up.

Halley: Okay, next question is from Eric B. in Indiana. Eric wants to know, "How did your characters come to like each other, when in the beginning they hated each other so much?"

Ethan: I'm pretty sure, deep down, Jill still hates Aaron.

Leigh: I mean, after how he [expletive] left her hanging in the finale, yeah, I'd say so. [laughter]

Ethan: But honestly, I mean, maybe they just moved past it?

Leigh: [steeples her fingers] Bear with me for a second, I'm going to say something kind of unpopular.

Ethan: Oh no.

Leigh: No, really. Okay. Here goes. I don't think Aaron and Jill ever really hated each other. [gasps from the audience]

Ethan: You're going to get so much hate mail for that. [wraps his arm around her shoulders]

Leigh: Hear me out, okay! [swats his hand away] I don't think Jill and Aaron hated each other. I think they didn't understand each other. And once they got to know each other—truly, honestly bonded—they realized that maybe they were never that different.

Ethan: Huh. Okay. That's fair.

Halley: Sorry, I don't mean to rush through this, but we've only got time for one more. Sharon J. in Vermont has the question we've all been wondering. She asks, "If *Warship Seven* had had a season two, do you think Aaron and Jill would have ended up together?"

[silence]

Ethan: [thinking] Yes. I think they would have.

Leigh: Do you?

Ethan: Absolutely. You don't?

Leigh: I don't know, honestly. [audience boos]

Ethan: Ouch. Way to bruise my fragile ego.

Leigh: Okay, no, shut up. I have a point. I swear.

Ethan: Sure you do.

Leigh: [presses a hand over his mouth, then recoils in disgust when he licks her palm] Gross, Ethan. [wipes her hand on his jeans] I mean, people are complicated, and it's a complicated question. Who could know the future?

Ethan: About eight thousand fans in the Lewton tag on the *Warship* forums would disagree with you.

Leigh: But I do think, in the end, Jill and Aaron's feelings for each other were real. And that's what matters. [audience cheers]

Ethan: Yeah, who cares if there isn't a season two? If you hate the canon, write your own. You fans have done a great job writing your own endings—yeah, we love the fics.

Leigh: Even the dirty ones.

Ethan: Especially the dirty ones.

Leigh: But really, it's true. If you don't like what's written in the canon, make your own. That's all anyone can really ask in life.

✦ ACKNOWLEDGMENTS ✦

Shipped would not exist without the support and encouragement of so many people.

A million thanks to my amazing agent, Sarah Landis, who has always believed in my writing, and without whom none of this would be possible! I am so grateful you took a chance on me. And thank you to everyone at Sterling Lord Literistic for always being so wonderful and supportive.

To my amazing editor, Ari Lewin at Penguin: Thank you for all your support, and for believing in this nerdy story and helping to make it shine; Wesley and Stella wouldn't be here without you! And thank you to Elise LeMassena for all of your help with this book, and for all your support.

A huge thank-you to Jennifer Klonsky, Tessa Meischeid, and all the amazing folks at Penguin Teen and Penguin Random House who helped make *Shipped* happen. I am so grateful to have such a wonderful team in my corner!

Thank you to Ursula Decay, the amazing artist who designed my beautiful cover!

I would not be the author I am today without the endless support from my amazing critique partner and friend, Jamie Howard, who tolerates my bad jokes, constant texts, and awful rough drafts. I am so grateful we connected in 2014!

Thank you to my amazing friend Jennifer Stolzer for all your support and for talking through plot points with me. Thank you to my friends Elizabeth Unseth and Jen Adam for your brilliant notes on the beginning of this book!

A million thanks to Zoulfa Katouh, Jamie Krakover, Ron Walters, Annika Sharma, Amanda Heger, Marie Meyer, Julie Abe, Erin Craig, Rosaria Munda, Lyudmyla Hoffman, Kate L. Mary, everyone in #TeamLandis, Diana Pinguicha, Melody Robinette, Taryn Albright, Erin Callahan, Joanna Ruth Meyer, Emily Schroen, the Electric Eighteens, the Write Pack, the NAC, and everyone in the Twitter writing community—your support over the years has kept me going!

And thank you to my cousin Jon Siegel for taking my author photos!

Vincent—the second half of my IRL OTP. I would never have gotten this far without your endless support for me and my career. I love you so much. Thank you for all you do, and all you are, and for spending part of our Sicily trip reading my terrible rough draft of this book.

Thank you to my father, Paul Tate, and to my mother in Heaven, Jessica Tate, for always supporting me and my dreams. I am extremely lucky to have such supportive parents. I love you!

Thank you to Finley, the best furry companion I could have, even when you attack me with squeaky toys when I'm trying to edit.

Thank you to all the Tates, Rosses, Siegels, Servellos, Bombardiers, Pions, and Murrays for being the most supportive family I could ask for.

Thank you to my therapist, Janet.

Thank you to Caitlin Clark, Rebekah Mar-Tang, Kirsten Cowan, Kristina Rieger, Caitlin Stevenson, Sarah Winters,

Molly Hyant, Brett Roell, Alexis Carr, Audrey Desbiens, Corey Landsman, Katie Gill, Caity Bean, Katie Levesque, Andrew Shepard, Joanna Wolbert, Jill Schaffer, Paige Donaldson, Ashley Taylor Ward, Amy and Eric Lousararian, Monica Craver, Barbara Hemingway, all the Dame School folks and everyone else—you know who you are—you're all such wonderful friends, and I would not have gotten this far without the support of so many amazing people.

Thank you to Ally Davis for allowing me to name the high school in this book after her father, and by extension, thank you to my beloved high school principal, Gene Connolly, who I hope would have enjoyed this book.

Thank you to the amazing folks who work on the Lake Zurich transportation boats; it's hard to write on deadline, as I quickly learned, and I would never have completed this book had it not been for these wonderful boat tours and the people who work on them who tolerated me climbing aboard with my laptop and buying way too many lattes and cheese platters almost every day in summer 2019.

And finally, all my love and appreciation to the fandom community, which has often felt like home.